A Hairpiece Named Denial

S. Sal Hanna

A Hairpiece Named Denial by S. Sal Hanna
ISBN: 978-1-938349-95-9
eISBN: 978-1-938349-96-6
Layout and book design by Mark Givens

Excerpt(s) from Joyce, James. A Portrait of the Artist as a Young Man. New York: B W Huebsch, 1916. Print.

Excerpt(s) from Dostoyevsky, Fyodor, 1821-1881. The Brothers Karamazov. Russia, 1880. Print.

Excerpt from Pope, Alexander. "An Essay on Man,: Being the First Book of Ethic Epistles. To Henry St. John, L. Bolingbroke", 1733–1734

Lyrics from "Eyes Of A Painter" by Kate Wolf © 1981 Another Sundown Publishing Company. Used by permission.

Excerpt from "Little Gidding" from FOUR QUARTETS by T.S. Eliot. Copyright © 1942 by T.S. Eliot, renewed 1970 by Esme Valerie Eliot. Reprinted by permission of Houghton Mifflin Harcourt Publishing Company. All rights reserved.

First Pelekinesis Printing 2019
For information: Pelekinesis, 112 Harvard Ave #65, Claremont, CA 91711 USA

Library of Congress Cataloging-in-Publication Data

Names: Hanna, S. S., 1943- author.
Title: A hairpiece named denial / by S. Sal Hanna.
Description: Claremont, CA : Pelekinesis, [2018]
Identifiers: LCCN 2018039521 (print) | LCCN 2018043140 (ebook) | ISBN 9781938349966 (ePub) | ISBN 9781938349959 (pbk.)
Subjects: | GSAFD: Humorous fiction.
Classification: LCC PS3608.A715567 (ebook) | LCC PS3608.A715567 H35 2018
   (print) | DDC 813/.6--dc23
LC record available at https://lccn.loc.gov/2018039521

www.pelekinesis.com

A HAIRPIECE NAMED DENIAL

by

S. SAL HANNA

This book, written at
Stone Clover Cottage,
is dedicated to:
Tracy and Paul,
Katie, Sami, and Todd.

— ❧ —

And, of course, to Tata
for her
wisdom, humor & love.

CHAPTER ONE

ALICE, A WRITER OF COMIC PROSE, PRINTED ON the title page of a manuscript: *Guaranteed to make you laugh or your sense of humor back*; she mailed the manuscript to an editor who, in her words, "misinterpreted the guarantee and sent the manuscript back."

Alice Princeton Goe and her husband Frank were a wealthy couple who had kept their fortune a private matter. No one living in Samsville, their small town located on the wide-open, wind-ransacked plains of central Kansas, knew of the millions they had tucked away in a bank in the big city of Wichita.

February 26, 1980, Alice informed her literary club, composed of twelve college-educated women who met weekly on Tuesday evenings, about what she had done with a young man she'd hired.

"What I did with this fellow," Alice told the women gathered in the drawing room of her clapboard Victorian house, "is a first for our town—at least I *think* it's a first."

"Tell us what you did," the vice-president of the club said, "and we'll tell you if it's a first."

"Fair enough," Alice said.

"It better be good," someone added.

"I know some of you have cleaning ladies," Alice said. "Well, I finally decided to hire one, but I hired *not* a lady but a man."

"A man?" asked a woman sitting near a stained-glass window.

"What you're saying," another added, "is you're the first Samsville resident to hire not a cleaning lady but a cleaning *lad*."

"Exactly," Alice said.

"That's a first all right," the vice-president said. Others agreed.

"You say," someone added, "he's a local boy?"

"Lisa Jaycubson's balding husband, Jack," Alice said. "He's been looking for work for a good while, and he can't find a job—even part-time."

"He's a fine young man," one woman sitting in an oak rocking chair said. "They come to our church, you know."

"He's *not*," someone said, "your tall, dark, and handsome type."

"And he's *not*," Alice quickly added, "short, fat, and fair either." She paused, looked around the room, then said, "He's what you might call a deluxe cleaning lad."

"*Deluxe* cleaning lad?" someone said, quizzically.

"Yes," Alice responded, "he's educated, witty, and unemployed."

"Where did he go to school?" the vice-president asked.

"K-State," Alice said, "and he majored in philosophy."

"That's a noble major," a woman added, "that'll guarantee you unemployment around here."

"And elsewhere," someone said. "No, I better say—*every*where."

"Poor guy," Alice said, "his wife insisted he get a hairpiece, thinking that'll help him get a job. He hated doing that, but he wanted to please her. He knew that the philosophy major (and not the hair follicles) had prevented him from getting a job. *What I've got now,* he told me during his interview, *is not a full-time job but a head full of store-bought hair.* I knew I'd get along with him when he spoke about his major, his job problems, and his Elvis-pompadour hair-piece. Yes, yes, my dear friends, Jack suits my purposes just fine."

Alice didn't elaborate on her purposes, and none of the women asked. She had specific goals to pursue with Jack. One of them was to have an intelligent and regular partner with whom to share her coffee, ideas, remembrances, and literary pursuits.

Above all, she hoped Jack would help her in solving what she had discussed in a long diary entry titled: "My Weird and Wicked Problem."

The problem: how to give away seven million dollars now that four years had passed after Frank's death. Alice had left all the money in a bank account in Wichita, and she started to search hard for ways to give away the millions. "Jack," she told herself, "will be able to help. Maybe."

— ℰ𝒻 —

Alice asked Jack to come to her place every Friday for eight hours: to clean house, do yard work, and run errands.

"I'll pay you $12.50 an hour," she told him. The expression on his face led her to ask: "Are you wondering why the pay is that much when the standard rate is around three dollars an hour?"

Jack nodded and said, "Lisa will be shocked by the amount."

"Well, let me explain," she said. "You may recall reading in our paper the feature story on my lighthearted, creative-nonfiction book *Editors and Their Turkeys*—where I posit: *Writers are turkeys, editors trim them to Cornish hens.* My editor at *Garvin, Akers & Sheridan* tells me the book is selling well, very well, far beyond their expectations. So, your pay," Alice smiled, "is thanks to my turkeys. You might say it's a poultry-based bonus."

At the interview, she also told him, "Included in the eight hours, you'll have three paid breaks: one in the morning, a second for lunch, and a third in the afternoon. I'll prepare cookies and coffee (or tea) for the breaks, and I'll also prepare lunch. I suspect the breaks will be rather long. If you don't mind, I'll join you, and we'll talk about all sorts of topics. Any questions?"

"No, not really," he said. "I'm still shocked and overwhelmed by the pay."

"Overwhelmed with joy, I hope."

"Oh yes, Mrs. Goe, incredible joy. Lisa will feel that joy."

"Each Friday before you go home to see your Lisa and have supper, you'll receive not a personal check but a crisp picture of Benjamin Franklin, my thanks, and if all goes well—memories galore."

Unlike her husband, Lisa Jaycubson had a full-time job. She grew up in Samsville and, after graduating as valedictorian from Samsville High School where she had leading roles in several plays and musicals (among them Maria in *The Sound of Music*), Lisa attended Kansas State University where she earned a degree in math education. There she met Jack, a varsity football player from Conroe, Texas who had become a backup player and philosophy major in college.

One evening at supper, Jack offered Lisa a frank assessment of his football career: "I went from a big star in high school to a doughnut in college," Jack said. "I became like the doughnut spare tire they place in cars these days—the coaches knew I was there, but they hoped *not* to use me."

A month after Lisa and Jack had graduated from college, they were married in the only Presbyterian church in Samsville. Lisa felt her best wedding present was a full-time job to teach math and direct drama at her old high school.

— ❧ —

As a writer, Alice kept an extensive diary. In an entry for Friday

March 14th, 1980, she wrote while Jack was vacuuming: "This morning, I ate a maple-covered doughnut; New Yorkers call it: French Cruller. Out here in the Samsville Café with the high antique tin ceiling, the farmers are far more poetic. They call it: Tractor Tire."

Later in the entry, she added: "Jack is here to clean house. He also wants to do yard work this afternoon. During the break, I plan to ask him for ideas on how to solve my weird and wicked problem. If I don't ask today, I'll do it next week for sure. Soon I'll join him on his break."

Alice left her diary—actually, it was the forty-fifth volume of a combination diary-*literary* notebook that she had faithfully kept for more than fifty years—on the dining room table where she often wrote, and she joined Jack who was taking his mid-morning coffee break in the spacious cabinet-lined kitchen.

Both sat on wooden chairs next to a round oak table whose edge rested a foot away from a picture window with a view of the back-yard's two-acre lot that had four Autumn Blaze Maple trees, a green picnic table, a brick barbecue pit with a metal grill, a brass horizontal sundial set on a stone pedestal, a rusty burn barrel, and a wooden bird feeder that, in her words, "is the size of a fat-midget's coffin."

The eighty-two-year-old Alice had moved to Samsville from a small town in western Kansas in 1927, the time her husband had accepted a job as a teacher at Samsville High School. Alice and Frank Goe bought a late nineteenth-century Victorian house on Main Street.

The white house had a staircase and unpainted woodwork, two fireplaces with marble mantles, dark-oak furniture with pillars and beveled mirrors, bookshelves and hand-carved Victorian antiques. It also had an inviting, charming silence about it that Friday morning in March, the kind of silence that's difficult to describe but that's as distinctive and appealing as the aroma of a new car.

One would expect the two to be drinking tea, but coffee was their drink of choice. Alice took hers black in a teacup, Jack white in a ceramic mug. Unlike the women in her literary club who would drink weak coffee (so weak that Alice felt they were drinking not coffee but brown water), she enjoyed strong coffee: "coffee with an attitude," as she once told Jack, "the kind of coffee that talks back to me in the morning."

They talked about many topics that morning—life at the high school; the grass growing in the tennis courts; why Alice disliked the label *Fu Manchu* for a moustache and preferred instead an *Arc de Triomphe*.

They reflected on a new artfully painted sign in a neighbor's front yard. The sign:

HOUSE FOR SALE
BY
BY OWNER'S WIFE

"That's Edna for you," Alice said. "Her for-sale sign can also be a poem."

"About divorce, or a husband with Alzheimer's?"

"Neither," Alice said. "Most people around here will assume the repeated word *BY* is a mistake."

"It's not?"

"I'm *sure* it's not."

"What do you mean?" Jack said, reaching for his coffee mug.

"The sign is crafted in such a way that if the repeated word is read slowly and with a certain intonation, a poetic wink emanates from it."

"Who connects with that?"

"The women at club," Alice said, referring to her literary club, "and other folks who traffic in odd comic twists."

"You know why they're selling?"

"Moving to Florida to be with their son, the physician."

"Wow, Florida," Jack said. "How nice."

"Edna calls it, *The nation's geriatric ward.*"

"Do you think the sign bothers her husband?"

"I doubt it. After fifty-two years of marriage, I'm sure he's used to her wit. She's by far the wittiest woman at club. Wit is to her as foam is to beer."

"Fifty-two years..." Jack mused. "That's a long time to be alive, let alone married."

"That it is," Alice said.

Jack took a sip of his coffee. "Yesterday, I called grandpa Jaycubson to wish him a happy birthday."

"How old is he?"

"Eighty-five."

"I'm three years younger."

"Like you, he's still active and in good health," Jack said. "I asked him about his secret for living a long life."

"Oh, what did he say?"

"Get lots of physical activity."

"Agree with that."

"He got his working construction."

"What else?"

"Don't smoke or drink."

"Good advice there."

"And live a modest tension-free life, so you can get lots of sleep."

"That's also good," Alice said. "Add to that a vegetarian diet and you've got my formula."

"Interesting," Jack said. He bit into an oatmeal cookie, chewed it, and said, "Tasty, very tasty, Mrs. Goe. Thanks for baking these. Grandpa also told me he had a wonderful life—a life with no regrets."

"Now, now, wait a minute, my friend," Alice raised her voice slightly. "With all due respect to your grandpa, I find *that* hard to believe. Regrets are the rummage sales of life, and if we're honest about it, we've all held many of them."

While they were talking, Alice would silently remind herself that Friday is the dawn of the weekend, and people rejoice in that day. But she dreaded it. She told Jack that morning: "Weekends are hard on widows." She reasoned her observation this way: "During the week, the husband had to go to work, and the homemaker had her routine at home, but during the weekend, the couple did things together."

Alice and her late Frank had done that. They shopped together; went to dinners, concerts, art shows, lectures, movies, plays, and church together; and they drove together to big cities and university towns to visit used bookstores (Alice's love).

Thanks to the ways of that gentle and intelligent Texan, Alice had started to look forward to Fridays. His presence on that day began to make a difference in her life and outlook.

— ❡ —

Near the end of the morning coffee break, Alice told Jack about a lecture on the economic crisis at the family farm that she and the town's librarian had attended on Wednesday afternoon at a university in Wichita.

"The lecturer had a wild handlebar moustache," she said. "He was introduced as a farmer's son, now teaching at an Ivy League university. He began his remarks by saying with a smile: *In our house, kids make investment decisions: they want their dad to invest in scissors and blades.* The scholar, an author of two books published by a major university press, advanced a controversial position on how to improve the struggling economy on the family farms and the small towns of the Great Plains."

"How was he received?"

"Respectfully," she said. "People listened with care. But when the question-and-answer period arrived, several men in the packed hall stood and charged after the soft-spoken scholar."

"They asked hard questions, I presume," Jack said.

"That and more. At one point, two middle-aged men stood up—farmers equipped with just enough knowledge of *Robert's Rules of Order* to sound parliamentary—to grill the poor professor."

"What do you mean?"

"I'll explain *and* illustrate," she said. "A visibly angry, bearded, and husky fellow, who identified himself as a long-time wheat farmer, began his comment/question by saying: *Professor, point of information...*"

"Okay," Jack said, sipping more coffee.

"And later," Alice added, "another fellow, shorter than Napoleon but not by much, stood up, headed to the microphone, grabbed it as if it were an ear of corn, and referred to what he felt was a garbled comment made by the speaker. He began his question: *Point of clarification, sir...*"

"That *is* funny!"

"There was lots of tension in the room," she said, "but an older portly fellow sitting in the back of the room magically defused it. The fellow didn't go to the front of the lecture hall and use the microphone that was set up for those who wished to ask questions. Instead, he stood in place, tucked his thumbs in his blue suspenders, and spoke in a booming voice: *Sir, your main idea intrigues me. May I speak to it from the rear?*"

"You may speak," the professor said, "from anywhere you can."

Jack laughed and raised his mug to Alice.

"As you can imagine, that comment lit up a roar of laughter in the audience. When the laughter subsided, the questioner surprised me and shocked many others by endorsing—yes, *endorsing*—the basic idea presented by the Ivy League professor who was standing behind the lectern, twirling the right side of his dark and unruly moustache."

"That endorsement was unexpected?"

"Totally unexpected. It led the bearded wheat farmer to rise again, look up, point an index finger at the ceiling, and exclaim in a loud and assertive voice: *Point of disgust!*"

At the end of the coffee break, Jack took his mug to the sink and said, "It's good to see our farmers challenge an Ivy League professor out here on the Great Plains."

— ❧ —

That evening after supper, she listened (much as she had done for years Monday to Friday) to the *CBS Evening News with Walter Cronkite*. When the depressing news of the day ended and Cronkite dribbled with charm and authority his famous sign-off: *And that's the way it is...*, Alice headed to the study, picked up her fountain pen filled with green ink, and wrote in her diary reflections on her discussions with Jack:

> At the morning, lunch, and afternoon sessions with Jack, we talked about many topics ... But I still need to get his opinion on how to give away the seven million dollars.
>
> I continue to ask myself: "How should I submit my question to Jack without letting him feel I've got that kind of money?"
>
> My answer: "Whatever you say, emphasize the word hypothetical." But I keep repeating to myself: "What if he asks if I have that kind of money hidden away? How should I respond?"

I can't lie. I won't lie. Pastor always reminds us, perhaps his subtle way of alluding to small-town gossip, "The Bible teaches—the devil is the father of lies."

Yet I don't want Jack to know that I have the seven million. If he does ask the dreaded question, I'll have to ad lib—with integrity—my way around it.

Like her departed Frank, Alice coveted her privacy. She felt that their wealth—inherited or otherwise—is a private matter, and it should remain that way. Still, she hoped her handyman would help her deliver it to a worthy cause.

— ☙ —

At Jack's morning coffee break the following week, Alice mustered the courage to share with him her problem.

She planned to stick to her strategy and present it not as a real but as a *hypothetical* one, and she hoped to gather ideas from Jack's thinking.

The break began with a look at a physician's odd behavior.

CHAPTER TWO

AFTER SOME SMALL TALK AT THE MORNING COFFEE break, Jack trotted out the ways of a doctor as they clashed with the antics of Jack's brother-in-law Dan, an orderly.

"Let me tell you," Jack said, "about a new doctor in the Gluesiville hospital who drives a silver-colored Jaguar."

"That's a strange car out here."

"Sure is," Jack said and bit into a gingersnap cookie.

"We're in the made-in-America land of Chevys and Fords," she added. "Aren't we?"

"Sure are. Mechanics in the small towns around here refuse to work on foreign cars, you know."

"Frank," she said recalling her late husband, "used to make that same observation. That's why he never bought anything other than a Ford. One year he was tempted to buy what he called a *Dinah Shore Chevrolet*, but he resisted. He loved that song, 'See the USA in Your Chevrolet,' that Dinah Shore made famous on her TV show."

"Well, the Jaguar is far from a Ford or a Chevy," Jack said, "and the fellow who drives it is a foreigner."

"From what country?" Alice asked and bit into her Fig Newton. "Love these cookies. They look like the bed of a pickup truck, but

I find them tasty—Cadillac of cookies."

"I don't know the doctor's native country," Jack said. "Dan says he's a slender handsome fellow who dresses neatly at all times and has lots of shiny dark hair. Three out of the five doctors in that hospital are from overseas. Did you know that?"

"I read that in the *News-Free Gazette*," she said, referring to the weekly newspaper that resulted from the merger of the *Samsville News* with the *Gluesiville Free Gazette*. "But I didn't read about a Jaguar there."

"Well there is," Jack said, "and all of Gluesiville is talking about it, and now our town is talking about it, thanks to what the doctor did with his Jaguar and—more importantly—thanks to what Dan did to the doctor."

Alice leaned forward and asked, "What in the world did Dan do?"

"I'm getting to that. As you know, the hospital in Gluesiville has a spacious and nicely lined parking lot; the spots near the hospital's entrance are reserved for doctors and clergy."

"You're right," she said. "That's common at most hospitals."

"But this new doctor refused to park his Jaguar anywhere near the hospital's entrance, using one of those spots," Jack said. "Instead, he'd park it in an unlined area as far away from the entrance as possible. It was a *very* lonely car parked at the *very* edge of a *very* large lot. The car reminded me—and this reference to football might not mean much to you, Mrs. Goe, but I'm sure it would've connected with your late husba—"

"Hold on," she interrupted. "That's a stereotype. I'm a football fan from way back. Anyway, what did the Jaguar remind you of?"

"Army's Lonesome End," he said. "That's the end who played on the Army football team, the player who never came back to the huddle but had the plays signaled to him. He's now part of college football legend."

"Yes, he is," Alice said, adding, "that was Bill Carpenter, and he was a wide receiver on those great Army teams of the late fifties. I recall watching him play on television."

"The Jaguar," Jack said, "was a lonesome car on that large lot."

"Let's be more poetic and say: *a lonesome cat on the prairie.*"

"That is more poetic, Mrs. Goe," the philosophy major agreed.

"Thanks," she said. "Now let me try to defend the guy's behavior: either the good doctor wanted to exercise by taking a longish walk, or he feared another car door would dent his Jaguar."

"Dan, the orderly, diagnosed the doctor's behavior and came up with a definitive conclusion," Jack said. "First, you've got to understand that Dan is a heck-of-a-nice guy, but a bit on the strange side. He feels the doctor is way too *pompous.* That's Dan's word, not mine. So, one day Dan took his blue rusty beat-up '64 Ford and parked it as far away from the hospital's entrance but as *close* to the doctor's Jaguar as possible, making it extremely difficult—but not impossible—for the doctor to open his car door without denting Dan's Ford. This ingenious, really bizarre, move got the pompous doctor's attention, and he started to park his Jaguar in a spot reserved for doctors and clergy: next to other cars, between yellow lines, very close to the hospital's entrance."

Alice squinted, bit the tip of her left thumb, and spoke deliberately: "I *think* I see behavior modification here." She smiled, made eye contact with Jack, reached out, and held his arm. "All of this tells me that your brother-in-law is more than a humble underpaid orderly: he is—and I'm going to be a bit earthy now—a pompous-ass adjuster."

Jack rocked back in his chair, laughed, and spoke in a loud voice: "Mr. Daniel Q. Henderson, *the pompous-ass adjuster of the Great Plains.* Why if he hears this majestic label, he'll make himself a business card!"

— ∽ —

After they pursued other topics, Alice decided to go back to what was on her mind: the seven million dollars, and Jack gave her the perfect opening.

"Yesterday, Lisa's other brother, Bill, the vice-janitor at the high school, got a check for an article he did for a magazine, and now he thinks he can make it in the writing business. Lisa reminded him of the adage: *One can make a fortune from writing, but you can't make a living from it.* Her advice to him: *Keep your day job.*"

"Speaking of a fortune," Alice said, "I've got this *hypothetical* question that I've been pondering for a while. I'd like your response to it."

"I'll try. What's the question?"

"If you have, say, seven million dollars to give away and you're not allowed to give any to family or friends, who'll get your money?"

"Wish I had that terribly disturbing problem," Jack said, reaching for a cookie.

"Let's—for fun—*assume* you do. Where would your money go?" She tucked her tiny chin in the index fingers and thumbs of her hands. "*Hypothetically.*"

Jack hesitated, admired the furrows in Alice's round and handsome face, cleared his throat, and asked, "Why're you so curious?"

"Why?" She spoke with hesitancy. "Why?"

"You're not working on another short story, are you, Mrs. Goe?" he said with a tone that accused and teased Alice. She smiled and reached for her coffee cup. He made eye contact with her blue eyes when he said, "You're not searching for a plotline, are you?"

The two questions reflected Jack's knowledge of Alice. He knew that she was an accomplished writer who had published a major book with a prestigious New York publisher. What Jack *didn't* know—or even suspect—was that she was a wealthy woman.

— ✑ —

Most people in Samsville knew the Goes to be humble folks: ordinary, gentle, sports-loving, hard-working, reserved, salt-of-the-earth Methodists, who vigorously supported the cultural and athletic activities of the local high school, and that's the image with which the Goes felt comfortable, and the one they had cultivated.

No person in town knew of the Goes' wealth. Alice and Frank believed in the unwritten rule of country living: *Never stand out and never show off your wealth.* All the money that they had was a burden to them, and they seldom tapped it. Frank's teaching salary met their needs, and in retirement, his Social Security and pension were more than enough for the two. The Goes had no children and, in effect, no biological heirs.

The two had written their last will and testament with the help of an attorney from Wichita. (To safeguard their privacy, they refused to use Samsville's only attorney, a member in their church.) The Goes' inherited money would go first to the surviving spouse, and following the spouse's death, to Winterpeace College, a four-year liberal arts institution in western Kansas where both had earned degrees and where Frank had earned five varsity letters: two in baseball and three in football.

"Because we cherish our privacy—and indeed our freedom—we are not sending a copy of our will to the college," Alice wrote in her diary. They left a sealed copy of the will in a safety deposit box in the Samsville State Bank on Main Street and another copy in the office of their church, "in the event both of us die together," Alice wrote in her diary.

In 1976, her husband died of a heart attack at age seventy-eight. "When people around the country were buying Bicentennial souvenirs such as flags, plates, coins, mugs, hats, and books," Alice once told her literary club, "I bought a plot and buried my beloved Frank in the Spa." (Even Alice used the acronym for *Samsville's Peaceful Acres.*)

She kept their will intact after Frank's death, but on a cold day in January of 1980, she read in the *News-Free Gazette* a story dealing with the impending death of the Goes' alma mater Winterpeace College.

"The college's death," as the newspaper put it in an article dated January 25, 1980, "resulted from a declining student population in the Great Plains, weak academic programs, increased competition for the small pool of available students, a depressed farm economy, a low endowment for the college, and a high inflation rate."

Winterpeace's death disturbed and pleased Alice. It disturbed her because it presented her with her weird and wicked problem: what to do with all that money. It pleased her because it gave her an opportunity to be adventurous, to search for ways to give away the money, to dream and experiment and interact with others, to break out of that cycle of loneliness that she had started to feel after Frank's death.

Jack didn't know that the Goes had intended to leave a huge sum of money to Winterpeace College, money the college would now never see.

— ❧ —

At first, Jack was of little help in supplying her with ideas on what to do with all that money—though he tried.

"Now let me see if I understand you correctly. You're saying, one can't give the money to family or friends?"

"Right. And it's not one or two or three, but sev—"

"Seven million," Jack interrupted. He paused, scratched his head, and added, "I get the point, and I see you've learned your numbers from watching *Sesame Street*, Mrs. Goe." He winked with his left eye, a wink that he frequently substituted for a smile.

"Not really. I've been reading William Shakespeare; he numbered his sonnets consecutively, you know. That feat inspired a critic to observe: *Such numbering is further evidence of his genius.*" Jack smiled as Alice lapsed into a British accent and added, "That, my dear, is a knee-slapper comment with the Bloomsbury set or *The New Yorker* crowd."

Both laughed at the knee-slapper remark. Alice, who had a strong interest in modern European and American literature, often made allusions that failed to connect with Jack, and he conveniently ignored them. He knew she was a voracious reader, an original thinker, and he admired her intellect and creativity.

"I wonder," he said, "what a *New Yorker* editor would do?"

"Forget them and let's talk about us Kansas folk," Alice said. "What would *we* do with seven million dollars?"

"I suppose we'd help bail out some poor farmers. So many are hurting these days," Jack said. Then he added, "Remember the article that was in the paper a while back about the closing of Winterpeace College? That school would've loved the money. From what Lisa says, it's a nice school. Her uncle, Tim, graduated from there."

"Frank and I did too," Alice said as her small, wrinkled hand shook. She slowly placed her coffee cup on the saucer, reached for a Fig Newton that was near the coffee pot, bit into the cookie, picked up her coffee cup again, and took a swig. Her soft voice trembled as she spoke, "Who else would get the seven million?"

That morning, Alice and Jack discussed setting up trust funds and college scholarships for the children of the poor in the small towns of the Great Plains. They considered supporting long-suffering missionaries they knew in Bolivia and Kenya. They also came up with traditional agencies to support, including The Humane Society, the Salvation Army, the Red Cross, the Goodwill Industries, and volunteer fire departments.

They even explored ways to nurture culture on the prairies. They considered setting up funds for starving artists, sponsoring more art shows, establishing publishing houses that cultivate regional writers, supporting organizations that sponsor visiting artists from New York and California.

From that coffee break, Alice smuggled a clue to help her in solving her problem. She wrote in her diary:

> The dreaded question never came up. When I asked Jack what he would do with seven million dollars, he wondered if I was searching for a plotline for a short story.

> In his quick response, I now see—and Dear Diary, please forgive me for resorting to a word that I only use when I write and never when I speak—fecundity.

> While it is important to find a place for my money, I must admit that I am gathering fodder for a novel.

> Rita Todd, my editor in New York, has been after me (given the ongoing success of our first book together) to write a second book that could, in her words, "be viewed as a companion to *Editors and Their Turkeys.*"

> Perhaps I could do an autobiographical novel, a slice from the life of a turkey, as it were: a wealthy writer of comic prose who doubles as a small-town philanthropist.

> If I do such a novel, I'd want to entertain the readers and to explore serious insights into the human condition. This will be my challenge for the years ahead.

> My motto will be: An old writer never dies—she just immortalizes her town in print.

For days, Alice searched for a plan to give away the money, a plan that could translate into a plot for a novel. And she finally came up with a seriocomic plan that had the potential to attract and repel a possible recipient. She felt the plan was, at once, tempting and repulsive, enticing and repugnant.

Frank would have vetoed her plan with firmness and vigor. But thanks to Frank's death, the plan in Alice's mind was veto-proof.

— ∽ —

She reflected on her plan and wrote two lengthy, somewhat philosophical, entries in her diary.

Most entries in her diary list a date but are without titles. These two entries carry titles. One is: "The Dead Are So Controlling," and the other: "The Dead Are Liberating."

She revealed her plan via a long letter.

CHAPTER THREE

ALICE WROTE A LETTER TO "A FINANCIALLY HORNY institution" (her words) on a sunny Monday morning, June 2 of 1980. She wrote it on a yellow legal pad, then she typed it using her green IBM Selectric typewriter.

Addressed to the president of Royalle College in Royallestown, West Virginia, the letter detailed her plan to give away the money and referred to her one-time visit to the college. The letter states:

> Dear Dr. Lynpeex:
>
> Permit me please to introduce myself. I am Alice Princeton Goe, an eighty-two-year-old widow: a writer and a literary-club organizer in a small town on the Great Plains.
>
> Years before my husband, Frank, passed away, we wrote a paper will that bequeathed seven million dollars to Winterpeace College, located on the Kansas prairie, a liberal arts college from where Frank and I had graduated way back in the twenties.
>
> And wouldn't you know it: Winterpeace College also expired. Of course, the college died unaware that it had our money coming. We valued our privacy and refused to let the college know about the status of our last will and testament for fear that the college's development officers

would pester us: visiting us often, whining at every visit, dining themselves (and us), and courting our money as we looked on.

Above all, we suspected that those development officers would want to enroll us in their favorite class: *Kicking the Bucket 101.*

When Winterpeace College folded, I looked for a cause to support, one that highlights a problem often encountered by senior citizens, especially women. In an allegorical way, the problem touches the lives of young, middle-aged, and older people no matter where they live in our great land.

I devised a plan to give away the money, a plan that may sound peculiar to you and you may *not* wish to pursue it. If that's the case, I only ask that you inform me via a quick note, so that I may pursue other colleges until I find a taker.

As you well know, few people these days give away large sums of money without some strings attached. I don't expect you to be puppets in my hands, but I *do* expect you to promise to do something and to carry through with your promise before my large prospective donation is given to your institution.

I'll admit that my request may sound strange. But to senior citizens, golden agers, senior saints, silver threads, Bengay geezers, or whatever other euphemism informs your thinking, the request is *not* strange: it speaks to a troubling condition (and more).

Twenty years ago, when Frank was alive, we attended at your college a conference on Virginia Woolf. The conference, sponsored by your English Department, was held in what was then a new building that had more glass than brick. It seemed to be the campus's showcase. The building had on the first floor, as I remember, two state-of-the-art bathrooms.

During our four days at your college, we stayed in a nineteenth-century stone mansion that (we were told) was built for the college's founder, W. J. Martyn-Royalle, and later converted with taste, I might add, into a marvelous and inviting Bed and Breakfast Inn.

My proposal is this: I am prepared to give your college a gift of *seven million dollars* provided you and a male vice-president (or a male assistant) agree to wear for one academic year tie clips that proclaim a cause that is dear to senior citizens everywhere.

The tie clips will be custom made for our purpose. One clip will be the size of a fifty-cent piece. The other will be the size of a quarter. The allegorical-philosophical factor that I wish to highlight is alluded to by the words that will be engraved on the tie clips.

Now you're probably wondering what the words would say. The words, which must be lettered in large type, should say: "CONSTIPATED" on the small circle, and on the big circle: "NON-CONSTIPATED."

The words must be printed on the tie clips, and the clips must be worn daily for a year. The clips worn on a given day should reflect your BMWs: (Bowel Movement Waves).

In Nathaniel Hawthorne's masterpiece novel titled *The Scarlet Letter*, Hester Prynne, you might recall, is required to wear on her chest the scarlet letter "A." Likewise, you and your assistant or a vice-president of your choice would wear more than a letter: you'll wear a flock of letters—tie clips full of letters that spell out your condition for a given day.

If you find this proposal enticing, we will later explore all the relevant issues that must be discussed. I am thinking of the color of the tie clips, the font and size of the letters, and the reason a *male* assistant must join you.

I have also devised a method to monitor and police your daily wearing of the clips. My method borrows its philosophic underpinning from the ways of the prestigious stores and restaurants that often employ "secret shoppers."

My method would appoint and pay a decent salary to a "secret stalker." Such an appointment, rare in academic circles, would be of the one-year, non-tenure-track variety. More on all these matters later—should you agree to my proposal.

For now, all I need to do is see if the general outline of the tie clips plan meets your approval. If the plan appeals to you, I shall be happy to commence a dialogue with you. Kindly reply to me in writing. Please: no calls or visits—I repeat, NO calls or visits—at this stage. I shall be happy to write back if you invite me to do so.

Right about now, if your mind feels as if a wickedly spinning Frisbee had slashed it and spun out, I understand. So, calm down. Finish reading this letter. Re-read it, if you are having a hard time believing what you had just read.

Meditate upon your response. Then write me when you are in a calm and rational state.

In order for me to feel free to pursue other colleges, I am willing to give you three weeks, twenty-one days, to reply. You'll have an exclusive, as it were.

If I don't hear from you on or before the twenty-third of this month (I just checked and marked my calendar, and that's a Monday), then I shall assume that my request is too bizarre-sounding for your comfort level, and you're totally uninterested in pursuing it. If that is the case, I'll feel free to pursue other small needy liberal arts colleges.

I shall look forward to hearing from you at your earliest convenience. Contact me IN WRITING. I repeat: please NO phone calls and NO visits—at this stage.

Now, take a deep breath, relax, and fling the Frisbee back at me.

Sincerely,

Alice Princeton Goe

P.S. If you feel you're going to be acquiring a Princeton education, you're right. Let's call this course—*Privacy 101.*

Alice proofread the letter several times, and when she felt it was error-free, she mailed it. Then she began what writers know all too well: the wait for a response.

"As my philosopher-cleaning lad knows," she wrote in her diary, "Voltaire once said: *History is a bag of tricks that we play on the dead.* In that spirit, Alice Princeton Goe says: *Happiness is a bag of tricks that we play on the living.*"

Her plan from the beginning was to deal with two males: the president of Royalle College and (as she insisted in her letter) a *male* administrative assistant or vice-president.

She wanted to educate them on a variety of topics and to surprise them with a startling move. She also wanted to entertain the men. She had calculated all her moves for their good—and hers.

— ∽ —

Whether the men would view her moves in that light remained to be seen. She felt empowered by all that money, and—being a strong and sagacious woman and a brilliant writer of comic prose—she wanted to wield her power on men in power.

CHAPTER FOUR

WHILE WAITING FOR A REPLY FROM THE PRESI-
dent of Royalle College, Alice enjoyed her conversations with Jack.
At Alice's insistence, Jack's breaks were getting increasingly longer
each Friday. "In our breaks," Jack once told his wife, "we talk and
talk: Mrs. Goe would rather have me listen to her than see me work."

At one conversation, Alice reflected on the death of her husband,
Frank, and concluded her thoughts by telling Jack, "My mother
used to say: *He who dies first gets the longest rest.*"

"Never heard it put that way," Jack said. "But I think you're right.
That's the kind of rest I can do without."

During one afternoon break, they talked about travel. Jack reached
for an oatmeal cookie that she had baked for him and said, "You
and Mr. Goe did a lot of traveling. Didn't you?"

"Sure did," she said. "In our day, we've been to Europe and Tangier
and Mexico and Canada and many other places at home and abroad.
For a paranoid man, my dear old Frank had an unusual streak in
him: he loved to travel."

"Did *you*?"

"Yes indeed," she said, "but I certainly don't enjoy traveling now
without him. Besides I'm much older now."

"So, what was your most memorable trip?" Jack said.

"At home or abroad?"

"Home for a start."

She considered telling him about a trip to Bradenton, Florida in the late 1950s when she and Frank had flown down to see the then Milwaukee Braves in spring training. She thought of mentioning a trip to West Virginia where the two had attended a conference on the work of her beloved Virginia Woolf. Finally, she decided to take a chance on shocking him by telling him about a trip to Las Vegas, Nevada, but she cushioned the shock by couching it in a story about a trip to visit Zion National Park.

— ❡ —

"One summer in the late sixties," she said, "we visited southern Utah and hiked the trails at Zion National Park and admired the impressive cream- and pink- and red-colored sandstone cliffs. Grand old cliffs. We don't have anything like that around here."

"Utah," Jack said, recalling the time in college when his football team had played a game against the Utes of the University of Utah, "is Mormon country. Isn't it?"

"Sure is, but it didn't take us very long to drive from the state of Latter-Day Saints to the city of Current-Day Sinners. In a couple hours or so, we were in Las Vegas."

"Don't tell me you went there. Did you guys really go to Vegas?"

"Sure did, though Frank didn't like that kind of information getting out here in town, so we'd usually say to friends or people at church that we went out West, and we'd focus the conversation on Zion and other innocent and wholesome places," she said. "Las Vegas will shock way too many people around here. The mere mention of it would trigger the town's gossip mill, leading the good people to their knee-jerk condemnation."

"I hear you on that, Mrs. Goe. My dear Lisa would also agree with you—strongly agree with you."

"Yet you'll be surprised, Jack, when I tell you that in Las Vegas we saw, met, and talked to many people who were visiting the city from such places as Muncie, Indiana; Green Bay, Wisconsin; Canton, Ohio; Bismarck, North Dakota; Davenport, Iowa, and similar places. We saw many—and I mean many—middle-class families and retired folks, tourists who've got money to spend."

"Older or younger tourists?"

"Both age groups," she said and took a deep breath. "The sight of a middle-aged or older church-going woman with her purse on her lap, sitting at a slot machine is not an uncommon one in Las Vegas, and it's one I haven't forgotten. As we walked through the casinos located in strategic and highly visible parts of the hotels, we were shocked by the sight of all those middle-aged and older people from middle America who were out there in Vegas recklessly spending their children's or grandchildren's inheritance."

"They weren't really *spending* but giving away the inheritance," Jack said. "I've been to casinos, and I know how that goes."

"Giving it away—*not* to missionaries, mind you, but to machines," Alice said. "Blowing it away is an even better phrase. I say that because in the three days we spent in that inglorious Sin City, we walked through numerous casinos—you can't get anywhere in those massive hotel buildings without going through those casinos—and in those days, we never saw a single person who had won anything. Not one."

"Did you or Frank play any of the machines?"

"Absolutely not."

"Go to the shows?"

"We went to one, but my dear Frank found aspects of the language, especially when spoken by women, to be *utterly repulsive*—his words."

"Too frank, you might say?"

"I'd say that if I were in pursuit of cheap humor."

Jack smiled and said, "Okay what's your general impression of Vegas?"

"To us, the city was a sensory overload, a morally bankrupt place," she said. "In the three days we were there, we felt as cut-off from the real world and the genuine culture of day-to-day life in America as the Amish must feel. I know comparing Las Vegas to the Amish sounds strange, but that's the way we felt. Vegas is a culture all its own."

She talked a bit more about Las Vegas, pointed to all the lights and glitter and the fact that the strip never closes, and answered a few more of his questions. "Now remember, Jack, the Vegas I've been telling you about is the Vegas of the late sixties; we're starting the eighties now, and if anything, the morality had degenerated and will continue to do so."

"I suspect you're right on that. It'll continue to go south with the drifting years."

"From our brief stay in Vegas, all sorts of images took residence in our minds," she said. "To this day, I can still see the smile-deprived faces of older and middle-aged women reaching up for those smooth black balls crowning shiny chrome-colored handles of slot machines at the casinos, reaching up again, and again, and again—pumping them as if they were rusty outdoor water pumps on the family farm. Such images lingered with us and will continue to do so."

"And by *us*, you mean you and Frank?"

"Exactly," she said. "Frank was as uneasy with the entire place as I was." She winked and paraphrased Joseph Conrad's *Heart of Darkness* by saying, "*Mistah Goe—he dead.* So, when I say, *us* now, I mean *me.* Let me re-word that and say: Those images lingered with me. And I'm absolutely certain that many of them—and now

I'm referring not to the machines but to the women—were faithful churchgoers."

"You're probably right. Gambling tempts a lot of us, but there's nothing in the good book that prohibits it. Or is there?"

"Don't know," Alice said. "But I do know this much: whenever we invest money in the stock market, we're gambling. Aren't we?"

"Guess so," Jack said. "That's a defense those women might use."

"Some images from life," Alice said while smiling, "stick with a person and continue to grow like one's ears, which I'm told never stop growing. The Vegas image is one of those for me."

Jack smiled, reached up and touched the earlobes of his large ears.

— ❦ —

That afternoon, she told him about a time in Barcelona in July in the early sixties.

"I'll never forget," Alice said at one point, "the sight of a little boy who was standing on the sidewalk clutching the bars of a dark wrought iron fence and looking at children his age playing on the playground of their Roman Catholic school during recess time."

"This was in Barcelona?" Jack asked. "In Spain, right?"

"Yes. Not too far from the harbor where Frank and I were walking to board a ship and begin a voyage to Tangier, Morocco. The children, dressed in their school uniforms, were playing on the grass of a well-kept playground, climbing the shiny monkey bars, pushing each other on the swing sets, rising and falling on the seesaws, playing kickball or soccer. They were clearly the children of well-to-do folks in Barcelona, those who could afford to send their little ones to expensive private schools."

"What a warm and inviting scene," Jack said. "And I trust it was a sunny day?"

"It was," Alice added. "I still remember all those lovely, happy, cheering kids, enjoying their recess time on a breezy sunny afternoon. When the little boy saw Frank and me approaching him on the sidewalk, he stopped clutching the fence, reached down on the ledge and picked up a box of Chiclets, the size of a hardback book. The box had tiny yellow boxes in it, each box being the size of a domino, with four Chiclets squares in it. The boy offered to sell some to Frank and me."

"Did you buy any?"

"Oh yes, we bought several," she said. "Frank scrambled the long dark hair of the dirty but beautiful boy with olive-colored skin and large brown eyes, and both of us said *muchas gracias* and refused to take any change resulting from the price of the tiny boxes we bought."

"What a tender scene."

"After we took a few steps away from the boy," she said, "Frank and I, almost at once, turned around and looked at the boy to see what he was doing following his transaction with us."

"And what did he do?"

"He placed the Chiclets box back on the ledge near the fence; then he clutched the iron bars of the fence and reconnected with his activity of looking at the kids in the playground." She paused, then added, "But that's *not* the end of the incident."

"What else could've taken place that day?" Jack said.

"What took place dealt with a question that went through my mind," she said. "I asked Frank: *How would a sociologist—or a math teacher—explain what we had just seen and done?* Frank thought, tilted his head and looked at the sky, and then responded: *Sociologists might resort to clichés to explain the scene: 'Rags to Riches,' or 'Progress and Poverty,' or 'Have and Have-nots,' and so forth.*"

"He's right, isn't he?" Jack said.

"Yes, he is. But you know what a writer who had witnessed that scene might say? Or at least, what your A. P. Goe would say?"

"What?"

"A writer might ask: *What was going through the mind of that little boy as he clutched the dark iron rods and looked in?*"

— ☙ —

"Speaking of writers," Jack said, "Lisa started *Editors and Their Turkeys* the other day, and I'm going to read it after her. She says she loves the wit in your writing style."

"Thanks."

"Your light touch in a book on the writer's craft is unique. Isn't it?"

"Unique is a strong word. Let's say *refreshing*."

"Lisa claims your title telegraphs the book's upcoming humor."

"She's right," Alice said. "I hope the title invites readers to see that the interaction between editors and writers can be viewed from a comic perspective."

"And if the readers don't see that in the title?"

"They'll probably assume," Alice smiled as she spoke, "that the book is about editors having Thanksgiving dinners with cranky relatives."

"The title does both to me," Jack winked. "Are you working on another book now?"

"Strange you should ask," she said, and decided to be suggestive and not definitive. "I'm working on a novel, one set right here in Kansas."

"Autobiographical novel?"

"More or less. Many first novels tend to be."

"I'd love to read it when it's completed."

"Why?" she asked. "First novels tend to be boring. I bet you think you're going to be in it, eh? You think a one-time star Texas quarterback in high school who is now a cleaning lad with an Elvis-pompadour hairpiece—that befits a talk-therapist—will make a good character in a novel?"

"Yes," he said, delighted to see her associate him with such a noble profession. "Yes, yes," he playfully stretched the hissing sound of the "s."

There was a long pause. "Well, you're right, my friend. But there are other men in my life who will also be in it. One is in the grave but the others are still kicking."

Sensing a shift in her demeanor, Jack didn't ask about the other living men. Instead, he said, "When do you think you'll finish the novel?"

"In a couple years or so."

— ❧ —

That afternoon, they talked about other topics related to the weather, car mechanics, baseball, and an upcoming retirement party—topics that interested them.

She didn't bring up the topic that had galvanized her creativity and absorbed all her attention. That topic appears in the letter that had just been received by the president of Royalle College in West Virginia.

CHAPTER FIVE

WHILE ALICE AND JACK CONTINUED TO TALK IN Samsville, her letter baffled Timothy Lynpeex in West Virginia. When he recovered from his initial shock, he chuckled. He saw the letter unfurling an honorably devious request.

The glass building that Alice had referred to in the letter is Addison Hall. On the first floor are the offices of Lynpeex and his administrative assistant, Bob Toyzol. The college, founded in the late nineteenth century by W. J. Martyn-Royalle, a Roman Catholic industrialist, had 614 students in the fall of 1980, with varsity teams in football, basketball, and baseball for men and basketball and softball for women.

Ten years earlier, when Dr. Lynpeex became president, he hired his friend Bob Toyzol and gave him the title of "administrative assistant," a post with low status in the minds of the faculty ("that's a secretary with a fancy title," as one person put it), but in the president's mind, Toyzol was an unofficial "chief of staff," entrusted with overseeing the work of the college's four vice-presidents. Toyzol's office was adjacent to Lynpeex's.

On the first floor of Addison are the offices of the college's Registrar, three conference rooms, a large auditorium, and several classrooms. The literary conference on Virginia Woolf that Alice and

Frank had attended was held, for the most part, on the first floor of Addison Hall.

The second floor houses the offices of four departments. The third and fourth floors consist of classrooms used mostly by students from the business, humanities, and education fields.

— ❧ —

Dr. Lynpeex, as the college's leader and chief fundraiser, would often assign a prospective donor with whom he didn't wish to deal to the college's vice-president for development.

"Our development fellow," Lynpeex once confided in his wife, "is a reasonably *incompetent* gentleman, but I don't have the heart to fire him; after all, he's a faithful member of our church who cheerfully carries out everything Father asks of him, and he has (in true Catholic fashion) seven children under twelve years of age that he and his wife need to support."

More importantly, the promises of Alice's potential donation had tempted and invigorated Lynpeex. So, he charged out after her challenge. After discussing with Toyzol the contents of Alice's proposition, Lynpeex dictated to a compact cassette an initial response. It states:

Dear Mrs. Goe:

Thank you so much for your letter, which arrived this morning. We are most appreciative of the donation that you wish to make to Royalle College.

As an institution, Royalle has been educating young people for nearly a century. We are most eager to pursue the entire matter with you, Mrs. Goe. We feel honored that you have selected our college as the possible recipient of your extremely generous gift.

We will do all that we can to please you. We are here to serve our students and to work with individuals, such as you, who care deeply about young people living and studying in Appalachia.

The Virginia Woolf conference that you mentioned in your letter was held in Addison Hall, the building that houses my office as president. Your witty reference to Addison's "state-of-the-art bathrooms" made me chuckle. (I've never heard that expression applied to bathrooms.)

We would like to ask you, Mrs. Goe, to allow us several days to discuss your extraordinary request among ourselves and to see what we can do to find ways that will accommodate and implement your request.

Frankly, we have never had a request that resembles yours, though I must confess that we have had several very unusual requests in all the years I had served as president. I have been here in West Virginia at Royalle College for ten happy and challenging years, and if the board wishes to keep me, I hope to remain here until retirement.

We will be in touch with you in a few days, and at that time, we will have some very specific suggestions to make to you. When I say "we," I refer to Robert Toyzol, my administrative assistant and myself.

Both of us will address the concerns that you had mentioned in your kind and unusual letter—a letter that, I might add, captivated us.

In the meantime, please be assured of our strong interest in pursuing this matter with you. We would like to kindly ask you to refrain from contacting any other college or university until you hear from us.

Needless to say, we will be excited to see what is in store for our relationship with you in the days and weeks and years ahead. For now, we hope you like our new motto (see below). My assistant and I came up with it.

We look forward to hearing from you.

All the Best,

Timothy Lynpeex MBA, Ed.D.

President

Lynpeex asked Toyzol to type the dictated letter on the presidential stationery.

The words "Office of the President" appear below the sketch of the building that for ten years had housed Dr. Timothy Lynpeex's office. At the foot of the letterhead is a thin red line, and below the line, the motto of the college is centered and printed in italics. The motto proclaims: *Educating Heirs to the Throne of Culture.*

CHAPTER SIX

"WE'LL BE PATIENT AND CREATIVE IN OUR PURSUIT of the money, but we *can't* be devious," Lynpeex told Toyzol during a meeting in the president's office after lunch on a Monday.

"Sounds good to me, boss."

"In matters of this sort if the money is fated for us, we'll get it sooner or later. If it's not, we won't. It's that simple."

Lynpeex, son of a Mexican mother and a French father, is a pious Roman Catholic who attends Holy Mass and takes communion— *daily*. Many learned professors at the religiously unaffiliated college respect his piety, but several secular humanists with advanced degrees would often ridicule it, albeit in private.

Robert Toyzol, an Irishman whose ancestors had emigrated from County Galway (and dropped the O and the apostrophe from O'Toyzol) is also a very pious Catholic who attends Mass and takes communion daily. His daughter, Livi, is now eleven years old.

Like Lynpeex, Toyzol is stocky, five feet eleven inches in height with a full head of white hair. In graduate school, the two had roomed together much as they had done in their undergraduate years. He earned an MBA from the same university that his boss had attended. His low status frees him from ridicule by Ph.Ds in need of house-training.

Both men often met to discuss college matters in the president's office. An unframed newspaper-size oil painting of a 1939 bright-red Ford pickup truck with an oval barrel-shaped grille hangs on one wall between two leather armchairs, and a large wood-framed oil painting of the quartzite-capped ridge of West Virginia's North Fork Mountain hangs on another wall. Near the mahogany desk, a bookshelf and a file cabinet are placed.

On the wall directly behind the desk's swivel chair are degrees that Lynpeex had earned: one a doctorate in education (an Ed.D.) and the other an MBA. Both are from a university in West Virginia, and both are matted and framed in wooden frames with non-glare glass.

The office has a thick tan carpet, so thick that a hardcore teetotaler would appear tipsy strolling on it. Neat and spacious, the office also has an expansive picture window that creates an indoor/outdoor space, a window that invites a great deal of sunlight. The window frames three scenes: the center of the tastefully landscaped campus, the massive sculpture of two bronze hunters with coonskin caps sitting next to a campfire, and the only Collegiate Gothic building on campus—Mountaineer Hall.

Lynpeex dislikes (and never uses) his office's two fluorescent lights anchored to the ceiling. He prefers the soft light of a lamp with a silk drum shade.

— ⌘ —

In Kansas, Alice was writing in her diary an entry dealing with what she had *imagined* her counterpart, Timothy Lynpeex, to look like. She felt he's likely to be slender, close to six feet, with brown or blond hair.

"An art professor, a scientist, or a writer," she wrote, "can get away with a wild, bushy head of hair or even a head with no hair. But a male chief executive of anything these days, much like a politician or an actor or a television announcer, needs a full head of hair. If you lose your hair, you buy some from a store and tack it on."

In reality, Lynpeex was six feet tall, stocky with a firm belly. He had his mother's brown eyes and dark Mexican complexion.

As for hair, Lynpeex is bald. He never claims to be bald, but he never denies it either. At times, he'd say, "Some people part their hair in a straight line; I do mine in a circle." Other times, the Catholic in him would lead him to claim that: "The Lord created so many perfect heads; the rest he covered with hair."

Such self-deprecating remarks (not uncommon among bald men) are part of Lynpeex's jovial nature, but for the most part, he is one serious fellow—and he certainly took Alice's proposal seriously.

— ભ —

"We've got to keep this entire project confidential," Lynpeex told Toyzol. "Highly confidential, until payday that is."

"Good idea," Toyzol added. "I'll type whatever letters we send, whatever papers we sign. I'll keep Kathy out of all of this."

Kathy is Toyzol's administrative assistant. She attends all letters addressed to Robert Toyzol, but letters addressed to President Timothy Lynpeex are opened and read by Toyzol, who has been Lynpeex's administrative assistant for ten years.

Lynpeex's business sense, nurtured during his MBA program, helped redirect the financial affairs of the school; he led Royalle to a more stable financial base. During his ten years at the college, Lynpeex improved the salaries for faculty and staff, but the college remained too dependent on tuition.

As Alice had suspected, the college was still "financially horny," but thanks to Lynpeex's leadership, it was moving towards a serious relationship with fundraising. His fundraising vision—executed with determination, wisdom, care, and old-fashioned hard work—was set, in his words, "on fat felines and major foundations."

Both men saw Alice Goe as a fat feline who drifted their way. They wanted to handle her with extra-special care.

As the two men sat in the president's office, a concerned Lynpeex asked: "Kathy didn't see Goe's letter, did she?"

"That's right; she did *not* see it."

"How about my reply?"

"Nope, I typed that. I had enough sense to do that."

"Great." Lynpeex said. "Let's give this project a name, a sort of code that we could refer to on certain occasions."

"Sounds good."

"What do you suggest?" Lynpeex asked, as he rocked in his padded swivel chair. He leaned over and fiddled with his cherry-wood smoking pipe, jamming it full of fibers of Flying-Dutchman tobacco. He rocked back, lit the tobacco, and spoke between puffs, "We really need a name, a good name for the project."

"How about the Peculiar Educational Project?" Toyzol said as he slouched in an armchair across from the desk. "The acronym is PEP."

"Okay, that's a possibility," Lynpeex said. Then he thought for a moment and added, "Scratch that idea, Bob. PEP is too close to *Pepto*, and we certainly don't want that name. With that, we'll be falling right into her trap," Lynpeex said as he blew smoke from the right side of his mouth. "What else is out there?"

Both looked up at the holes in the white cork ceiling. Toyzol spoke up, "How about calling it simply the *Peculiar Project*?"

"Sounds so-so."

"Only so-so?"

"Yes," Lynpeex said, stretching the word.

"It has alliteration."

"Maybe that's why I think it's only so-so."

"Well, it's another start."

"If we go with that," Lynpeex said, "we'll probably end up calling the project by its initials PP. That'll wink at your prostate problems, Bob."

Both laughed at that remark. The sweet aroma of Flying Dutchman filled the office, mingling with the sulfur released from the matches. Some cigarette smokers chain-smoke, Toyzol thought to himself: pipe smokers chain-light. The aroma of Lynpeex's now-lit, now-unlit tobacco conspired with the sulfur odor and persuaded Toyzol to release the gases that had accrued in his system from the beans he had eaten with his hot dogs for lunch at the college's cafeteria.

Tobacco and sulfur, Toyzol felt, stamp the prohibition on releasing gas in a president's office when two persons are present as *Null and Void*. Accordingly, Toyzol bombed away. To align the angle of a descending bomb, he would occasionally lean on his left buttock, but the ethic of equipping the bombs with silencers remained intact—no matter what competing (and dominant) fragrances were present in the office.

"How about the Kansas Donation?" Lynpeex said, as his teeth bit the pipe's mouthpiece. He rocked back in his chair, placed his feet on the corner of the desk and his palms behind his head.

"Sounds like we're making a big donation to Kansas University," Toyzol said. "Like *we're* the fat felines and not the beggars."

"Exactly," Lynpeex said. "That's precisely what I intend for it to sound like. Normally, we're considered the charity, but we sound like the rich donor with that name. I like it. What do you think?"

"Sounds good. We'll name it: *Kansas Donation*."

"Now the big question remains," Lynpeex said. "How do we get the money and maintain our integrity—"

"And sanity. Her strings are strange, crazy."

"On our Bizarre Gifts Barometer with strange strings attached," Lynpeex said, "this one has got to be off the charts."

— ∽ —

Lynpeex's phone rang, and his wife was the caller. Sensing that, Toyzol left the office to give them some privacy.

After using the restroom and chatting with Kathy for a moment, he knocked and entered the office. They exchanged a couple of trivial remarks and refocused on Alice's request.

Lynpeex stood and stretched as if he were in a baseball game participating in the seventh-inning stretch.

"In our line of work," Lynpeex said, as he returned to his swivel chair, "we've come to expect unusual requests every now and then."

"And almost all our requests, no matter how strange and unusual," Toyzol said, "have been converted into cash."

Lynpeex was busy lighting his pipe again. Toyzol's nose itched, so he scratched it; then he stuck his right pinky into the right fender of his nose and confronted the restless ways of a nagging booger.

He smiled inwardly at the release of another silencer-equipped fart and thought, "Tim lights his pipe, I light some gas, and all is well with the brass of Royalle College. Things will really be unwell with me if Tim declares his office to be—*a fart-free zone.*"

CHAPTER SEVEN

"Do you remember our *COCKROACH-MILLIONAIRE*, as we used to call old-man Gilbert?" Lynpeex asked.

"Sure do—an unforgettable fellow."

The *cockroach-millionaire* was a Royalle alumnus who had played football at the college in the early nineteen-twenties. He had expressed interest in giving the college a gift of two million dollars if it agrees to change its nickname from, in Gilbert's words, "the un-original and staid Royalle *Guards* to the attention-commanding Royalle *Cockroaches*."

The alumnus from Wheeling, West Virginia, told Lynpeex and Toyzol that he wanted "to be in a position to hear the radio announcer say at the beginning of a football or a baseball game, . . . *And now, onto the field go the fighting Cockroaches of Royalle College.*"

Even for two million, there was no way Lynpeex and Toyzol could have gotten such a change approved by the board of trustees of the college and the athletic department and the faculty and the student body. So, they did all that they could to get Gilbert to change his mind.

When they visited him at his mansion in Wheeling, he kept telling them: "All kinds of cats and dogs, bulls and bisons, lions and even trees are used for nicknames. Why not a cockroach?"

He went on and on and reasoned why cockroaches would make a remarkable name. He argued: "Cockroaches get attention; no one dares to ignore them; it's hard to get rid of them; they're everywhere; they're frightening, intimidating, elusive, vigorous, indestructible, mean. Cockroaches inflict pain on all who come in contact with them."

"At one point in our conversation with old-man Gilbert," Lynpeex said, placing his cherry-wood pipe on a spur-shaped bronze ashtray, "I recall him saying something to the effect that the word *ache* is in cockroaches; in other words, the Royalle cockroaches inflict *pain* on their opposition. Do you recall that, Bob?"

A smiling Toyzol said, "I do. And as I recall, you told him that *ache* isn't the only word in cockroaches. The old man laughed out loud." (That allusion led Toyzol to feel the urge to urinate, but he struggled to hold it. He, in effect, succeeded in trapping his discomfort.)

Both gentlemen reminded themselves that in the end, they did get the cash, and as Toyzol put it, "we *did-and-didn't* end up changing our nickname." They negotiated and finally changed the college's nickname from *Guards* (one word) to eight words, making the tiny West Virginia school, as Lynpeex boasted to Gilbert, "*Number One* in nickname length." Thanks to a donation of two million dollars, the college's formal nickname became: *The Spiffy and Majestic Royalle College Palace Guards.*

It didn't take long for the students and the radio announcers and the college's newspaper editors to shorten the name to: *Spiffies.* "Outsiders don't know what a *Spiffy* is," Lynpeex told Toyzol. "And I don't know what a Georgetown *Hoya* is, or what an Oklahoma *Sooner* is, or what a Virginia Tech *Hokie* is. They're just silly nicknames. It took a little persuasion to get our precious *cockroach-millionaire* to contribute in a big way to his alma mater."

"Just a *little*?"

"Well, a lot-of-little persuasion worked on old-man Gilbert."

"Whether such persuasion will work on our wealthy widow from the Great Plains remains to be seen."

"You said it, man," Lynpeex spoke raising his voice. "We've got to come up with a game plan, a strategy, that'll work on Mrs. Goe."

"Seven million is an incredible amount."

"Sure is," Lynpeex said. "It'll be nice to get it for the old *Spiffies* of West Virginia's College Royalle."

— ☙ —

After a long moment of silence, Toyzol asked, "Well, where do we go from here? What should be our next move?"

"We've got to make sure Mrs. Goe is real."

"Real?"

"We've got to make sure she exists and that this isn't a stunt that some frustrated writer is pulling on us."

"Good point."

"Yeah, some writers carry out their research by doing things to see how people react to them, then they write about what they've done, the people's reactions, and so forth. I remember one time reading about a fellow who held up a bartender at gunpoint, and later in court tried to defend his action by telling the judge that he didn't intend to kill the bartender but was simply collecting material for a novel."

"Oh."

Lynpeex continued, "We've got to somehow learn a lot more about Mrs. Goe, make a psychological profile of her before we approach her with a visit and a plan of our own."

"And how do you propose to do that, Tim?"

"Oh, there'll be all sorts of ways. We've got to look for and explore those ways." Lynpeex reached to the side of his desk, picked up Alice's letter, and re-read a segment of it. "It says here that she wants no phone calls or visits—and the *no* is repeated and printed in all caps."

"She also claims," Lynpeex observed, "that she's a writer, and you know what that means?"

"What?"

"That she corresponds with herself. My nephew claims to be a writer, and he's forever enclosing self-addressed stamped envelopes with all the manuscripts that he sends out—and the manuscripts come back to him with *disturbing faithfulness*, as he jokes. He's an odd dude: he claims the often-maligned post office is an extremely efficient operation because it never lost or damaged any of his rejected manuscripts. Never. I wouldn't say all this to Mrs. Goe—not at this stage anyway. If we discover that she, like Paul, has a sense of humor about the writing profession, then we can unleash some of that humor on her."

"For now, let's get serious, Tim."

"Okay, let me say this: we can learn a lot about a person from reading his or her writings. We'll have to check her name in the library and see if she published books or poems or stories or essays or what not."

"Our library probably won't have her literary work."

"We'll go to Morgantown if need be," Lynpeex said, referring to the town where the University of West Virginia is located.

"They've got a good literature program down there, don't they? If I remember correctly," Toyzol added with a double cough, "a couple of our *beloved* English professors have their doctorates from there."

"For a seven-million-dollar donation for our college," the president said, "I'll go to the Library of Congress to hunt up stuff that she may have published—if that'll help us get the money."

"What if all her writings are unpublished?"

"Then we'll ask her to send us some unpublished stuff, and we'll see what it says," Lynpeex replied. "What we've got to do, Bob, is draw a psychological profile from her writings and her letters to us. All I'm saying is we can't go in there cold to meet her and expect to freelance our way: unusual requests require unusual preparation. She doesn't want to be courted, yet she has this strange request—"

"And to us, a spectacular amount of cash."

"I'll drink to that," Lynpeex said and stood to stretch. His dark, double-knit suit opened and closed around his stout six-foot frame. He stuck both thumbs under his belt buckle, anchoring his belly with his fists. He took several steps away from his chair; then he walked back to it. "Let's start by calling her town's directory assistance to make sure she's a real person—not a phony-baloney writer using a pseudonym. And if she is, see what else you can find out about her, and we'll talk at lunch tomorrow."

CHAPTER EIGHT

Moments after leaving the first meeting on the *Kansas Donation,* Toyzol went back to his office and his telephone rang. Lynpeex told him, "Please come back, Bob: I've got an idea on what to do with our *Vespa-man.*"

The *Vespa-man* was a tenured professor in the English department, and Lynpeex felt the professor might be able to assist the Royalle College administration in its pursuit of Alice Goe's donation.

The professor, a fellow in his early sixties, would come to the campus riding a Vespa with its small wheels and open U-shaped front. The professor insisted on calling it a motorcycle (but others at the college considered it to be a motor scooter), and he always wore a helmet and a dark leather jacket. The jacket, Lynpeex felt, might go nicely with a big and muscular rider straddling a Harley-Davidson, but it looked weird on a delicate man sitting and leaning forward with knees a dozen inches apart.

Lynpeex's idea had the professor wearing the Goe tie clips on the lapel of his leather jacket for at least one year. In doing so, the professor would help earn his salary and that of others in that department.

The English department wasn't Lynpeex's favorite department. It was overstaffed with six full-time professors: all male, all tenured.

The *Vespa-man*, who grew up in the Northern Panhandle of West Virginia, was the only religious person in the department: a practicing Catholic who attended every Sunday the church where his wife grew up in a town near Royallestown. He was also a Virginia Woolf scholar who had published extensively on her work. He organized and led the college's conference on her writings, the conference that was—joyfully—attended by the Goes.

"That guy," Lynpeex said, referring to the English professor, "is more suited for the tie clips than we are. We're just lowly administrators. He's a full professor with a Ph.D. from a major university. The clips on him would be most appropriate. After all, if you stop and think about it, when he rides his Vespa and spreads his feet apart and leans forward, he looks like a man sitting on a moving toilet stool."

"Never thought of it that way," Toyzol said. "But now that you mention it, I can picture that."

"If we tell Mrs. Goe about this guy and about what he looks like when he rides his Vespa," Lynpeex said, "she might like our idea, and she might expand on it and say: *Get that old guy to wear not tie clips but a leather vest with the appropriate wording on it.* And if she makes such an outlandish request, our job would be to try to convince the old professor that he's got to wear such a vest for the benefit of the *Ol' Spiffies* of Royalle College."

"Your idea is a good one, Tim. Problem is—that old fart would never do it even though his cooperation could mean seven million dollars for the school, and all his buddies would benefit from that."

When Toyzol says "buddies," he is in a subtle way reminding Lynpeex of Royalle's situation: all but one of the college's tenured faculty were male. (The one tenured woman was a librarian.) Lynpeex and his assistant were committed to getting more female scholars on tenure-track appointments, and they were succeeding, however slowly. Their hope was, in Lynpeex's words, "for more male profes-sors to either move on or retire or go on academic—i.e. mental—disability. We're stuck with too many men who've degenerated into tenured teachers of dated knowledge."

"Love that phrase," Toyzol said.

"I'd pay to see what Alice Goe thinks of my *Vespa-man* idea," Lynpeex said.

— ❧ —

Toyzol went back to his office and placed on the Zenith Console Stereo a vinyl disk that featured the clarion voice of Hazel Dickens, his favorite West Virginia artist who blends pure mountain-inflected ballad singing with traditional-country and bluegrass influences.

With Dickens playing the guitar and singing in the background, Toyzol began working on what he called, "Early Profile of Mrs. Goe." That's the label he scribbled at the top of a yellow legal pad that he always carried in his briefcase.

Toyzol called the Samsville directory assistance (located in Wichita, Kansas) and asked for Alice Goe's telephone number. He also asked for an address, but the operator said, "Sorry, sir, we're not allowed to give out street address information."

He hung up and again called Samsville information and hoped to get a different person working the directory-assistance desk. Sure enough, he did, and the second operator also refused to give the address. So Toyzol read Goe's Main Street address from a copy of her letter, which he had reproduced earlier and placed in a file. The operator responded, "Yes, sir, that's her correct address."

He thanked the operator and asked for another number: the number of the Samsville Public Library. He called it to see what published items might be there under the name of Alice Goe.

"Of course, I know her," the person who answered his call said.

"Miss. Stuneburn, our head librarian, knows her very well; she'll be able to help you, but she's not here at the present time."

That comment led Toyzol to assume that he was talking to the head librarian's assistant. He asked the assistant if she knew of any books, fiction or nonfiction, that Mrs. Alice Goe might have published, and the woman gave him the relevant publication data on what she called, "the only book ever to be *professionally* published by a resident of Samsville: *Editors and Their Turkeys*."

Toyzol noted the data on the book then asked if Mrs. Goe had published other literary works, and the librarian said, "No other books, but she's published many stories, poems, and articles in all sorts of places. Mrs. Goe is a very prominent and productive member of our WLA."

"What's that?" Toyzol asked.

"Women's Literary Association, our town's writing-literary club. Lots of towns and cities have reading clubs, book clubs, but we've got a writing club instead."

"I suspect they also read. Don't you think?"

"Yes, they do," the librarian answered. "If nothing else, they read their own writings, I suppose."

"Could you tell me where she's published her creative stuff?"

"I could," she said, "but that'll take me a good while to research; I certainly can't do that research now. I'm the only one at the desk now, and we've got other patrons waiting to be assisted."

"Is there someone else who knows where she published her writings?"

"Yes, there is."

"Who would that be?"

"Mrs. Goe."

"No, no, other than her."

"Call the librarian at the high school. Mr. Goe used to teach there. I know that for a fact because my husband and I sat under him when we were students there."

Toyzol listened and thought: *You'd probably be a better couple if you sat beside him.*

"So, Mr. Goe was a high school teacher? Does that pay well?" Toyzol asked.

"Not as much as we'd like, but it's a living."

"Did Mr. Goe have another job? Or another source of income?"

After a pause, the librarian replied, "Call Tripod at the high school. He knows about Mrs. Goe's writing and Mr. Goe's teaching. He'll be able to help you with all of that."

"Tripod" is the nickname of a part-time English teacher, part-time librarian, and part-time football coach. He is a neighbor of Mrs. Goe, and both are members of the only Methodist church in town.

"Would you please be kind enough to give me his phone number?" Toyzol asked. "I urgently need it, and I'd really be most appreciative of your kind assistance."

The librarian took a deep breath, blew in the phone's mouthpiece, and said, "Just a minute, sir."

Toyzol thanked the librarian, placed the receiver on the hook, and wondered aloud: "How could Mr. Goe, a teacher in a high school in a small town in Kansas, amass all that wealth?"

— ∾ —

Toyzol had hoped to get a first and a last name for Tripod and to use the "Mr." label with the name, but the assistant at the public library told him: "Everyone in town uses his nickname. His real name will confuse people."

Toyzol called the library at the high school and asked to speak to

Tripod. And, after the usual introductory formalities, Tripod got to business. "From what I know," Tripod said, "Mrs. Goe writes a heck of a lot, and she always reads her stuff at a club for the old ladies around here." Tripod paused, then added, "Other than her book on writers as turkeys, she has published works in *Pens of the Great Plains* and other literary quarterlies, but I don't know where off-hand. I know she's got an excellent book collection of American and European writers whose works were published in the first half of the twentieth century. I've seen the collection at her house, and I've even borrowed several books from it. She's a kind and generous woman."

"Thank you, Tripod," Toyzol said. "May I ask one last question?"

"Sure."

"If Mrs. Goe's husband is so wealthy, why did he teach school?"

"Who told you he's wealthy?"

"You mean he's not?"

"Mrs. Goe's husband is dead," Tripod said. "Mrs. Goe lives in a nice and spacious Victorian house on Main Street. She lives four houses down from us. Her old man was a teacher for many years; I sat under him. All of us who knew him felt he was on the paranoid side: if he was rich in anything, he was rich in his paranoia. Still a hell-of-a-nice fellow."

"Got you," Toyzol said. "Thanks for your help."

After placing the phone on the hook, Toyzol received an urgent call from his prostate. He answered it in the bathroom where he found himself asking the urinal's handle: "Why do people sit *under* people in Kansas?" He laughed at his question while pulling his zipper north.

When he returned to his desk, he asked himself: "How can I find out if Mrs. Goe is indeed wealthy? Is she assuming that posture in order to trick us at Royalle College, in order to write a comic novel or a short story about us?" He took a deep breath and added: "Tim suspects that could possibly be the case. Is he right? After all, Mama Lynpeex didn't raise a dummy."

Toyzol looked at the birds frolicking outside his office window. He placed his feet up on the corner of his desk and told himself: "Some people tug their chins or brace their cheeks or suck their pipes when they think, but I place my feet on the desk, not as picturesque a posture as that of others, but it does the job. I'll have to think all this through with Tim tomorrow. I'm sure he'll have ideas on what to do."

— ❧ —

Toyzol wondered what his boss would think of the information he had gathered from his investigation.

Alice had a game plan to deal with the men, and they, in effect, were formulating their plan to deal with her. Before long, the two plans would collide.

CHAPTER NINE

At the afternoon coffee break, Alice told Jack about two greetings with peculiar responses she overheard at the grocery store.

"The cashier asked Curley Hayward," Alice said, referring to a retired farmer: "*How're you doing*? and Curley replied: *Living the dream*! Curley paused before asking, *And you, son*? The cashier quickly replied: *Certifying the nightmare.*"

"Who's the cashier?" Jack asked.

"Your neighbor's son-in-law, Tommy Wyse—the one with all the tattoos."

"You know that guy majored in English at Fort Hays State. For a full-time job around here, that's almost as good as a philosophy major. I suppose he could write for the newspaper if he wanted to. I know his wife would love that."

"Love those tattoos on his arms," Alice said. "I see modernity in them, but to people around here, they probably look like chicken wire."

"So many people here have tattoos these days."

"Even my Frank had one that led him to claim: *Tattoos are our way of saying*: '*We can make bad decisions with the best of them.*' "

"Tattoos, nicknames, and country music are big out here on the plains. Aren't they?"

"Sure are."

"And everyone seems to have an opinion on them."

"You should hear the women at club when these topics come up."

"We're a two-person club here," Jack said, "so let me ask: What do you choose to listen to in music?"

"When I'm writing, I usually listen to an FM radio station from Wichita that plays sacred and classical music from Bach, Mendelssohn, Mozart, Handel, Vivaldi, and others. I don't have a collection of classical music records, but I do have several LPs of Gregorian Chants that I listen to on occasions. And from the contemporary sphere, I have every record produced so far by an extraordinary folk singer from California whose tunes penetrate and engage every facet of my being, and whose riveting and poignant songs are first-rate poems."

"Who's *that*?" Jack asked.

"Care to guess?"

"Bob Dylan or John Denver?"

"No. Wrong gender."

"Judy Collins or Helen Reddy?"

"No to both. Though I love Helen Reddy's *I Am Woman*. I see poetry in that song—really, it's an anthem—and I love the energy she feels when she sings it. Give up?" He nodded, and Alice added: "Kate Wolf."

"Never heard of her."

"You did today," Alice said. "Someday I'll play you one or two of her albums. I love the way she strums a guitar and weaves her pure and angelic voice through image-laden poems that form her songs."

— ∽ —

In time, the conversation drifted to the Wednesday evening retirement dinner party held at the Methodist church for the town's only veterinarian who, as Alice said, "called it quits at sixty-five."

Many people from the community had attended the party. Alice was there, but Lisa and Jack stayed home to play board games with two other couples from their church.

Lisa's parents also went to honor the veterinarian. The pastor of the church served as master of ceremonies, and several people spoke— among them the town's mayor, four farmers, the town's barber, and the two brothers and only sister of the veterinarian: a widower.

"It wasn't a potluck dinner but a catered one," Alice told Jack. "Highlights of the evening were the gift presentations."

"I hear the vet got a nice rocking chair," Jack said. "Lisa's old man says, *Doc was also given a new typewriter that has no moving carriage but a little testicle in it.* Is that right?"

Alice laughed and said, "It's a green IBM Selectric typewriter, like the one I have, with a typing mechanism that looks like a golf ball or a large marble or a ping-pong ball. Oh, Lisa's dad can be so colorful."

"He sure can," Jack said. "Even though he doesn't laugh much, I love his sense of humor. Lisa nicknamed him *The Smiling Factory*."

"Love the irony in that, my friend," Alice said.

"I do too," Jack added. "With the typewriter gift, I'm assuming someone heard the old vet was planning to do some writing."

"I *know* he's going to try," she said. "The other day at church, he asked me what I thought of his project."

"He's got one mapped out already?" Jack asked. "The fellow just retired, and he wants to go to work in another field?"

"Oh yes," she said. "He wants to write a book and dedicate it to his late wife, a book that evokes the work of an English vet by the name of James Herriot, the author of the bestseller *All Creatures Great and Small*. But our vet wants to title his work *Ill Creatures of the Great Plains*."

"That's because he heals *ill* creatures out here, I suppose."

"It's because he doesn't know what he's doing," she quickly said. "*Ill Creatures*, I told our vet, is an off-putting concept, a negative one. A book publisher won't use that title, however evocative you think it's going to be. The folks in marketing will shoot it down. Needless to say, our vet didn't like my response; he'll be looking elsewhere for advice. And that's fine with me. He'll soon discover that writing a book is a lot harder than coming up with a bad title and a dedication for it."

"I'll say. It's tough enough to write a short story, let alone a book."

— ❧ —

Following the coffee break, Alice went to the study, sat on the Victorian armchair, and wrote in her diary an entry dealing with the literary aspirations of the newly retired veterinarian.

The entry refers to the vet's wife of forty years, Lucille, a retired high school English teacher who had passed away seven months earlier:

> This afternoon, during a conversation with Jack, I regret coming down hard on our Dr. Trumbollie and his attempt to write a memoir. If his Lucille were still alive he would have first consulted with her on the title.
>
> Lucille, a member of our writing club, would've asked— really ordered—him to "sleep on his Ill-title idea." He would've interpreted that to mean, "Think it over." But she would've meant: "Put it to sleep."
>
> Anyway, now that the obligatory six months had passed since her death (that's the duration that must elapse if

one desires to follow our town's unwritten but widely accepted widower-dating etiquette), the pie caravan from the eligible widows had started in earnest.

I'm too old to be part of that caravan, but widows from the Presbyterian church and ours are busy baking.

From what I sense, we're in for some "interesting times" in little Samsville, America, as Chen Lee would say.

When she finished writing, she started to wash dishes in the sink. Even though she had a KitchenAid dishwasher, she seldom used it. She washed by hand the dishes that would result from her coffee sessions with Jack or from the lunch that she would cook for both.

— ∾ —

With the dishes washed, she sat alone near the kitchen table and held a round mirror, the size of a teacup saucer, that she kept on the windowsill.

She fiddled with the mirror, tilting it one way then another and another until she began to siphon sunlight with it—sunlight she would splash on items on the dining room walls. She landed on a large framed oil painting of a one-room clapboard schoolhouse in western Kansas that she and Frank had attended as kids. The painting had been hanging near a round chrome clock in the same place for more than fifty years.

Near the painting were three black-and-white photographs, one of her mother, one of her father, and one of Frank's parents. All three photographs were well-preserved and placed in oval wood frames. In these photos, all of the parents appear to be observing a moratorium on smiles.

Below those was a black-and-white photograph of Frank dressed in his Winterpeace College football uniform. Next to that was another one of him in his college baseball uniform with a Louisville Slugger wooden bat on his shoulder. Both pictures were neatly set in dark tin frames, bought years earlier at the local Ben Franklin store.

While fiddling with the mirror, Alice recalled Frank and his blue eyes and portly five-foot-seven-inch frame. She remembered his days playing football and baseball in high school, and she remembered seeing him play both sports for the Ice Storms of Winterpeace College.

She also recalled the time she (and six other women students) had campaigned for a mascot for their college. "Our unofficial mascot now," they argued sarcastically, "is a time period: *the dead of winter.* We suggest using a real person: *a meteorologist,* one who predicts the Ice Storms of Winterpeace College."

The campaign won, and a happy Alice wrote in a letter to her parents: "Our beloved Winterpeace College is now the only institution of higher learning on the planet that has a woman meteorologist for a mascot. And if truth be told: most of our students don't know what a meteorologist is or does, so our mascot also serves as an educational tool."

Looking at those pictures from around the early nineteen-twenties, Alice remembered that Frank had blond hair as a young man and during his years in college, but he saw most of his hair disappear shortly after graduating from college. With the Soviet Union, of all places, gentle on her mind, Alice thought: For a few years, my Frank had parted his hair in a line straight as a hammer's handle; then the good Lord, without Frank's consent, transformed the part into a sickle.

She remained seated near the window in the kitchen, splashing all those items with sunlight and mulling over the past.

CHAPTER TEN

Lynpeex and Toyzol sat in a large rectangular restaurant. The restaurant's main dining area had several wooden booths with Siamese benches, the kind where opposing buttocks share a backboard.

Lynpeex felt the place was "attractively ugly"—ugly in appearance but attractive for their purposes in that it was large and sparsely populated, offering them the desired privacy. Both ordered hamburgers with fries and two glasses of Coors beer.

"Well, Bob," Lynpeex said, "what did you find out about Mrs. Goe?"

"Not all that much, frankly."

"Specifically?"

"The name and address are real," Toyzol said.

"Good."

"Got a phone number."

"That's good, too."

"I also got the title of the one book she's published," Toyzol said. "I checked, and we don't have it in our library, but we can get a copy, I'm sure."

"That's good."

"I was told by two librarians that she'd published a lot of other stuff in magazines, but they wouldn't—couldn't—give more on that," Toyzol said. "We can hunt that up, however."

"Yes, we can."

"Ooops," Toyzol said and pounded his forehead with the palm of his right hand. "I forgot to tell Kathy that we decided to come out here. Should I call her? They have a phone booth outside this place."

"Nah," Lynpeex said. "Let's enjoy our meal."

"But she hates it when I don't tell her where I'm at; I know I'm going to hear about it," Toyzol said, expecting to have Kathy reprimand him on his return to the campus. In a strange way, Toyzol feared his administrative assistant far more than he feared Lynpeex, his boss.

"Anyway, a librarian in town told me that Mrs. Goe is a member of a writing club for ladies in Samsville. It's one of those clubs for old ladies in small towns; my mother belongs to such a club back home, except hers is a reading club, I think."

Both men looked out the window and saw a strange car with three wheels go by. Lynpeex said, "What I hear you saying is that she's an author with a recently published book and—"

"A writer with all sorts of other pieces in magazines," Toyzol said. "What magazines? That I don't know."

While trying to read the expression on Toyzol's face, Lynpeex said, "You look a bit concerned, Bob. Did you learn something that disturbed you?"

"Well, yes, and I might be wrong on this: I don't think she's rich."

"What makes you say that?"

"The librarian, who works at the high school, told me he knew Frank Goe and knew him well, and the old man wasn't rich. If Frank was rich in anything, the librarian said, he was rich in his paranoia."

"Ok-kay," Lynpeex said as both watched the waitress place their hamburgers and fries before them. "Thank you," both men spoke at once.

"Enjoy your meal, gentlemen. I'll be back to check on you," the waitress said and left.

"Bob, we've got to get that money, man; it'll do miracles for us. Seven million is a huge gift, a gigantic gift for Royalle," Lynpeex said. "To us, it's job security for a few more years. After all, this is our job: raising money for this place. That's about it."

Lynpeex spoke as if he was sure the money was there, but Toyzol guided the discussion to his personal doubts.

"I agree," Toyzol said, biting into his burger.

"We're talking seven million big ones," Lynpeex said, his eyes wide open, his arms fully outstretched as if they were poised to collapse into a bear hug.

"But frankly," Toyzol said, chewing a morsel of food, focusing his eyes on a pickle, "yesterday's preliminary research helped me establish some doubt as to whether the money is even there. The librarian at the high school seemed very blunt about the entire matter."

"What do you mean?" A suddenly concerned Lynpeex asked.

"The high school librarian seemed to think that the Goes are ordinary people, not people with money; they live a comfortable life, a school-teacher's life—but scarcely more."

"Don't let that bother you."

"It does."

"It shouldn't."

"What do you mean?"

"Trust me, it shouldn't."

"Be more specific," Toyzol said.

"The ethic in small-town life is this: *If you have it, don't flaunt it.*"

"Well, if the money is in property," Toyzol said, "I could make some calls to verify that information. But Mrs. Goe says the money is in cash."

Lynpeex pulled out of his briefcase Mrs. Goe's letter, and he read—first to himself—the parts about the money; then he read those parts aloud to Toyzol. "There's absolutely no way," Lynpeex said, "for us to call the bank, obviously. That information is more private than your penis. And if yours isn't, it should be."

"How about if I visit her neighbors in Samsville and ask about the Goes' wealth?" Toyzol asked, bit a pickle with goose bumps, and winced.

"That might hurt more than help. She might get upset and paranoid if she finds out people are in Samsville checking on her. She'll assume it's devious, however innocent and noble our motives are," Lynpeex said, took a large bite from his burger and chased the morsel with a swig of beer. "That's probably not such a good idea."

"You know, Tim, you've got me concerned already. I hope the librarian doesn't go to her house and tell her everything I asked about; I'm afraid our project would be kissed goodbye—if she does."

Lynpeex ignored Toyzol's fears and said, "The only way is for us to be honest and up front. Let's write and tell her we're now intensifying our pursuit of the donation, but we need to verify a few things first: and one of those *minor* things is the presence of the wealth—the seven million dollars—that she proposes to donate to Royalle College."

"What if she flares up in anger," Toyzol said, "and cuts us off?"

"No risk, no gain, but we've got to be honest."

"I'll drink to that," Toyzol said, raised his beer glass in a manner that reminded him of his corpulent urologist who would often lift and tilt his patient's specimen towards the room's light in search of that amber color. That image of his doctor was so vividly etched in Toyzol's mind, he gave it a label: "The unmistakable toast of urologists."

Toyzol's prostate had made him all too familiar with the ways of urologists. The raised beer glass led Toyzol to excuse himself and head to the men's room. When he returned, he told Lynpeex, "I thought of collating her unpublished pieces and publishing them for her as a book."

"That's a good idea, buddy."

"Thanks."

"We might even start a literary magazine for our college and call it *Review Royalle*, and in it we could feature her work," Lynpeex suggested. "That'll drive your boys in that English Department nuts."

"Sure would."

"After all, they're the scholars and writers who should be starting magazines, not us. We're the guys with those worthless MBAs."

"You're right about that. All those angry men in that department are so full of themselves, someone ought to drive them nuts."

"I thought I did it one time, but I *lost*."

"Refresh my memory on that, Tim. I don't remember."

"I'll do when I come back," Lynpeex said, stood, and added before heading to the bathroom, "I don't know if it's this beer or this morning's coffee, but it's rushing through me."

— ℰℐ —

When Lynpeex returned to the table, he spoke about the role that the *Vespa-man* had played in embarrassing him publicly. "I'd never forget what that guy did to me in front of the entire faculty at a meeting during our second year here. He embarrassed me in a most memorable and disgusting way."

"Oh, what did he do, Tim? As you know, I never attend those

long faculty meetings that drive you nuts."

"I must've told you the day it happened, and you forgot."

"Refresh my memory," Toyzol said smiling.

"You know how I'm a neat freak? I love everything to be neat and clean and organized and in place. That's the *business* part in me."

"That you are."

"Well, one day I tried to impress that sense of neatness on the entire faculty in some impromptu remarks that I was making during a Thursday afternoon meeting," Lynpeex said.

"Fair enough."

"I stood in front of them and said: *It's very important for you to keep your offices neat and clean and organized.*"

"That's a harmless-enough request."

"It is," Lynpeex said, "but it got harmful when I added: *When I make an unexpected visit to your office to talk about a college matter, the state of your desk will tell me a great deal about the state of your mind.* I emphasized my pronunciation of the word *mind* and felt so happy with the comparison. I thought the comparison reflected my views of what it means to have a neat, clean, and organized office. But that's not the way the *Vespa-man* took it. He made fun of me in front of the entire faculty."

"Oh, what did he do?" Toyzol asked. "I don't recall you telling me any of this. Not a word of that exchange."

"He was sitting in the back of the room, where he always sits, and he used his booming voice when he spoke. *Now, Dr. Lynpeex, all the times I've come to your office to talk about departmental matters, your glass-covered desk was always so neat and clean and organized: it had nothing on it.* The faculty members there made the connection and roared with laughter."

"What did you do?"

"Touched and wounded by his humor, I laughed and changed the subject," Lynpeex said. "What could you do when you're insulted like that in public? I simply dissolved the insult in my mind and took it as humor and laughed. Can't wait for him and his colleagues to retire. We'll replace them—each and every one of them—with women scholars; our wonderful students deserve to learn from women and not just from those old codgers we now have teaching. We desperately need many more women professors in our little college in the mountains. Sorry for my *Vespa-man* rant."

"No need to be sorry. I think what he did to you is funny."

"Yes, and it's one of the reasons that I'd love for him to be the one who wears the tie clip, or vest, for the Kansas Donation. But first we need to lock down the funding source," Lynpeex said. He spoke slowly, "I think the book idea is a good one. The literary-review idea is also a good one. Both are very good ego-stroking ideas that I suspect she'd like. If I learned anything in doing my job as president, it's this: if you stroke enough egos enough times and if you do it with the right touch and sensitivity, you'll get that happy feeling we call cash and more cash. That might be the origin of the old metaphor that people in the fundraising business love to use."

"You mean," Toyzol said, triumphantly, "she's our cash cow."

"I sure hope," Lynpeex replied, smiling, "she's not a dollar donkey."

— ❧ —

They talked for a while longer about their views of Mrs. Goe. "I'll write her a letter tonight, Bob. Let's meet in my office at eleven tomorrow, and we'll see what I come up with. You may, of course, make suggestions, as you always do."

CHAPTER ELEVEN

In Samsville, Alice was speaking with Jack:
"Let me tell you about a reading group experience that took place at the fellowship hall of a big Presbyterian church in a suburb of Wichita immediately after *Editors and Their Turkeys* came out. I was a speaker for the group, but they used me as a fundraiser too."

"Fun or *fund*?" he said.

"Both," she said and reached for an oatmeal cookie.

"Love those Wichita stories—stories from the big city, the cultural hub of the Great Plains." He said with a smile.

"I was invited to speak to a reading group composed of women and men on the topic: Getting a Book Manuscript Professionally Published. In the letter, I was told by the group's president: *We don't want to hear about how to get a manuscript privately printed or self-published, but about the challenging task of professional publication.* I loved the topic."

"And you obviously accepted?"

"Sure did," she said. "And I was told in the invitation letter that I'd be given an honorarium of two hundred dollars."

"Got you so far," Jack said, reaching for his coffee.

"My friend Paul," she said—referring to a single middle-aged man from town who had written a comic book manuscript on animal behavior titled *The Way We Appear on Animal TV*; a man with whom she felt destined to establish a literary institution that would benefit their town in a major way—"drove me to Wichita. He was also my guest at dinner. We sat at the head table with the officers of the club, and I spoke to a crowd of close to one hundred adults. The woman in charge, the club's president, boasted of the fine turnout when she introduced me."

"Isn't that a big number for a reading group?"

"Yes, it is," Alice said. "And that's precisely what I asked the president who sat next to me at the head table. She told me that the large group at dinner divides into small discussion groups of twelve in each group for weekly meetings, and they also meet as a large group once a month and have a dinner in the fellowship hall and listen to an outside speaker. These are the perks of big-city megachurches." Then she added with a smile: "Where we live, we have perk-free microchurches."

"So, you were their outside speaker that evening?"

"That I was," she said. "And I spoke on some of the difficulties and hurdles that all unknown writers must deal with as they try to get a book professionally published."

"There are many hurdles, I suspect."

"Sure," she said. "And they're faced head-on by herds of unknown writers of first novels or memoirs or autobiographies or books of poetry or works of creative nonfiction."

"Such writers formed your audience. Right?"

"Yes, they did," she said. "After the speech, several flared up at the publishing industry and at me: the messenger. Some made mini speeches that trotted out their frustrations with the book publishing industry, and the speeches would end with questions for me to answer. Others didn't even bother to end their comments with a question: they simply wanted to publicly attack the industry, an industry that, with all due respect, they didn't know much about."

"I hear you. So, you ended up in a megachurch in Wichita, Kansas, defending the mega New York-based book publishing industry?"

"Yes, I did. After all, I knew something about it; I even wrote a book about it, one that led the group to invite me to be the speaker, but I unwittingly angered some pe—"

"You say you *angered* people?"

"Yes," Alice replied, "and you're wondering how I did that?"

"Sure am."

"Well, I did it partly by leavening my speech with several witticisms, and those witticisms offended some in the audience."

"For example."

"Okay, here's one I used. I said: *You've all heard the often-quoted expression: 'Everyone has a book in them.' In my opinion, many who hear this expression should dismiss it as an acoustical mirage.*"

"That's funny, subtle—but harsh. How did they react to that?"

"With hushed laughter," she said. "I carefully embedded my take on that expression in my speech. I wanted them to see the many challenges in getting a book professionally published by a major New York press."

"Too many people these days," Jack said, "fancy themselves as potential authors with major publishing houses. Is that what you mean?"

"Yes, sir. Back to the unexpectedly heated question-and-answer session... when that ended, the president who introduced me tried to calm the storm with humor. Her tactic was a classic. She spoke slowly and enunciated each word with extreme care, and she spliced her remarks with long and short pauses, those urgently needed pauses that supply humor with its necessary ingredient: timing."

"Interesting," an attentive Jack said, "very interesting."

"And here's what she told the group: *If you enjoyed what our distinguished author, Ms. Goe, had to say about the book publishing industry, then you'll want to support her in a big way.* Then the president paused, looked around the room, collected her thoughts, leaned to her right and looked at me and added: *And if you didn't enjoy what Ms. Goe shared with us this evening,* (another pause), *then you'll want to make sure we have the resources to get her out of town as quickly as possible.*"

"Did people laugh?"

"Does it snow in Alaska?" Alice replied. "The people who probably laughed the loudest were those who had attacked the hardest. After the laughter subsided, the president said: *All kidding aside, please consider giving generously in the wicker baskets placed at your tables.* Guess how much money they collected that evening?"

"I don't know."

"Submit a guess," she said. "Now remember this is a big suburban Wichita church, and a Presbyterian one—not a Baptist or a Nazarene."

"Okay," Jack said, "I'll say three hundred dollars or so."

"You're way off," she said. "In her handwritten thank you letter, that told me what I had spoken on, the witty president of the reading group informed me that they had received more than two thousand dollars that evening and the church's bookstore just ordered twenty *Turkeys*."

"That's what happens," Jack said, "when those who love you and those who dislike you give to your cause." Both laughed at that remark. "That might *not* happen in political gatherings, but the ways and means of writing groups in the wealthy suburbs of Wichita, Kansas are different."

— ❧ —

They talked about other topics that Friday morning: some significant, others trivial. One topic dealt with the shocking behavior of Alice's late husband, Frank, when he had taught math at Samsville High School.

"At breakfast yesterday," Jack told Alice, "my dear Lisa spoke about her mom's days as a student in the high school. Her mom wasn't exactly a math whiz; she didn't care for numbers, but she loved words; she's good in literature, you know."

"Oh, yes, I know," Alice said. "Lisa takes after her in all sorts of ways, but in the math business, she takes after her dad, the engineer."

"Her mom tried to do her best in math, yet her best was atrocious. Sorry to say that about my mother-in-law, but it's true. Lisa said that her mom dreaded her days in math, and she wasn't the only one. Other kids in the class found math to be very difficult, but they had to take it if they wanted to go to college."

"Yes, I know. Kids must take math if they want to go to college, and math can be tough to some."

"Her mom claims that in the late forties, Mr. Goe—bless his soul—had managed to find a way that inspired the students to hate math, and hate it with a passion," Jack said. He paused, made eye contact with Alice, and added, "Mrs. Goe, please forgive me if I seem to be speaking ill of the dead. That's not my intention. I'm simply telling you what Lisa said about her mom's experience in your late husband's math class."

"No need to apologize, my dear. I'm aware of the limitations of my departed husband."

"Yes, but what Lisa's mom was speaking about isn't a limitation," Jack said. "She called it, *a clumsy attempt at creativity*."

"Creativity and Frank?" Alice laughed and clapped as she spoke. "That's like finding a fish alive in a wheat field. You've got to get serious, my friend."

"Okay, I'll tell you just what she told me, and you decide if his behavior was creative or otherwise."

"Fair enough. Please continue."

Jack did. "On the day when Mr. Goe would return the tests in an algebra or geometry class, he'd do something that most students dreaded. I say most and not all because the students who were good in math probably loved Mr. Goe's tactics."

"Pray tell," she said, "what did he do? Now I really want to know. You've taken a drama-free man and injected him with drama—at least in the mind of his octogenarian widow."

"Here's what Mr. Goe would do." Jack reached for his coffee mug, took a swig, and continued. "He'd return the graded tests to the students in descending order of achievement or score. The student with the highest score would receive his or her test first; the person with the lowest score would receive his or her test last. He'd read each student's name *and* earned score."

"How dreadful. That's just utterly dreadf—"

"Not only that," Jack continued, "but he'd ask the student with the highest score to stand and *remain standing*, and the person with the next highest score to also stand and remain standing, and so forth. The students would continue to stand and remain standing until the last person's name was called and he or she received the graded test."

"I can see humiliation avalanching on those poor students who remained seated for a long time."

"And Lisa's mom," Jack said, "was among those. She was often last in the class, and Mr. Goe would spice up his humiliation, to use your word, by twisting and freshening a cliché."

Alice laughed, "Frank freshening a cliché! A strange act for him."

"But he did it," Jack insisted. "Here's what he'd say when he'd get to my mother-in-law's test score: *And now, class, we have last and ALSO least* . . . He'd linger and pronounce with care the word *also*, and then he'd call her name and her score, and he'd march to her desk and hand her the graded test."

Alice laughed, for she instantly recognized the *last-but-not-least* cliché. "Sorry to laugh," she said. "I shouldn't have laughed."

"I also laughed," Jack said. "I've been last on many occasions."

"I suppose Frank must've thought that to be cute," Alice said. "To me, that's not cute but cruel." She looked down at the floor and spoke: "It's stupid—stupid and insensitive. It's sad, very sad, to hear how brutally insensitive my Frank was. And I didn't know about this *routine*. If I did, I would've put an end to it, of course. Believe me, I would've."

"I know you would've. You're a sensitive and caring woman. But to be fair, I don't know if what Mr. Goe did was a *routine* that he did after every test. Maybe it was something that he did once—or once in a while."

"Let's hope it was done infrequently," Alice said. "If it were done often, the town people would've heard about it, and the parents would've complained at the PTA meetings." She paused then added, "You know, Jack, my dear old Frank would *never* be able to get away with that kind of behavior in the classroom these days. *N-e-v-e-r.*"

"Why do you say that?" Jack said. "Don't teachers have academic freedom in high school like they do in college?"

"Oh, they do," she said. Then she spoke slowly and softly, "A teacher with that kind of behavior can plead academic freedom 'til he or she is blue in the face, but there's absolutely no way a teacher could get away with that kind of behavior these days."

"Why?" he asked. "Just why do you say that, Mrs. Goe?"

"Because these days, my dear," she said, leaned forward, and made eye contact with Jack, "high school students who struggle (or excel) in math or any other subject for that matter expect a teacher to respect their privacy." After a long pause, she added: "There's a Federal law that protects the privacy of a student's education record."

"Didn't know that," he said.

"It's called FERPA."

"I'm assuming that's an acronym."

"It stands for the Family Educational Rights and Privacy Act, the golden legacy of the short-lived Ford administration."

— ○ —

"I'll have to share all this with Lisa tonight, and I'm sure she'll enjoy passing your observations to her mom."

CHAPTER TWELVE

LYNPEEX SAT IN HIS STUDY AT HOME AND PLACED on his Philips Stereo set a 1978 album by Emmylou Harris titled *Quarter Moon in a Ten Cent Town*. Then he began to draft a letter to Mrs. Goe.

When the song "Green Rolling Hills of West Virginia" came on, he stopped writing, for he was touched by the poignancy of that song. Being the son of a coal miner, Lynpeex felt his eyes becoming moist when Harris's moving voice began to sing about the hard life of a coal miner facing hard times. Lynpeex paused for a good while, then resumed writing. Given its sensitive topic, the letter, written in pencil on a yellow legal pad, turned out to be longer than Lynpeex had expected. It stated:

Dear Mrs. Goe:

Greetings. We here at Royalle College hope and pray you're doing well.

Mr. Robert Toyzol, my administrative assistant, and I have been hard at work on the preliminary details that need to be worked out before we can accept your generous financial donation to Royalle College.

Some of those details could be worked out via a telephone conversation or through a personal visit to your home in Samsville. But since you asked us to do neither of the two at this time, we are now resorting to a letter format and specifically to this letter.

In writing you about a most serious concern that has occupied our interest, we must first apologize for even expressing this concern. But we have to express it, and we're doing it with the awareness and realization that you, as a published writer, will understand and sympathize with our significant concern.

You are an accomplished writer as indicated by your book *Editors and Their Turkeys* and by your other published work as well. My nephew, by contrast, is a frustrated writer. He is very successful at getting rejected. But bless his soul: he has the capacity to laugh at himself. All writers need that. Don't they, Mrs. Goe?

From what we understand, writers of fiction often devise elaborate and highly entertaining schemes for their novels and short stories. Frequently, those schemes grow out of experiences from real life. These experiences are often intriguing tales that they would have spun with innocent and benign motives on unsuspecting but gullible and highly vulnerable people.

We as the administrators of Royalle College are among those extremely vulnerable people. We are not rearranging chairs on the Titanic, as the old saying goes, but we are in desperate need of cash to support the many programs in our beloved small college in Appalachia. Certainly, we do welcome any gifts that come our way.

But what concerns us and what we need to know before we can proceed is this: we need to make certain that you are in a position to make the substantial donation that you wrote us about in your thoughtful letter.

To put it bluntly: Are you acting from your role as a writer in search of material for your fiction, or are you acting as a donor who has no heirs and would like to adopt us and have your name or cause memorialized with our college? If you're in the former role, then shame on you, and do NOT answer this letter.

But if you are in the latter category, please consider forwarding us formal documentation that will convince us of the wealth that you have and that you wish to donate to Royalle College.

Please realize, Mrs. Goe, that we remain most appreciative of your interest in us. We feel we can work out all the necessary details that are essential for us to establish a harmonious and pleasant relationship. We have had some good experiences in dealing with donors who wish to attach strings to their donations.

It would be an honor for Royalle College to have your name associated with our institution: with our fine students, professors, staff, alumni, and administrators. Our motto *Educating Heirs to the Throne of Culture* is one that I am sure you approve of, Mrs. Goe.

Mr. Toyzol and I will be seeing this entire matter through to what we hope will be a very happy conclusion to you and to us.

Given the unusual strings attached to your donation, please be assured that this entire matter will remain strictly confidential with us, and we hope with you.

Thank you so much, Mrs. Goe, for your interest in Royalle College, and we look forward to hearing from you at your earliest convenience. We hope this letter finds you happy and in good health.

Cordially,

Timothy Lynpeex MBA, Ed.D.

President

TL / rt

The next morning, at their scheduled meeting at eleven, Lynpeex read the letter to Toyzol. No changes were made. Toyzol typed the letter, made two copies for their files, and brought the original to Lynpeex "for your hand signature." (Lynpeex detested the expression John Hancock.)

Lynpeex predicted: "If she's serious, she'll reply right away and enclose the appropriate documents. But if she's a fly-by-night writer, she'll ignore us, or she'll probably hoist a few drinks and write a letter prolonging the issue, dodging our questions, asking more questions, tantalizing us with her imaginative gifts. And if she does that, we'll just have to ignore her. We'll see in a few days," Lynpeex said.

Toyzol listened and shook his head. "This has got to be, by far, the weirdest request we've had since the *cockroach-millionaire*. That request was profitable and got us the nickname *Spiffies*. I can't wait to see what's going to happen with this one."

"I can't either, Bob."

"What's your gut feeling?"

"Oh, that's easy," Lynpeex said. "She's a real person *and* a writer."

"I think she's real too, but whether she's got the money is another matter. I'm like that Samsville librarian: I doubt her wealth exists."

"Well, I think she's real *and loaded*. I do, I do," Lynpeex said.

"Can't wait to see her response to your letter." With that remark, Toyzol left Lynpeex's office and went back to his, to continue work on other, more conventional, college duties for the day.

— ∞ —

The next day Lynpeex found himself sitting in his office and reflecting on his job. He buzzed his assistant and asked for a cup of dark coffee.

Toyzol followed orders. He came with two coffees. The two sat across from each other on leather armchairs that had been part of the office from the day Lynpeex had moved in as president. Between them was a lit lamp set on a small, rectangular cherry-wood table.

Lynpeex said, "Book editors juggle writers."

"You're right on that," Toyzol said.

"And as fundraisers, we court and juggle our prospective donors," Lynpeex said. "Don't you agree?"

"Sure do."

"Some donors," Lynpeex said after taking a sip of coffee, "are a piece of cake: very orthodox in their approach to donating money."

"An example would be—*who*?"

"Is he a Japanese donor that I don't know about?" Lynpeex said and smiled at his own remark.

"Yeah right. Seriously, give me an example."

"My golfing buddy," Lynpeex said, adding the name of a wealthy man from their church. "He's orthodox, caring, and generous. An ideal donor, and like us—a Pittsburgh Steelers fan."

"You're referring to Aiden Kaimitchell?"

"He's the one," Lynpeex responded. "Then we've got those unorthodox givers, the bizarre-strings-attached donors."

"The *cockroach-millionaire* was unorthodox. And now we've got our dear Mrs. Goe. In courting her, we could be courting disaster."

"We could," Lynpeex said. "But I'd like to think we're in a terrain that could be labeled safe but wickedly unorthodox . . ."

— ❧ —

As they continued their discussion of Alice Princeton Goe as a promising "cash cow," their letter to her was making its way to Samsville, Kansas.

In the meantime, Alice was telling Jack during a morning coffee break about the son of a friend of hers, a newspaper reporter in Wichita, who had come by the house after church on a late Sunday afternoon, and she asked him to stay for supper. While eating, the reporter told her about a feature story that he had written the previous winter.

Alice told Jack: "The reporter informed me: *City life in the winter can be brutal on the elderly, especially if they don't have money.* Then he went on to tell me about an assignment he had the previous winter. His editor assigned him a feature story on the people in Wichita who didn't have gas to heat their house on a cold night in January. The editor gave him several names of people whose gas was turned off, and she instructed him to focus on one person and use that person as the illustrative example for the feature story. Are you following me so far?" Alice asked Jack who nodded and she continued. "The reporter selected an elderly woman who lived in the old section of town in an old walk-up flat. He called the woman, identified himself, and told her that the newspaper would like to do a story on her and the heat-cold situation."

"Did the woman agree?" Jack asked.

"Yes," Alice said. "And she gladly suggested two o'clock in the afternoon as a meeting time. At three minutes before two, the reporter climbed the stairs leading up to the dark walk-up flat. He knocked on the door and was invited in by the poor woman who had no gas heat. At first, the woman and the reporter visited on trivial matters, and then the reporter asked her how she had managed to stay warm the previous night when the temperature outside was in the low teens. He followed the question by saying: *It's twenty-two outside now, and I'm cold just sitting here talking to you.*"

"What did the woman say in response?" Jack asked.

"The woman—a widow—replied *not* with bitterness and anger, but with resignation and acceptance of her lot in life. She told the reporter that even though she had no gas, she has a small electric space heater, but it's incapable of heating the entire flat, however cozy it is. She added that in late August, she had requested that her gas be turned off because she had no money to pay the bills. Her meager income, she said, consisted of a Social Security check that she used for the rent, food, and medicine. She also contributed to her church and paid the electric and phone bills. Her limited income had led her to cancel her gas services."

"Oh, such a sad situation," Jack said. "Very sad indeed."

"The reporter continued by asking her about how she stayed warm the previous night. And her response was gripping and moving. Here's what she said: *Last night was really cold, and it was a tough night for me. Thank God I made it, though I didn't sleep in my bed.* The woman pointed to the open closet in the small living room of her flat and said to the reporter, *See those coats in that closet: they belong to Jim, my late husband of fifty-two years. He passed away three years ago. To stay warm last night, here's what I did: I put the iron on low, then took that grey wool sport coat that he used to wear to church, wrapped it around the iron, and plugged the end of the iron's cord into the electric socket. I sat on this couch, hunched over, and hugged the iron all night to stay warm.*"

A long stretch of silence set in. Jack's eyes became moist, and he glanced at the bird feeder outside.

"That's a really memorable story," he said. "A very *moving* story. The image of the woman leaning forward and hugging the iron will stay with me. It sure beats the spectacle of an old Baptist preacher from Texas pounding the pulpit and shouting about how bad poverty is."

"Now, now," Alice said, "there you go again—being hard on your

Texas roots. I'm not saying anything about Baptists."

"I know you're not," he said. "You create such a powerful image. In the words of my old lit professor: *There's power in a poignant image*, and your image has that."

"Thanks," Alice said. "And I'm so happy to hear your response." She made eye contact with Jack and smiled as she added: "I made up this story yesterday afternoon, and I plan to read it at our next club meeting. What you just heard is the story's basic plot."

"Are you kidding me?" he snapped, raising his voice. "You made all that up? You had me believing this whole thing was real and true."

"In a manner of speaking it is," Alice said. "After all, you've heard the old saying: *Fiction is a bag of lies that we use to tell the truth.* What I just told you is a slice of life from the big city."

— ❧ —

When the morning coffee break ended, Jack went outside to do yard work, giving Alice time to reflect on her plan with the men from West Virginia.

"Does my plan exhibit a legitimate way to do research for a novel? Could I turn all that research to serve the greater good? Can I maintain a straight face and act out my role if I should ever meet the men when they play their embarrassing part in the plan?" She saw herself writing the novel and—if all goes well—sharing the proceeds from it and a chunk of her wealth with the college.

She constantly reminded herself by saying, "My plan may be summed up in the way I tweaked Voltaire's dictum. All I'm doing is changing the word *History* to *Happiness* and the word *dead* to *living.* My mission now is to show that: *Happiness is a pack of tricks that we play on the living.*"

Alice loved to coin words. To capture her mission, she coined the word "*voltairize*"—meaning: *to beat the wit out of someone.*

In her diary she wrote: "In my plan, I hope to voltairize two men, to engage them in some viciously entertaining and instructive moments, and to make them squirm—in fun, to be sure."

— ❧ —

The following Friday, Alice and Jack, "my talk-therapist" (as she started referring to him), discussed a variety of topics growing out of the national and international news, and out of life in small-town America.

Writing and publishing, however, were the two topics that came up often, and Jack peppered Alice with questions. After all, a prestigious New York publisher had made her an authority on those topics.

One day, she told him about speaking on writing at his alma mater.

CHAPTER THIRTEEN

"I don't think I ever told you," Alice said, "about the time I spoke at your alma mater in a creative-writing class in fiction. The professor invited me after my book *Editors and Their Turkeys* was published. The professor, a delightful young scholar and an author of a first novel published by Random House, had read and liked my book and wanted me to share some insights on writing and publishing with her students. I was happy to go; after all, it's not often when college kids get to hear an octogenarian speak. Besides, I wanted to push my book."

"How did it go?"

"It was different," Alice said. "Let's just put it that way: it was an unusual experience for me, a bit shocking also."

"Oh, get more specific, please."

"I seldom speak to college kids," she said. "Reading or writing group composed of middle-aged or older people usually invite me to speak. So, when I was asked to speak to a college class, I thought I'd do something different: educational and entertaining at once. And here's what I did."

"Can't wait to hear this."

"After the usual introductions," she added, "I handed out white index cards and conducted a survey. I told the kids: Suppose you go to a garage sale in a little town outside of Wichita, and at the sale you buy a framed dirty painting for seven dollars, thinking that the wooden frame alone is worth that much. Let's also suppose that after you take the painting home and clean it up and examine it, you do research on the artist and you discover that the painting is worth more than seven dollars. You take it to a well-known art appraiser and she says that the garage-sale painting is worth at least seven hundred thousand dollars."

"Okay, I'm with you so far."

"I also told the class," Alice added, "suppose you sell the painting and receive nine hundred thousand dollars for it. What would you do with the money? That's what they were to write on those cards: just a few words on what they'd do with the money. Then I collected the cards, and I read them aloud to the class."

"And I bet the responses were all predictable."

"Not only predictable but disappointing as well," Alice said. "Very, very disappointing."

"Why do say that? What did they say?"

"Pay off student loans, or travel, or buy a house or a new car or a fancy boat. Some said they'd invest the money. One person wanted to buy a Cessna aircraft from the plant in Wichita where his dad works."

"That's disappointing all right."

"Only one person out of the twenty-three students in the class said what I was looking for," Alice said. "Just one."

"And what was that?" Jack asked. "Give some of the money to the poor or to an orphanage or what have you?"

"No, but that's close," she said. "Here's what one person wrote: *I'd go back to the person from whom I bought the painting and give him*

a check for six-thousand dollars and explain all that had happened.
You see, I saved that response to last, and after I read it, I told the class: Now that's a response that's decent and noble and honorable—and it's one that might give rise to a plotline in a story."

"How so?"

"Well, if the person who had sold you the painting for seven dollars takes the check, cashes it, and then sends you a thank you note for being so considerate, you don't have much of a story."

"I see that much."

"But if he takes the money," Alice said, "and heads to his attorney and the attorney convinces him to go after more—much more—money, then things begin to complicate themselves, and a storyline with tension and characterization begins to take shape."

"I see what you're driving at," Jack said.

"Now that I told you all this," she said, "it might not be a bad idea for a story, eh? Maybe one of us should work on it."

— ✑ —

"Speaking of college stories," Jack said, "let me tell you about some *inadvertently creative* teaching that I had experienced during my senior year. The teaching took place in a drama class, and it was done by a distinguished visiting scholar from Oxford."

"Is that the class where you first met Lisa?"

"No, no, I met her in my freshman year in a history class."

"I see."

"She would've liked to take the drama class, but it conflicted with her student-teaching responsibilities. The course was outside my major, but it interested me."

"Got you," Alice said and reached for her coffee cup.

"The professor," Jack said, "was an exceedingly brilliant research scholar with numerous books to his credit. He was invited to be a visiting scholar at the university for a year, and he was assigned one class to teach. That's the one I took. The one I'll never forget."

"Why won't you?" she asked.

"Because it was so darn strange—unorthodox, you see."

"I don't see anything. You'll have to explain."

"I'll be happy to," he said. "The professor, a slender gentleman who was a little over six feet tall with lots of blondish hair parted in the center, walked into the first floor classroom building. He was dressed in a dark suit and a green tie. He stood behind the podium, looked at the twelve students who had enrolled in the class, and then said, in his perfect British accent: *I'm not going to take a long time and use the lecture method to tell you how bad the lecture method is in teaching. Enough said.* He passed out a document that he called, *The Course Outline.* He said: *The document in your hands lists fifteen books.* After a long pause, he added: *The last book on the list is optional. The rest is required reading. We'll meet again in this room for the course's final, and only, examination to be held at the time scheduled by this university. Sorry, but I have no time for office hours.* The man then left the room, and we all tightened our eyebrows and looked at each other. Most students decided to drop the class."

"Did you?" Alice asked, and quickly corrected herself. "You obviously didn't since you're telling me about the class."

"You're right. Only five of us stayed in the class, and we stayed home and read the books, including the optional one."

"That makes for what—almost a book a week?"

"About that," he said. "Still, we didn't have to go to class or write papers or listen to lectures or participate in class discussions. All we had to do is stay home, sit on our rocking chairs, put our feet on padded stools, and read and read—and read."

"What happened when the examination time came?" she asked. "The joys of reading came to an end, didn't they?"

"They did. All five of us wondered what the exam would be like. A day or so before the exam, we had a couple of beers at my off-campus pad in the student ghettos, and we tried to come up with some questions that he might ask. We were hoping he'd give us twelve or more questions and ask us to select four or five and write essays on them in the two-hour exam period."

"Did you get your wishes?"

"What do you think?"

"I'd say you did."

"And I'd say you're wrong," Jack said. "The day of reckoning came, and the exam was at eight in the morning. The learned bloke, to use the British label, strolled into the classroom with a fistful of blue books. He gave three to each and set the rest on the table on which the lectern was placed. *If you need more blue books*, he said, *they're up here. Please come up and help yourself.* After a pause, he added: *When you're done writing your essays, slip your blue books under the door of my office located on the third floor of this building. I'll be there working.* He said all this, but failed to give us questions to answer. No one dared to ask."

"So, what happened next?"

"He started to leave the room," Jack said, "and as he was nearing the door to exit, he slapped his forehead with the palm of his left hand and said aloud: *Oh, you need questions to answer and explore, don't you?* No one said a word. He actually smiled. I liked him better without a smile. He looked at the five of us and said: *I'll write the question on the board.* He proceeded to write a three-word question."

"What?" Alice said. "Did I hear you say, *a three—*?"

"Yes, it was a three-word question that stated: *Is tragedy enough?*" Before leaving the room, he said: *I very much enjoyed teaching this class, and thank you very much indeed for having the courage to stay with it. May your local postman bring an evaluation of your work that will please you and your parents. A final word: you may take as long as you wish to complete your essay, much longer than two hours, if you desire.* That's what he said before he left the room—smirking, I think."

"Wow," a flabbergasted Alice said. "That has got to be the most bizarre college class that I ever heard of. What did you do ?"

"All of us wrote and wrote," Jack said. "I felt he expected us to formulate a thesis in our responses and to develop the thesis with many references to the studies that were listed on the course outline and that we had read during the semester."

"I can see how you arrived at your *inadvertently creative* label for his teaching method. What I'm curious about now is your grade."

"First let me tell you," Jack said, "I filled six blue books in my response to that three-word question. Others did likewise, give or take a blue book. All of us stayed at least three hours, and we all received the same grade: 'A'; and we all think—maybe I should say, we all *believe*—that the scholar never read our essays. No time for us. We might be wrong, of course. I hope we are. But I must emphasize, we were all pleased by our performance in the course, and speaking for myself, I'll say this: I learned more in that class than I had in any other class that I had taken during my four-year college career. If that sounds strange, it's still true."

"You know, Jack, you could write a piece of creative nonfiction that captures the essence of that course, and the piece could be published in a major forum that deals with higher education."

"Oh," Jack said and placed his fists on his cheeks and elbows on the table: "an article on that?"

"As you were speaking," Alice continued, "I kept wondering what would happen to an American professor without tenure—or, for that matter, one with tenure—if he or she tried such a radical teaching method. Would that original teaching method test the limits of academic freedom? Would the American be fired at once? Something to think about, eh?"

"I think you're right. There might well be an essay in my experience, and only five students—who had nicknamed the Oxford fellow *The Phantom Professor*—could write about it as a true experience."

"In a manner of speaking, that guy gave you a taste of what it feels like to be homeschooled while in college."

"That's an interesting take on that experience."

"An incredible experience," she said.

"You gave me an excellent idea for an essay, Mrs. Goe," Jack said. "As the British would say: *Thank you very much indeed.*"

— ❧ —

Alice enjoyed sharing her short-story idea with Jack, and she loved listening to his account of his drama course.

She hoped to connect—before long—with *inadvertently creative* teaching of her own, given her forthcoming encounter with the two men from West Virginia. Whether her teaching would reach that coveted level remained to be seen.

Her next move was to respond to the men's last letter.

CHAPTER FOURTEEN

A DAY AFTER RECEIVING LYNPEEX'S LETTER, Alice took to the typewriter and replied to it. She wrote her thoughts on paper, revised them, and then typed them out on her green IBM Selectric typewriter. Her letter states:

> Dear Dr. Lynpeex:
>
> Thank you so much for your thoughtful letter, which arrived yesterday. I am most appreciative of your legitimate concerns.
>
> First, I want to assure you that I have the necessary money to donate to Royalle College provided, of course, your institution—in this case, you and your administrative assistant—comply with my extraordinary and pressing request. This is the first thing that's on my mind, and should be on yours.
>
> Second, I thought of what might be a good piece of documentation to send to you, and I came up with several items: bank records, a copy of our previous will to the late Winterpeace College, or my tax statement for the past year. I have a trusted accountant who prepares my taxes every year. In fact, he has been doing them for us for the past thirty years.

I thought I'd make a copy of last year's tax returns and forward that to you as proof. Accordingly, enclosed is my tax statement of the past year. You'll note from the interest earned by the various accounts that there is quite a bit of money in my name in a bank in Wichita, and it is from that account that I would transfer the promised sum to your college if my terms are met.

So, let's get down to business and pursue the donation-exchange that I had suggested in my initial letter to you. Thank you, again, for your letter, and I look forward to hearing from you.

Sincerely,

Alice Princeton Goe

Alice placed her neatly typed letter in a white business envelope; she printed with a felt pen Timothy Lynpeex's address at Royalle College, walked to the post office, bought and placed a stamp on the envelope. She slid it into the outgoing First-Class Mail slot and sauntered home, feeling that she had started to solve her problem in earnest.

— ✁ —

Toyzol whose task was to open all letters addressed to his boss refused to open this one on his own. Instead, he took the envelope that had the name of Alice Princeton Goe, hugged it like a child hugs a security blanket, and headed to Lynpeex's office.

The time was nine-ten in the morning, and Toyzol strolled in with two mugs: one filled with coffee, and the other with a big smile.

"I bet you, Tim, this is what we want," Toyzol said as he handed the envelope to Lynpeex and sat on one of the armchairs in the office. "You said: *If she wrote right away, she's for real.*"

"Let's see if we're right."

"Let's," Toyzol said and watched his boss sit on the other armchair. Toyzol took a sip of coffee and added, "Tim, when I first saw the letter, my knees started to shake, and I felt weak. I just can't believe all this. It's incredible."

"Incredible is the word," Lynpeex said. "I've got to go to the bathroom and take a leak."

"I do too."

Both headed to the bathrooms adjacent to their respective offices. Thanks to his prostate problems, Toyzol had a difficult time convincing his urine stream to leave his body. He lingered in the bathroom for a good while.

When he returned to Lynpeex's office, he said, "My knees are weak, and we both had to take a leak." The rhyme scheme led him to repeat the words several times, to dribble them, as it were. He laughed and added, "I can't believe what I'm about to see."

"Isn't it strange how Mother Nature tells us when we're nervous?" Lynpeex said, slid the blade of the tiny red knife on his keychain under the flap of the envelope, and slit the sealed flap.

"Strange indeed," Toyzol said, as he watched Lynpeex pull the letter out of the envelope.

"Let me read this aloud," Lynpeex said. He read the letter, leaned back and adjusted his testicles, then read the highlights of the tax figures.

Toyzol could not contain himself as he blurted, "Hot Hoover!" He was way too pious to use the word, *damn,* and if he did, he knew Lynpeex, who was even more devout, would scold him. "I don't believe this, Tim. I don't. We're halfway there."

"No, no, we're ninety percent there," Lynpeex corrected Toyzol.

"What about her conditions?"

"We'll get her to adjust her expectations."

"What if we can't? Old ladies can be stubborn, you know."

"We've got to do all that we can to talk her out of them," Lynpeex said. "We'll offer her different symbols of honor and recognition, kind of like what we did with our *cockroach-millionaire*. Remember how we finally talked him out of, in effect, calling cockroaches *Your Highness* and ended up with the longest nickname on record for a college?" He smiled and added, "How many times do I have to remind you of that, Bob?"

"We'll see if something like this works with Mrs. Goe."

"You'll see," Lynpeex fired back.

"We're beginning to sound like optometrists now," Toyzol said and laughed.

"I feel like dictating a letter to her right now," Lynpeex said. Toyzol asked him to speak slowly for he was unaccustomed to taking dictation. Lynpeex agreed and began with a sentence that was spoken in a manner and a pace that resembled those of an auctioneer in the Mountain State of West Virginia. Both laughed as Lynpeex drifted to his normal voice and pace while dictating the following letter to Mrs. Alice Princeton Goe of Samsville, Kansas:

> Dear Mrs. Goe:
>
> I have read with great interest your letter and the material you enclosed relating to your financial donation to the college. Of course, Mr. Toyzol and I are looking forward to meeting you in person at your convenience.
>
> Regarding your donation to Royalle College, we would like to visit you in Samsville and to take you out to dinner to discuss the donation in more detail. We have plans and ideas that might be of interest to you.
>
> We would appreciate it if you would be so kind as to suggest a date that might be convenient to meet with you in Samsville.

Also, if you would like to spend some time with us here, please be assured that Mr. Toyzol and I will be very happy to pick you up and bring you to our friendly campus here at Royalle College.

Perhaps a visit to our campus will help you connect with the memories you have of that superb Virginia Woolf conference that you attended with your late husband.

Again, thank you for thinking of Royalle College, and we look forward to hearing from you.

Cordially,

Timothy Lynpeex, MBA, Ed.D.

President

After Lynpeex dictated the letter, he told Toyzol: "Please type the letter later this afternoon. Bring me a copy, and let's sleep on it tonight, and we'll mail it tomorrow unless we get second thoughts. This, I think, is the best course of action. What do you think?"

"Sounds good to me, boss."

Toyzol gathered his materials and returned to his office. He started to type the letter. Lynpeex returned to what he called, "my conventional Royalle College duties for the day."

— ℰ✥ —

The next day, Toyzol brought the neatly typed letter to Lynpeex who read it, signed it, and enclosed his cream-colored business card.

On the back of the card he wrote his private office phone number and invited her to call him at any time.

Little did he know what Alice would, in time, fling his way.

CHAPTER FIFTEEN

WHILE WORKING ALONE IN HIS OFFICE, LYNPEEX heard his private office phone ring. His wife always uses this line. He picked up the phone, leaned back in his swivel chair, placed his feet on the corner of the desk, and in a loud, slow, distinct, and even playful voice, said his usual: "Hell—o."

"I'm so glad you put an 'o' at the end of that word. May I speak to Dr. Timothy Lynpeex, please?" She pronounced his last name as if it were *Lyn-peeks*. The correct pronunciation is *Lyn-pee*, with the 'x' at the end being silent, as in Grand Prix.

He didn't bother to correct her. So, her first words to him sent him through an identity crisis, but he didn't mind that.

His first word to her had almost sent her to an undesirable place, but he quickly snapped to attention and said: "Speaking, ma'am."

"Dr. Lynpeex, Alice Princeton Goe here."

"Oh, yes, Mrs. Goe, so pleased to hear your voice. I'm so happy to talk to you."

"I received your letter today."

"Yes, good."

"And remember what I told you in my earlier letter: I don't want to be courted. Frank and I never told Winterpeace College about our will because we didn't want the college's bigwigs to visit us, to court us, to take us out for dinner, to congratulate us about caring for young people, and then to leave—and leave disgusted with the fact that we go on living, hanging on and on and on."

"I see."

She continued, "One wealthy woman at a manor in Texas once told a visiting male vice-president from a small college in Nebraska that *Heaven is my home, but I'm not really homesick.* The VP returned to the college and held a bemoaning festival with his staff. He told the staff that he'd love to enroll her in the course of his dreams: *Kicking the Bucket 101*, which, I might add, is frequently mistaken by many wealthy donors with *Kicking the Bucket AT 101*."

"So you say," replied Lynpeex. He didn't know whether to laugh or just smile. "I am familiar with the situation—I think."

"I like my men to be bald as ice cubes and to be able to *think*," she said. "You claim you do. That, my son, is good, very good, especially for a small-college president."

"Thanks," he said and thought: I'm thanking her for insulting me. But what else can I do? "I'm a woman of action, Dr. Lynpeex," she said. "And I have a plan, distinct and attractive as the expansive pate of a bald man as opposed to one whose head is choked with hair."

"I see," he said, even though her rapid-fire comments and images seemed to dazzle him. Lynpeex saw in her comments a comforting clue: she seems to like bald men, he thought, and stroked his smooth head. I already feel a plus in that.

"And that means, I've got the money—in cash—and I've got a plan and a cause, and I'm willing to exchange one for the other. Now, when do you want to come up?"

"Any time that's convenient with you, ma'am."

"Next week, I'm flying to Decatur, Georgia, with my good friend, Alivia Figinston, for her fiftieth college class reunion. We plan to be back at the end of June," Alice said. "Why don't you suggest a date now? Quickly check your calendar and suggest a date."

"How about Tuesday the first of July at four, and we'll go out for dinner that evening and you'll be our guest, of course?"

Alice checked the small brown calendar that she had carried in her handbag and said, "That'll be fine with me; I'll look forward to it: a dinner date with Dr. Timothy Lynpeex."

"Mr. Toyzol, will come along, if you have no objections."

"That's fine," she said. "For a variety of reasons—none of which I'll discuss with you at this time—I'd prefer to deal with two men instead of one. Will you boys be flying or driving?"

"Both. We'll probably fly to Wichita, rent a car, and drive to Samsville if that's okay with you?"

"That'll be fine," Alice said. She felt the urge to baffle him, to be enigmatically literary, so she asked: "Would you permit your daughter to marry a man whose engagement ring he crafted out of his kidney stone?"

"What was that?" Lynpeex asked. "Could you please repeat—"

"No need to do that, darling," she said, stretching the endearment. "I know it's a loaded question with lots of ramifications. Remember, in addition to being a small-town philanthropist, I'm a writer, through and through."

"Yes, I know."

"And you'll soon find out more about me."

"We're looking forward to that." Before closing the conversation, Lynpeex confirmed the date with Alice and told her that he'll get back to her if there's a change in time. They said their goodbyes, and Lynpeex placed the phone on the hook and spoke to himself: "Boy, oh boy, I hope we can pull this off."

— ∾ —

Lynpeex then buzzed Toyzol and asked him to come to his office at once. Toyzol did. "Bob, you wouldn't believe who I just finished talking with."

"Your wife?"

"C'mon."

"Mrs. Goe, of course."

"And—"

"I tell you, she's serious about that donation."

"How about the tie clips stuff?"

"I didn't dare ask about that," Lynpeex said. "But I suspect she's serious about those tie clips too."

"So, there's no chance we could change her mind?"

"Really don't know."

"And we can't give in to her demands, of course?"

"Not even for twenty million," Lynpeex said.

"What could we substitute for the tie clips?"

"I've been thinking about this for awhile now," Lynpeex said. "Write these down, please." Toyzol reached for the yellow legal pad on the desk, yanked a pen out of his shirt pocket, and wrote what Lynpeex dictated: "Naming a building after her is a possibility."

"Okay, that's one."

"Maybe naming the auditorium in Addison Hall in her honor or in the honor of her late husband or both."

"Okay, that's two."

"Maybe granting all sorts of scholarships in the Goes' names for years and years to come."

"Okay, that's three."

"Let me see," Lynpeex said, thinking aloud. "Any others? How about publishing all her unpublished writings in the *Review Royalle* that we could start with part of her funds?"

"Okay, that's four."

— ❧ —

"Man, oh man, what a problem. Would you like coffee?" Toyzol asked. Lynpeex said no and began to fill his pipe with tobacco.

Toyzol excused himself, went to the secretary's office next door, and came back with a mug full of black coffee.

"Bob," Lynpeex said while lighting his pipe, "at one point in the phone conversation, she hit me with a weird question that she said had lots of ramifications, but I failed to understand the question."

"Did you ask her to repeat it?"

"She ignored my request. The question had a kidney stone in it."

"With her kidney stone and my prostate: we'll get on swimmingly, as they say." Toyzol smiled as he spoke. "Wouldn't it be splendid, Tim, if Mrs. Goe assumed that all the handsome administrators at Royalle College—that means both of us—have colostomies?"

"That sure would solve our problem in a hurry," Lynpeex said. "The distinction that she clearly wants to make suddenly becomes a distinction without a difference," he added, lapsing into the rhetoric that he had used as an undergraduate student in the only philosophy class that he had taken in college.

"I like that," Toyzol said. "A distinction without a difference."

"That was my philosophy professor's favorite phrase," Lynpeex continued. "He'd use it over and over, so much in fact that the students often quoted the phrase in a flippant manner. That phrase became the professor's theme song, as it were. All professors have favorite phrases that they regularly trot out and defend with their wisdom, you might say. I'm beginning to sound like Mrs. Goe," Lynpeex said, congratulating himself while trying to incite in his good friend a little envy of his rhetorical flourish.

Toyzol ignored Lynpeex's rhetoric and kidded, "If you suggest naming a building in her honor and she chooses the name Colostomy Hall, what would you do?"

"Use it, of course," Lynpeex said. "People will just assume it's named after Joseph P. Colostomy. For seven million, I'd do that in a heartbeat, Bob. Wouldn't you?"

"I would."

"One of the four options we discussed is bound to click," Lynpeex said.

"I hope so."

Both stayed in Lynpeex's office for a while longer. They talked about other matters growing out of their responsibilities as officers of that small liberal arts college located in what the cars' license plates proclaim: "West Virginia: Wild, Wonderful."

— ℰℐ —

To the two men, other college matters seemed trivial compared to what Alice had dangled in front of them.

To them, thinking about her prospective donation was becoming as unshakeable as a paranoid man's delusional disorder. But unlike that man, Lynpeex and Toyzol welcomed their predicament.

CHAPTER SIXTEEN

Alice was preparing herself a dish of vegetarian spaghetti. The sauce's recipe called for fresh parsley, onions, fresh mint, walnuts, green peppers, tomatoes, roasted garlic—all finely chopped and mixed in extra-virgin olive oil and lemon juice.

While chopping away, Alice came up with a short story idea that was stimulated by her daily Scripture reading. Part of what she had read that afternoon came from the King James translation of Psalm 127. Here the psalmist writes: "Lo, children are an heritage of the Lord: and the fruit of the womb is his reward. As arrows are in the hand of a mighty man; so are children of the youth. Happy is the man that hath his quiver full of them." Alice felt that a quiver full of children on the Great Plains means more hands for work come harvest time.

Her idea focuses on a wealthy widow. In the story, the widow expresses her love for first names that come fully equipped with superfluous letters: names like Jay or Dee or Kay. And she acts on her love in an unusual way.

Once a week, she goes to her small town's Carnegie Library on Main Street and looks in the newspapers for names and pictures of babies who had been born in her town in central Kansas and in neighboring small towns. She also consults the towns' phone books and records the parents' street addresses.

At home, she types a given address on an envelope that she stuffs with a three-line note typed on a white unlined index card. No date or salutation or signature would appear on the card. The note states:

> Congratulations on the recent birth of your child. Please accept the enclosed for your newborn from a small-town philanthropist who is determined to remain anonymous.

Enclosed would be some cash. The baby's parents would receive *at least* five bills, each being a hundred dollars: these are "the birth-bills," given to all the parents of newborns on the small towns of the sparsely populated Great Plains.

An additional five bills would be given to parents if their baby's first name has one superfluous letter. So, a name like Brooke or Sue leads the philanthropist to send a total of ten bills of a hundred dollars each. A name like Jay would bring in fifteen bills, thanks to the two superfluous letters. Each superfluous letter earns five hundred dollars.

If a family had named a newborn daughter Kaye (and spelled it in the newspaper that way, as in Danny Kaye), then the family would find twenty crisp pictures of Benjamin Franklin in the mailbox.

As Alice neared the end of her vegetable chopping, she realized that the story-idea needed fiction's *what-if-factor* to spin tension and interest in it. So, she kept chopping and thinking.

"*What if*," she asked herself, "a math teacher at the high school discovers and breaks the philanthropist's superfluous-letter code? If that happens and the towns' residents become aware of it, would the generous unknown philanthropist continue her giving? And if she continues, would the pursuit of the lucrative superfluous-letters rewards bring a burst of fresh creativity to name-selection for newborns on the Great Plains? What might the story say about the creative process?"

— ☙ —

The next day, Alice was invited to have supper with the Jaycub-sons at their two-bedroom house located two blocks from hers on Main Street. After Jack had started working for Alice, Lisa would call and invite her over for supper once every two weeks or so.

As the months went by, Alice would join the Jaycubsons for supper once a week, sometimes even more often. Out of respect for Alice's food preferences, Lisa would always cook—for all three—a vegetarian dish culled from Thai or Indian or French or Mexican or even Seventh-Day Adventist cookbooks that she had acquired. Lisa would always preface their gathering by saying, "Thanks to Mrs. Goe, we're all going to be eating a healthy supper."

Jack would typically offer grace before the meals—and he did so that evening. The conversation at supper dealt with issues growing out of life in Samsville and especially Lisa's upcoming year at the high school. The selection for the annual musical was on her mind.

"Frankly, I try to select a musical," Lisa said, "that involves many people and especially children. This way, we'll have the parents and the grandparents and the aunts and the uncles and the neighbors and even the Sunday school teachers at all the shows, assuring us of a full house every night of the performance."

"Not only a full house," Jack said, "but a full house of the same people night after night. Maybe I should say, *almost* the same."

"In business," Alice said, "they call that *repeat customers*. And that's the way culture gets cultivated in small towns on the Great Plains." Then Alice addressed Lisa by saying, "I'm absolutely certain that other small towns throughout the country do the same thing. It didn't take you long to discover the formula, did it?"

"You're right on that," Lisa said. "I learned it from my high school drama teacher."

Supper continued and Lisa conveyed another story, one of an incident that happened in her homeroom during the previous semester with the yearbook photographer: Samsville's own *Kodak-Kojak*. (The photographer was given this nickname because he had a bald head resembling that of Telly Savalas, star of the television crime drama of the seventies, *Kojak*, a popular show in Samsville.)

"*Kodak-Kojak* is a fussy photographer," Lisa said. "He'd ask a student to sit two or three yards away from the camera, then he'd go and adjust the camera, return and adjust the student's face, and he'd repeat that cycle—camera, face, another adjustment on the face, then the camera again, then the face—until the head had just the perfect tilt."

"We've all encountered such photographers in our day," Jack said.

"Well," Lisa said, "I had one joker in the class who played to the attention of other students who were standing and watching and waiting their turn. This guy frustrated *Kodak-Kojak* by shifting his head moments after its tilt was adjusted for the camera."

"I can see a joker doing that," Jack said, "especially if he felt the other students were watching and expecting to be entertained."

"And they were," Lisa said. "Finally, after two or three minutes of head-adjusting, as it were, *Kodak-Kojak*—the very serious and elderly gentleman—was ready to snap the picture. So, he informed the student: *Please keep looking straight at the camera. Don't blink. Now, please smile and say—'Yes.'* The student followed orders—sort of."

"What do you mean by that?" Alice asked.

"The student jumped out of his chair, looked directly at the camera, took one giant step forward, pounded his right foot on the wooden floor, raised his clenched right fist into the right-angle salute, shook his arm, and yelled and hissed a prolonged and tortured—*Yes-sss...sss...s.sss.* The other students standing and waiting, jumped and clapped and laughed, but the angry photographer lectured the rude student, scolding him for what he had done."

Alice laughed and said, "I suppose the student did that because dear old *Kodak-Kojak* forgot to tell him *not* to move. Is that the case?"

"That might be," Jack said. He had heard the story on the day that it happened, so he added, "But, Mrs. Goe, there's one more thing the student did: he gave a reason for his startling response, and it's a classic."

Alice stopped eating and listened as Lisa added, "Oh yes, the rude student had some manners. He waited for *Kodak-Kojak* to finish his tirade, and then he calmly informed everyone in the room about his upbringing: *My mother raised me to be an EMOTIONAL child.* Needless to say, our dear *Kodak-Kojak* wasn't amused by the entire episode."

— ❦ —

When Alice went home that night, she sat in her study and reflected on her forthcoming meeting with the men of Royalle College, the two MBAs who were about to embark on a journey to the Great Plains of Kansas, a journey in pursuit of cash for their tiny college in West Virginia.

That evening, she wrote Lynpeex a two-page letter in which she confirmed their July 1st meeting day.

In the letter, she told him: "This afternoon I wrote the first draft of a short story that deals with the ways of an elderly woman, a philanthropist whose love of superfluous letters in babies' names leads her to bring joy to ordinary people living in small towns on the Great Plains. The story—with its quest for creativity—might not mean much to you now, but it might after a while. If this sounds enigmatic, so be it. I titled the story: *Where There's Smoke, There's— Someone Smoking.*"

The next day, Alice walked to the post office and mailed the letter to her man in West Virginia. That evening, the story, or *Kodak-Kojak*, or her talk-therapist weren't on Alice's mind as much as the two men of Royalle College.

In West Virginia, the men had just accepted an invitation to serve as the grand marshals for the parade of the Preston County Buckwheat Festival. But the annual festival wasn't on their mind as much as Alice.

— ☙ —

In her letter to Lynpeex, she also wrote: "Please don't be shocked if I call you from Georgia. I might call—if for no other reason than to stay in touch. I'm taking your private number with me."

After reading that passage, Lynpeex told himself: "I wouldn't be surprised if she calls."

In time, she used the number.

CHAPTER SEVENTEEN

ALICE PRINCETON GOE TUCKED TIM LYNPEEX'S private telephone number in the purse that she took with her when she flew with Alivia W. Figinston to Decatur, Georgia.

At three-ten in the afternoon, Georgia time, while Alivia was attending one of the ceremonies in the gardens of her alma mater, Alice used her room's phone and called Lynpeex's private number.

Following the usual telephone conversation formalities, Alice said, "We're here, and Alivia is at one of those *so-good-to-see-you* afternoon ceremonies."

"Did you have a comfortable flight?" Lynpeex asked.

"Oh, yes."

"Are you staying at a hotel near campus?"

"Not too far."

"What are the highlights of your trip so far, Mrs. Goe?"

"It's strange that you'd ask, but I joked with Alivia about a problem that nags many senior citizens. At one point I even asked her: *Wouldn't it be fun if colleges divide the restrooms in their buildings into two categories: Male/C and Male/NC, with the C standing not for average but for Constipated?*"

"What was her response, if I may ask?"

"She called it *borderline crazy*, if I may reply."

"That means she liked it?"

"That means she loved it," Alice said. "She's a bit like me, you know: she loves the witty side of life. But she did say that some people even in these liberated times might consider the wording vulgar."

"What was that word?" Lynpeex asked. "The last one."

"Vulgar."

"I thought that's what I heard."

"But no one," she said, "considers laxatives as vulgar; they're all over radio and television commercials."

"You're right on that, though if you listen carefully to those ads—and I've been doing that lately—they often make a distinction between laxatives as such and laxative *science*. Believe me, Mrs. Goe, I've been doing my homework and listening to those ads lately."

"Good," she said. "The reason that I called you, Dr. Lynpeex—"

"Please, please, just call me Tim. All my friends call me Tim." Then for some mystifying reason, he added, "My enemies in the college *doctor* me. They're aging male profs who don't really care for me, you see. We're overstaffed in several departments, and I want to make cuts, but I can't: they all have life tenure."

"Okay," she said, paused, then added, "Tim, the reason I called you now is to see if we could possibly delay our meeting from the first to the seventh of July. I scheduled a doctor's appointment for the first."

Lynpeex quickly checked his calendar and said, "That's a Monday. That'll be all right with us. Hope all is okay with you, Mrs. Goe."

"Physically, I feel fine for my age and condition."

"Good."

"Doc Addison," Alice said, referring to the town's only physician, "allowed me to make this trip, but she wants to see me after I return."

"Aha."

"She plans to admit me and run a few tests."

"Please tell me where you're going to be so that I might send you a get-well card."

"Now that won't be necessary. A card never gets you well."

"You're right on that."

"When you get to be my age, every day is a bonus. I just hope I have enough bonus days, as it were, to see my ideas through with Royalle College or with *another college* in our land."

Mention of the two words "another college" shook up Lynpeex. He began to wonder if Alice, the writer, was doing what his nephew and other writers often do and that is: submit manuscripts to multiple publishers. So, he asked her in his sensitively blunt manner: "Mrs. Goe, forgive me please for asking: Are there other colleges who are now seriously considering your tie clips idea?"

"Now? No. But if you reject it, others may be contacted."

"They may?"

"Oh, yes, but I hope you jump on it because if you do and if you take out a patent on the idea, you'll get the fee from those who imitate it."

"I see," Lynpeex said. He paused, tapped his fingers on the desk, and again said, "I see."

"You keep looking," Alice said. "I'll call you from the hospital if my visit is going to be a long one; otherwise, the seventh will be the day of reckoning for us."

"That's fine. Hope all goes well."

"Thank you. Bye," Alice said.

"Thank *you*, Mrs. Goe."

"Bye, Tim."

"Bye Bye," he said and looked at the receiver in his right hand.

— ∾ —

"What now?" Lynpeex asked himself after he hung up the phone. He lit his pipe, placed his feet on the corner of the desk and looked at the ceiling; he remembered how peculiar older folks with millions of dollars to give away could be.

He remembered the Royalle College cockroach request, and he remembered a true story about a woman who had left her cat millions of dollars. Lynpeex sat in his office, looked at the painting of the pickup truck on the wall and brooded: he entertained thoughts on topics that hopscotched from recruiting athletes, to class-reunion celebrations, to Tums-for-the-tummy commercials, to pompous hats with feathers that his grandmother used to wear to church, hats that ladies in England still wear. To relax, he buzzed Toyzol who walked in with a big smile.

"Bob, I just got another call, and it's a baffling one at that."

"From who, Tim?"

"Mrs. Goe called from Decatur, Georgia, and she wants to delay our get together. She pushed it back to the seventh unless—"

"Unless what?"

"Unless her doctor keeps her for a longer stay in—"

"She's sick?"

"I guess so."

"But she's in Georgia now?"

"Yes."

"What's making her sick?"

"I really don't know. Maybe she's just getting old, Bob. The doctor allowed her to go on this trip, but insisted on seeing her when she returns."

"What else did you learn from the conversation?"

"More disturbing news."

"Now wait a minute, Tim. A doctor's visit isn't that disturbing to us."

"That's right; it isn't. But that's not the disturbing news that I'm referring to. As you know, one of the standard jokes among presidents and college-development officers has them gathering around and moaning the longevity of the people they love so dearly. It always seems the bigger the donation, the longer the donor hangs on and on."

"Got you. Okay, what's the disturbing news?"

"The disturbing news is far more serious than her age or the state of her health."

"And that is?"

"We're *not* the only pebble on the beach."

"Well, she's right about that."

"Doesn't sound good, Bob, not at all."

"Not at all?"

"Well," Lynpeex said, "we've got to be as sharp as we can; we've got to be resourceful. In a bind, Bob, we've got to freelance and do it with creativity and flair." Lynpeex, who had a tendency to repeat Toyzol's first name in a conversation especially if he felt nervous, was alluding to their forthcoming visit to Samsville.

"What you're saying is that Mrs. Alice Princeton Goe of Samsville, Kansas, isn't your typical prospective donor that college-development officers are familiar with. Is that right?"

"That sure is. She sounds like a tough nut to crack. But by golly, we're going to crack her. We're going to have that seven-million-dollar donation as part of Royalle College, come Havana or high water."

"But remember what you said earlier, we've got to be honest as we've always been—"

"And will always be," Lynpeex said. "You bet your life on that. Honesty has its own rewards. Believe me. We'll never take the money unless we agree to her demands, but what we've got to do is try to get her to *change* those demands so that they're acceptable to us, to our college community, to our honor, and to the public at large."

— ❧ —

Following their meeting, the two decided to go to the racquetball court at the college's fieldhouse.

Strolling to the gym, Lynpeex told his sidekick, "It'll be nice to put on our trunks and beat up on that small and lively blue ball by way of releasing some steam."

CHAPTER EIGHTEEN

IN GEORGIA WITH ALIVIA W. FIGINSTON, ALICE
wrote a brief letter to Tim Lynpeex and enclosed three literary items
(and a quick concrete poem) that she felt might be of interest to him
and his long-time colleague. The handwritten, one-page letter stated:

Dear Tim:

You know how it is with writers: they either connect
with the Muse or make love to a snake.

The last couple of days, I've experienced the former.
What a delight to create while on the road in Decatur,
Georgia.

Enclosed is the result of that encounter: a poem titled
"At a Café in Tangier." My late Frank is in it, and I'm there
obliquely. Hope you enjoy it and its paradoxes.

The poem is part of the Café Series that I've been
writing for the last few months. That series deals with
trips that Frank and I had taken long ago. On those trips,
we'd often stop at cafés in Paris, Madrid, Pula, Trieste,
Rome, Dublin, Prague, Florence, London, Venice, Barcelona, and Tangier.

We were in Tangier to see and visit Paul Bowles, a

writer and a musician and a friend of Gertrude Stein. Paul Bowles lived for a good many years in Tangier. Among his books are *The Sheltering Sky* and and a book he translated titled *Love with a Few Hairs*.

I also took the liberty to enclose an item from my LSB Series: these are part of a genre that I invented called "Literary Sound Bites." These pieces are more suggestive in a poignant—and I trust, memorable—way.

I didn't expect that the Muse would visit me in Decatur, Georgia. So, consider the enclosed to be a treat. I look forward to the 7th.

Below this letter's postscript is a suggestive concrete poem. I'll conclude my signature sign off with a *rebus*: ~~~ ya.

Regards,

Alice

Like the letter, the poem that she had enclosed was handwritten with care, using a fountain pen that Frank had bought for her during their stay in Paris in the late twenties. She cherished that pen and always filled it with green ink and took it with her. The poem:

AT A CAFÉ IN TANGIER
Old ladies on tour
buses wilt rapidly.

. . .

They left their "Go Big Red"
alumni caps with their wilting
wives at the Hilton, and with
golf slacks mesmerized
high over their pancake bellies,

they waddled to the *medina*
snowballing in their wake
shoe-shine boys specializing in sandals,
street peddlers boasting the
highest-low prices in town,
tour guides reeking with the sauce
and legend of the place,
newspaper boys chanting "extra, extra
read all about it," and even
pimps, surprised pimps, surprised to
be hotly in pursuit.

. . .

In the *medina*, they entered a shop,
shedding an entourage that would return
swift and sure as a
band of flies cahootsing with
a pile of dates.
They priced items in dollars,
spoke broken English, felt a
curious fluency in the dialogue.

. . .

They entered empty-headed,
emerged wearing red fezzes with
black tassels
instant and proud graduates into
the Moroccan way.
They languished in a classy café
with transparent windows.

They smiled as their snowball,
sporting glacier proportions, melted
ever so slowly.

. . .

Inspiration comes in spurts.

. . .

That day, a local café-poet
began an ode:
    "Little do they realize
    that we know otherwise."
Hours later, they left as
the poet added:
    "A fez and a beer belly
    Cohere into a classic anomaly."

After he read the cover letter and the poem, Lynpeex read the *Literary Sound Bite* titled: "An Ode to the Pastor at the Corner Church." It wasn't an ode as such, but a fragment of prose. It notes:

> In those days, we used to leave our church doors open for prayer and meditation until the homeless started drifting in and staying. Their stench lingered like expensive perfume, leading us to a realization more riveting than rumble strips: It's time to start an airwave ministry.

— ❧ —

After reading and re-reading the two pieces, Lynpeex invited his sidekick to come to his office for a quick review of the literary offering of Alice Princeton Goe.

"Well, Bob, you read the pieces before I did," Lynpeex said. "What did you think?"

Toyzol sat on his usual chair, glanced at his Xeroxed copy of the letter, the poem, and the literary sound bite, and said, "Oh boy."

"What's a paradox in poetry?" Lynpeex asked. Hearing no response, he added, "Do you know?"

"No."

"Who's this Bowles fellow?"

"How should I know?" Toyzol said.

"Do you think he's real? Do you think she made him up and gave him a name that evokes the toilet bowl, a name that resonates with all that bathroom humor that she seems to like? What do you think?"

"I don't know. They don't teach you this stuff at the MBA schools. Do they?"

"They surely don't," Lynpeex agreed.

"He must be a figment of her imagination, Tim. I don't think a writer would title a book *Love with a Few Hairs*."

"Be careful there, buddy. I like that title," Lynpeex said, stroked his pate, and smiled. "But you're right: that can't be a *real* title. Or is it?"

"What about the literary sound bite?"

"I don't know," Lynpeex said. "I can't figure out if she's critical of radio and television evangelists—and heavens knows we've got thousands of them nowadays, and they're all over the airwaves—or if she's critical of the pastor on the corner church. I'm puzzled again. And that might be her intention: to get the readers to ask questions. And if that's the case, she's got us in her vice, and she's smiling and slowly tightening her grip. We're surely asking all sorts of questions that her work is stimulating, aren't we?"

"And what in the world is a concrete poem?"

"That's what she calls the word-tree design that follows the post-script."

"I can see some homework coming on."

"You're right again," Lynpeex said. "I tell you what: you look up that Bowles fellow; try to establish if he's real; and I'll look up the word *paradox* in the context of poetry in a book on literary terms that I have, and we'll compare notes tomorrow."

"What about that concrete-poem stuff?"

"Yeah that," Lynpeex said. "Let's both see what we can find on it. I've got a feeling that's her sarcastic way to look at what kids do in freshly poured cement. You know, how kids carve their initials, or love-hearts with arrows through them, or coded messages to friends. That must be big in Samsville, Kansas, and we get a lot of it around here. You even see it in some of our college sidewalks."

"I think you're right on that. How can words designed in the form of a tree make a poem?"

"That's what we're going to find out," Lynpeex said.

They broke up their meeting and Toyzol headed back to his office.

— ❧ —

When the two administrators met the next day for lunch in the college's cafeteria, Lynpeex was surprised and pleased to hear that Paul Bowles was a real person, and the books that were mentioned in the letter were actual literary works, and Gertrude Stein was a friend of Paul Bowles.

In a curious way, Bowles's existence strengthened the two men's faith in the availability of the money and the desire of Alice Goe to make her donation.

"If the two men in the café poem are her husband and a friend," Lynpeex said, "then her husband must have been a fat fellow, with a belly that had expanded over the years like a pancake does in a frying pan."

"Fat as we are, we'll probably appear trim to her," Toyzol said. "Not trim as a breakfast-sausage link, but close."

"Maybe a Polish sausage," Lynpeex added. "And those guys in the poem didn't seem to be too appreciative of foreign cultures, did they?"

"Certainly not."

"And if the occasion comes up, we better not act like hicks from West Virginia: we better act appreciative to please her," Lynpeex said. "By the way, I looked up the word *paradox* in the context of poetry, and it is *an apparent contradiction that is nevertheless somehow true*."

"Could you give an example from the poem?"

"Yes. *Speaking broken English and feeling fluent* is one, I think. Here's another, not from her poem but from the book I consulted. It gave as an example: *less is more*, referring to clever description in poetry or prose. And in our situation, if we come close to getting the money but we still don't get it, then we can proclaim: *We came so close, yet so far away*. That, I think, would be a paradox, a disturbing paradox, one that I hope is *not* a prophetic one."

"I do too," Toyzol said. "What about the concrete-poem stuff?"

"I found a little on that," Lynpeex said. "One writer defined it as a *visual poem* where you play around with the appearance of letters and create enigmatic words or images that if solved (or if they connect with the readers) will leave them with a poetic feel."

"So, they weren't poetry in concrete."

"Not at all," Lynpeex said. "Quite the opposite: they're poetry in the abstract, kind of like abstract art. But they're supposed to be visual."

"Ok-kay. I think I get it now. I even get her sign-off poem, Tim. She wants us to visualize *waves of the sea* in saying: *see ya*."

"So, that's a visual play on words. Is that what you're saying?"

"Exactly," Toyzol said. "Now, she calls that a *rebus*, but that's probably a form of concrete poetry. I think I'm right on that."

"Well, I'm sure I'm right on another thing: Monday July seventh will be here before you know it. And I can't wait."

"Neither can I."

"We'll either get the money," Lynpeex said and stood as he spoke, "or we'll be making love to a snake."

— ✌ —

Alice had tucked the letter and other material in a big yellow envelope because she didn't want to have the sheets folded. The folds, in her view, "would have ruined the impact of the concrete poem" that she had lettered below the postscript which states:

"Hope you enjoy this poem. My publisher has agreed to publish a book of my poems, all of which are epitaphs that I continue to revise, under the title: *Waiting for the Mail*. That publisher is pressing me to do a first novel to go along with my first work of creative nonfiction that seems to have found a big audience. And I'm working on that novel right now—if you know what I mean. (wink-wink)."

The men didn't know what to make of the postscript and the concrete poem below it. "Do you reckon," Lynpeex asked Toyzol, "she's using us to do research for a novel? After all, it's about writers."

"Probably not, but how are we to know?"

"Even if she is," Lynpeex said, "I really don't care. All I care about now is getting lots of money for our beloved college. This much we know: she's an imaginative and mighty creative cookie."

"Sure is," Toyzol added. "Back to the epitaph: why would anyone want to have an epitaph that's without punctuation and that looks like a Christmas tree? Is it her way of getting us to connect with her prospective *gift* to us? Probably her way of saying: *Merry Christmas, boys!*"

Here's what Alice had lettered below her brief postscript:

he

lived

with a measure

touch-and-go tenderness

similar to *Playboy* in braille

he died

waiting for the mail

Below the poem she wrote—and Lynpeex read this out loud: "If you know anything about the struggles of unknown writers who lived during the first eighty years of the twentieth century and served as the unsung heroes of postal subsidy, then you'll resonate with part of the focus of this poem. The other part remains for you to decipher."

Lynpeex took a deep breath and said, "Your Christmas gift idea, Bob, might well be the *other part* in her focus. Let's hope it is. I tell you, that waiting-for-the-mail comment reminds me of my nephew, who works hard at the writer's craft. My sister says: he always waits and waits for the mail."

— ℰℐ —

"The truth is," Toyzol exclaimed, "we really don't know much about known or unknown writers."

"And we're having a hard time figuring out her literary output, even in these small samples," Lynpeex said.

CHAPTER NINETEEN

WHEN ALICE AND ALIVIA RETURNED FROM
Georgia, Alice wrote a story about a murder on the Great Plains.

The murder occurs in a small town similar to Samsville. Told from
the point of view of an elderly widow, the story is set in Kansas in
the late nineteen-seventies.

It begins by detailing the harsh economic conditions tyrannizing
life at many family farms. It continues by profiling the difficulties
endured by a farm family of four.

One day, the family's ten-year-old son, twelve-year-old daughter,
and their mother are found shot to death: murdered in cold blood
in the basement of their house while they were watching television.

The father and husband of the dead people—a farmer who works
hard and is religiously devout—is brought in for questioning by the
police. No gun is found, and the case remains unsolved.

The elderly widow feels sorry for the sensitive, well-read, bearded,
soft-spoken, and handsome farmer who had lost his family. She invites
him and his parents (who are retired farmers and members of her
church) to a Sunday lunch after church at her house on Main Street.

She cooks a ham for them, and presents it with steamed broccoli,
mashed potatoes, garden salad, bread, butter and homemade rolls.

During dinner, the son excuses himself and goes to the bathroom.

While the son is away, the elderly widow asks the parents how their son is dealing with the horrible murders.

The son's mother replies: "It's been hard on him. He's probably in the bathroom throwing up what he just ate. He's been having a hard time keeping food down. He can't work. He seldom sleeps. He stays only at our house. It's been almost two months, and he hasn't been back to his house. He's devastated, to say the least."

The son returns to the table, eats more food, speaks very little, and coughs more than usual. The four move to the living room to eat apple pie and watch on television a professional football game that's in progress.

At the end of the exciting game, the three guests stand to leave. They hug the widow and thank her for the dinner and her hospitality.

The next Sunday when the widow strolls to her mailbox to pick up the Sunday newspaper of a nearby big city, she pulls the paper out of the box, unfolds it, stands and stares at the picture on the front page.

In the picture, the bearded farmer's hands rest on his back in hand-cuffs. On each side of him is a law-enforcement officer in uniform. The banner headline reads: HE CONFESSED. The newspaper story goes on to note that the farmer told the police: "My confession is typed on a card, tucked in a hardback book on the shelf by our bed in the farmhouse. The book is titled *The Grandeur and Misery of Man* by David E. Roberts."

The authorities check the book and find an unsigned, neatly printed note addressed to the farmer's parents. They release the note to the press:

Dear Mom and Dad:

I love you dearly. The times are hard, and I am unable to provide for my family. The gun is buried seven feet away from the pump towards the house. This simple note is my confession. When the time comes, I will plead guilty and ask to be killed at once. Bury me next to my dear family. And on a stone from the farm, please paint these words:

Their father loved them

Fate foreclosed on them

This letter ends Alice's story. She considered using the entire epitaph as a title for the story (on occasions, she used long titles); she also considered the epitaph's last four words, or the motto: "Live Free or Die." In the end, she chose: "Look Who Came to Dinner."

— ❧ —

Because Jack liked to read murder stories, Alice thought of reading her story (close to five thousand words) to him during one of his coffee breaks or after lunch when they would frequently sit and visit.

His critique of the story, she felt, will help her improve it. She was developing a deep respect for his critical faculties and witty comments.

In critiquing her literary pieces, Jack was always tactful but frank. He'd often preface his comments with what he felt was "a cute remark." One afternoon, for example, Alice read Jack a section from a long poem that she was writing, a poem that attempts to capture moments from life with her late husband. Titled "Mental Plumbing," the section states:

Monday, he replaced

in the basement's ceiling

two termite-infested boards

and declared:

"No one will ever

notice what I did: it's like

buying new underwear."

The rest of that week in April,

fear shredded his life, making

his paranoia distinct as the

aroma of asparagus-spiked piss.

"I see in this section a touch of the creative overkill in Super Bowl commercials," Jack spoke to himself. Then he told Alice about an incident that had occurred in his college days: "Near the end of a fall semester, a philosophy professor—a nice guy, but a poor teacher—gave us forms to evaluate the course he had taught us. It was then when a student asked: *Will you drop our highest grade if we're honest?*"

That comment made Alice smile. She laughed aloud when Jack added, "Before launching into a critique of your poem, Mrs. Goe, permit me please to ask: *Will you dock my pay if I'm honest?*"

He went ahead and offered her a searching critique of the poem and his unease with the poem's last line.

— ✄ —

She thanked him and told him of another short story she had written and titled "The Parable of the Rich Dentist." She planned to submit it for publication.

"The story," she said, "deals with a wealthy dentist in a small town on the Great Plains, a town not unlike Samsville—but triple its size. The dentist loves to spend money on expensive items, so one day he flies to San Francisco, California, and buys a new car that has the colors of his favorite professional football team, the Pittsburgh Steelers. The color of the car is black and gold, and the make is a Lamborghini.

"In time, the stylish—maybe I better say, pompous—dentist starts taking his twelve-year-old daughter to school in their new Lamborghini, and every morning he drops her near the front door of the school in the same area the other parents drop their kids."

"Okay," Jack said, "I'm with you so far."

"The story gets complicated," Alice said, "when the daughter starts to beg her dad to drop her off a few blocks away from the entrance of the school. The father refuses, for he is aware of the older students who, early in the morning, stand on the periphery of the school and smoke and use language that refers to body parts, and what students do with them."

Jack laughed and said, "Please continue."

"Much to his daughter's anger and dissatisfaction, the dentist refuses to grant his daughter her request—even though she begs and pleads with him to do just that. Finally, one morning the father asks his daughter why she insists on being dropped several blocks away from the school's entrance. He pleads with her to be brutally honest. The girl agrees, and what she says stuns him. Her innocent observation forms the pivotal part of the story." Alice pauses for a long time.

"Well," Jack said, "are you going to tell me what she said?"

"By all means. The lovely and sensitive daughter simply says: *Daddy, all my friends have such nice cars—Fords or Chevys or station wagons or trucks, and we've got this thing.* That remark slaps and startles the dentist. The next day he goes out and buys a green used rusty Chevy pickup truck—a truck that injects immeasurable joy in his daughter's life."

— ☙ —

Following this account of Alice's story, Jack recited (from memory) a poem that he had been working on for some time.

"If you don't mind, I'd like to see the poem typed on a sheet of paper," Alice said. So, she asked him to use the typewriter in her study. As he began to type, she told him: "It'll be easier for me to follow the flow of the poem and to interact with what you're saying in it."

Jack interrupted his typing to say, "This playful poem deals with small-town life, but it wasn't inspired by a small town on the Great Plains. Its inspiration came from the time our football team flew to Huntington, West Virginia to play the Thundering Herd of Marshall University."

"That explains the reference to West Virginia?"

"Right," he replied. "And I know poems don't usually come with footnotes, but this one does. You want me to type the footnote too?"

"By all means," she said. "In poetry, they're called endnotes, and some poems can't live without those endnotes. I'm thinking specifically now of *The Waste Land* of T. S. Eliot."

When he finished typing the poem, he handed it to her. She read the title: "Spermville U.S.A." Then she began to read the poem:

On the outskirts of West Virginia
dipping gently into Virginia proper lay
the town of Spermville USA.

. . .

On a breezy Indian-summer
evening in late October,
the good people of Spermville
gathered at the river
to frolic at their annual autumn
picnic in the park
and dedicate their brand-new
red-brick health clinic before dark.

• • •

Not far from the railroad tracks
at the foot of Cemetery Hill,
the women prepared the tables
while the men worked the grill,
barbecuing their picnic staples:
hamburgers and hot dogs,
mushrooms and onions,
green peppers and opinions.

• • •

In time, the town's sole physician
corralled the folks' attention
after being introduced as
"the evening's main attraction."
The bald and dashing physician
uncorked a gesture-driven oration
that rambled all over creation,
flirting with one finally after another
only to have the last one
twist and transform
a dull oration into a classic one.
"And finally," the doctor proclaimed,
"we must all remember
those who are buried in this hill,
those who died against their will,
those who died in the paths of
silver bullets."

. . .

"Objection, objection, objection,"
someone fired from the rear,
"The earth is for the living not the dead,
the great Virginian once said.
Besides, where will we
residents of Spermville be
without silver bullets?"

. . .

The objection, needless to say,
was sustained in Spermville, USA.

She read the poem twice. She began to smile early in the first reading and stayed smiling throughout both readings. Then she glanced at the ceiling, at Jack's beard, at the paper in her hand, and said, "My dear Jack, with a little tweaking here and there, you'll have in this work not a poem as such—but a ballad."

"You mean one that you could set to music and sing?" Jack said, disbelief coloring his voice. "That kind of ballad?"

"Yes, a folk ballad."

"That's *not* what I had in mind when I wrote this, but I can see Lisa strumming a guitar and singing it as a song—if I dare show it to her. The title alone will set her off, you know."

"C'mon, she's not that—"

"Yes, she is, Mrs. Goe. She'll scold me for using what she'll call a *shock-title*, and she'll say: *I don't like it. I just don't think it's any good*, and there's no way to argue with that, of course."

"I guess she's entitled to her opinion," Alice said. "But all that

* Letter from Thomas Jefferson to James Madison, dated September 6, 1789

148

surprises me, especially for one who's in charge of drama at school."

"I hear you. Do you see the kind of plays or musicals she selects? If they're in the slightest bit suggestive or *risqué*, she'll edit them. That's my dear Lisa."

"Our small-town culture probably influences her decisions, but I'm not your Lisa, and I'm okay with the Spermville title and all."

"That's good to hear," he said. "Unfortunately, Lisa isn't literary like you, but a math teacher—more like *Mr. Goe.* I'd love it if she were like you, having your literary taste and temperament."

"Before you jump to conclusions," Alice said, "I must tell you, your poem or ballad has potential, but you've got to work a bit more on the rhythmic flow of the piece. At this stage, it's one of those poems or ballads, and we get a lot of them at our club, that's working hard to be creative." After a long—and to Jack, a perplexing—pause, Alice added: "There's *something* in your splendid poem that's troubling me, and I know what it is, but I can't discuss it with you at this point. Maybe I will in the near future. Who knows?"

"Do you see your influence on me in the poem?" he asked. "I'll be more specific: Do you see an allusion to that fat Ivy League professor, the one who gave that lecture on the farm economy at a university in Wichita? Do you recall the fellow I'm referring to?"

"I do." She felt the allusion was to the parliamentary-procedure rhetoric that followed the professor's lecture. "If you don't mind, Jack, I'd like to keep your ballad because I *might* have uses for it— uses that won't mean anything to you now, but mean a lot to me."

"I don't mind," he said. "I hope next time when I come back to clean and do yard work, you won't be loaded for bear and tear after me for writing what I think is a playful and fun poem—and *not* an attack on our small-town life."

"I don't see it as such," she said. "I love life in a small town, and I tend to be defensive about that. But yes, I'll make that promise."

"In that case," he said, "please keep it—and enjoy."

Alice wanted to see if there is a way she could use the poem in her forthcoming meeting with the men from West Virginia, given the poem's reference to their state.

— ❧ —

In her diary that evening, Alice wrote about her anticipated visitors from the Mountain State of West Virginia.

"When I meet the men, should I share my slice-of-death story with them? Should I be: playfully mean or simply kind?" She answered: "For now, it might be best to wait and go with the flow."

She looked forward to the meeting—and the men did also.

CHAPTER TWENTY

AT SIX IN THE MORNING ON MONDAY THE SEVENTH of July 1980, Lynpeex and Toyzol drove from their small town in the Mountain State of West Virginia to Pittsburgh, Pennsylvania, and flew (coach-class nervous) to Wichita, Kansas.

Once there, they rented a white Ford at the airport and drove to Alice Goe's house on Samsville's Main Street. Her house was less than two hours away from the Wichita airport, and the drive to Samsville would introduce the men to the terrain of the Great Plains.

Toyzol drove, and Lynpeex looked at the flat land and the wheat fields. "All you see out here," Lynpeex said at one point, "is field after field after field, and the way the wheat sways in the breeze leaves one with a soft, gentle, and peaceful feeling."

"I'll say," Toyzol added. "Sunsets must be beautiful out here on the plains, Tim. No mountains with trees to obstruct one's view."

"And those huge, circular white silos are lighthouses for a sea that turns from green to amber waves of grain: they're pillars on the prairie."

"I bet those silos measure twenty-five or thirty feet in diameter, and they must be over a hundred feet in height," Toyzol said.

"If anything, your estimate might be lower than the actual size,"

Lynpeex said. "These silos, whether they're made out of concrete or tile, are impressive indeed."

As they drove on, they also noticed huge sprinklers set up to pump underground water, and in some fields, they noticed oil wells. "Not all farmers out here are suffering," Toyzol said. "I bet some are rich."

"Rich is the word," Lynpeex said.

Their visit to Kansas was a first for both. Many times they had flown over the Great Plains, but now they were in flyover country, driving on the prairie: they were filtering their impressions of Kansas and looking forward to meeting a long-time resident of the Sunflower State.

— ❧ —

They arrived in Samsville at ten minutes after four. The men wanted to get a feel for the town, so Toyzol drove around for two minutes, and at twelve minutes past four, they climbed the steps leading to the front porch of Alice's house and rang the doorbell.

"Come in, gentlemen," said the elderly woman who had answered the bell by opening the door. She glanced at the grandfather clock in the well-lit foyer and added, "I see you're fashionably *late*."

Lynpeex and Toyzol smiled. She ushered them to the living room and ordered them: "Please be seated—*here!*" She pointed to a couch.

Without formally introducing themselves, the nervous men followed orders and sat on the Victorian couch, and she went back to her easy chair next to the living room's window, collected her white index cards, placed them in their slots in the shoebox, and walked them to a small table with a Tiffany lamp set near the windowsill.

"The cards I just took over there are trunk thoughts," she said. She was standing; they were seated. "Do you, gentlemen, know what trunk thoughts are? And if you don't, do you care to guess?"

"I can't say we know," Lynpeex said.

"Are they thoughts," Toyzol guessed, "that you store in an attic-type trunk?"

"Nope," she said. The manner she sealed and popped her lips by way of pronouncing that word took twenty, maybe forty, years off her age in Lynpeex's mind at least.

"Are they a variation of popular elephant jokes?" Toyzol said, submitting another guess. "Thoughts dealing with elephant trunks?"

"Nope," she replied again as she walked to the wooden chair set across from the men. She moved the chair closer to them, sat, made eye contact with them, and listened.

"Are they," Lynpeex said and leaned forward from his position in the couch, "thoughts that you can staple to tree trunks like they do around political campaigns?"

"Negative there too," she replied. Her hip-sounding rhetoric continued to intrigue Lynpeex and to whittle away at her age in his mind.

"Well, we give up," Lynpeex said, speaking for the two. Toyzol fidgeted in his seat.

"Speak for yourself," Toyzol said and looked at the woman sitting across from him. "I want to try one more guess."

"That's what I like about this man," she said, pointing to Toyzol. "*A winner never quits, and a quitter never wins.* I know that's a cliché, but it applies. All your guesses so far have been good, but wrong."

"I got it, I got it," Toyzol said. He raised his voice and connected with that special excitement that certainty generates in a guessing game. "Are they thoughts that one places on *gym trunks*?" Toyzol paused for a second or two, then added, "Like people do with t-shirts or hats."

"You're close there," she said. "Close but no cigar."

"But I'm close?" Toyzol pressed on.

"Yes, indeed you are. You're close."

"What do you mean?" Lynpeex said. "I'm lost."

"Well, look at it this way," she said, leaning forward and making eye contact with Lynpeex. "People use gym trunks to cover their butts, and they use trunk thoughts for a similar task—more or less."

"They cover *butts*?" Lynpeex asked, surprised to be using such a word in the presence of an older woman that he had just met.

"They sure do; they cover the butts of *cars*," she said, leaned back and smiled. "They're thoughts to be placed on the trunks of cars; they're a new literary genre that I'm pioneering in American letters. Who knows if they'll catch on?"

"Could you please," Lynpeex said, "give us some examples?"

"Sure," she said. She retrieved the shoebox, pulled a card, and said, "Here's a literary trunk thought for poets and writers. I'm sure you heard Hemingway's famous six-word story: *For sale: baby shoes, never worn.* Now I'm no Hemingway, but I wove his technique into this trunk thought:

> *Translators detest this six-word story:*
> *Mother tongues father the best poetry.*

Here's one from the theologic sphere that folks interested in the issues in religion might have on the trunks of their cars:

> *When death visits those who frolic in unbelief,*
> *Will the Balm of Gilead ever touch their grief?*

Here's a third example that many sensitive people can understand:

> *The tumor grew and grew, killing his wife,*
> *Whose biggest tumor was a source of life.*

Oh, my, my, these last two are *downers*, sorry! Here's a trunk thought that's a bit on the lighter side, thanks to heavy people. It's an *upper-er*, you might say. It addresses a male's torso by stating:

> At one time, he was a handsome fellow
>
> Now he flaunts a belly—soft as Jell-O.

So, gentlemen, what do you think of what you've heard so far? Are you connecting with these trunk thoughts?"

Both were stout, somewhat portly fellows in their early fifties; their bellies were hard, not as hard as those of fine-tuned athletes, but certainly not as soft as Jell-O, so they didn't feel offended by that trunk thought.

"Frankly," Lynpeex said while gently tapping his belly, "we've never heard of trunk thoughts."

"No one has," she said. "I gave birth to the genre. That's French, but I don't have to say, *pardon my French* because it *is* French." Both men looked at each other; they appeared nervous. To intensify their nervousness, she asked, "Would either of you like to ad-lib a trunk thought?"

They glanced at each other again. Lynpeex pointed to Toyzol and said, "He will."

Looking at Toyzol, she said, "Your sidekick either kicked you or volunteered you, depending on your perception. Let's hear your first contribution to this genre."

"You just want two lines that rhyme?" Toyzol asked, unsure of his abilities to come up with a trunk thought on command. "Is that it?"

"For now it is," she said and paused. Then she added, "In a crude sense, that's what a trunk thought is. I say *crude* because trunk thoughts deal with poetic images, ironies, paradoxes, insights, subtleties, figurative language, and so forth. But two lines that rhyme might do for *now*."

Lynpeex looked at his buddy and mumbled: "Come on, man, you can do it. I'm pulling for you."

"Okay," Toyzol said. "Here I go with my first attempt ever at trunk thought creativity:

There once was a boy who was tall

His mom made him play basketball

Well, what do you think, folks?" Toyzol asked, turning toward Lynpeex and then in the direction of the woman. Lynpeex smiled and said nothing. His smile telegraphed to Toyzol the message: "Good job, buddy!"

"You at least had him playing the right sport. Tall boys who are athletic do play basketball (and that's big in Kansas, you know); they certainly don't play shuffleboard," she said. "Droopy old men do that."

"I suppose a trunk thought like that," Toyzol said, "will go on the car trunk of a basketball coach or a player. Right?"

"Yes, sir," she said.

Lynpeex spoke to himself, "We're in for a strange stay in the land of the thinking cars." He looked at the elderly woman and said, "But let me see if I understand you correctly: You believe his trunk thought is a good one?"

"Not exactly," she said. "You've got to refine it and inject it with some literary or philosophic elements—or even a comic twist."

"Comic?" Lynpeex said in a puzzled tone.

"Yes comic," she replied, smiled, paused, and stated, "as in:

The dog took the question-mark posture,

And some still questioned its departure.

That's a versatile trunk thought: animal lovers might place it on their cars, and it might interest philosophers or skeptics—or even constipationalists."

The men laughed as she returned to her earlier critique. Pointing at Toyzol, she said, "His is a working-class trunk thought, perfectly suited for the NE crowd but not the NY folks."

"You mean," Toyzol asked her, "it'll be a hit in Nebraska and not New York? Is that what you mean?"

"Not really."

"What precisely do you mean?" Toyzol persisted. "I'm curious."

"I'll explain," she said, stood, and took a step towards them. "What I mean is your trunk thought will be accepted as a decent trunk thought by the *National Enquirer* crowd, but not by the good folks at *The New Yorker*: two national forums with two vastly different audiences. Do you see?"

"We do," Toyzol said. "I'm sure I speak on behalf of Tim when—"

"Did I just hear you say *Tim*?" she interrupted. "This reminds me: we never *formally* introduced ourselves. Let's do that now. She pointed at Toyzol. He stood up. She extended her right hand and said, "You're—?"

"Robert Toyzol, ma'am." He smiled when he spoke. He reached for her hand and bowed, a gentle and respectful bow.

She smiled as she noted the tiny gap in the center of Toyzol's upper teeth, a very distinctive mark, she thought.

"Love your little hyphen," she told Toyzol. "These days, some people hyphenate their names, but you do your beautiful teeth. A hyphen between the upper teeth is like a dimple in the cheeks. When I see such a hyphen in a man, I respond positively to it because it reminds me of the great football coach Vince Lombardi, one of my favorite people, a hero of mine."

"I thank you, ma'am, *I think*," Toyzol said and smiled.

Lynpeex was also smiling and now standing. She turned to him and said with her hand extended, "And you're the one who's not using your hormones to grow hair, you're—?"

"Timothy Lynpeex," he said. He too bowed and shook her hand.

He smiled and stroked his shiny bald pate and bowed again and again as if he were not in Samsville, Kansas, but in Sapporo, Japan.

"And I'm Margaret *Trunk-Thought* Fuller, a colleague of Alice in the WLA, a housemate and friend of Mrs. Goe. In a minute, I'll go and get Alice. She's looking forward to meeting you, gentlemen."

— ❧ —

The woman left the room. She went to the kitchen, opened the refrigerator, poured herself a glass of prune juice, and drank it slowly.

Lynpeex and Toyzol looked at each other. They were speechless. Stunned. Baffled. Confused. Shocked. They didn't know what hit them. They were too shocked to be angry.

When she returned, she said, "I was just teasing you, gentlemen; I *am* Alice Princeton Goe, as I'm sure you had assumed, and I hope you weren't offended by my response to your striking features: striking *indeed*, as the British would say. They love that word *indeed*. Don't they?"

Lynpeex sighed—a huge sigh—and confessed, "I'll be honest: you stunned us with that move. You squirted us with mace—verbal mace that is."

"James Joyce works with epiphanies," she told them. "You just felt the reverse of that, but I don't have a neat label for it. You, unwittingly, gave me such a label: *verbal mace*. I like that as a literary label. Now I'll have to define the contours of this new literary technique—*verbal mace*. Thanks for the homework, gentlemen."

She looked at both, and they remained silent. So, she added, "And how did you like my two-word, hyphenated nickname? Nicknames are really big in the small towns of the Great Plains, and two-worders are in fashion these days."

"Yes, they are, ma'am," Toyzol said. "We've got an English professor back home who has a two-word nickname: we call him the *Vespa-man*."

"Speaking of English professors," she asked: "Did you find the literary pieces I sent you from Georgia to be delightfully enigmatic?"

"Delightfully enigmatic?" Lynpeex said.

"Yes," she replied, "as in Kafka's *Hunger Artist.* Kafka feels, *A book should serve as the ax for the frozen sea within us.* Frankly, I only like new or old books that are sold in quality bookstores."

"I see," Lynpeex said.

"Both of you just came from an airport, and you probably know the type of books they carry at a book-and-souvenir shop. They don't carry great literature there, do they? Airport-type books often resemble those sold in adult shops. Those books *serve as the zipper for the simmering passion within us.*"

The mere mention of the word *zipper* nudged Toyzol's highly sensitive prostate, and he struggled to hold his urge to urinate.

"You're right, ma'am," Lynpeex said. "Please tell us about life in this charming small town."

CHAPTER
TWENTY-ONE

"Life in Samsville would be dull and lonely if it weren't for books," Alice told the men. "Books, you see, connect us with the outside world and the life of the spirit and the human condition."

"We too share a respect for books," Lynpeex said. "But I'll be quick to confess, we're not as learned as our Royalle College professors: we're humble college administrators, you see."

"A year or so ago," she said, "our literary club had an assignment to explore in any form—poem, short story, essay, or one-act play—life in a small town on the Great Plains, and one woman wrote an essay about life in Samsville, and she used an acronym that I still remember to guide and discuss her observations."

"And that was what?" Lynpeex asked.

"FACTS," Alice replied.

"And the letters stood for what?" Toyzol said.

"The 'F' stood for faith," Alice said. "The woman felt—and I'm sure she's right—that faith, the Christian faith, is a central part of life in our small town. We have no Roman Catholic church here, a town nearby does, but we have active Presbyterian, Methodist, and

Baptist churches with good Sunday school programs for all ages and good Vacation Bible School in the summer. Outside of town, there's a small Mennonite church. Our churches are much more than spiritual health spas: they form our community, and they attend to the needs of the poor, the widows, and the orphans—what the Bible teaches should be the role of true religion."

"Amen to that," Lynpeex said. "In our town in West Virginia, we don't have Mennonites, but we've got the other denominations, and we also have churches for Catholics, Nazarenes, and Assemblies of God."

"The 'A' in our woman's essay," Alice continued, "stood for athletics. That's big around here. High school football, basketball, and baseball are the three sports that rule the town, and Little League baseball and adult softball and American Legion baseball also play a role in our town's life."

"We've got all that in West Virginia as well," Lynpeex said.

"The 'C' the woman claimed stood for our culture," Alice said. "She pointed in her essay to our literary club's activities with our weekly meetings and creative pursuits; she also wrote about the plays at the high school; she singled out the work of our library in fostering culture with its varied activities for children and adults; and she pointed to the high school band and other musical activities."

"We've got all that also," Toyzol said.

"The 'T' in the acronym stood for television," Alice said. "It's sad to say, but television governs the life of many around here, and I detest that."

"TV also tyrannizes our people," Lynpeex said. "Sad but true."

"And the 'S' stood for scouting," Alice said. "Boy Scouts and Girls Scouts are big around here. There are other clubs as well such as 4-H and rodeo, but scouting rules the day in the life of the kids out here."

"Clubs are a great way for kids to get together, and to stay connected in later life," Alice said. "Many older people here in town and out on the farms are lonely."

"I see," Lynpeex said.

She continued, "Some watch lots of television, and some listen to preacher after preacher on the radio—they don't come on TV here except on Sunday morning. The radio preachers seldom if ever play hymns or sacred music: such music would no doubt intensify the sad and real loneliness of those older people who live by themselves. Instead, the preachers preach. They *speak*. Their voices are the voices of real persons. The lonely people here on the Great Plains of Kansas and in other parts of small-town America feel as if someone out there is talking to them daily. Now, I understand this might be an odd explanation for the way some older folks alleviate their loneliness around here, but it's my explanation, and I'm sticking to it."

Lynpeex and Toyzol nodded their heads. "How's the weather around here?" Lynpeex asked.

"The heat out here is dry," she said. "We get days, many days, when the temperature goes beyond a hundred degrees in the summer and dips close to zero in the winter—even below zero at times."

"That's cold," Toyzol observed.

"But the highlights of our weather are those ever-present dust storms that frequently punctuate our days in the summer. There's never really an end to dust on the Great Plains, and dusting, as my cleaning lad would agree, is an ongoing activity."

"I see," Lynpeex said.

"And in winter, we get windstorms," she continued. "I recall many days in winter, when my husband Frank would walk to school to teach. He'd come home and say: *The wind was blowing so hard over the snow this morning that I had to stop and catch my breath every ten steps or so. Sometimes I'd lean against a house or a porch and stay there for a while: I'd get some rest and catch my breath.* That's how hard the wind can blow on the mean but lovely prairie."

Toyzol looked at Lynpeex and sneaked in an "I see" of his own and smiled with his eyes as she continued speaking.

"One especially cold and windy afternoon," she continued, "Frank came coughing and complaining about the cold. He cleaned the snow off his cowboy boots and said: *This weather is for the birds.* But I quickly corrected him and flushed that cliché out of his system by saying: No, it's not. The birds are smart: they headed south before it came."

Both men smiled and nodded in agreement.

"The people here," she continued, "are wonderful but ordinary and predictable farmers and middle-class and working-class folk; they make good citizens, easy sociology, and bad literature." After a long pause in which she made eye contact with both men, she added, "You see, there's little meaningful tension in their lives. Good literature, as I'm sure you know—and if you don't, you'll be finding out soon enough—requires individuals to grapple with tension. During our get together today and tomorrow, you gentlemen will get—and I hope you'll be kind enough to forgive me for saying this—a Kansas education."

"And I hope," Lynpeex whispered softly to Toyzol, "we get that Kansas dona—"

"Say that louder, Dr. Lynpeex," she spoke with authority. "I heard you. You'll soon learn that this alert eighty-two-year-old woman can hear the *farts of the ants.* You're after that big Kansas dona-tion. Aren't you?"

They felt another squirt of verbal mace and said nothing. Both nodded ever so gently and chuckled under their breath. "Your language is extremely colorful, Mrs. Goe," Lynpeex said. "Yes, I'm sorry. The 'farts of the ants.' That's good. Yes, the 'Kansas donation' *is* what we hope to get."

"Well, that's what I plan to give—provided the conditions we discussed are met."

— ❧ —

She stood up (they did also) and said, "How about a tour of our white clapboard Victorian house? I love this place. We've lived here since the summer of '27, the year the immortal Babe Ruth hit his sixty home runs."

"And a delightful home it is," Lynpeex said.

"It's a *house*, Dr. Lynpeex," she said, raising her voice and looking up at the men. She paused then added, "A house is not a home. A *home* is a word with an entirely different connotation and meaning."

"Sorry," Lynpeex said. "It's a delightful *house*." He pounced on his pronunciation of the disputed word much to Alice's evident pleasure.

"Now why would you say it's a *delightful* house?" she asked him. There was a long silence. She repeated: "Why would you say that when you haven't toured it yet? You've seen it from the outside as you walked up, and what you saw were clapboard and windows with useless shutters. Is that what you mean by *delightful*?"

"No, ma'am," Lynpeex said. "I didn't mean that. I'm wrong."

"That's like saying that a book is delightful just from seeing the cover and reading the title." She made eye contact with Lynpeex and said, "You don't want to do that, do you, *Dr*. Lynpeex?"

"No, ma'am," Lynpeex said and wondered if he had already blown the donation by his rhetoric and inability to assess her hearing powers.

"Some British folks," she said, "give names to their houses."

"Out in West Virginia," Toyzol said, "the farmers name *not* their houses but their pickup trucks, and they usually give them female names."

"That's sad," she said. "Our farmers do likewise around here.

They think it's cute. Years ago, Frank and I gave our house a name."

"Which is?" Toyzol asked.

"*Remembrance*," she replied. "The name is a Biblical allusion, as I'm sure you're aware."

"And a poetic name as well," Lynpeex added.

"Thank you for mentioning that, Tim," she told Lynpeex. "I agree. It was my idea, and Frank reluctantly agreed to it."

— ∾ —

On that note, the tour of the Goes' house in Samsville, Kansas, began in earnest.

Alice was the tour guide, and the gentlemen from West Virginia (minus the obligatory cameras dangling on their belly buttons) were the interested—albeit slightly shook-up and baffled—tourists.

It was a tour laced with unique lessons.

CHAPTER
TWENTY-TWO

ALICE TOOK THE TWO MEN ON A DETAILED TOUR
of the various rooms, the passageways, and the alcoves in her house.

She pointed to the chandelier in the dining room and the one in the study, to the original unpainted woodwork, and to the sturdy banister. She pointed to the well-preserved stained-glass windows and to some built-in cabinets and to a four-stack oak barrister bookcase.

She pulled from the case a thick hardback copy of James Joyce's *Ulysses*, stroked the dust jacket, and said, "At Joyce's request, the two colors used here are those of the Greek flag. You have the blue cover and the white lettering. Simple but beautiful. We bought this in Paris in 1927 from Sylvia Beach's bookstore Shakespeare and Company. In those days, *Ulysses* was banned from entering our country, so Miss Beach offered to cover the copy we bought with the dust jacket of *Shakespeare's Works Complete in One Volume* or with that of *Merry Tales for Little Folks* . She used to do that with her American customers. She even wrote about it in her memoir. But my brave Frank refused her offer and ended up tucking *Ulysses* between his socks and underwear. He told Miss Beach: *If customs confiscate the book and arrest me for bringing it in, so be it."*

"They obviously didn't confiscate it," Lynpeex said.

"Didn't even open our suitcases, not one," she said.

Alice took the men to the drawing room and spoke about the four paintings there that she and Frank had bought "from artists in the historic Latin Quarter in Paris—again in 1927," as she put it.

While the three stood in the drawing room, Alice noticed that a large painting captivated the attention of the men. "An Irish artist," she said, "did that painting and titled it *The Field Is a Cage*. The poet in me calls that melancholy and serene painting *The Antenna of Our Age*. My Frank used to call it *Juxtaposed*. He saw in it a beautiful Kansas wheat field juxtaposed with hunger and starvation, symbolized by the skinny fellow squatting at the periphery of the field with his large blue eyes staring at the wheat, his long blond hair flowing in the prairie breeze, and his thin hairy legs folded like nutcrackers."

Alice paused, and then spoke slowly: "That painting will stick with you like the dead flies you saw stuck in that sweet brown corkscrew ribbon on the front porch. My dearly departed Frank used to call that *a suicide strip*." She paused again, then added, "If you want a less oppressive image, then let me say: This painting will visit you as often as a smile does a happy face. Understand?"

The men remained silent. She took them to the well-kept, spotless bedrooms and bath on the second floor. She offered to skip the sweltering attic and guided them to Frank's favorite place: the basement. She showed them built-in bookcases: solid oak cases designed and crafted by Frank. The cases held her collection of works from modern literature and her prized collection of literary books published by the Hogarth Press when it was owned and managed by Virginia and Leonard Woolf.

She pulled from a shelf and showed the men two issues in mint condition of the literary journal *Blast: Review of the Great English Vortex*, printed in folio format in 1914 and 1915. She and Frank had bought the rare copies from a bookshop in London's Bloomsbury section.

"Many of our modern writers," Alice said as she stood next to the bookshelves and addressed the men, "acquire a kind of a mystical mustiness down here." She paused then corrected herself, "The writers don't acquire that, do they? Their books do. Writers live on long after they die, and they live on and on—thanks to their books."

The two MBAs seemed impressed. They were dealing with a woman of culture, a learned and creative woman.

— ❦ —

Finally, she took them outside to the yard where the three stood and talked about the weather, the antique dealers in the area, the plans to re-surface the town's two tennis courts, and other topics.

Alice pointed to the large wooden bird feeder that Frank had made. "God rest his soul," she said referring to her husband. "My Frank insisted on making that thing much larger than a traditional bird feeder."

She complimented Lynpeex on his embroidered leather cowboy boots. He thanked her, "I call them, *cockroach specials*, because with their sharp pointed toes, I can trap and murder a cockroach in a corner."

She laughed and complimented his olive-colored tie. "It's a Wembley tie from the late fifties," he said. "I got it from my father." Thin as a yardstick and 100% wool, the tie was straight at the bottom.

"My old Frank used to wear ties like that," she said. "I didn't think anyone else is wearing them these days. What I especially like about those ties is that they're square-cut at the bottom; I frequently call them, those *morally sensitive* ties from the fifties and sixties. These days," she added while looking at Toyzol's conventional red-and-blue tie from the seventies or eighties, "all ties come to a point at the bottom; they subliminally focus people's attention to all those items below the belt: that's too suggestive for my taste, I'm afraid."

"Mine too," Lynpeex said. "But to be honest with—"

"Oh, oh, my dear Dr. Lynpeex," she interrupted, "you should never use that phrase: *to be honest with you* because it implies that when you don't use it, you're being *dis*honest with me."

"Good point," Lynpeex said. "From now on, I'll refrain from using it. Good advice, excellent in fact."

Toyzol noticed two squirrels in pursuit of each other. He watched the squirrels and listened to Alice as she continued to speak to Lynpeex about the urgency of using language with extreme care.

"Our language," she said, "is full of such phrases and expressions. Here's an example. You'd never want to say: *Do all things in moderation*. People say that all the time."

"Yes, they do," Lynpeex said.

"But as moral citizens," Alice said, "you two don't want to do adultery or bank robbery in moderation. Do you? And please don't ever say: *We've thrown God out of the public classroom*. Radio preachers and others use that a lot, but it's an ill-advised expression."

"We hear that in West Virginia all the time," Lynpeex said. "We've got a lot of country preachers in the mountains, you know."

"Oh, I know that," she said. "But my point is God is not a football that you can hold in your hand and then ask Jackie to open the window so that Jim can throw God out the window. The Bible teaches in Psalm 139 that our God is an omniscient God, and he's an omnipresent God. He's also, as I'm sure you know, an omnipotent God, one who can throw us around, but we can't package and throw him out of a classroom: public or otherwise. Do you see how foolish such expressions can be?"

"Oh, yes I do, Mrs. Goe," Lynpeex said. "I sure do. I pledge to be careful with my use of language from now on."

"Let me give you a couple more expressions from our language," Alice said. "And you'll see how silly some common expressions tend to be. I'm on a crusade to purge such expressions from the language."

"I'd love to hear a couple more," Lynpeex said. "Careful use of language is a good thing for a college president."

"Certainly comes in handy these days, especially in small-town West Virginia," Toyzol added with a smile.

"You heard, I'm sure, the expression: *small world* used by people when they meet and talk about other people they know in common?"

"Yes, I have," Lynpeex said. "I've even used it myself."

"But think about it," she said. "Isn't it silly? Your room might be small, your college might be small, your town *is* small. But the world? That's the biggest thing on this bloody planet, Tim."

"You've got another good point there," Lynpeex said.

"Thanks," she said. "Let me give you guys another example."

"Okay," Lynpeex said.

"You've heard the expression: *Don't cry over spilled milk.*"

"Sure have," Toyzol said. "My wife uses it all the time."

"Mine too," Lynpeex said.

"When you guys go home," she told them, "you've got to tell your wives to stop using it. Crying is good therapy. They *should* cry, for after all—the kids have no milk, and there's a mess to clean up."

"Not a fun task," Lynpeex said, smiling.

"I'll say," Toyzol added and thought: Now that's corny!

"Here's another," she said. "People often say: *Life is short.*"

"Yes, they do," Lynpeex said.

"Have you ever used that expression?" she asked both men.

"Yes, we have," Lynpeex said, speaking for both.

"I want to get him on the record," Alice said, pointing to Toyzol. "Did you also use that expression?"

"Yes, ma'am. Used it many times."

"Well, that's the dumbest thing I've ever heard," she told both. "A baseball game might be short; the college years might be short. A vacation might be short. But life? Think about it. Are you, gentlemen, listening?"

"Yes," Lynpeex said. "You're talking about how long life is."

"Life is," she said "the *longest* darn thing that anyone ever does, no matter how brief their life is. See how foolish-sounding a phrase like that can be? See why I'm on a crusade against such expressions?"

"We sure do," Toyzol said, speaking for both.

"Look how long I've lived, and I thank the good Lord for that," she said. "Now, do you see why I think that's a silly phrase?"

Lynpeex wanted to correct her and say: "Hey, that's *not* a phrase: it's a three-word *sentence* with a subject and a verb." (He remembered his boyhood days in a Roman Catholic school in the hills of West Virginia when the nuns would make the kids recite over and over: *A sentence has a subject and a verb.*) But Lynpeex held back his urge to correct her. Such a correction, he reasoned to himself, might kiss those seven million dollars goodbye—an expensive kiss, to be sure. He bit his tongue and nodded in agreement. "We won't use those expressions from now on."

"I'll give you one last expression *not* to use," she said, "and this one might trigger some laughter. You hear this all the time when someone is happy and can't stop smiling. Another person would say: *Look at that smile on her face.* I heard that the other day at the hairdresser."

"Yes, you're right," Lynpeex said. "We hear that all the time."

"Now here's why it's ill-advised. You don't need to say: *her face.* The cheeks of the face are the *only cheeks* that can support a smile."

Both men laughed. "Got you," Toyzol said.

"Language lesson adjourned," she said, smiling.

— ∽ —

The twenty-minute tour—and even the mini lectures on books, art, common expressions, and the uses of language—jibed with the men's expectations far more than did their first ten minutes or so in the house.

As Alice climbed the porch's stairs leading them into the house, Toyzol poked Lynpeex's left thigh, leaned his head towards his boss's left ear and whispered, "Step on that ant, man."

After the tour and the small talk in the yard, Lynpeex told Alice, "We've made reservations at the Holiday Inn outside of town. With your permission, we'll check in, rest a bit, take showers, then come by at a time convenient to you so that we could go out for a fine dinner. You know the good places around here—or we could go to Wichita."

"I'd rather stay around here for tonight," she said. For dinner-time, she suggested seven that evening, and they accepted. "Some women from our literary club," she told the men, "are driving to Wichita tonight to hear a popular movie star speak about an auto-biographical book he was told *he* had written, but it was really written by a ghost." She paused then added, "The women adore the star's good looks. He's a celebrity. Most people, in my opinion, buy the books of celebrities not to read them but to keep them as memorabilia items."

"I agree," Toyzol said.

"Celebrities, as I'm sure you know," she added, "are the best book pimps around. But I'll be with you guys tonight. You're the big fish in the small pond of Royalle College: you're handsome celebrities in your own right—in your tiny town in West Virginia."

"That we are," Toyzol said, smiling.

"Our wives," Lynpeex said, "don't consider us as such. We're just Bob and Tim, whose job is to go and beg for money to try to keep the old college afloat. You see, Mrs. Goe, we've learned that tuition income just won't do it in West Virginia. The good people of Appalachia are poor."

"But if you wish to see us as celebrities, and handsome ones at that," Toyzol smiled as he spoke, "we're grateful for that recognition."

Before they said their goodbyes, Lynpeex asked: "Does the inn where we're staying have a good spacious dining room?"

"Yes," she said, "and it has *good* food. Let's go there for supper."

— ❧ —

They agreed to come back to her house at seven to pick her up for an evening meal together.

Her parting remark to them: "I'm really looking forward to our first supper together, and I trust you are also."

CHAPTER TWENTY-THREE

WHILE DRIVING TO THE HOLIDAY INN, TOYZOL listened as his boss spoke of the *eerie sensation* that he felt when they were standing in the drawing room looking at one of the four paintings the Goes had brought back to Kansas from their trip to Paris in 1927.

"Bob, here's what I see in that painting," Lynpeex said. "First, it's almost the size of a picture window—a large painting for a house. For a museum, it's a perfect size. But a house, it's a bit much."

"But the size is trivial. Isn't it?"

"Sure is," Lynpeex agreed. "What gripped me were the wheat fields' amber waves and the amber-colored hair of that emaciated young man with the residue of a handsome face. If he were standing there, the painting wouldn't have bothered me, but he's squatting there at the edge of the field with his long hippieish hair flapping in the breeze and his long thin legs folded like nutcrackers—to use her words. That canvas grabbed me in the throat, man."

"That's a haunting painting," Toyzol agreed. "It's going to linger with me. Powerful art can do that to you, so she claims, and she's right, absolutely right, Tim."

"How can you forget those blue eyes of that guy in the painting?" Lynpeex said. "Do you reckon she sees him as the antenna of our age?"

"Who knows?"

"I don't know if he is, but the entire painting might represent that to her."

"Yes, sir, it might," Toyzol replied. "If that painting is a reflection of her character and sentiment, then I see an extremely caring person in Alice."

"Not only that," Lynpeex added, "but she's learned as well. Weren't you impressed by all those books throughout the house? That's an impressive library, to put it mildly."

"I don't usually notice this type of thing, but most of the books I saw were hardbacks."

"Come to think of it, Bob, you're right."

"And, Tim, did you catch her reference to smuggling a banned book that she and her husband bought in Paris in the twenties?"

"I did. Bad people smuggle drugs. Good people smuggle literature, I suppose. But you're right on that. She broke the law."

"Don't you dare bring that to her attention," Toyzol said. "She'll be offended."

"She sure went hard after all those country preachers, didn't she?"

"She did, especially those who use language carelessly."

"She even went after my use of language," Lynpeex said. "From now on, I'll never use that phrase *to be honest with you*. That's one of my favorite phrases, but it's no more. She made such a good point there."

"And other good points regarding idioms and clichés."

"I don't know if they're good points," Lynpeex said. "More entertaining and playful than anything."

"But fun points—thanks to her wit and vision."

"Oh yes. I loved it when she complimented my square-cut tie and called it a *morally sensitive* tie, but called yours an immoral one because it points to your penis."

"When she said that, I felt that annoying urge to piss," Toyzol said. "The good old prostate started to nag. I'd say my prostate and bladder and whatever else I've got down there nagged the minute she squirted us with what you called—and brilliantly, I might add—*verbal mace*. She liked that phrase."

"I do too, Bob. And I don't know where it came from."

"Let's just say you connected with the Muse, and you proved that you can do that with the best of them," Toyzol stated. "With that phrase, Dr. Lynpeex, you certainly didn't make love to a snake."

— ❧ —

At the Holiday Inn, Lynpeex and Toyzol carried their suitcases to the front desk, checked in, and were assigned a room on the first floor not far from the indoor swimming pool.

Their room was one of sixty-eight rooms in a two-story red brick structure built in the late nineteen-sixties near the highway on the outskirts of Samsville.

Resting on the only dresser in the room was a green hardback Gideon Bible. Toyzol got up and walked towards the dresser, picked up the Bible, glanced at its title page, and said, "Yep, it's the old King James translation."

"All those Gideon Bibles are," Lynpeex said as he plopped himself on the bed. "Years ago, I spoke to the Gideons of Royallestown and learned that recent translations are protected by copyright laws. One must pay to use them. The King James is in the public domain. Any organization can reproduce it for free."

"Didn't know that. I like recent translations."

The cleaning staff had placed on the dresser a locally produced glossy magazine titled *Sunflower Views & Reviews.* "Please hand me that magazine, Bob."

Toyzol did and headed to the bathroom.

Lynpeex flipped through the magazine and began reading about a Tuesday morning heist at a bank in Hennyisville, a nearby town of ten thousand. When Toyzol came out and saw his friend reading and smiling, he asked, "What's up?"

"You won't believe this: a bank in a nearby town had installed brand-new state-of-the-art cameras and pointed them at the tellers' area, where people stand and move once they're inside the bank. On the outside of the bank in the drive-thru area, the cameras are pointed to the cars as they pull up and park so as to capture the faces of the drivers and others in the cars."

"Interesting," Toyzol said. "Pretty shrewd as well."

"According to this," Lynpeex added while shaking the magazine in his hand, "it's *not* shrewd at all."

"How so?"

"A fellow robbed the bank," Lynpeex said, "but he didn't walk into the bank to rob it, and he didn't drive a car outside to rob it from the drive-thru window. Instead, he rode a red Harley-Davidson to the area of the drive-thru, dismounted, walked gingerly as close to the wall as possible so the mounted camera failed to capture him, handed the teller a bag and a note that demanded five thousand dollars."

"Okay," Toyzol said.

And Lynpeex continued. "There was no gun, and no threat to shoot—simply a handwritten demand prefaced with a *please* and ending with a *thank you*; a gentle demand, as it were. The sheriff dubbed the fellow the *Polite Robber*, and that's the title of the story."

"He got his loot?"

"Almost. His bag had a little more than four thousand big ones. He rode his loud Harley and escaped, probably off to Dodge City or Colorado. Those state-of-the-art cameras were mounted outside and pointed to capture a car and its driver—and not a wiry man who'd sneak up next to the outside wall of a teller's window."

"How fascinating is that," Toyzol said.

"According to the story," Lynpeex added, "the teller didn't recognize the robber's face and failed to get a license plate number from the Harley as it sped off—cash tucked away in that compartment behind the chrome sissy bar."

"I bet," Toyzol said, "the fellow won't be caught out here in these wide-open spaces." Then he added, "Tim, why would a small town need drive-thru banking?"

"Don't know, but that's got to be one of those classic robberies that small-town people can come up with. When we get home, I'm going to tell the story to Aiden," Lynpeex said, referring to Aiden Kaimitchell, his friend who is president of the Royallestown State Bank. "He'll get a kick out of the ways of a polite robber on the Great Plains."

"And since drive-thru banking hasn't hit us yet in Royallestown," Toyzol said, "Aiden doesn't have to worry about aiming outside cameras at Harley-Davidson riders."

"Or, more precisely, at outside customers who park their bikes and sneak up to the teller's window, carefully avoiding the camera's range," Lynpeex said. "I've always believed that some criminals— especially the polite ones—are smart, and this Kansas outlaw is certainly no dummy."

"Well," Toyzol said, "at least he straddled a Harley—and didn't sit on a Vespa."

Lynpeex and Toyzol laughed.

"Is that a true story," Toyzol continued, "or is it, as I suspect, a work of fiction that's made to sound real?"

"It doesn't say fiction under the title, but there may be something in the writer's bio. Let me see," Lynpeex said and turned to the back of the magazine. He read the writer's biographic note and added: "You're right, buddy, it's fiction, a made-up story that's commenting on (or satirizing) drive-thru banking that's becoming popular in bigger cities and even some smaller towns. The writer is a recent graduate with an English major from Pittsburg State University out in Pittsburg, Kansas. Didn't even know there's a Pittsburg out here. Did you?"

CHAPTER
TWENTY-FOUR

ROYALLE COLLEGE'S PRESIDENT AND HIS ASSIS-
tant sat in their hotel room and spent the good part of an hour
discussing their chances of getting the money.

During a stretch in the discussion, both sat on the edge of their
respective beds. They faced each other as they spoke. Lynpeex said,
"We're in for a treat with Mrs. Goe."

"It's that *cockroach-millionaire* stuff all over again."

"Speaking of roaches, how did you like her take on ants?"

"That's a classic."

"Well, we learned something from that, didn't we?"

"Sure did."

"Bob, we just can't be whispering; this old woman can hear."

"Did you like my trunk thought?" Toyzol asked. "My first ever."

"All that trunk thought business," Lynpeex said, "could really
help us in sketching our psychological profile from her writings."

"You mean to say, our elusive psychological profile?"

"Our non-existent profile, if you will."

"Yep," Toyzol said, popping his lips Alice-style and smiling. "You know, Tim, we should've made an effort to look up that book that she had published—*Editors Eat Turkeys*, I think, is the title. That book might've helped us somewhat."

"It's still not too late," Lynpeex said. "We can ask her about it at dinner. She'll probably have a lot to say on it."

"Good idea. Really a good one."

Both stared at the silent television, at the light-blue curtain, at the red carpet in the room. Neither said a word for about three minutes.

Lynpeex stood up, stomped his right foot, and shouted, "Shucks, shucks, shucks!" He paced the room, looked in the mirror, felt pleased by what he saw (a belly firmer than Jell-O), and glanced at the genuinely bad imitations of art that decorated their room.

"You know, Tim, she had a whole card file in a shoebox, full of those trunk thoughts. I made a mental note of the cards when we entered the living room, and I stared at the box when she started quoting from it."

"If we could only get our hands on them," Lynpeex said. "Maybe they'll help us to get to know her better."

"I doubt it. We're not good at drawing insights from the writings of old ladies having intimate contacts with ants."

"You're right, Bob. Hate to say it, but you're dead right."

Toyzol paced the room; when he stood near the window and looked out at the parked cars, he said, "I just got an idea."

"Let's hear it."

"Remember those options we isolated earlier as substitutes for her *C* slash *NC* tie clip stuff? Now we can add another—and a good one at that. At least I think it's a real good one."

"What's that?"

"Not trunk thoughts, but Royalle thoughts," Toyzol said. "They'll be written, of course, by Alice Princeton Goe."

"And what would *we* do with those thoughts?

"We'd place them on cars, vans, trucks, and buses owned by us."

"You might have something there, Bob, but I wish your label, like her trunk thoughts, had some alliteration to it. She likes alliteration."

"Okay, how about: *Crown Couplets* from Royalle College," Toyzol said. "You'd think she'd go for that idea?"

"Inter-es-ting, my friend. Now you're cooking with gas."

"But not, I hope, the gas of the Samsville ants," Toyzol said.

"We can even plaster her *Crown Couplets*," Lynpeex said, "all over campus: in the student union, in the classrooms, in the washrooms, in the gym, at the football field's press box. She'll name it, and we'll place it. For seven million big ones for Royalle College, her *Crown Couplets* will be everywhere. That'll show off those English profs who, in my mind at least, are in desperate need of an attitude adjustment."

"My mind too," Toyzol said.

"Too bad there's no such thing as attitude surgery. Back to your idea: I sure like, really like *Crown Couplets*, oh buddy."

"I feel better already, Tim," Toyzol said, plopped on the bed and spread his legs in the victory sign.

Lynpeex paced the room, looked out at the parked cars, fiddled with the curtain. He tried to catch a program on television, but gave up quickly. "Afternoon soap operas," he said, "aren't my cup of tea now."

It was five forty-five, and they weren't in the mood for a nap or a shower or television viewing. So they strolled to the dining room to get a feel for its atmosphere; then they headed to the coffee shop, located just off the dining room, to continue their impromptu strategy session.

— ❧ —

"So, you think this will be a good place to eat?" Toyzol said. "It's where she wanted to come."

"It's cozy, dark, candle-lit and romantic," Lynpeex said. "It has enough middle-class touches to make it very Holiday Inn-ish. These Holiday Inns, you know, are truly the nation's innkeepers."

Toyzol put sugar in his coffee and began to stir the aromatic dark brew. "How should our approach be tonight?" He looked at his coffee and thought: caffeine is a mind-expanding drug, and it's legal.

Lynpeex started to laugh. "I just remembered a cartoon that I saw in a magazine that had an elderly widow by the name of Mrs. Sullivan. The cartoon showed Mrs. Sullivan and a bank clerk. The clerk had just spotted Mrs. Sullivan approaching his window. When she stops to talk to him, he pulls out a gun, points it at the woman and says in the words of the caption: *Mrs. Sullivan if you put in or take out those two hundred dollars one more time, I'll. . .*"

Both laughed. "We really needed this belly laugh," Toyzol said.

"We'll be in good shape tonight, Tim. We've got all sorts of options for her to consider."

Lynpeex and Toyzol had a second round of coffee and talked more about their upcoming meeting. Then they walked to their room. In order to feel fresh at six-thirty, they both took what Toyzol called "feline naps."

When they arose, they shaved for the second time that day. They showered and dressed in their elegant and conservative-looking gray suits, then drove to Alice's house on Main Street.

They arrived there at seven o'clock sharp. They didn't want to be scolded again for being fashionably late. They rang the doorbell, and she appeared at the door, dressed in a modest red dress.

"You're *disgustingly prompt!*" Alice said. I expected you to be fashionably late again. I'm still not ready; I'll be out in a few minutes."

Both waited on the front porch. "All these wheat fields out here on the plains are so beautiful," Lynpeex said. "And when the wind blows, the fields appear to be so sensuous and attractive. I really like the fields."

"I can see where the phrase *amber waves of grain* comes from," Toyzol said. "The fields look like waves. They really do."

"Their fields here are like our mountains in West Virginia."

"Out here on the plains, those sunsets must be a thing of beauty."

"I bet they're pretty," Lynpeex said. "A sunset here probably looks like a cantaloupe slit in half, with the golden half dipping slowly at the end of a long oak table." He paused to process his try at ad libbing a poetic image laced with figurative language and added, "The table's color would be dark in autumn when the fields are plowed, and blond in summer when the fields acquire their amber waves of grain at harvest time."

"With all due respect," Toyzol said, "when it comes to writing poetry, you're no A. P. Goe. I don't know if slitting cantaloupes to make an image of the sun is very poetic. In that, I see making love to a snake. My little Livi can do better: *she sees sunsets as fires in the sky*."

Lynpeex winked and smiled, for his thoughts, like his sidekick's, connected with Alice's Muse-snake reference to creativity.

— ∾ —

Toyzol said, "Alice didn't seem to have makeup on. You think she's in there putting on some perfume?"

"If she is," Lynpeex said, "I'll resist all temptations to classify the aroma; I'll even stay away from grandma's Bengay jokes that would often highlight our annual Thanksgiving dinners."

The two agreed to be on their best behavior.

CHAPTER
TWENTY-FIVE

ALICE OPENED THE DOOR, SMILED, AND STEPPED onto the porch. "Greetings, gentlemen," she said. "Glad to see you."

Her red dress dipped slightly below her knees, and an artfully tossed blue scarf highlighted her neck.

Lynpeex glanced at her and said, "You look nice in these colors."

"These colors along with my white hair," she said, pointing to her head, "make me appear organically patriotic, eh?"

Lynpeex smiled and ran down the stairs and stood next to the car. Toyzol who remained standing on the porch popped his left arm so that it became a handle; she reached up and held Toyzol's arm as he guided her down the stairs.

"Though I don't need it, it's nice to have a moving railing for a change," she said as the two made their way down the porch's steps.

While the three stood on the sidewalk, Alice asked, "We're going to the Holiday Inn, right?" The men said "yes" and gently guided her into the front seat of the Ford.

Lynpeex decided to drive, and Toyzol sprawled in the back seat. Lynpeex located the ignition key, put it in place but didn't start the engine, for he felt Alice was getting ready to make a comment. She turned slightly towards Toyzol and said, "I just love, absolutely love, Tim's gorgeous bald head. I can't deny it." She wanted to reach up and stroke it, but she resisted.

"Thank you," Lynpeex said.

"Bald men, you know, often have extremely attractive daughters," Alice said, smiling. "But their sons, in general, tend to be average or slightly above in looks."

"Didn't know that," Lynpeex, the father of two teenage daughters, said. "I'll have to share that unusual bit of information with my wife and with Tressa and Sarai."

"Trust me, Mrs. Goe," Toyzol added, "Tim's daughters are very pretty and striking, and they're popular at the high school."

"So, you're saying, I'm right on that?" she said, as she turned slightly and addressed Toyzol.

"Yes, I am," Toyzol said.

Lynpeex listened with interest and said, "Permit me please, Mrs. Goe, to ask you: From where did you acquire your data on the pretty-girls-bald-men equation?"

"Why do you ask?" she said.

"Because I'd like to share your ideas with my wife."

"Fair enough," she replied. "I received my ideas from a character in my fiction, a delightful and learned editor who works for one of the women's magazines in New York, and she in turn received the unusual information from an extensive survey that was done on the finalists in the Miss America contests and the hair-follicle status of their dads. Does that answer your question?"

"Yes, ma'am," Lynpeex said. "There's something very impressive, and at times convincing, about a survey, especially if the survey reaches the results you're hoping to get—and for a bald man like me, the results you give are positive and reassuring."

The three buckled their seat belts, and Lynpeex turned the key in the ignition and finally began the drive to the Holiday Inn.

— ∽ —

While driving, Lynpeex noticed two boys, wearing green t-shirts with the words *Samsville Stallions* lettered on them, playing what he felt was a familiar—yet strangely unfamiliar—baseball game in a spacious backyard located several blocks away from Alice's house.

The game attracted Lynpeex's attention. He pulled the car to the side of the road, and said to Alice: "The game these boys are playing intrigues me. Do you know much about it?"

"Yes, I do," she said. "And I know the two boys out there—Paul and Sam Artsusu. They're twelve-year-old twins who play on the town's Little League team. Out here on the Great Plains, our boys are creative and active: they love the outdoors, especially in the summer."

"That's always good and healthy," Lynpeex said.

"You'll see many basketball hoops here. After all, this is Kansas. But what you're looking at is a *baseball* backboard: a game invented by the twins," she said, pointing at the boys with long dark hair. "That game occupies them for hours," she said. They come out here every day with their bats and balls and gloves, and a jug full of water and ice, and their aging Collie follows them and sprawls on the grass and watches them play. Their friends from the Little League team often join them—and they all play together for hours on end without a coach. The boys call this *Plywood Baseball*."

"I see," Lynpeex said.

"That's a way kids in small towns bond at an early age," she said.

"*Plywood Baseball*," Lynpeex said. "How did the boys come up with that?"

"Their dad came up with the name," she said. "He's a baseball coach at our high school, and an art teacher. He took a sheet of plywood, the size of a door, and painted it all blue. Then he drew a white square in the center of the board. Being an artist, he also painted a decorative abstract in the upper-right corner. He nailed the plywood on two posts and planted the posts in the ground, as you see here. He built a backstop on the edge of the spacious yard, using chicken-wire and treated wood."

"Isn't that interesting? So, this area here, in front of the plywood," Lynpeex said, "became the home-plate area?"

"You got it," she said. "Then he took a thin log, two feet long, and planted it on its belly fifty feet away from the backstop. Do you know what that became?"

"The pitcher's rubber," Lynpeex said.

"You're right," she said.

"You can see it from here, Tim," Toyzol said.

"I see it," Lynpeex added.

"So the dad designed the field, but the game they play," Alice said, "was designed *not* by their dad, but by those two handsome boys."

"How is it played?" Lynpeex asked.

"It calls for at least two players: a pitcher and a batter. That's your one-on-one *Plywood Baseball*. A pitcher would step on the log, and he'd wind up and pitch the tennis ball overhand. The boys use a tennis ball and not a hard ball, and they pitch it overhand, much as a baseball pitcher does in a hardball game. If a batter swings and foul-tips or misses the ball, that would be a strike. And if a batter doesn't swing and the ball hits *inside* the box painted on the plywood, that too would be a strike. Anything outside the box would be a ball. And as in conventional baseball, four balls would lead to a walk. And three strikes would make an out."

"I see," Toyzol said while watching the boys at play.

"How would they score?" Lynpeex asked.

"That's a good question," Alice said. "I too wondered about that, so one day after church, I asked the boys, who with their delightful parents come to our church."

"And what did they say?" Lynpeex asked.

"They told me: *In scoring, a team has to force in a run.* They explained that a walk gets one to first base; a ground ball gets one a single. A ball that bounces once and then hits the back of the family's sprawling red-brick ranch house located about forty yards away from the batter counts as a double. A ball that hits the house on the fly counts as a triple. And a ball that sails over the house is a homerun."

"And outs are made in the usual way an out is made in a baseball game?" Lynpeex said. "Is that correct?"

"Yes, it is," she said. "An out is made by catching a fly ball or a line drive, and by striking out. An error is made by dropping a fly ball. An error gets the batter a single base and no more. If, for example, the bases are loaded and the batter hits a pop fly to the pitcher and the pitcher drops the ball, only one run scores. If the bases are loaded, and the batter drives a ball that hits the house on the fly, that drive would be a triple that will force in three runs."

"That's easy to explain to players who had never played *Plywood Baseball*," Lynpeex said.

"I forgot one thing," she said. "It takes only one out to retire the side for an inning, not three outs, as in a conventional baseball game."

"Interesting," Toyzol said.

"The boys also told me," Alice added, "the number of outs per inning may be negotiated before the game starts. The players decide."

"That's fair enough," Toyzol said. "That happens in a lot of sport activities that are a variation of the accepted rules of the main sport. It happens in flag football, playground basketball, etcetera."

"And in *Plywood Baseball*," Alice added, "the game may go on for an agreed-upon number of innings, and the teams may be made up of one person or more on each team."

"That'll involve other kids," Lynpeex said.

"Exactly," Alice said. "The more players who are in the game, the more fielders will be out there to catch the balls."

"And I can see," Lynpeex added, "that more players could lead to three outs per inning instead of one."

"True," she said. "And from what I understand, that happens a lot when their buddies come over and join them—and they do so often."

"Nice," Lynpeex said.

"What's also nice," Alice added, "their dad took a rectangular slab of slate and artistically painted the field's name on it and hung the slab in the center of the backstop. Back up a little, Tim, and you'll see the sign."

He put the gear in reverse, moved the car back, and read out loud: "*Frank Goe Memorial Field*. Well, that is quite an honor."

"Frank often teased the boys at church when they were growing up. I know he would've been touched—and impressed—by the work of the Artsusu family members who took a sheet of plywood and transformed it into a sports-culture artifact on the Great Plains."

— ❧ —

"How wonderful and moving is all that," Lynpeex said, placed the car's gear in drive, and headed to the Holiday Inn. Both men listened as Alice spoke about other facets of life in her small town.

When Lynpeex noticed the neon sign of the Holiday Inn, he

flicked on the left-turn signal, slowed the car to a halt, and began to turn into the motel's parking lot. The driver behind him, who had tailgated him for a mile or so, slapped him with a vicious, loud, and obnoxious horn.

"What an idiot!" Lynpeex shouted. "A royal stupid idiot!" Then he quickly added: "I'm sorry, Mrs. Goe. Forgive me if I sound rude."

"Don't let that bother you," a calm and embarrassed Alice said. "Tim, permit me please to offer you my explanation of what just happened: you're driving so slowly, that when you finally decided to turn left, the guy behind you decided to thank you in a most dramatic way. Out your way, you've got those hillbillies. Out here, we've got our own breed of troublemakers, and you, my friend, just interacted with one of our—plainbillies."

"My wife," Toyzol said, "usually yells at a driver like that and asks: *What else did you get for Christmas?*"

"What just happened to you," Alice added, "would often happen to my dear Frank. He was like you, Tim: a slow and lumbering driver, a very slow dri—"

"Now wait a minute," Lynpeex interrupted. "I'm *not* slow: I was simply obeying the speed-limit sign."

"Yes, I know," Alice said. "But nobody does that out here on the wide-open plains, you see. That's not country culture, understand?"

"Didn't know that, Mrs. Goe. I really apologize for my impulsive and ill-considered response," Lynpeex said. "People obey the speed-limit signs in West Virginia, where the roads are narrow and winding and are near the tops of mountains."

"And if they don't obey the speed limit," Toyzol added, "they'll likely end up in heaven: hence the phrase that John Denver made famous in his song 'Take Me Home, Country Roads.' Remember how the song opens? *Almost heaven, West Virginia.* Beautiful song, isn't it?"

"Oh yes, that song is beautiful," she said, "very beautiful."

"It put our poor state on the national map," Toyzol said. "If I had my way, I'd make it our official state anthem."

"No, no," Alice said. "For an anthem you'd want a song that brings out the spirit in your state's motto: *Montani semper liberi*. Don't you think that's a great motto?"

"Tell you the truth, I didn't even know we had a Latin motto," an uneasy Lynpeex said. He turned slightly and asked, "Did you, Bob?"

"I didn't either," Toyzol said, smiling. "If you two don't mind me saying this, with all due respect, that Latin motto Mrs. Goe just mentioned is *Greek* to me."

Alice laughed and told Lynpeex: "You've got a witty sidekick in this Robert of yours. Frank and I came across that motto when we visited your lovely college."

"I wonder what it means in English," Lynpeex said.

She paused, glanced at both men, and said, "In English, the motto means: *Mountaineers Are Always Free*. Frank loved that motto."

"Oh, I see now," Lynpeex said. "I *know* the English version but not the Latin one."

"I do too," Toyzol said. "That's familiar."

"Speaking of Frank," Lynpeex asked: "What would he tell that jerk who just blasted me with his horn?"

"Nothing," Alice said. "While riding with Frank, I've seen him get many road-rage horns. He'd always tell me in a soft, unflappable, almost lackadaisical tone: *Well, my dear, I've just been informed that I won*."

"Your Frank, Mrs. Goe, surely had a sense of humor," Toyzol said.

"Thanks for saying that, Bob," she said. "Sometimes he'd get far more than a horn: a fellow would roll down his car or truck window, customize his left fist, and stab it in the air. And Frank would say, calmly: *Bad news for that guy. Tethered birds don't fly.*"

"I like that," Toyzol spoke in a cheery manner. "That, Mrs. Goe, sounds like a trunk thought to me."

"Nice of you to say that, Bob," she said. "Never saw it that way." Then she addressed Lynpeex by adding: "Should everything work out, you've got to give this perceptive man a raise—a hefty raise."

Lynpeex drove around the motel looking for a parking spot near the motel's entrance. He couldn't find one. The place had no vacancy, so the parking lot was full. Finally, he located an empty spot ninety yards away from the motel's main entrance.

"Do you want me to drive to the entrance and have the two of you jump out while I come back and claim this spot?" Lynpeex asked.

"No," Alice said. "Let's just park here, and we'll walk." After they exited the car and stood in the parking lot, she said: "Let's see, we're parked next to a red car. You should always remember the color of the car parked next to yours, especially if you're in a crowded lot."

"Why should you, Mrs. Goe?" Toyzol asked.

"That's a window into my wit, son," she said.

Lynpeex spoke silently to himself: "I see we're in for an unusual dinner with our golden parachute on the Great Plains."

CHAPTER TWENTY-SIX

When the three arrived at the Holiday Inn's entrance, Toyzol rushed to the front, opened the door, smiled, and told Alice, "You might say, I'm now the doorman."

"Sure like your *new* uniform, Mr. Doorman," she said.

Flanked by the two men, Alice headed to the dining room. The hostess took them to a small round table with armchairs. Toyzol held, pulled, and gently guided Alice's chair and invited her to sit.

She thanked him, looked up at Lynpeex, and said, "Our doorman has been transformed into a *chair*man—who around here is often confused with an upholstery dealer."

"I don't mind this confusion," Toyzol said, as the contentious ways of a department *chair* at the college cruised his mind.

The three sat on sturdy padded vinyl seats of ladder-back wooden chairs and began to look over the menu handed to them by the hostess. Alice announced her eating preference, and she did it in her distinct manner: "I'm sure you gentlemen know that the eating world has three types of eaters—Cannibalists, Animalists, and Vegetarians. I'm happy to be ensconced in the third group."

That Holiday Inn had, on the opposite side of the *Kids' Menu*, a section labeled, *Vegetarian Version*, featuring traditional meals with a creative variation growing out of a substitute for the meat.

"When Frank was alive, we used to come here often," she told the men. "I still do, but now I come with my friend the librarian, almost once a week, and on occasions with several members of our church, especially after Sunday services."

"What church do you attend, Mrs. Goe?" Lynpeex asked, while glancing at the menu.

"Guess," she said.

"Episcopalian?" Toyzol said.

"Lutheran?" Lynpeex said.

"No," she replied. Her eyes focused on the menu.

Both men knew that Episcopalians and Lutherans tended to be the denominations that had people with money. Farmers and working-class people tended to belong to the Baptist or the Nazarene or the Assemblies of God churches. This sociological classification, in the men's opinions, applied to West Virginia, and they assumed it applied to Kansas. So, they ruled out the working-class denominations. "I'll give you a clue," she said. "I'm a long-time member in what some might consider to be a brand-name church."

"I got it," Toyzol said. "Presbyterian."

"That's close," she said, "a cigarette but no cigar."

"Okay, okay, I got it this time," Toyzol said. "Methodist."

"Bingo," she said. Her voice was uncommonly loud.

— ❧ —

Alice asked, "Are you guys originally from West Virginia?"

"We are," Lynpeex said. "Born and bred in the Mountain State. Our fathers were coal miners."

"Interesting," she said.

"As a writer, Mrs. Goe, you might be interested to know that my late father, Philippe Lynpeex, was born in the tiny town of Hillsboro, West Virginia, birthplace of Pearl S. Buck."

"Is that so?" she said, noting that the "x" in Lynpeex is silent.

"Yes, it is. Not only that," Lynpeex added, "but both were born around the same time."

"For all we know," Toyzol said, "they might've had the same doctor, or most likely—the same midwife."

"How fascinating is that," Alice said.

"Both of us," Toyzol added, "went to grade school, high school, college, and even graduate school in the Mountain State."

"Out here on the Great Plains," she said, while making eye contact with Lynpeex, "we live in what I call America's *net-serve culture.*"

"What culture?" Lynpeex said.

"Net-serve culture," she said. "That's my label for our culture compared to the country's culture at large," she said. "Imagine the country as being a volleyball court or a ping-pong table or a tennis court, and people on the east and west coast are volleying ideas, music styles, lifestyles, clothing styles, etcetera. That's the dominant culture. What doesn't go over and hits the net is what we get out here, forming part of what I call our net-serve culture. Notice: I say *part* because we also make our own distinctive contributions to culture."

"Could you please give us some examples?" Lynpeex said.

She began: "In clothing, one-hundred-percent polyester double-knit leisure suits and turtle-neck t-shirts for men are big out here, but I don't think they are on either coast. In music, Bluegrass is big out here, but I don't think it's that popular on either coast. In recreation, board games are big out here, and in hairdos, it's the beehive for women and hairspray for men. In dog matters, both coasts have laws on the books relating to those red plastic pooper-scoopers—the artifacts of modern culture in their region. Out here, we have no such laws. Or artifacts. We've got Dada."

"Dada," Toyzol said. "What's that?"

"Something that has prevented me and many other good citizens in town from getting dogs," Alice said. She smiled at Toyzol.

Toyzol nodded and glanced at his boss.

"Well, it stands for: *Dogs always defecate anywhere.*" Alice paused then added, "When Frank and I were in Paris in the late twenties—at the height of their *Dada* art movement—their dogs did it on all the sidewalks and you had to gingerly step around their output—or you'd end up walking with it. People around here, like the Parisians of old, don't scoop up their dogs' output and take it home with them much as they now do in the cities and suburbs and small towns of the east and west coasts."

"I see," Lynpeex said.

Alice, playful Alice, slipped in a word that she felt might amuse her guests. She said: "The accoutrements of dog-care culture that bring sophistication to both coasts haven't reached us yet. Probably never will." Then she asked: "Get the drift of all this?"

"Sure do," Lynpeex said. "The *net-serve label* is very descriptive."

"You'll hear a lot more about it, and I'll probably come up with many more examples, during your visit as we flesh out this entire matter that's before us." She alternated in making eye contact with the men. "What I'm saying is that we differ from either coast in many ways, enough to form another culture—and *not* a subculture, mind you. To many wise people, a subculture indicates inferiority, but ours is an alternate culture: a net-serve culture."

— ❧ —

The waitress came to their table, left them glasses of water, and took their orders. Alice ordered lasagna from the *Vegetarian Version*, a dish that she had eaten there before and was a favorite of hers. (Her late husband used to love "the full-octane lasagna," as he called it: the one with meat.)

Lynpeex ordered Prime Rib and requested that it be "as rare as *rare* could be." Toyzol asked for a T-bone steak and said, "I like mine the opposite of his: as well done as *done* could be."

For side dishes, one ordered broccoli and mushrooms; the other requested baked potato and mushrooms.

"You know," she informed them, "mushrooms out here on the Great Plains (or anywhere else for that matter) can either nourish you or perish you."

"Hope we get the nourish kind," Toyzol said, smiling.

"How much is your T-bone going to cost?" Alice asked him.

"I forget," Toyzol said. "More than ten dollars, I know."

"The other day," she said, "when Alivia Figinston and I were at a restaurant in Decatur, Georgia, I saw a large sign on the wall that stated: *T-bone ninety-nine cents—with meat eleven ninety-nine.*" The men smiled.

"As a vegetarian," Toyzol asked, "you eat a lot of pasta?"

"Sure do," Alice said. "I want to be as creative as the Italians—by far, the most creative people in the world. They eat lots of pasta. Does that contribute to their creativity? I say, *maybe.* I believe different nationalities excel in different fields. The Swiss, for example, are great financiers, but in terms of creativity: what do they have besides the cuckoo clock?"

Both men laughed. Then Alice spoke about a trip that she and a friend had taken to Abilene, Kansas to visit the *Dwight D. Eisenhower Presidential Library, Museum, and Boyhood Home* and a dog museum: *Greyhound Hall of Fame.* The conversation also drifted to other topics among them a peculiar television ad for *Braniff International Airways.*

While talking and waiting for their food to arrive, the three noticed an elderly couple, in their early seventies perhaps, as they walked into the dining room and claimed a table near theirs.

The woman had an unusual hairdo in that her long white-and-dark hair was parted in the center and braided into two long braids that dangled on her back.

Toyzol's eleven-year-old daughter, Livi, often wore braids, but the sight of a distinguished-looking older woman in pigtails led Toyzol to whisper to Lynpeex, "Hey, Tim, check out that *unique* woman walking in."

"Oh, my dear," Alice said, raising her voice slightly, "I'm so glad you said unique and not *antique.*"

Both men laughed, and Toyzol said, "Thanks."

"Next time, don't whisper, *daaarling,*" she said. She smiled at the way she dipped and stretched the "dar," for she felt that her pronunciation imitated an elderly self-assured woman she had seen in a Hollywood film. "Remember? I told you guys: I can hear the *burps of the cockroaches.*"

"No, no," Lynpeex interjected. "That's *not* what you said earlier."

"What did I say?"

"What you said," he responded, "dealt with the gas of the ants."

"Oh," she said. "C'mon."

"It did," Toyzol chimed in and smiled.

"But I didn't say *gas*, did I?" Alice said, as she reached for her glass of water. She looked at the woman with the braided hair and didn't recognize her. "The couple might be passing through town," she told herself. Then she spoke to Lynpeex, "What did I say?"

"You used the other word."

"Which one?" Alice said. "Be specific."

Lynpeex said, "The one that rhymes with *parts.*"

"That's a clever way to avoid being earthy," she said, smiling. "College president sure have a way with words, eh?"

"I'd say," Toyzol added while smiling. "Even college presidents in tiny towns in West Virginia have got to watch what they say these days."

"Whatever," she said. "Back to the ways of our two insects: burps of the cockroaches, you might say, is a variation on a theme."

Both men laughed. But Lynpeex felt nervous. He had been traumatized by "variations on a theme" in his humanities class in college, and even though she applied it to body language, he felt Alice might be getting ready to weave into the discussion references to classical music, an area—like literature and art—in which he felt his knowledge was weak. So, he tried to change the subject, but Toyzol started to laugh again.

"What's the matter, Bob?" Lynpeex said.

"Nothing," he replied. "I just think Mrs. Goe is so entertaining and witty. Her language is so colorful. I'm sorry."

"You shouldn't be sorry about that," Alice scolded him by saying. "You should be happy that's the case. Right, Tim?"

"Of course, you're right, Mrs. Goe."

"You know," Alice said, "in many ways Tim reminds me of a fellow I know who crowns his handsome bald head with a dark Elvis-pompadour hairpiece that only his wife, his barber, and the rest of the world know for sure." She paused then added, "He doesn't *look* like Elvis. He has one of those Amish beards without a moustache. If anything, he looks like an Amish-Elvis. Anyway, he's a very bright fellow, a philosophy major in college, a witty guy who named his hairpiece—*Denial*."

"An Amish-Elvis on the Great Plains," Lynpeex exclaimed, laughing at his own remark.

"Hey, Dr. Lynpeex, you just gave me a splendid title for a short story or a poem or even a novel: *An Amish-Elvis on the Great Plains*. Thanks for the incidental suggestion, my friend." Alice winked at Lynpeex. "Aren't you glad you didn't take the hairpiece route, given the extremely attractive horseshoe atop your head?"

"Here we go again," Toyzol said, smiling. "Never heard of a halo referred to as a horseshoe. That's a first for me—and I love it."

"It's an example," she said, "of net-serve culture *rhetoric*."

"I see," Lynpeex said and gently stroked his bald head.

"Look at Tim," she told Toyzol, "he's caressing his horseshoe and tapping its edges with his fingers. He's probably feeling it to see if there are any nail holes up there." She grinned as she teased a smiling Lynpeex then added: "My Frank was bald just like you, and I absolutely loved that.

"At the conference that Frank and I attended at your college," Alice continued, "we met the fellow who had organized the event, and what a delightful Irishman he was. His head was bald as a white button mushroom. The guy introduced himself by using *not* his first name but his doctor's title. *My name*, he said, *is Doctor C. W. O'Hare.* He quickly added: *The students who dislike me call me 'Dr. No'Hare,' and the faculty members call me the 'Vespa-man' because I always ride a motorcycle around town and on campus. My friends call me 'CW,' and you all should feel free to call me that.* He said all this in a charming manner while lapsing into your classic West Virginia twang."

"Interesting," Lynpeex said. "Very interesting."

She continued. "After Frank and I came home from that splendid conference on Virginia Woolf, I wrote and published a long article titled, *The Beautiful Children of the Poor*. I sent a copy to your *Dr. O'Hare*, and he was kind enough to acknowledge that by sending me a thoughtful letter thanking me for the article and praising my *observations and wit*, to use his words. I still recall how kind and gentle and sensitive that gentleman-scholar was—or maybe I should say, is. After all, he might still be working at your college. Is he?"

"Oh yes he is," Lynpeex said, a bit uncomfortable hearing Alice mention the *Vespa-man* in such a warm and positive light. "He's got life tenure at Royalle."

Lynpeex hoped that Alice would not want to talk about literature, art, and classical music.

If she does, he felt, she'll be having roast administrators for dinner.

CHAPTER TWENTY-SEVEN

WHEN THE FOOD ARRIVED, ALICE ASKED LYNPEEX to offer grace, and he gave a brief prayer.

The conversation continued; it dealt with life in Samsville. At one point, Alice turned to Lynpeex and said, "Pretty soon when your mouth is full and you're busy chewing a morsel and shouldn't speak, the server will come by and ask: *How's your food?* and you're expected to say something."

"And, Tim, you're not allowed to say: *None of your business,*" Toyzol kidded, much to Alice's delight.

"Why not?" Lynpeex asked.

"Because *it is their* business," Toyzol replied.

"He's right, my dear Dr. Lynpeex," Alice said while reaching over and touching his arm. "Out here, what you put in your mouth is the business of the one who serves it to you."

"Ok-kay, you two, I get it. I'll just nod or make a harmless remark."

"And believe me, Mrs. Goe, it will be harmless. Tim is a very gentle and considerate fellow, very tactful."

"Will he be tactful even if his food is bad?" she asked.

"Yes indeed," Toyzol replied. "The prime rib he has now is nicely done, just the way he likes it. But if it came burnt, and if the server asks him: *How's your food, Sir?* Tim will speak softly, complaining in a witty, creative, and suggestive manner."

"How would he do *that?*" she asked.

"First, let me say this: Tim won't lie. A lie would offend God."

"You sound like our pastor now," she said.

"And he won't offend the server by saying: *This meat is awful. Just awful. It's dark as charcoal. It's burnt!*"

"Oh," she exclaimed. "What would he say?"

"He'll say something like: *I didn't know prime rib could be cooked like this.*"

All three laughed. And Alice added, "So what I hear you saying is that Tim treats food servers everywhere in a manner that differs vastly from the way he reacts to horn-happy drivers on the Great Plains, eh?"

"You got it," Lynpeex said, flashing a reluctant smile. "Permit me please to change the subject. I wonder if you'd mind if I ask you, Mrs. Goe, of other places you considered giving money to—now that Winterpeace College had unfortunately closed?"

"Now wait a minute," she said. "The fact that Winterpeace College had closed its doors is *not* unfortunate for you, is it?"

That question puzzled Lynpeex. He regretted using the word *unfortunate* and he tried to anticipate what she was likely to say. So, he remained silent for a moment or two. She repeated the question, and he felt obligated to respond.

"We feel it's sad to see an institution of higher learning die," Lynpeex said.

"Even Winterpeace?" she said.

"Yes," Lynpeex replied.

"If they didn't die," she said, "you wouldn't be here."

"You've got a good point there," Toyzol said. "How's your pasta, Mrs. Goe?"

"Just fine," she said. "Thank you for asking." She maneuvered the pasta with her fork and knife and took a bite.

Lynpeex and Toyzol were busy cutting their meat. More people continued to arrive to the dining room. Lynpeex looked up in the direction of Alice and re-asked his question: "Did you consider another college?"

"No, sir," she said. "Not yet."

"Another non-profit institution?" Toyzol asked.

"No."

She took a bite of her garlic bread and started to toy with them, "You won't believe this, but I thought of starting a business."

"Oh," Lynpeex said.

"The problem with all that was that the business would beget more money, and as you can see, I'm having a hard time giving away the money I now have."

"What specific business did you have in mind," Lynpeex asked, stuffing his mouth with a bite of baked potato.

"I thought of starting a business that manufactures and makes fancy stickers out of those trunk thoughts that I write; I've got hundreds of them written, and I can write more each day," she said.

"Sounds interesting," Toyzol said, "the business venture that is."

"And I'm sure," she added, "it would be a profitable business. Just look at how well bumper stickers sell, and bumper stickers aren't all that great. Trunk thoughts are a cut above bumper stickers, and I'm sure they would sell better, much better, especially to thoughtful people."

"Agree," Lynpeex said. "Did you have a name for the company?"

"I had a descriptive, working name—*Trunk Stickers*, but I would search for a more poetic catchy name when the company launched." Alice glanced at both men and then at her food. "While in Georgia, I wrote a trunk thought that you may share with all your English faculty members, especially the poets on staff. It states:

The true poet triggers, graphs, and shows
Goosebumps flowing like falling dominos

I'll give you two copies of this trunk thought when we get back to the house; I've got several typed on index cards that I plan to give to women in our writing club."

"I've been thinking about your trunk thoughts ever since you and Tim asked me to come up with one at your house," Toyzol said, "and I now see *at least* two things in them that are absent from bumper stickers."

"Oh, I'm so glad you've been thinking about my trunk thoughts," she said. "What're the two?"

"Wisdom and rhyme," Toyzol said. "You know, my mom back home in Weirton participates in a fine program called *Meals on Wheels*. Volunteers bring food to her house. Likewise, your fine trunk thoughts, Mrs. Goe," he leaned in her direction and added, "bring food for thought for drivers and riders, especially those who often get stuck in slow-moving traffic. You might call them *Wisdom on Wheels*."

"Love that label, *Wisdom on Wheels*," she said, and touched Toyzol's hand. Toyzol breathed a sigh of relief, thankful that the conversation was moving in the right direction. Eventually, it landed on football.

— ∾ —

Alice and her late Frank loved to watch professional football on television. "Football is a drama in four acts and one intermission," she told the men. "People go to see a drama by, say, Eugene O'Neill or Tennessee Williams or Noel Coward even though they had read the play and know the plot and the characters."

"So true," Lynpeex said.

"But in a football game," she added, "one doesn't know the plot or even some of the characters, and one has no idea what the characters are going to do in the upcoming game."

"Right," Toyzol said.

"And during a tense, hard-fought contest, one feels numerous (and different) emotions," Alice continued. "The spectators at the game are likely to soar to the heights of joy at the scoring of a touchdown, or they could collapse at the feet of despair if an interception occurs at a crucial moment.

"Throughout the game, the fans are likely to feel a variety of other emotions. Sadness, for example, if a player is hurt. Anger if a player is ejected. Laughter if a pass drills the back of a receiver's helmet or if a fumble takes wicked and weird bounces. Disgust if a coach decides to punt on fourth down and inches. Disbelief if a Hail Mary pass is caught for a winning touchdown."

"All that is so true," Lynpeex said. "I absolutely love your perspectives on all of this."

"One year when Frank was teaching at the high school," Alice began to reminisce, "an exchange student from a small town in Sweden came to live and study for a year. Ingemar stayed with the family who owned the Samsville State Bank. (They had a son and a daughter in the high school.)

"Like others in town, we'd invite the Swedish student to our house for supper. One evening while we were eating, the topic of football came up. Ingemar noted: *I went to a high school football game here, and I found it confusing, especially when you compare it to what we know as football.*

"Frank asked: *Why do you say that?* And Ingemar replied: *Let's start with the name—Why do you call it football?* Frank said, *That I can't answer, I'll have to look it up.*"

"I would too, come to think of it," Lynpeex said.

Alice continued by quoting the Swedish boy: "*In the game I saw, the players seldom used their feet to kick the ball, as they do in football in my country.* After a long pause, Ingemar added: *The players here carried the ball and ran with it, and sometimes they passed it. And when I finally saw a player's foot kick the ball, they didn't call that football, but a punt, a field goal, or an extra point.* Frank and I laughed.

"Frank tried to explain the game to the Swedish student who listened and even asked questions. At times, Frank seemed pleased with his explanations of how the game is played and scored, but at other times, he became tangled and confused.

"At one point, I teased Frank and stirred his frustrations by telling him: *Okay, you've explained how field goals and touchdowns are scored: now try explaining to Ingemar how a team scores without having the ball.*"

"How's that?" Lynpeex and Toyzol spoke at once.

"You guys are as puzzled as Frank was; he too looked up at me and asked: *How's that?* And I replied, *I'll be more specific: explain to Ingemar how a team scores a safety.* Frank hesitated then replied: *On that, I'll pass.*

"I tried to explain how a team scores without the ball, and much to Frank's delight, I too got tangled up. So, I changed the subject."

CHAPTER TWENTY-EIGHT

LYNPEEX BEGAN TO EAT HIS SALAD. "I'M LIKE THE French: I eat the salad last, not first."

"Frank and I had spent two months in France," Alice said, "and I can perfectly understand your eating the salad last. I might add, they've got good salads here: no iceberg lettuce."

"The French are sensible that way," Lynpeex said. "We've talked about a lot of things, but not about what we must talk about: and that's about our correspondence and your plans. We can talk about that while we eat dessert; or we can go back to your house, Mrs. Goe, if you prefer, and we can talk there. I'm certainly open for suggestions."

"Let's start here when the dessert comes," Alice said. "And play it by ear from there. We'll continue at my place if need be."

The three finished their main dish, and the waitress came and showed them a dessert menu and suggested that drinks from the bar could also be ordered. The three requested cheesecake. Alice and Toyzol asked for coffee, but Lynpeex—who loved to drink *fine spirits*, as he would often say, but never drank excessively—asked Alice if she would mind if he ordered a drink from the bar.

"Not at all," she said.

"Good," Lynpeex said and ordered a Brandy Alexander.

"I'm a hardcore teetotaler—have been all my life. Frank was also. We never cared for alcohol, but I don't find it distasteful if others drink liquor in front of me. Scientific studies claim that drinking red wine in moderation with meals can be healthy for you. Out here in the land of the net-serve culture, many people frown on drinking. I'm not one of them." She paused, fiddled with her napkin, and added, "You two are probably puzzled by my behavior, aren't you? I ask Tim to pray before we eat, and then I permit him to order liquor after supper. These moves might lead you to wonder if I'm a conservative or a liberal on social (and political) issues: a right-wing or a left-wing sympathizer. Am I correct in all this?"

"Yes, you are," Lynpeex said, and Toyzol nodded.

"You can't pigeonhole me as right wing or left wing," Alice said. "Thoughtful people need both wings to fly. On some issues, they might be right wing, others left wing. One has got to read intelligent thinkers and be informed. I subscribe to *National Review* and *The New Yorker*, you see."

"On drinking," Lynpeex said, "I wish my wife agrees with you."

"Why do you say that?" Alice asked.

"At home," Lynpeex said, "Gloria allows me to drink just one glass of red wine with dinner—no hard liquor is permitted in our house."

"He's lucky that way," Toyzol said. "My wife doesn't permit that. Even though she's Roman Catholic now, she's a hardcore prohibitionist as strict on me as her Fundamentalist Nazarene parents were strict on her. She doesn't want our kids to ever *see* liquor in our house. Ever."

"I'm just happy," Lynpeex said, "you're not objecting to my Brandy Alexander. That's my favorite out-of-the-house drink."

"In town," Alice said, "you can't get a drink of hard liquor or wine or beer. Samsville is a dry town. Has been from day one. But because this place is outside the town limits, they have a license to serve hard liquor. They wouldn't have located here if they didn't get that license."

— ❦ —

While waiting for the cheesecake to arrive, all three focused their eyes on a woman in her late twenties as she walked into the dining room flanked by a tall and fair-skinned young man with a slender body and a bald head with the color, shape, and fuzz of a cantaloupe.

The man was wearing a brown turtleneck t-shirt. The couple was escorted to a table in the center of the restaurant.

"Look, look, gentlemen," she said, as she glanced at the man who had just walked by their table. "Isn't it interesting how a turtleneck t-shirt dovetails with a bald head and a slender body? To me, that combination is downright poetic." Neither fellow said a word, so she reworded her subtle observation: "A bald head, crowning the upper torso of a man, dressed in a turtleneck t-shirt—all conspire to create a gigantic sinep."

Both men had no clue what she was talking about; they appeared baffled and curious. "They create a gigantic *what?*" Lynpeex exclaimed.

"Sinep," she snapped and smiled. Then she added: "That's what you get from trying to read Joyce's *Finnegans Wake* out here on the lonely and lovely prairie. Go ahead and tap your college days in literature classes in those green rolling hills of West Virginia, and you'll figure out what I mean."

"I have no idea what you mean," Lynpeex said. "Maybe he does."

"I don't either, Tim."

Alice smiled and told the men, "I'm desperately trying to make you gentlemen into *poets for a night* by asking: What does a tall bald man, with a firm slender torso, dressed in a turtleneck shirt look like? Puzzled? Remember you came here on a fundraising journey, but I'm taking you on a *literary* journey as well. A bonus, as it were."

— ❧ —

Lynpeex pulled out a handkerchief from his suit pocket, sneezed, looked at Alice, and said, "Excuse me."

"No need to excuse yourself," she said. "Sneezing, my friend, is one of the three joys in life. I even have a trunk thought that proclaims that. Care to hear it?"

"Sure," Lynpeex said, "I can go for another trunk thought from you, but I'm not so sure I can take another one from Bob."

"Oh c'mon, Tim," she said. "Bob's trunk thought wasn't bad." Toyzol fidgeted in delight; he glanced at his boss and smiled. She touched her napkin, made eye contact with Lynpeex, and said: "It was abysmal."

"Would you guys like to hear one of my *risqué* trunk thoughts?"

"Why, of course, we would," Lynpeex said. "We'd love to hear one. Didn't even know they existed."

"Oh, they do," she said. "I can't believe I'm sitting here dining with you guys and sharing one with you. Anyway, it proclaims:

When a non-cold-related sneeze is lit

A warm orgasmic feel flutters from it

Now you see why I say with absolute confidence that *Sneezing is one of the three joys in life.*"

"If sneezing is one of the three joys in life," Lynpeex dared to ask, "what're the other two?"

"*Acceptance* is number two," she said. "Yes, *acceptance*. Acceptance of a marriage proposal; acceptance to a prestigious college; acceptance for employment; acceptance for joining a select club or society; acceptance for publication: be it an article, a story, a poem, a book manuscript, or what have you. To me, *acceptance* is definitely joy number two. As I'm sure you know, James Joyce's *Ulysses* ends with a flourish on the word *Yes*—a flourish that indicates *acceptance* to me."

"And the number one?" Lynpeex asked, with a mischievous smile (as if to say, drumroll please), for he was expecting a predictable one-word *risqué* response—and not a nuanced one.

"The number one joy in life," Alice spoke in an authoritative tone, "depends on one's age, inclination, and status." After a pause, she added: "What's number one to young people differs vastly from number one to older folks—and so on.

"For me, in case you're wondering, my number one joy now is *intrinsically* related to my number two joy: *acceptance*." She placed one hand on top of the other on the table, leaned forward, made eye contact with each man, and said: "I'm now looking for a college to *accept* my seven-million-dollar-strings-attached donation."

— ❧ —

When the cheesecake finally arrived, there was a long stretch of silence, and then the three began to partake of their dessert.

"Could we now," Lynpeex said, "put the donation in front of us? I'd love to move on to that topic."

Alice agreed but with some stipulations.

CHAPTER
TWENTY-NINE

"First off," Alice said, "I really don't like the naked word *donation*."

"We've been calling it the *Kansas Donation*." Lynpeex asked, cutting a clip from his cheese cake.

"I prefer to call it *SAD*," she said.

"Sad?" Lynpeex exclaimed. "I don't understand."

"It's an acronym," she said. "By now you should know what it stands for: *Strings Attached Donation*."

"Quite frankly, Mrs. Goe, for us to wear those tie clips for a year would be most uncomfortable and embarrassing," Lynpeex said, leaning forward and slightly in her direction.

"I'm sorry to hear that," she said, cheesecake near her lips.

"It'll be horribly embarrassing to wear them for a month or for a week or for *even a day*," Lynpeex said. "It'll be tough on us. Impossible."

"We'd be," Toyzol said, "the laughing stock of all the faculty and staff and every college and university in the area."

"We'll make all three national TV networks and the wire services,"

Lynpeex said. "We'll be in every newspaper in the country, and we'll even make the *Tonight Show Starring Johnny Carson* and *Saturday Night Live*. You name it, and we'll make it, and you'll make it with us, for you're the one attaching the strings, and people would want to know all about you."

"Wonderful, just wonderful," she said. "National publicity would be priceless for *Editors and Their Turkeys*. My publisher would love that. That'll be gigantic and incredible publicity, my friends. That book will continue to sell and sell, and ultimately, you'd benefit from all that. The money I earn will be money you keep. I don't need more money to live on. Social Security, book royalties, and interest from a CD, and Medicare are way more than enough for me. Most old widows around here survive this way, but I don't know any who receives royalties from a book."

"But you don't understand," Lynpeex said. "We'll make all those places, but we'll make them in a negative way, not a positive one." He looked at Alice whose face flipped from cheerful to sad in less than three seconds. "Mrs. Goe," Lynpeex added, speaking in a soft, solemn-sounding voice, "the manner we'll make these programs will *not*—I emphasize, will not—dignify your donation."

"You mean dignify SAD? Please don't call it simply a donation, call it SAD from now on. Will you please?" Alice said, her voice was soft, her pace slow, her eyes focused on her cheesecake.

"Sorry," Lynpeex said.

"Yes, ma'am," Toyzol offered. "Dr. Lynpeex is absolutely right. He knows what he's talking about. People from all walks of life—living in either coast and even in the *net-serve culture* will simply laugh and laugh at us. Royalle College will be the laughing stock of the country, pure and simple."

"Dr. Timothy Lynpeex and Mr. Robert Toyzol, I want to tell you something, gentlemen," she said while raising her voice, which had a serious and didactic tone to it. "I want to tell you something that I hope you'll never forget. This comes from the wisdom of old age." Both men finished their drinks and looked at her. They listened intently as she said: "Other people's heads is an odd place to look for prosperity and happiness. Who cares what people think or say? If they want to laugh at me and Royalle College, let them: you'll have the seven million, and you'll be laughing all the way to the bank, to use a cliché."

"Ma'am," Lynpeex leaned over and said, "ma'a—"

"Yes," she interrupted.

"We seem to be spinning our wheels on this donation bit."

"No, we're not," she said. "We need to come to a *yes* or *no* answer. Will you, honored gentlemen, accept or reject my offer as it was submitted to you in writing?"

"To tell you frankly, Mrs. Goe," Lynpeex said, "my reaction—and I suspect Mr. Toyzol shares it—resembles a poster that spells out in all caps the word YES using the word NO. So, there you have it: that's the way I feel in my current capacity as the chief executive officer of West Virginia's College Royalle."

"You just gave an example of a concrete poem, Tim," she said. "You *connected* with the Muse and *rejected* the snake." She repeated that, emphasizing the rhyming words. Then she added: "How do you like this internal rhyme? Congratulations, my dear friend, my poetic and creative friend! Perhaps you're right. Perhaps we are indeed spinning our wheels here. How about continuing this in my house?"

— ᴄ⌒⌒ —

Lynpeex paid the bill. Toyzol helped Alice out of her chair. Lynpeex told Toyzol: "When we arrive at the entrance, we'll wait in the lobby and you go and get the car."

As they sauntered near the pool, they passed two little girls sitting in a stroller that their mother was pushing. Alice looked at the girls' hairdos and told Lynpeex, "How cute! The poet in me would label one a touchdown hairdo and the other: an Eiffel Tower."

"You're so poetic, Mrs. Goe," Lynpeex said and recalled the mural on the library at the University of Notre Dame in South Bend, Indiana, the colorful mural that the students had nicknamed *Touchdown Jesus.*

As the three continued strolling, they noticed a large man, who Alice felt looked like a cookie jar, munching (but definitely not smoking) a cigar and sitting on a lounge chair in the restaurant's bar area.

"That fellow's massive size," she told the men, "reminds me of the great English writer G. K. Chesterton. He was a huge fellow, a massive man. Absolutely massive. Let me give you an analogy that'll capture his size: if you compare most people to ants in size, G. K. Chesterton would be a cockroach. But what a magnificent cockroach: eloquent and witty. He once wrote: *It is impossible to be fat in secret*, and this man proves that."

"That he does," Lynpeex said, smiling.

Toyzol laughed and left to get the car. The other two lingered in the lounge area and Alice turned and took another look at the fat man, then urged Lynpeex to look at the man's moustache and feet. Lynpeex did and asked, "What am I supposed to notice?"

"The man's thin and dark moustache," she said. "Is that really your typical masculine moustache, or is it simply a misplaced eyebrow, or even a caterpillar on a diet? Don't you dislike such thin moustaches?"

Lynpeex didn't respond. So, she added, "And those feet: Aren't they tiny for such a huge man? Chesterton's feet were small also.

Few people know why those massive men with the Hula-Hoop physique have such tiny feet. Do you know why?"

"I can't say I do," Lynpeex said.

"I'll tell you why their feet are so small," she said.

"Why?"

"Because, you see, limbs—and now I'm using net-serve culture humor—don't grow well in the shade."

Lynpeex laughed and begged her to share her remark with Toyzol. "He'll find it very witty, Mrs. Goe. He doesn't smoke now, but when he did, he smoked Chesterfields. And his very fat uncle, who Bob says *resembles a Hershey kiss on toothpicks,* has tiny feet."

— ℰℐ —

While standing near the front door waiting for Toyzol to drive up, they exchanged some small talk dealing mostly with the weather.

"Wonder what's taking him so long?" Alice said. "The car isn't that far."

"Mrs. Goe," Lynpeex spoke softly and slowly, "forgive me please for saying this: our dear Bob has been having problems with his prostate, and before going out to get the car, he probably made a detour to our room to use the bathroom."

"I can understand and sympathize with that," she said. "My old Frank had his share of plumbing problems."

"Plumbing p—"

"Yes," she said. "As he grew older, he'd go to the bathroom more often. And at times, he'd wrestle with a reluctant stream; other times—rare times—he'd make those golden suds: the kind of bubbles and suds he used to make as a vigorous young man and an athlete, a football and baseball player for the Ice Storms of Winterpeace College:

the kiss-of-the-hops-type suds, as they say in beer commercials."

Lynpeex laughed and found it fascinating, even strange, that a wealthy elderly woman would use such metaphors, so he told Alice to ask Bob about his "plumbing problems."

"You really think I should?" she said. "He won't be offended?"

"Not Bob, he's a thick-skinned fellow with a marvelous sense of humor, and he'd love your metaphor."

The instant Lynpeex uttered the word "metaphor" Toyzol arrived. Lynpeex motioned for him to come out of the car. The three stood in front of the inn's entrance and talked.

"I'm sorry it took me so long to get here," Toyzol said. "I had to make an unplanned visit to our room's bathroom, and I stayed there much longer than I wanted. Believe me, I'm sorry in more ways than one."

In keeping with Lynpeex's request, she asked Toyzol about his "plumbing problems," and he laughed and told her all about them.

"Men with such problems, not unlike bald men," Alice said as the three continued standing next to the rented Ford, "tend to have a delightful sense of self-deprecating humor—and I see you've got that in abundance. And I believe that's good and healthy."

"Oh, Bob surely has that about his prostate," Lynpeex said, stroked his shiny pate, and added as he smiled, "I hope I've got that for my head."

"My Frank had prostate problems and was bald, so he had the best of you," (she touched Lynpeex), "and the worst of you," (she touched Toyzol), "combined in one. Seriously, I've observed this phenomenon in other men in town and elsewhere."

— ∝ —

Lynpeex told Toyzol to sit in the back seat and added, "Mrs. Goe and I will sit in the front, and I'll drive. I hope we won't get a horn this time."

"Or what Frank used to get," Alice added, smiling. After a pause, she turned to her left and told Toyzol: "He could get both—a presidential bonus on the prairie, as it were."

Lynpeex drove the speed limit and listened to Alice speak.

CHAPTER THIRTY

"How cool," Alice said, resorting to words often used by young people in Samsville. "Here I am again riding shotgun on the Great Plains. I never do that with Jack and Lisa."

While they were leaving the motel's lobby, Alice noticed in a newspaper a banner headline dealing with nuclear weapons. After sitting in the car, she brought the headline to Lynpeex's attention, then added: "Our most brilliant minds—the scientists—create very sophisticated and powerful weapons and ways to deliver them. And what do we end up doing with their remarkable creations?"

Lynpeex interpreted that to be a rhetorical question. He waited for her to answer it as he continued the drive to her house.

She answered it by saying: "We take those incredibly devastating weapons and place them at the disposal of the politicians, not exactly the brightest folks in our society, not the sharpest tools in the box."

"I see," Lynpeex said.

"If you don't believe me," she said pursuing the politicians, "take the IQs of nine hundred of the most brilliant and creative scientists in our great land and compare them with the IQs of nine hundred of the most brilliant politicians that you could find. You'll no doubt note that the scientists will win by a huge margin—a gigantic margin, Tim."

"Good point," Lynpeex said. He wasn't fond of politicians either.

She continued addressing Lynpeex: "My point is that our destiny as a nation, indeed as a world, is *not* in the hands of our brightest thinkers, but in the hands of people with modest intellect—in the hands of public *servants*. I'm sure you'd agree that servants, public or private, are *not* known for being great intellects. Most politicians we send to Washington are, as some say, *crooks or creeps*. They're not great minds, are they?"

"Not the ones I know," Lynpeex agreed. He continued driving. She continued talking about the politicians and other topics.

When they arrived at Alice's house on Main Street, she exclaimed: "Well, folks, we made it home—horn-free and bird-less."

— ເວ —

The neighbor's daughter, a senior in college, was sitting on her porch's wooden swing reading Jane Austen's *Pride and Prejudice*. Alice greeted her and placed the key in the door.

She invited the men to sit in the living room. Lynpeex and Toyzol sat on the Victorian sofa with flowered upholstery and carved woodwork. She walked to the study, came back with a pillow, placed it on a matching Victorian armchair, and sat across from the men.

"Two months from now," she said referring to her neighbor's daughter, "Nancy plans to get married to one of the basketball stars at her college; her marriage is stirring a lot of discussion around town. She told me the young man is the third person she had fallen in love with this year; she spends a lot of time with him."

The men listened as she continued, "My observation of Nancy's situation, and that of others in our culture, has led me to posit and explore an unusual theory of love. I refuse to share my theory with Nancy, for fear it might offend her. Would you, gentlemen, like to hear about it?"

Both men looked at each other, hoping that Alice would not launch into an explanation-discussion of her theory. Still, they needed to keep the conversation going and on topics that interested her. The men felt it would be best if Alice brought up the money idea. They remained silent.

Alice broke the silence, "As I told you, Nancy claims to have fallen in love three times this year. I will posit that *this can't be*."

"Oh?" Toyzol said, recalling that he must have fallen in and out of love a dozen times or so before he finally met his current wife.

"I maintain *that can't be*," Alice continued, "because a person can only fall in love once." She raised her index finger. "Just once."

Toyzol asked, "Just once?"

"Yes," she said.

"What about these other times?" Toyzol said.

"Those are *illusions* of love," she replied.

"What about the fourth or the fifth lover?" Toyzol said. "You know, the one you end up marrying?"

"That's *not* a marriage out of love but convenience," she answered.

"What do you mean?" Toyzol asked, placed his right elbow on the sofa's arm, and braced his chin with his palm.

"Oh, you can marry out of convenience. In some cultures, parents arrange marriages for their kids, but in other cultures, such as ours, the kids arrange their own marriages. You can have a happy life, with children and all that, and you can grow together and stay together and end up playing shuffleboard together in the nursing home, but all of that is the result of convenience, not love. Love would've vanished with the first person you had fallen in love with: you've got to harness it then or never. It's that simple. You can only fall in love once."

"What if it's a woman's third love, but it's the man's first love, and what if the two marry, would that be a marriage of love or convenience?" Toyzol asked.

"Convenience, of course," she replied.

"So, it's got to be the first time for each?" Toyzol asked.

"Right," she said.

"Then, our culture," Toyzol said, "has few real marriages of love?"

"You're right again," Alice said.

"And that," he said, "might account for all the divorce we have?"

"You're right for a third time," she said. "You're on a roll."

"And if people knew this," he said, "there'll be fewer divorces?"

"You're right for a fourth time," she said. "Yes, you are."

"But, Mrs. Goe," he said, "that's a hard theory to accept."

"It is," she said, "and few abide by it. The life of James Joyce, one of my favorite authors, is one example that illustrates my theory. He fell in love with a remarkable Irish woman, Nora Barnacle, and he eloped with her in 1904, had two children together, and years later, in 1931, they were formally married for *will purposes*."

A long moment of silence set in. Both men seemed to her to be attentive and introspective. Lynpeex broke the silence by stating in a slow and perplexed manner: "You can only fall in love once. Right?"

"You got it," Alice said, pointing to Lynpeex. "I know my theory isn't popular; it goes against everything that Hollywood portrays in its movies, and against all the tendencies in our secular culture as it grapples with issues of sex, love, and marriage. The ways of our culture lead us to the disasters of divorce."

She looked at both men and seemed unaware of how garbled and strange her theory sounded to them.

— ⁊ —

Toyzol stood suddenly and said, "Believe it or not, illuminating discussions like this one work on my prostate. Do you mind if I excuse myself and go to the bathroom?"

"The guest bathroom is straight and to your left."

Toyzol said, "Please, please, you two, don't talk on this topic until I return. I'm intensely interested in Mrs. Goe's wisdom on all this."

"You're so kind, my dear," Alice said. "My late Frank used to say when his prostate would act up: *My chestnut has a migraine.*"

"That's just what my urologist calls a prostate," a smiling Toyzol said. "But unlike your Frank, he doesn't connect it with aspirin."

"I should apologize again for Bob's prostate problems," Lynpeex said. "They're not life-threatening as such, but as you can see, they're extremely annoying."

"I hear you on that," she said. "My Frank's prostate did a number on him as well. Many times we'd be traveling out here on the wide-open plains, and he'd pull the car to the side of the road, go out and stand near a tree. You see, out here our roads aren't busy enough to have many rest stops as they have in the east or west parts of the country." She paused. "Is that why Bob didn't have a drink at supper?"

"I think so," Lynpeex said. Then he corrected himself, "I know so. Hard liquor works on his system, leading to frequency of urination. In fact, *any* drink leads to frequency with him. If I had a dollar for every time Bob urinated in a given day, I wouldn't be out here in Kansas fundraising, Mrs. Goe. I'll be one happy, wealthy man."

She smiled and said, "As I told you earlier, your Bob with his prostate problems and you with your chrome dome remind me of my Frank, and that, my friend, is a good thing—a very good thing indeed: a treat I failed to anticipate."

— ❧ —

Toyzol stood near the Goes' toilet and recited to himself words he had seen written above the urinal in a hotel in Wheeling:

No matter how much you shake and dance,

Those last drops will end up in your pants.

After he pulled his zipper north, he told himself, "This sounds like a good trunk thought , but the stakes now are way too high for me to risk sharing it with the others."

He returned and greeted the two with an apology.

CHAPTER THIRTY-ONE

"I'm sorry," Toyzol said, "these prostate problems can be embarrassing, needless to say. Forgive my interruption."

"Did everything come out all right?" Alice asked.

When the two men stopped laughing, Lynpeex said, "A question that might be potentially offensive crossed my mind. Do you mind if I ask it, Mrs. Goe?" He looked deep into her bright-blue eyes and said, "Is your falling-in-love theory a reflection of love in *real* life, or is it as it appears to characters in your fiction?"

"You, my friend, are far more perceptive than I thought," she said, complimenting and insulting Lynpeex in a slap. "It's the latter, of course. Still, it's too easy to make fun of my odd, perhaps troubling, love-theory analysis as filtered through the eyes of my extraordinary, sometimes bizarre, characters. My theory shocks people at first. They see it as too paradoxical."

"Too para—"

"—doxical," she interrupted Lynpeex. "True, yet contradictory. Life pulsates with all sorts of paradoxes. I absolutely love paradoxes," she said. "Our Lord used them all the time to jar people's attention. For example, when Jesus says something like this: *If you lose your life for my sake, you shall gain it.* That's a paradox. When he says:

The first shall be last and the last first is another. The Apostle Paul also uses paradoxes in second Corinthians when he says: *For when I am weak, then I am strong."*

"We're puzzled," Lynpeex said, speaking on behalf of both men. "We're lost."

"Let me *un-puzzle* you so you can find yourselves," she said. "I'll give you some perspectives that—in the minds of clever poets—have the potential to be molded into paradoxes."

"That'll be helpful," Lynpeex said.

"Look at authors," she said. "If you ask an author why she writes nonfiction books, say, a book like my *Editors and Their Turkeys*, and if she replies: *In order to get my articles published*, then you've got a classic paradoxical feel in that response. Now you say: *Paradox number one."*

"Paradox number one," the men spoke in unison.

"Look at freedom," she said. "The more famous you become, the less freedom you enjoy. Paradox number two."

"Number two."

She scolded them for leaving out the word paradox.

"Look at a soccer coach who motivates her players during a rigorous practice by saying: *It hurts to win*. Paradox number three."

The men enunciated: *"Paradox* number three."

She smiled and added, "Look at silence: if our discussions tonight and tomorrow get really serious and tense, and if at one point I tell you: *Let silence speak*, that'll be a paradox, you see. Paradox number four."

"Paradox number four."

"Look at those American tourists," she said, "who speak broken English in a foreign country in order to feel a fluency in the conversation. The poet in me crafted that in a poem I sent you. Paradox number five."

"Paradox number five."

"Look at Proverbs 17, verse 28: *Even a fool, when he holdeth his peace, is counted wise.*" She smiled, looked up at the ceiling, and added, "Paradox number six."

"Paradox number six," the men stated, even though they felt uncomfortable with her smile and the implications of that paradox.

"Look at silver bullets," she said. "My cleaning lad, a poet in his own right, sees silver bullets from two perspectives: one, they can take life; two, they can give rise to life. He articulated that in a poem on small-town culture titled *Spermville USA*. That's paradox number seven."

"Paradox number seven."

"End of the seven-paradox drill," she said. "I hope one or two of these paradoxes will linger with you, helping you understand what I mean when I say: *My theory of love has a paradoxical feel to it.*"

— ❦ —

After a long pause, Alice said, "Enough for now of these literary matters. Let's move to our main concern: SAD."

"That's where we need to be," Lynpeex said.

"Oh, by the way," she interjected, "I forgot to tell you, the guy Nancy is marrying lost his job before school closed for the summer; he was working in a pizza place in Wichita. Lots of people made placards and demonstrated outside the place; all those students—and even some learned professors from the university—demonstrated, thinking he was dismissed on racial grounds. Many of the men who had demonstrated—and I saw them on the television news—had long hair and unshaved cheeks—facial, that is. Their signs accused the pizza owner of dismissing the fellow on racial grounds. They chanted and shouted and tried to intimidate people from going in to buy their pizzas. The story was all over the evening news on the boob tube."

"Oh," Toyzol interjected, appreciating the net-serve culture term for television.

"The demonstrators," she continued, "demanded an explanation, and the owner of the place gave a brutally honest and detailed explanation, one that the owner knew might hurt the business, but the explanation put an end to the demonstrations. And you wouldn't believe the explanation. It's an unusual one. Would you like to hear it?"

Lynpeex, who had become impatient reciting her paradoxes and listening to her mini speeches, fidgeted in his seat, took a deep breath, made eye contact with Toyzol, and spoke slowly, even sarcastically: "What was it, *Mrs. G?*"

"Don't call me that!" she snapped. Toyzol wet himself. "My name is composed of three letters, and one of those letters is superfluous, but you're trying to make two out of the three that way. That, my dear, won't work with me. It's a good try, though," she added. "Now please don't misunderstand me; you can have a three-letter name with two superfluous letters: Kay is one, Dee is a second, Jay is a third, Gee is a fourth, but my name is Goe—not Gee, you see."

"I see, and I apologize," Lynpeex said, feeling the urge to piss. "I really, really apologize for my poor choice of words. I simply—and innocently—felt that would be an *endearing* name."

"I accept your apology, Tim," she said. "And I trust you see my point: I'd understand if someone abbreviated my name to *Mrs. G* if my last name was a long one, say, Mrs. *Giysilvsnreowrkentruwayski*, a difficult name to be sure, one that would cry out for verbal circumcision. But you want to abbreviate a three-letter word that already has a silent letter. Shame on you."

"Sorry, Mrs. Goe," Lynpeex said, contrition all over his voice. "Please forgive me. Please, please, Mrs. Goe. I'm really, really sorry."

A storm of silence set in. Both men were shaking. Finally, Toyzol gathered himself enough to ask: "Forgive me, but why did the kid lose his job?"

"Thanks for asking," Alice said. "The management discovered and documented—by use of state-of-the-art hidden cameras—the fact that he was allergic to flour. His allergy led him to sneeze on the pizzas."

Both men tried to stifle a laugh. "Please forgive our laughter," Lynpeex said.

"I do," she said. "But what's so funny in all this?"

"I can't speak for Bob," Lynpeex said, putting his opened right hand in front of his mouth, "but to me it's the sneeze."

"Me too," Toyzol said. "That sneeze was a costly one."

"Sure was," Alice agreed.

"Would that sneeze in the pizza dough qualify as one of the three joys in life?" Lynpeex said. "It cost him his job."

"It did," Alice said. "Is there work for him, gentlemen, at your college?"

"No, ma'am," Lynpeex said, "we're cutting back, not hiring. In fact, last week after much soul-searching and tough decision-making we had to let go three people from the staff. Two were high school graduates, the third a high school dropout. All are married, with six or seven kids each, and more in the oven. Believe me, it wasn't easy to let them go. Those dismissals broke my heart."

"Broke mine too," Toyzol added. He touched his heart.

"Well, gentlemen, that's what I think is wrong with our country," Alice said, paused and looked at both men.

"What's that?" Lynpeex asked.

"High school dropouts, as well as politicians, have a litter of kids—five, six, or seven—but the physicians, the professors, the brilliant scientists, the pastors, the engineers end up with one, two, or in many cases, none."

"I see," Toyzol said.

"To sum up: the people who in my humble opinion should have lots of kids, don't. And the people who shouldn't have lots of kids, do," she said, pleased to have offered the men her observations on life, love, marriage, and on the ways of unenlightened demonstrators in the streets of Wichita, Kansas.

"With your permission," Alice said, "I'll go to the powder room—that's our net-serve culture euphemism for bathroom."

"I hate to say this," Toyzol snapped, "but I've got to go *again*."

"Since you're familiar with the guest bathroom," she told Toyzol, "you go there, and I'll use the one in the basement. As for you, *Dr. L*," she stared at him, leaned over, smiled, and lovingly slapped his left shoulder, then asked: "Do you see how hostile that sounds, my dear friend?"

"Sure do," he said. "I'm sorry. I made a mistake."

"Oh, Tim, please, please don't ever say that. I know people say that all the time."

"Say what?"

"*I made a mistake.* Sane and thoughtful people like yourself simply don't set out in life *to make* mistakes: you might stumble into a mistake or be pushed into one, but you don't decide to go out and *make* a mistake for the sheer joy and rewards in such an act. Do you see what I mean?"

"Sure do now: I stumbled and ended up in a blunder," he tried to smile as he spoke. "How's that?"

"Much better, my friend. Please sit—not *tight,* as they say, but sit and relax—waiting for us to return, refreshed and ready to explore the big topic on our agenda."

"Will do."

"And if you start talking to yourself—"

"Oh, Mrs. Goe, I'm guilty of that: I talk to myself all the time, especially if I'm nervous."

"From what I can tell, you're a bit nervous now."

"Yes, indeed I am."

"Don't let that bother you, for even if you're nervous: *when you talk to yourself, you have a pretty good audience.*"

Lynpeex smiled and said, "Your observations are instructive and, dare I say—true."

"Thank you," she said and headed to the bathroom.

— ☙ —

Lynpeex talked to himself: "Fluency in broken English is a paradox." "Comic people are highly sensitive." "Should've used her full name." "It's foolish to say: *I made a mistake.*" "Grandma in Hillsboro used to say: *Coal can warm a hand or blacken it.*"

Toyzol returned seconds before Alice. When she joined them, she smiled and said, "This clean old woman is back and ready to tangle."

CHAPTER THIRTY-TWO

"AND NOW, WHAT WOULD YOU GENTLEMEN LIKE to talk about?" Alice asked. Before they could respond, she said: "How about a three-letter word that starts with 's' and has a vowel in the middle?"

That stunned them. They didn't respond.

"You'd think you'd want to talk about that topic by now," she said. They said nothing. "I can't believe this, I simply can-*not* believe it: two wholesome and handsome, very handsome, American men with MBAs sitting right here in front of me, and I get no response. You certainly know what I mean by a three-letter word that starts with 's' and has a vowel in the middle. Don't you?"

Neither one replied. They looked at each other. Lynpeex began to giggle; then he burst out laughing. Toyzol did likewise.

Lynpeex calmed himself and tried to say something, but he burst out laughing again.

"There you go again," she said. "Laughing at me."

"It's not you," Lynpeex said, "it's the topic."

"What's wrong with this *good* topic?" she said, raising her voice. "Think, boys! Think for a change! What I have in mind is on the mind of most people in our culture, young or old alike. Think!"

"I can't say it, Mrs. Goe," Lynpeex said. "I just can—*not*."

"Neither can I," Toyzol quickly added.

"Okay, I'll go ahead and say it for you," Alice said. "Are you ready for this? Let's at last talk about SAD. After all, money is on the mind of most people, and I trust it's on your minds as well. Correct?"

"Yes, indeed," Lynpeex snapped to attention.

— ✸ —

"I've been trying," she said, "very sensitively and gently to steer the conversation to SAD, and all you do is laugh. Now isn't that a shame? SAD is what I want to talk about—the Strings Attached Donation, the seven million dollars, my friends."

Lynpeex leaned forward and said, "I'd like to level with you, Mrs. Goe, on this donation matter. What I want to say is this: there are all sorts of things we can do for you for the money you wish to donate—all sorts of noble, honorable, worthy, deserving, and conventional things."

"Such as?" Alice said.

"Naming one of our fine buildings after you," Lynpeex said. "After you and your husband, of course. The name would be Goe Hall."

"So, when the building deteriorates the memory of the Goe family deteriorates with it? Is that your intention, Dr. Lynpeex? Tell me, please. Tell me, sir."

"That's certainly *not*—I repeat, not—our intention," Lynpeex said. "Our intention is to keep the building in tip-top shape."

"Frankly, I don't like that idea," she said, leaning slightly forward as she spoke. "A plaque on a building nails down some donations, but not that of Frank Goe's widow."

"Okay, how about this?" Lynpeex said. "We'll offer substantial scholarships for years and years to come to students in your name."

"Too conventional for my taste," she said. "I'm such a peculiar woman, I'd have to interview everyone who receives such a scholarship, and that's an endless, tedious job."

"You'll get," Toyzol said, "lots of writing material from them."

"True," she added, "but I'm too old to be in search of writing material. My past has so much in it that I still need to tap, and even my present experiences offer—and are offering—a lot to write about."

The twinkle in her smile was a dagger aimed at their thoughts, but they dodged the point—more or less.

"So," Lynpeex said, "your reaction to that idea is...?"

"Negative," she said.

"Well, how about establishing a literary review in your honor and publishing your material, all your material, in it?" Lynpeex asked. "We'll call such a journal *Review Royalle*. A classy-sounding name, wouldn't you say? And over the years, we'll feature in each issue material from your unpublished writings."

"Sorry, but I'll have to say 'no' to that," she said. "That sounds like vanity publishing, and I'm certainly not into that."

"Ok-kay," Lynpeex said. "Here's my last suggestion, and it's a variation of my first: we'll rename our Collegiate Gothic Mountaineer Hall in your name. How's that?"

"If you really mean that," she said, raising her voice and looking directly at Lynpeex, "then why didn't you say that first?"

"I didn't think of it first," Lynpeex said. "I'm very sorry about that, Mrs. Goe."

"He's keeping the best to last," Toyzol interjected. He spoke in a soft voice.

"Stay out of this. Hear me?" she snapped at Toyzol.

"Sorry, ma'am," Toyzol said, "I was just trying to be helpful." A trace of sarcasm punctuated his voice as he whispered, "If that's possible at this stage."

"Watch that tone, son," she said as Toyzol cowered in his seat, feeling like he had just dropped a crucial and easy touchdown pass and the coach had pulled him out of the game. Toyzol hoped for a hole to suddenly appear in the ground and swallow him.

Toyzol refused—feared—to even glance at his boss. He felt as if he had, unwittingly, blown the seven million dollars.

"Fine, ma'am," Toyzol said. "I'm really sorry. I apologize. I really, really apologize."

"He's reminding me," she told Lynpeex and pointed at Toyzol, "of those famous eight lines in James Joyce's brilliant little book titled: *A Portrait of the Artist as a Young Man*:

> Pull out his eyes,
>
> Apologise,
>
> Apologise,
>
> Pull out his eyes.
>
> Apologise,
>
> Pull out his eyes
>
> Pull out his eyes,
>
> Apologise.

"I accept your apology," Alice said.

"Renaming Mountaineer Hall is so tempting," she said to Lynpeex, "and I might consider that if I get negative responses from other colleges on my tie clips offer."

"You mean if we don't come to terms tonight, we're done?" the good Dr. Lynpeex said. "You're going to pursue other colleges?"

"Yes, sir," she replied. "That's exactly what I mean; you're a perceptive gentleman indeed."

Toyzol felt the urge to warn her to watch her tone, but he resisted much as a religious teen gets the urge to look at his father's pornographic materials but somehow resists that urge. Lynpeex paused and thought about a response to her last comment.

"So, there's not much," Lynpeex said, "that we can do but wait, is there?"

"The great poet Milton would agree with you on that," she said. "He wrote, somewhat paradoxically: *They also serve who only stand and wait.*"

"So, there's nothing more for us to do, is there?"

"Of course, there is," she replied.

"What?" Lynpeex said.

"Come to terms with SAD," she said. "My terms, of course."

"That's a virtually impossible demand," Lynpeex said.

"It's possible," she said. "Your reaction makes it impossible."

"I tell you what, Mrs. Goe: why don't you hold off making other contacts until we get back to you in a week or so," Lynpeex suggested, stood up, and marched around the room somewhat authoritatively. Then he added, "For now, what I suggest we do is go back to West Virginia, the two of us," he nodded towards Toyzol and pointed at himself, "involve our board members in this matter, and then form a subcommittee to study this extraordinary matter. We might come up with a compromise that might be pleasing to both of us."

— ☙ —

"I've been silent for a while," Toyzol said. "Do you mind if I make a suggestion?"

"Go ahead," Alice told him.

"It deals with your trunk thought idea."

"My trunk thought idea?" she said.

"Yes," Toyzol said. "Your excellent idea."

"Not a sarcastic take off on it, I hope," she said.

"Oh, no, not at all," Toyzol said. "It's a modification of it."

"Pray tell, what's that?" Alice said.

"It's *Crown Couplets from Royalle College*," Toyzol said. "We'll place all your couplets on all our vehicles: the vans and buses that our athletic teams use; the cars that the administrators and staff drive; the trucks that physical plant uses; we'll even place them in the classrooms and the gym and the bulletin boards: you name it, and we'll place it there. What do you think?"

"*Trunk Thoughts*, Mrs. Goe," Lynpeex said, "is a great name with alliteration and all, but it limits your thoughts to car trunks. Mr. Toyzol's suggestion would expand the range and reach of your original idea. You'd include other vehicles and places in your thoughts." After a long pause, he added, "The name of your literary invention will still have alliteration, and the word *crown* will fit in nicely with our college's name: a lot better—if you'll forgive me for saying—than trunk thoughts."

Alice reflected for a moment. She looked at her shoes, then at the ceiling, then she glanced at the bookshelf in the study. The new name might work.

In her mind, *Crown Couplets* as a label had a delightful ring to it. She looked up again at the ceiling as if to invoke the muses to descend; she looked down at the carpet as if to apologize to any muses that she and the men might have stomped on, and she came up empty both times.

"Both of you, good gentlemen, have got me in a bind now. Half of me is saying: *What a clever idea*. The other half: *What a crappy one*." She spoke slowly and distinctly.

She shocked both men when she rose out of her seat, walked towards them with her right hand raised in the courtroom-salute manner, and invited them to exchange high-fives. The men stood, bent their knees a bit to shrink their height, and exchanged high-fives.

At their daughters' softball games, the exchanges would have been appropriate; but in Samsville, Kansas, with an aging millionaire-widow, the exchanges seemed downright bizarre—at least to the slightly portly and totally baffled men of Royalle College.

When all three reclaimed their seats, she told them, "Permit me please to say, you're *not* the first ones to suggest an alternate name for my poetic genre."

"You mean others did before us?" an anxious Lynpeex asked. He wondered if other college officers have been on the same ride.

"Not others," she said. "Just one other person."

"Do you mind if we ask who that person was?" Lynpeex said.

"Oh, I don't mind telling you," she said. "Not at all. The fellow is my cleaning lad."

"So, it's not another college administrator?" Toyzol said.

"No, no," she said. "You're the first administrators I've dealt with on this SAD matter."

"Your *cleaning lad* came up with the alternate label?" a perplexed Lynpeex said.

"He's not your typical cleaning person," she said. "This guy has a college degree in philosophy with honors."

"I see," a smiling Lynpeex said.

"And I hasten to add," she said, "he's unaware of my immense wealth. No one in this town knows a thing about my wealth. My late husband's pursuit of privacy was fierce—downright ferocious. And on the matter of privacy and wealth, I agree with him."

"I see," Lynpeex said.

"I'm curious," Toyzol said with a smile: "Is his label better than *Crown Couplets*?"

"It is, and it isn't," she said.

"What do you mean?" Toyzol said.

"In the context of Royalle College's name," she said, "I like yours a lot better than his. Your *Crown Couplets* as a name works well with your college's name. But as a name for the genre outside of your college's context, it's pretentious."

"Please tell us his label," Toyzol said. "I'm curious."

"It was," she said, "a good label: *Moving Poetry*, and I liked it better than my *Trunk Thoughts*, but my dear old Frank loved alliteration, so I stayed with the car's rear end. And you," she added while pointing to Toyzol, "came up with a superb alliterative name at dinner. It was an ingenious name that evoked the food-for-thought idea: *Wisdom on Wheels*. But, I must admit, *Crown Couplets* tops them all!"

Lynpeex smiled and wondered: "Well, where do we go from here? What do you think, Mrs. Goe? Do you think the Crown Couplets might take the place of the tie clips in our arrangement?"

Once again, Alice looked down at the carpet; she was pensive; she seemed to lean towards the idea of *Crown Couplets*, yet she also seemed a bit hesitant. The men sensed her hesitancy, and rather than push her, Lynpeex said: "Mrs. Goe, why don't you sleep on the idea, and we'll do likewise. We'll come back tomorrow after breakfast, and we'll see what you've decided. How does this sound to you?"

"Sounds fine with me," she replied. "How about at ten tomorrow morning? I usually eat breakfast at eight. We'll have a cup of coffee, and we'll wrap things up."

"See you then, Mrs. Goe," both men said at once.

They stood and she led them to the door. After she shook their hands, she locked the door and chained it.

Most people in Samsville took pride in the safety of their small community and never locked their doors. But thanks to Frank's paranoia, the Goes were in the habit of locking and chaining the doors when he was alive, and Alice held on to that habit after his death.

— ☙ —

At ten, she relaxed and watched on television (from Wichita) what she playfully called "Fire-Trucks Time," the late evening news. After that, she continued in a routine that she and her late Frank had started in 1962: faithfully watching the *Tonight Show Starring Johnny Carson*.

CHAPTER THIRTY-THREE

BACK IN THEIR HOLIDAY INN ROOM THAT EVENING, Lynpeex and Toyzol disagreed as to their chances of getting Alice to drop her peculiar tie clips demands in a manner that was categorical and final.

Toyzol at one instance told Lynpeex, "She's stubborn, Tim; she'll never budge. I hope I'm wrong, but—"

"Hope you're wrong, Bob, but I tell you that *Crown Couplets* idea of yours hit her in a sensitive place. I've got to take off my hat to you, old buddy. It's a brilliant idea," Lynpeex said, standing next to the window and looking out at the parking lot. "A real stroke of genius, if you'll permit me to flatter you in a way that'll expand the size of your head from a cantaloupe to a watermelon,"

"I don't know why I feel she's *not* going to buy it," Toyzol said. "During our conversations in the restaurant, an idea flew by me and lit up my thoughts for an instance, and I saw clearly a motive of hers that disappeared as suddenly as the light appeared," Toyzol added as he sat on the bedside and looked down at the carpet. "The idea reminded me of a lonely lightning bug on a hot summer evening back home. And the idea really disturbed me, really hurt."

"What was that idea?" Lynpeex asked. "What did it deal with?"

"Mrs. Goe. It dealt with her—with herself."

"Be more specific."

"Her condition, Tim."

"Her wealth?"

"No, no, her social and psychological condition."

"What about it?"

"She suddenly seemed to me to be a sad old widow: rich, lonely, creative, highly intelligent, and in desperate need of company—not the company that'll do little more than add another layer of gossip on her thoughts, but the kind of *intellectual* company that'll fire-up her creative instincts," Toyzol said. He took a deep breath, paused, then added, "Okay, here's what's likely to happen: we get a 'yes' to *Crown Couplets*."

"In that case, we would've gotten our cigars."

"We'll accept them with joy. Right?"

"Extreme joy," Lynpeex said.

"Yes, sir," Toyzol said. "But if she says no to the couplets, then we're back to square one."

"But I'm not going to give up on getting that donation and getting it honestly and with integrity, and without those silly, obscene, peculiar, downright vulgar labels," Lynpeex said, his voice becoming progressively louder. "But you're right, Bob. She might insist on the tie clips."

"That's what I fear, Tim. She might insist."

"I know it," Lynpeex said, his fingers tapping on the table, his voice subdued. "I know it."

"Now the ideal thing," Toyzol said, standing up and pacing the room, "would be for Mrs. Goe to say 'yes' to the *Crown Couplets* and 'no' to the tie clips labels. There's *bingo* in that for us. And you know what? We might hit the news and feature columns with those couplets, but only the local news back home."

"If we go with the couplets, we'll use all that she has, and we'll commission her to do more, as many as she can produce," Lynpeex said. "She'll probably like that."

"Keep talking, man," Toyzol said. "I'm beginning to think that's a great idea for us even if we don't get our hands on her SAD. We can involve a lot of people on campus in doing that. We'll show up those old boys in that English department after all."

"I hate to say this, Bob, but I agree. I can see us dabbling in those *Crown Couplets* of Royalle College. I really can."

"The trip out here might turn out to be more beneficial than we thought. Whatever the outcome, it's not a waste."

— ☙ —

"I've got one final idea that we had mentioned back home," Lynpeex said. "This one she might buy. You might not, but she might."

"Oh," Toyzol said. "You've got the magic formula?"

"This could be it," Lynpeex said. He glanced at the mirror above the dresser, a mirror that wasn't so much built into the wall as it was glued to it, and added, "This idea could be our Stogie." The word Stogie—cigars that Lynpeex had smoked in college—sent him scrambling for his pipe. He continued, "We can tell her that we'll be happy, very happy indeed, to wear the tie clips, but rather than have her words lettered on those clips, we'll place instead a certain agreed upon number code, like even numbers standing for consti-pated days, odd numbers for non-constipated. We're in despera-tion mode if we suggest this. Do you think she'll go for this idea?"

"Sounds good to me."

Lynpeex jammed Flying Dutchman tobacco into his cherry-wood

pipe. While lighting the pipe, he said, "I can see her asking: *How would the people at the college know what those numbers stand for?* Yep, she'd probably ask that."

"And our reply to that would be—"

"The explanation of the number code will be available in a statement that will be sealed and put in a safe place, and the statement won't be revealed until fifty years after Mrs. Goe's death. For all we know, this whole thing might give her yet another idea for a short story or for a chapter in a novel about us, no less. And who cares about that. What we care about is the money. What do you think?"

"Boy, Tim, your ideas are really flowing now; I think we've got a good one in this number-code business. I have a feeling she'll jump on it," Toyzol said. "She better jump on it. After all, we would've met her more than half way; the spirit of what she wants is there even though the letters, the easy-to-see letters, don't spell it out. We would've gotten the money and saved ourselves a tremendous embarrassment."

"A number code, a number code," Lynpeex said as he paced the room, puffing on his pipe. He stood near the wide window and looked out. "A number code, that's magic in the making," his teeth clenched his pipe, forcing his words to cascade through his nose. "I can already see the seven million dollars in our college account. Oh, Bob, I'm glad, so very glad you came along."

"Thanks, boss."

Lynpeex suggested they drink to that idea. He phoned the Inn's bar and asked for a Brandy Alexander for himself and a Diet Pepsi for Toyzol, whose prostate refused to allow him to negotiate with any liquor.

When the drinks arrived, Lynpeex gave a ten-dollar tip to the delivery man. "That guy hit us at a very happy moment," Lynpeex said.

— ༨ —

While drinking, they talked more about the promises of the number codes and the *Crown Couplets* and the other possibilities.

They even recalled the fat fellow at the lounge, the one who in Alice's opinion had tiny feet and a misplaced eyebrow for a moustache. "Do you recall," Lynpeex asked, "what West Virginians usually say about a comic remark that falls flat on its face?"

"What?"

"That went off like a lead balloon or like a pregnant pole-vaulter."

"Oh yes," Toyzol said. "I recall that. In fact, you often hit me with that comment."

"From now on," Lynpeex said, "we can say: *That went off like a pole-vaulting Chesterfield.*"

"I don't think the guy Mrs. Goe referred to was named Chesterfield, Tim. I remember the name she used by association: I associated the word 'ton' with heavy, and I'm sure his last name has a 'ton' in it. You got the first part right: that was 'Chester,' but the last part of the name has a 'ton' in it, and not a 'field,' I'm sure." Toyzol took a sip of his Diet Pepsi and said, "Did you notice the black sign on that large marquee advertising for help wanted in the restaurant?"

"What restaurant?"

"This one, the Holiday Inn's restaurant," Toyzol said. "The place where we're staying, in case you're wondering."

"I can't say I noticed anything unusual."

"Well, I did," Toyzol said. "There's a neat sign out there that uses those large and dark plastic letters that say, NOW HIRING ALL SHIFTS. I'm guessing that a disgruntled employee, and not the wind, popped out one of the letters: the 'F' letter—of all letters—is missing, man. I think that's hilarious, don't you?"

Lynpeex smiled. "That's life in small-town America," he said.

"We've got those characters in West Virginia, too. Long ago I learned that people who flip burgers at motel restaurants aren't there doing it because NASA wasn't hiring."

Toyzol laughed and said, "But burger flippers—out here or by us—can be mighty witty too. That's my point."

"And they often are. I'd venture to say, they can be wittier than a hairless, Vespa-riding English professor at a tiny college in the Mountain State."

Before going to sleep, Lynpeex and Toyzol called their wives and chatted for a while. The men looked forward to the next morning.

— ❧ —

Alice also looked forward to the next morning. Before going to sleep, she wrote a long entry in her diary detailing the activities of the day.

At one stretch in the entry, she reminded herself of how "urgent it would be for me to write a realistic novel, using many of the details that I'm encountering and recording. My hardest task—if I want my novel to be a good comic novel—is for me to get the readers to suspend disbelief. If I succeed in that, then the novel might work. National comedians use the national news in order to get their vast audiences to suspend disbelief. That's why *Saturday Night Live* has the Weekend Update segment, and comedians like Johnny Carson and others who appear on major television networks always refer to issues in the national news in their monologues."

She concluded the long entry by stating: "Getting my readers to suspend disbelief will be one of the challenges that I'll face in writing the novel—now that I know its basic plot and characters. Tomorrow should be fun. Maybe the good boys from West Virginia will advance the plot in ways I'm not anticipating. We'll just have to wait and see."

— ℘ —

Monday night July 7, 1980, Alice had problems falling asleep. So, she got up, lit the reading lamp on the nightstand next to her bed, and pulled from a nearby bookshelf *Editors and Their Turkeys*.

That night, her lighthearted prose magically transformed itself into an anesthesiologist's needle. The next morning, she confided in her diary: "Some people buy their sleeping pills. I publish mine."

CHAPTER THIRTY-FOUR

MAIN STREET IN SAMSVILLE, KANSAS WAS QUIET on that July morning when Alice was to reconnect with her visitors from West Virginia. At seven, she sat on her front porch and drank two cups of dark French-roast coffee.

At eight in the morning when Alice finished her morning reading from the Bible, Lynpeex and Toyzol awoke: they shaved, showered, and took their turn in acknowledging—to use the words of a senior citizen who is a character in an A. P. Goe story—"the power of the prune."

The two men from West Virginia felt that Alice Princeton Goe's huge donation might be only a few hours away from becoming a reality, connecting them with the joys of that three-letter word that starts with "S" and has a vowel in the middle: SAD. "That donation," Lynpeex exclaimed with a hesitant smile, "would be a spectacular climax to our first journey to the Great Plains of Kansas."

To be sure, they still had doubts about succeeding, but their doubts were minor ones, not strong enough to prevent them from enjoying their breakfast that also served as a dress rehearsal.

Lynpeex and Toyzol sat at the table near the indoor pool and immediately filed their orders for coffee, bacon, eggs, wheat toast, and orange juice.

The pungent odor of chlorine reminded Toyzol of vacation days with his family in recent summers. Lynpeex's thoughts were preoccupied by the potential Goe donation. They sat in silence for a good while.

Then Lynpeex spoke, "I'd love to teach Mrs. Goe what you and I had taught other wealthy and caring people over the years."

"And what's that, Tim?"

"Simply put," Lynpeex said, "we taught them how to spell Royalle College's name on a check."

"And in Alice's case," Toyzol added, "we'll have to teach her the same lesson. Got you."

"You know, Bob, I've been thinking about that number-code idea that we talked about last night," Lynpeex said. "I really think we've got a winner in that idea. I'll be surprised, in fact, if she says 'no' to it because it's one of those rare ideas that comes along every once in a great while, an idea that allows you to have your cake and eat it too."

"I hope you're right, Tim," Toyzol said, as he began to put cream into his coffee. "You just might be."

"How do you think we should approach her?"

"If I were you, I'd first present all the options that we'd talked about, one at a time—"

"Even the ones that she already said 'no' to?"

"Oh yeah," Toyzol said. "Those were the conventional and noble ones, and if she agrees to any of them, that'll certainly be our best avenue. Let her either approve or veto each."

"So, give her, in effect, what the folks she dislikes most—the politicians—call a line-item veto. Is that what you're saying?" Lynpeex said, sipping his black coffee.

"Exactly."

"Sounds good so far."

"And if approval comes early," Toyzol went on, "then we're in great shape, but if she begins to resort to that four-letter word—veto, veto, veto—then we've got to improvise one more time, and I'd be happy to submit the number-code bit."

Lynpeex yanked a pen out of his suit pocket, pulled out a business card from his left pocket and on the back of it wrote the word "Options" and underlined it. "Now, what do you think should be first?" A tense Lynpeex asked a surprisingly relaxed Toyzol.

"Naming a building or an auditorium or an athletic field after her," Toyzol said. "That's an acceptable exchange for a seven-million-dollar donation."

"Okay, *Name Change*," Lynpeex wrote. "What next?"

"There'll only be a next, assuming you get a veto on that one."

"Understand. I'm with you, Bob."

"I'd try establishing a scholarship fund to honor her. She might go for that if she comes to her senses." Lynpeex wrote: *Scholarship Fund*.

"That too is conventional and acceptable," Lynpeex said. "I'll make that as item two."

"Item three should be the *Review Royalle*. That's that literary journal we talked about earlier. She might go for that in a big way, this time. Who knows?"

"Got you," Lynpeex said and wrote that on the back of his business card. "What else?"

"Item four should be the *Crown Couplets* stuff," Toyzol said. "That's the idea she was sleeping on, you see. Maybe we should start with it. What do you think?"

"No, let's keep this order," Lynpeex said. "Let's be conventional before we become crazy. And if all the above fail, if I strike out with her, then you step up to the plate with your number-code bit. You might hit a homerun with that. But that has got to be our last resort."

"Sounds good to me," Toyzol said. "We're going in like good boys scouts: well prepared. Or like hopeful Little League baseball players."

They continued drinking their coffee. When the food arrived, they began to eat it slowly and chat about other matters.

— ✧ —

"Let's get back to the donation," Toyzol said after a long stretch of silence. "Suppose you get a veto on the first four items. What's next?"

"She'll probably drift back to the clearly labeled tie clips."

"What do we do then?" Toyzol asked. "Accept her tie clips demand?"

"No way, absolutely no way."

"If she insists—"

"We desist."

"Tails between our legs. Her tail wagging."

"Seriously," Lynpeex said, "if she insists that's when you come in and suggest your number-code idea. Make it sound fresh and new and spontaneous. At first, I'd appear as if I'd reluctantly—emphasis now on reluctance—consider it, and maybe even accept it."

"I'm with you," Toyzol said. "What next?"

A waitress with a beaker asked, "More fresh coffee, gentlemen?"

Both accepted, thanked the waitress, and Lynpeex continued, "I bet she'll try to transform my reluctance into an acceptance, and if she does, I'd slowly allow myself to be molded by her transformation agenda."

"Sounds good to me, Tim."

Both drank a second cup of coffee. They talked and tried to anticipate Alice's responses, working hard to get their minds in a positive frame.

— ∾ —

They paid for the food, stopped at the newspaper-candy rack, and picked up a copy of the *News-Free Gazette*. Lynpeex also paid for a roll of Tums, and then they headed up to their room, packed their suitcases, and as Alice would say, "assassinated time by watching television."

When Lynpeex got bored with morning television, he turned to the newspaper and glanced at the stories. An extensive feature story with the title *From Tantrum to Trial: A Story of Road Rage on the Great Plains* caught his attention.

He assumed it was a true story but when he finished reading it, he wasn't so sure. He found the story incredible.

In small-town newspapers, he felt, the editors often publish local talent, and the writer of the road-rage story was listed as "a recent graduate of Fort Hays State University, now working as an assistant to the editor of this newspaper." It was a long story that used elements from fiction such as dialogue, characterization, and scene setting.

Lynpeex read the story silently and then told himself: "Never thought road rage could be so entertaining, but it is out here."

As ten o'clock neared, they drove around Samsville's countryside for a short ride. For small talk, Lynpeex spoke about the road-rage story. It's a long story (that begins with an arrest and ends with a trial), and he summarized it in a few words.

"This guy in Wichita had stopped at a red light," Lynpeex began. "Then the light turned green, but the fellow failed to move. The guy behind him, a muscular fellow wearing a Wichita State University hat, gave him a sustained and angry horn—a horn that was *leavened with choice expletives* as the article puts it. The front driver—a burly man who had not shaved for a few days and looked downright ugly, but if he were a movie star, people would refer to him as *rugged*—put his car in park and reached under the seat. He grabbed a pistol, opened his door, walked to each tire of the car behind him, and shot a bullet in each. Then he told the angry driver: *C'mon, Mister, give me another horn!*"

"Reminds me of the horn you got yesterday, Tim, but thank God you didn't act like that,"

Lynpeex smiled and continued. "The police came and the driver with the pistol was arrested and taken to jail, and in due time, he was escorted to trial and found guilty. He was sentenced and given jail time and a fine. But before leaving the courtroom, the shooter asked the judge if he could say a few words, and the judge allowed him. According to the article, the shooter proclaimed—with delight—after hearing his fine: *Your honor, it was worth it.* It's a long feature, but that's the gist of it. Unusual, don't you think?"

Following that, they said very little to each other; they were getting mentally ready for the upcoming event. The main event. The big game.

Both had played high school football in West Virginia, and both knew the importance of silence before a big game. The bigger the game, the deeper and more introspective the silence became.

In going to Alice's house, they were heading to a big, big game, and they knew it. At the end of the game, they wanted to tell each other what their coaches used to tell them after a victory, "You done good, boys! You done good!"

— ⌘ —

At eight in the morning, Alice prepared her breakfast of fried eggs and wheat toast. Following breakfast, she began to write an unusual entry in her diary-literary notebook.

The entry summarized a hastily arranged lecture on nutrition that Alice had attended at the Carnegie Library in Samsville. The lecturer, a winsome young woman who was doing her graduate work at Loma Linda University in California, had returned home to attend her grandmother's funeral. She presented an engaging and well-attended lecture on the topic: "Developing a Healthy Relationship with Food."

— ❧ —

While Alice was writing, the phone rang. It was about the usual time that Martha, her librarian friend, would call. Alice refused to answer it.

She concluded the entry by metaphorically referring to food: "In a few minutes, I'll be grilling two impressive portabella mushrooms plucked from the mountains of West Virginia."

She looked forward to doing just that.

CHAPTER THIRTY-FIVE

Lynpeex and Toyzol parked their rented Ford in front of Alice's house, climbed the porch's wooden steps, and stood near the door. The time was one minute before ten.

Lynpeex pressed the doorbell and waited for a response. Lynpeex reached out and shook Toyzol's hand and said, "Good luck, buddy."

"Good luck to both of us," Toyzol said and waited for the door to open.

Lynpeex said, "I'm tense."

"I'm nervous," Toyzol said. "What do you think she's doing?"

"Probably thinking of more modern American or European writers that we've never heard off," Lynpeex said. "If she mentions just one more writer to us, I'm going to fire out at her and tell her how all these modern writers are worthless compared to Milton and Shakespeare."

"Don't you *dare* do a thing like that, Tim."

"Ah heck, I'm going to press it again," Lynpeex said and did. "What do we have to lose?"

They waited. Toyzol speculated, "She could be taking a shit, man. People do that, you know."

"When she opens the door," Lynpeex said, "and you ask her if she was doing that, she'll jump all over you and correct your English and say: *You go to the bathroom not to take a shit but to give one.* And she'll be correct with that, and I'll second her comment and dismiss yours. When it comes to rhetoric or English usage, I'll side with an author: A. P. Goe."

"You know our old *Vespa-man* back home never claims to *take a shit*—or *give* one, for that matter."

"What does he say when he goes to the bathroom?" Lynpeex said. After a pause, he added in a tone that appeared to be scolding his buddy, "Why do you even bring up that old fart at this time?"

"The *Vespa-man* just wandered into my thoughts," Toyzol said. "And just for your information, he'd say: *I'm going to make some money.* That's an original expression for that act, eh?"

"Where did you hear that?"

"He brought it up in a conversation at the faculty lounge one day," Toyzol said. "He broke up the room with the remark, and I corrected him: *You don't make money; the money is already made: you make a deposit.* For some reason, that incident wandered into my mind just now."

"We're going to make money," Lynpeex said. "I really like the sound of that. And we're trying to do that for all those people back home. The way our *Vespa-man* looks when he rides his scooter, he's making money at home and on the road. Those riders do look like they're sitting on toilet stools."

As they continued to wait, Lynpeex said: "Should I press it again."

"I would," Toyzol said and watched his boss do just that.

"If she were just a bit younger, we could've invited her to be a writer-in-residence for a semester or a year," Lynpeex said. "She'd be a great example for the students, and she'd show the English faculty what's expected from them in the publishing and research domain."

"Writer-in-residence," Toyzol said, "would be the proper position for her at the college." He paused then asked, "Which bathroom do you think she uses? She's got three in the house, you know."

"If she can't make it on the first floor or basement," Lynpeex said, "she'll try her luck at the higher altitude. We joke about all this, Bob, but constipation does bother my mother and aunt."

"Oh, I suspect it does," Toyzol replied. "It's a serious matter with older people, especially women. Still, it's a private matter, a very private matter. And that's the way it should be. That's what we're trying to tell and teach the old woman, aren't we?"

"You know what's my biggest and greatest fear right about now?" Toyzol said.

"What?"

"My prostate."

"Well, wherever I go, my prostate problems go with me."

"Mine too."

"But yours never misbehaves, Tim."

"And I'm grateful for that."

"Mine is worse than a priest's: it's always on the blink, it seems."

"You know what the best remedy for that is?"

"What?"

"More intercourse, frequent intercourse."

"Are you making that up, Tim?"

"As a matter of fact, no," Lynpeex replied. "I read an article on that recently, and the writer was making that argument."

"A credible writer?"

"A reporter who had talked to urologists. He cited some who claim that frequent intercourse and *not* masturbation is the best treatment for prostate problems—far better than the massage from a urologist's bird."

"Ok-kay," Toyzol said. "How interesting. Let's hope that today my prostate, unlike yesterday, will stay calm. But I'm afraid it's going to act up, especially after all the coffee I had this morning."

"If the discussion gets tense," Lynpeex said, "a nagging prostate might help defuse the tension. We'll just have to wait and see, my friend. We've got to play all this not by ear but by *prostate vibes*. Our hope is for that chestnut of yours to be on its best behavior."

— ∽ —

Moments later, the brown door opened, and a befuddled Alice appeared and said, "I had just finished taking a shower when the doorbell rang the first time, and I was brushing my teeth when it rang the second time. I'm sorry to make you wait."

"No problem," Lynpeex said. "No problem, Mrs. Goe."

"We'll see about that," she said. "Forgive the pun please, but I'm looking to put some clean teeth into this gathering. As my dear father used to say: *Fiasco, today is the day of reckoning*. And it's the day of reckoning with us. Right?"

"Right," Lynpeex said, as the two walked into the house.

"Right, ma'am," Toyzol added and shut the door behind him.

Lynpeex stared at her and asked, "Who's *Fiasco*?"

"That's the name of Dad's bull."

"Bull as in a male cow?" Toyzol said. The words slipped out of his mouth in an innocent manner, as involuntary as the twitch of an eye.

"What was your question?" she asked Toyzol.

He calmly and slowly repeated, "Bull—as in a male cow?"

"No," she shouted at him. "Bull as in bullshit!" The needle on his prostate-nagging barometer shot up to one hundred. "Of course," she added softly and with a big smile, "it's bull as in cow." Then she looked up at Lynpeex, continued smiling, and said, "Just for fun, I thought I'd shake him up."

"Bob is a good sport," Lynpeex said, reached out with his right arm and clasped his buddy's shoulder. "We love him and we tease him a lot at the college. You're right in step with the rest of us, Mrs. Goe."

Toyzol muttered, "Wish my prostate was a good sport."

Looking at Lynpeex, she said, "My deluxe cleaning lad, Jack, has some literary leanings. He started to write prose and poetry after he began to work for me. And his output shows real promise. Someday he might write a novel."

"I bet you stimulated his creativity," Lynpeex said.

"I like to think so," she said. "His wife probably has other thoughts on that.

"Anyway," Alice said, "Jack thinks that *Fiasco* would be a great name for a literary magazine. But hey, we're not concerned with literary stuff today. Been there, done that, eh? We've got some real work to do: we've got to talk turkey not *Fiasco*."

"That sure sounds like a good bird to me," Lynpeex said.

"Me too," Toyzol said with a smile. "If you two don't mind, I need to step into the bathroom for a few moments. The orange juice and coffee I had this morning bothered my prostate—"

"And my comic tantrum helped too, I bet," Alice said. She winked at Lynpeex and smiled as her eyes made contact with Toyzol's.

"Frankly, it did," Toyzol said, sheepishly. "Please wait for me to return before you two begin to talk turkey."

— ❧ —

Lynpeex sat on the couch, and Alice sat in the armchair across from him. She told him about an English professor at a nearby state university in whose classes she had spoken on two occasions on writing and publishing.

"The professor," Alice said, "is an elderly gentleman, a creative fellow, who's in the local news now because the college wants to dismiss him for what he's doing in his English composition classes, but the fellow has life tenure and doesn't want to retire."

"What's he doing?" Lynpeex asked. "We're college administrators and such a matter interests us."

"I knew it would," she said. "That's why I'm sharing it with you. Anyway, this fellow doesn't want to continue grading composition papers in the conventional manner by writing comments in the margin and at the end of the papers. So, he went out and had a rubber stamp made, and he bought a pad for it—a pad soaked in red ink."

"Mrs. Goe, I'd like Bob to hear this story. Can you wait until he gets back so you won't have to repeat it to him?"

"Once again," she said, "we're victims of the tyranny of a prostate. My, my, how well I remember those days with my dearly departed Frank." She smiled and added, "Sure, I'll stop and wait for him."

They talked about the "nice morning" and the "quiet streets" of Samsville. When Toyzol returned, he sat near his colleague on the living room's couch.

She re-introduced the professor and continued: "The rubber stamp consists of one word. He'll read a stretch of prose in a student's paper, and then he'll stamp—really pound—the word onto the page, if the prose he is reading deserves it. The fellow told me: *This way, I don't have to write a single word on a single essay. It's an original and fun approach to grading freshman papers. When you get to be my age,* the fellow added, *you either retire or you innovate.* He innovated."

"What's the one word on the stamp?" Lynpeex asked.

"It starts with a 'G' and ends with a 'D,' " she said.

"Is it, GOOD?" Toyzol said.

"No," she said. "It's longer than that. The second letter is an 'A.' "

"What's the third?" Lynpeex asked.

" 'R,' " she said.

"I got, I got," Toyzol said. "Is it GARBAGE?"

"No," she said, "but that's mighty close. You, son, have to work on your spelling. Garbage ends with an E not a D."

"GARBLED!" Toyzol shouted.

"He's right," she told Lynpeex while pointing at his sidekick. "The professor is pleading academic freedom, and the administrators are saying, *It's a classic case of abuse of academic freedom*."

"We'll side with the administrators—case unheard," Lynpeex said. "At Royalle, we've got some aging codgers of our own who should retire. Do you see it as an example of tenure abuse, Mrs. Goe?"

"I think it's a marvelous illustration of the adage: *Truth is stranger than fiction*."

Lynpeex smiled and added, "Ah, yes. We're even illustrating it now with you." Her smile relaxed them—a bit.

CHAPTER THIRTY-SIX

As they began to talk turkey, as it were, Lynpeex reached for a more conventional opening for the day. He said, "I hope it's been a good morning for you so far, Mrs. Goe."

"So far it has," she said. "Now let's hope it'll continue to be so. May I prepare you, gentlemen, some coffee?"

"We're pretty much coffeed out," Lynpeex said. "We had several cups at the Holiday Inn."

"And my prostate already testified to that," Toyzol said smiling.

The three found themselves involved in some small talk dealing with the weather, the nicely cut lawns on Main Street, the two large trees by the hardware store.

"Now," Lynpeex said, "let's talk about getting SAD."

"I hope you have finally made up your mind," she said.

"Well, we hope *you* did, Mrs. Goe," Lynpeex said.

"Well, I have," she replied.

"Oh," both men said at once. Silence followed.

"Care to share it with us?" Lynpeex asked, really implored, Alice. Another slice of silence.

"Yes," she said.

Both men looked at each other; they said nothing. Alice also said nothing, but she stared at them. The phone rang.

She excused herself and went to answer it. "Martha, I'll call you later; I'm extremely busy now in a very urgent matter." A slight pause followed; then the men heard Alice say, "No, I wasn't in the bathroom. Stay where you are; I'll call you back before long."

Martha persisted in asking Alice if anything was wrong.

Alice said, "No, no, nothing is wrong, and I don't need any help. I'm at the turning point of an urgent matter, a very urgent matter."

After Alice hung up, she went back to the living room to talk to the men on the couch. The brief telephone conversation didn't allow the men to exchange any comments or reactions. "Where were we, gentlemen?"

"We're waiting to hear your decision, Mrs. Goe," Lynpeex said, meekly. "Your decision means a lot to us."

"You're not going to like it, I'm afraid, but I hope *my* fears are unfounded," she said. "Indeed, I hope I'm dead wrong."

"What is it?" Lynpeex said, impatiently.

"Care to venture a guess?" Alice said.

"You'd want us to name—in your honor and the honor of your late husband, Frank—an auditorium or a building or even an athletic field?" Lynpeex said. "That was a possibility, wasn't it?"

"Yes, it was, but I really don't have that kind of ego," she said. "I'm not one to have things, buildings, fields, trees, diseases, statues, paintings, scales (as in Richter), or even auditoriums named after me; I realize I've got a very classy-sounding middle name in Princeton with lots of tradition in our culture." She paused for a long while, then added, "Just out of curiosity: you gentlemen would've agreed to name a building after me if my full name was Linda Lakabozo?"

"You bet," Lynpeex said smiling. "I like names that begin with 'L.'

Yes, ma'am. Absolutely. If that's your name, that's what we'll use."

"Well, that's honorable, gentlemen, but I must respectfully decline it," she said. "Sorry on that."

"So, the name change is out?" Lynpeex said.

"Yes," she replied.

"Absolutely?" Toyzol said.

"Unequivocally," she responded.

"Too bad," Lynpeex said. "We're hoping you'll permit us the distinct honor, Mrs. Goe, of re-naming one of our buildings, maybe even our Collegiate Gothic Mountaineer Hall, after you."

"No way," she said. "The name change is out."

Toyzol said, "I see."

"Giving scholarships in your honor?" Lynpeex said. "Would that be acceptable?"

"No," she said, "and for the same reasons I gave you yesterday."

Wow, Lynpeex thought, that's quick. So, he went to the next item. "When we left last night," he said, "you told us you're going to sleep on the idea of *Crown Couplets*, as a label to replace *Trunk Thoughts*, the literary undertaking that you're introducing into the American scene, as you so eloquently and impressively put it."

"Well, I did sleep on that," she said.

"And?" Lynpeex said.

"And I woke up from my sleep this morning," she said.

"We did also," Toyzol added. All three smiled.

"But did we all wake up on the same wavelength?" Alice asked.

"I hope so," Lynpeex said.

"You mean," she said, "you'd put my *Crown Couplets* on the college's cars and buses and in the classrooms and so forth and you'll wear my tie clips for a year? If so, we'll wrap up the deal right now."

"Just the couplets on the cars and buses etcetera," Lynpeex said. "We felt that those couplets would bring a unique dimension to our little college, and we'll be honored to have you write as many as you wish."

"Those couplets," Toyzol added, "might get our college featured in newspapers and magazines. You've got a unique idea in that."

"Thank you," she said.

A long silence set in. Lynpeex decided to forgo the *Review-Royalle* idea for it seemed to be a variation of the *Crown Couplets* possibility that they were considering.

"Mrs. Goe, I want to level with you," Lynpeex said, leaning forward. "There's *no way*—absolutely no way—we can wear the tie clips with the labels on them. What the labels proclaim is a private, a very, very, *very* private matter. No one should know that about people. There is some privacy that ought to be honored and preserved, you understand?"

"Oh yes I do," she said. "You wouldn't be here if I didn't."

Another long silence set in following her remark. Alice was silent and motionless as a statue. In a manner of speaking, she had enjoyed their company, and she didn't want them to leave. Yet in another sense, she wanted them to leave, for she had *just* made her point—indeed, they made it for her—and she had collected the material that she was in pursuit of.

— ✺ —

Toyzol felt *the* moment had arrived, so he said: "I've got one of my good suggestions to offer, not as a compromise, mind you, but a suggestion that acknowledges the essence of Mrs. Goe's idea and affirms it in a proper perspective. I think you'll like this, Mrs. Goe. I really do. I wouldn't even *think* of mentioning it, otherwise."

"Get to the point, Mr. Toyzol! What's your idea?" Lynpeex said.

"Let's go ahead," Toyzol said, "and wear those tie clips Mrs.—"

"See," Alice said, "I won him over." She jumped out of her chair (insofar as an eight-two-year-old woman can jump), dove at Toyzol, cupped his cheeks with both hands, and kissed him on the forehead.

A startled Toyzol froze and looked straight ahead. "Just a minute, Mrs. Goe," he said. "You won me over, but I haven't submitted my idea *fully*. That's only half of my idea."

"Damn it," Lynpeex shouted. "I don't want to hear it, Mr. Toyzol. We can never—*ne-v-v-ver*—wear those tie clips. Period. Absolutely not." He raised his voice and beat his right fist into the palm of his left hand and said, "Nev-er. Hear me. Nev-er."

"Wait a minute, Tim," Toyzol said. "Both of you are being unfair to me. I can't even finish a statement without being *kissed* by you and *cussed* by you." Toyzol pointed first to Alice then to Lynpeex.

"Well, go ahead, but if it assumes wearing the tie clips, I'd prefer you keep your ideas to yourself. Stay silent in other words," Lynpeex said.

Toyzol reached up to the left edge of his pursed lips, placed the index finger and thumb of his right hand there, and pulled them across his lips as if to *zip them shut*. Alice saw that, but she didn't smile and Lynpeex maintained an equally somber mood. Finally, she told Lynpeex: "I'd like to hear my dear Mr. Hyphen's idea, if you don't mind."

Toyzol said nothing. Lynpeex said nothing. Alice looked at Lynpeex, then at Toyzol as if she were watching two evenly matched tennis players at work. She never knew that silence could be volleyed in its own way. When she became uneasy with the silence, she told Lynpeex while pointing with her chin at Toyzol, "I'd love to know his idea."

"Here it is," Toyzol said. "We'll be happy to wear the tie clips—"

"Stop right there, Bob. No way. Absolutely no way!" Lynpeex said, raising his voice, kicking the carpet, and shaking his head.

"Let him finish," Alice ordered Lynpeex. "You remind me of a base-ball batter who had just struck out and is returning to the dugout, flashing his disgust moves. Let him finish, please."

Toyzol continued, "We'll be happy to wear the tie clips that Mrs. Goe wants us to wear, but instead of using a conventional word code, we'll use a number co—"

"No way," she said, "absolutely no wa—"

"C'mon now, let him finish. Please let's hear him out. Please!"

"Okay, continue," Lynpeex and Alice said, almost in unison.

"Odd-numbered tie clips could be for the days we're constipated, and even-numbered tie clips for the non-constipated days. See, it's that simple," Toyzol said. "The numbered tie clips will capture the spirit and essence of your plan, Mrs. Goe."

"And how will the academic community and the world at large know of these numbered codes?" she asked, her voice dripping with sarcasm. "How will they know what the numbers stand for?"

"That's easy," Toyzol said. "The appropriate explanation of the numbers will be fleshed out in a detailed statement that will be revealed to the public fifty years after your death and the death of Dr. Lynpeex, the chief administrative officer of the college at the time of the donation."

"Well, I'll have to think about Mr. Toyzol's plan," Lynpeex said. "Quite frankly, I'm not so sure I like it; in fact, I'm sure I don't, but I'd still like to give it some thought."

— ☙ —

Alice took a big sigh and said, "Here we are in 1980, four years after our Bicentennial celebration as a nation, and everything is a number these days." She addressed the men, and then she began to enumerate all sorts of items that have numbers on them.

"We've got a Social Security number, a checking account number, a student number, a birth certificate number, an insurance policy number, a typewriter serial number, a car serial number, a driver license number, a credit card number, a hospital treatment number, and, of course, a death certificate number: this one is highly coveted by those in the fundraising departments of small colleges." She smiled—even before she had finished her catalogue of numbered items.

And despite their mood, both men could not resist revealing a gentle smile. The men, sitting across from her, nodded and she continued: "You name it, and it probably has a number on it. Just think how everything about us is numbered. It's easier for others to trace us; it's easier for others to intrude into our lives and rob us of our privacy by knowing so much about us; it's easier for the bank executive, the hospital administrator, the internal revenue officers, the lawyers to get to know so much about us."

She personalized her reflections by adding, "My late husband, Frank, was the model citizen: law-abiding in every way, and he cherished his privacy. He felt that numbers were calculated to rob us of our privacy. They de-personalize us: but in a paradoxical sense, they make it easier for others to find out more personal things about us. Numbers are distinct. Names can be identical, you see. Out here in the net-serve culture of the Great Plains, we cherish our privacy. Understand?"

"You've got a good point in all this, Mrs. Goe," Lynpeex said. "We just have to go back home highly disappointed by our visit, but we thank you very much for your exceedingly kind and warm hospitality."

"Big Brother," she continued, alluding to George Orwell's *1984*, "is alive and well in this day and age. He's watching us all the time. The way so much is known about us by so many different people and agencies, we're *not* truly free anymore. I know I'm beginning to sound like my late husband, but that's how I feel. Sadly, there's no privacy left in our world. None whatsoever."

"I'll agree to that also, Mrs. Goe," Lynpeex said.

"I do too," Toyzol said.

"Mr. Toyzol, I hate to slam the door on your number idea, but I must! I must!" There was a long pause.

"Here's my final offer, gentlemen. If you accept it, we'll sit through lunch and supper and negotiate, and I'll sign my name on the appropriate papers et cetera; and if you refuse it, then I'd have to ask you to leave because I want to pursue other options."

"Well," Lynpeex said, his head tilted more towards the carpet than towards Alice, "I'm willing to hear your final offer."

"I'd love—I repeat, I *would* love—to give Royalle College the seven million dollars provided you wear the tie clips with the lettering on them as I had requested in my initial letter. You see, my first offer to you is now submitted as my final offer."

They said nothing. Both looked at the carpet and failed to make eye contact with her. To her they appeared sad.

But she continued speaking, "If you'd like me to frame all this for you in literary terms, let me quote a few lines from T. S. Eliot who claims:

> We shall not cease from exploration
>
> And the end of all our exploring
>
> Will be to arrive where we started
>
> And know the place for the first time.

You are two honorable men from the Mountain State of West Virginia, and you would make T. S. Eliot proud. You arrived, and you'll soon begin the knowing process. You might not know it now, but what you're doing is noble—and profitable: wink, wink—indeed." She smiled, and the men dismissed it as a sardonic smile.

Both nodded, and Lynpeex said a soft, "I see."

Alice continued, "The *Crown Couplets* sounded great yesterday. But today is the day to murder that label." The men seemed puzzled and angry. The expression on Lynpeex's face made it appear as if a thick squirt of Crazy Glue had just lined and sealed his lips.

She explained her harsh rhetoric: "In the writing craft, we have an expression that says: *Murder your darlings*, and by darlings we mean those glittering and lovely phrases that we fall in love with for a while but that don't say very much at all. 'Tis time to do that now, don't you think?"

Lynpeex stood. Seeing that, Toyzol also rose to his feet. Then Lynpeex said, "To your final offer, I respectfully say: *No, no, no, but thank you, ma'am.*"

"I hear you," she said.

Both headed towards the door. Alice followed them. She said nothing to them. When they pulled the door open to leave, the three exchanged a set of cordially cold goodbyes.

"Before you leave," she told Lynpeex, "I thought you might like to take with you some reading material for the long airplane trip back home." She handed him the typescript of a twelve-page short story that she had written and revised while they had corresponded about the donation. She titled the allegorical story: *Gladys of the Great Plains*.

There was a curious postscript at the end of the story: a postscript that would have—at once—pleased and puzzled the men.

Lynpeex accepted the story, folded it, and thanked her once again. He placed the story in his briefcase. After the two rambled down the porch's stairs, Lynpeex said: "There's no way I'm going to read that thing on the plane. I'm done with her."

CHAPTER THIRTY-SEVEN

As Toyzol drove the rented white Ford, he listened to Lynpeex filter his anger through some painful reflections.

Lynpeex fidgeted in his seat and exclaimed, "Darn it, we blew it!" Toyzol drove out of Samsville to the highway that leads to the airport. "Bob, I don't know if Mrs. Goe fits your image of the little old lady in tennis shoes."

"Oh, she does, and she doesn't. I never liked the wording of that image, to tell you the truth."

"I don't either," Lynpeex sighed and added: "I created in my mind an image of a wealthy widow on the prairie."

"Yea, kind of like—a little house on the prairie."

"But peopled by a potential donor for our college."

"A former potential donor."

"We're not going to give up on her," Lynpeex said. "That's round one, you might say."

"And in it, we got knocked down."

"Sure did, didn't we? But that's only round one. We'll have to get up and continue the fight."

"Sounds like a true champ."

After a long moment of silence on the way to the airport, Lynpeex said: "You know, Bob, I really shouldn't let you drive."

"Why do you say that?"

"Because you can't see."

"What're you talking about, Tim?"

"Don't tell me you forgot already. Remember, how she pulled out your eyes after you apologized?"

"Oh, that's when she quoted that one Irish writer. Correct? Well that writer, as I recall, is James Joyce. I'm an old Irishman, and he's a hero in our world, even though I don't know much about him."

"Yep, that's the guy."

"He (and Mrs. Goe) pulled out my eyes all right," Toyzol said. "Yet she also called me a nice guy during that exchange. That was, at once, utter hell and sweet music to my prostate."

Both laughed and recalled other prostate incidents. Throughout the car ride to the airport and the plane trip back to West Virginia, both men continued to evaluate their visit to Samsville.

— ❧ —

"You know," Lynpeex said as their airplane reached its cruising altitude, "we might've blown this thing so badly, she might just decide to give all her money to another small college."

"One like ours?"

"Yes."

"In Kansas or the Great Plains?"

"Yes, or elsewhere."

"At least we *were* honest," Toyzol said. "We didn't fall into the temptation of making promises that we couldn't keep."

"You're right. We didn't lie," Lynpeex said. "Thank God for our insistence in being honest."

"Father Jacob at church often says: *The devil is the father of lies*, and we stayed away from that temptation. And that's good."

"As she'd say, very good *indeed*," Lynpeex said, trying to connect with a smile. "We maintained our God-fearing decency through and through, and that was our intention all along. The temptation to lie and be devious never crossed my mind. Ne-v-er!"

The two men conspired to remain ethical throughout their pursuit of the huge donation. On the flight home, they congratulated each other on the success of their ethical pursuit. In sports terms, they felt good about the way they played, but they regretted the loss. They commiserated over losing the cash, but felt great about holding up the honor of Royalle College and maintaining their personal and spiritual integrity.

The men also evaluated the ways of A. P. Goe, "a gently wicked and creative writer," as Lynpeex called her. But they missed connecting with the poignancy of *her* pursuits.

At one point, they seemed to come close, especially when Lynpeex told Toyzol: "For all we know, she might've explored her tie clips ideas in some of her writings. Who knows what she might've done? Who cares? It might well be that she has stories with college professors having such labels as their tie clips. After all, we do assign to some professors the status of *full professors*, don't we?"

"Sure do," Toyzol responded. "That old *Vespa-man* is a full professor. He's one of those guys in that blasted department who's the reason we ended up coming here in the first place."

"Don't get me started on that guy now," Lynpeex said.

"It's all my fault, Tim, I should've drawn a better psychological profile of her. I didn't do good enough research on her."

"No, no, Bob, it's not your fault or mine. We can go on forever saying, we should've done this or that. All this is so painful. As the cliché says: *It hurts to lose.*" Lynpeex paused for a while, sighed, adjusted his testicles, then said: "Reading more of her literary work, published or unpublished, would've helped. Now I see meaning in that paradox that she had us recite: *It hurts to win.* Maybe you're right: we should've put in more time studying her literary work and forming a detailed psychological profile of her. All that research would've been hard work, and we needed to do that to win. Instead, we went there and tried to wing it. It's all my fault—not yours."

"We're crying over spilled milk now," Toyzol said. "Remember what she told us about that?"

"Oh, I do," Lynpeex said.

Both smiled, half-hearted, insincere smiles, the kind that defeated people often give at a time when they need to blend politeness with anger.

— ❧ —

When the airline steward staggered down the aisle handing out peanuts and soft drinks, the two men accepted the handouts, and Toyzol asked, "Well, what do you think? Will she get in touch with us again? Will she invite us back to Samsville?"

"Believe me, my dear *Mr. Hyphen*, these questions have been nagging my mind like urine does a damaged bladder or prostate."

"Should we get in touch with her again?"

"Another nagging question."

"Looks like we've got a lot to do when we get home," Toyzol said. "Alice Goe is likely to occupy our thoughts as we go back to square one. Is that what you're saying?"

"Yes, indeed it is, but she'd make life a heck of a lot easier for us if she contacts us and tells us she had seriously considered—and decided to cheerfully accept—one of the options we had suggested," Lynpeex stated. "I hope that'll be the case."

"Keep hoping." They talked for a good while on what to expect from her and what their next move should be. "Maybe we should consult her deluxe cleaning lad," Lynpeex laughed.

"Jobs in small-town Kansas must be hard to come by for boys educated in the humanities," Toyzol said. "But she obviously took pity on him and employed him."

"Remember that phone call she got," Lynpeex said, "when our negotiations got real tense?"

"I'd love to be a mouse in the room and listen to Mrs. Goe tell that woman about us."

"I'm sure she won't tell her much, Bob, because she told us none of the people in Samsville know anything about her wealth. I know people say *in small towns everyone knows everything about everyone*, but the Goes, from what I could gather, were smart and shrewd people, and they guarded their privacy. Of course, I could be wrong on that."

The two men talked more about privacy and the way small-town life impinges on it. Then they returned to the elusive donation.

"You know, *Mr. Hyphen*, I felt that we were going to have problems when we entered her house and your prostate problems kicked in: that was a bad omen."

"So, you think," Toyzol replied, "my behavior got her pissed off?"

"Not pissed off. She won't use words like that."

"What would she use?"

"Urined off."

Both laughed. Toyzol said, "I'm not so sure of that. She did use bullshit on me."

"She didn't use it, my dear friend," Lynpeex said. "She *slapped* you with it."

"And that's when my prostate went into overdrive, and I literally wet myself as an adult on the Great Plains of Kansas."

"Let's wait for at least two weeks before deciding what we should do next. We've got to reconnect with her—somehow."

"It would be great if she invited us to reconnect," Toyzol said.

"That it would, Bob. That it would." Lynpeex yawned. "I'm tired, Bob, I'd like to take a nap."

"Do you mind if I get her story out of your briefcase? I'd like to read it while you're napping."

"Please do."

Toyzol fetched the manuscript that explored, in words from the story, "the wickedly benign exploits of an elderly writer-philanthropist from the Great Plains."

He stopped reading the story after the third page. "Same old, same old literary shit," he told himself and joined his boss in taking what he felt was a much-needed nap.

The story had an enigmatic postscript addressed to the men. The postscript: "*They will depart—Special Delivery—the moment you leave.*"

— ❧ —

When the two men arrived at the campus and walked to their cars to drive home, Alice started writing in her diary-literary notebook a long entry for Tuesday evening of July 8, 1980.

"These two fine men," she wrote in one stretch, "no doubt feel that getting millions with bizarre strings attached isn't going to work for them. I hope they had as much fun in their journey to get the cash as I had in trying to give it away. I plan to remember them in a special manner: a manner that'll please them immensely. These next few days—thanks to our mail system—will be hard on the two men. By mid-week, however, happiness will strike them. I hope their anger at me doesn't freeze, but if it does, the plan that I have made will thaw it out."

She went on to sketch in that extensive entry her encounters with the good men of Royalle College and to reflect on the minuscule sense of privacy that remains in our culture.

"The men might not know this," she wrote near the end of the entry, "but some privacy *does* indeed remain in our culture, and those two wise and handsome men—unwittingly perhaps—seemed intent on preserving it. For that, they merit my utmost respect."

The issue of personal privacy—"a key pillar in our democracy," as she and her Frank had often noted—occupied her thoughts that evening.

That hot summer evening in July of 1980, Alice—like many other people in the culture—was unaware of the impending devastation that the fast-approaching World Wide Web would bring to the privacy concerns coveted by many thoughtful and law-abiding citizens, whether they were well-educated folks heading a small college in West Virginia or wealthy and creative people living in a small town in Kansas.

The last lines in that entry were positioned as a separate paragraph, almost as if they were a salute to privacy. The lines:

> The two honorable men with whom I interacted these last few weeks—the men from West Virginia—will go through life either constipated or non-constipated, and they will still navigate the halls of their campus: UNMARKED.

— ❧ —

Before going to bed, Alice Princeton Goe made plans to make yet another connection with the integrity-anchored men of Royalle College.

She suspected her connection would change her life (and theirs), but she didn't know the specifics of those changes, though she looked forward to them.

CHAPTER THIRTY-EIGHT

"WHEN A WOMAN GIVES BIRTH TO A CHILD," ALICE wrote in a tribute to Hank Aaron (published in Samsville's *News-Free Gazette*, three days after Aaron broke Babe Ruth's homerun record), "the excruciating pain of labor and delivery—though in the immediate past—recedes to a distant memory as the mother cuddles her newborn child, her bundle of joy."

She went on to add, "When a homerun hitter comes close to breaking a major record, the pain of all the hard work sets in, and when the hitter nears the end of his career and he or she struggles and struggles but finally hits the homerun that breaks the record, the hitter would no doubt trot around the bases with tears of joy—involuntary tears of joy. The pain of the athlete's pursuit would have been overwhelmed by the joy of the record-breaking performance."

Life has many moments when joy overwhelms pain. The men of Royalle College lived through one of those moments. The men were angry and hurt when they left Samsville; they had a long and sustained struggle but no positive results.

Alice Princeton Goc had taken them on a spectacular ride, but all they had to show for it was the pain of disappointment.

That pain lasted for only three days. While in West Virginia, in the office of the president in fact, Tim Lynpeex was handed a Special-Delivery envelope for which he had to sign. The envelope came from Samsville, Kansas, and in it was a card.

Designed by Alice, the homemade card consisted of a heavy sheet of cream-colored textured paper that she had around the house; she folded that sheet in half and wrote with a felt pen on the front of the card: "A calculated random act of generosity—Alice style." On the inside of the card and above her signature, she lettered these words from James Joyce:

> Apologise,
>
> Pull out his eyes
>
> Pull out his eyes,
>
> Apologise.

She drew two long but smiling faces, and underneath she wrote: "*Happiness is a bag of tricks that we play on the living.*" She signed using only her first name.

Tucked in the card were three bank drafts that she had acquired the day after the men had left her. (Her cleaning lad had driven her to Wichita "for an emergency," as she told him. He remained in the car while she was in the bank acquiring the three checks.) One bank draft was made out to Dr. Timothy Lynpeex and the other to Mr. Robert Toyzol. Each man's check was in the amount of twenty thousand dollars. The third check, consisting of two million dollars, was made out for Royalle College.

She also enclosed a note addressed to both men. In the note she thanked them for being "... extremely good sports in playing the role of the innocent participants who were *voltairized* by an octogenarian widow from the wheat fields of central Kansas, where the fence posts are made of stone and the land had muscle-tone.

"I hope the personal bank drafts will make you smile, and I

request—indeed I insist—that all the money must be used for the benefit of your families and not for the work of the college. The larger check should, of course, go for the work of the college, and you may use it in any way you wish."

In the note, she also mentioned her plan "to write a novel about the adventure we had undergone. My first book, *Editors and Their Turkeys,* did very well for its publisher, and my editor assured me—after reading the first fifty pages of our projected novel—of an advance that is slightly more than your combined bank drafts."

She concluded the note by writing: "The novel's storyline will be based on what we had done, but I promise to fictionalize every single detail. No one will be able to trace the story to you."

— ❧ —

Immediately after receiving the three bank drafts, Lynpeex called Alice to thank her. He spoke about her "creativity and extraordinary generosity."

During the phone conversation, he also told her: "On the flight home, I gave Bob a nickname that came from your description of the gap in his front teeth. You compared Bob's teeth to those of the old Green Bay Packer coach Vince Lombardi. Remember? *Hyphen* became Bob's nickname. His wife absolutely loved your original comparison." Lynpeex then told *Hyphen* to talk to Alice. He did, and he thanked her, profusely.

She responded by saying, "Love your nickname. Congratulations! Nicknames are the emblem of small-town, or should I say net-serve, culture. Out here in Samsville, the males have nicknames, and if you've got one, you've arrived."

"It's like that in West Virginia," *Hyphen* said. "You've got to find a nickname for Tim."

"I'll work on it, my friend," she said. "I promise. I will."

A happily agitated Lynpeex reclaimed the phone and informed her, "Both of us would absolutely love to fly to Samsville, to take you out for a leisurely dinner in Wichita's finest restaurant, and to express to you our deep gratitude in a more concrete way."

Alice invited them to come, but she insisted on "no gifts, please." They arranged for a dinner date in Wichita, "the dock of America's amber waves of grain," as Alice had once labeled the biggest city in Kansas.

— ❧ —

A week after that phone conversation, on a Thursday morning, the two men flew to Wichita (coach-class happy), rented a car, drove up to Samsville, picked up Alice, and drove back to a restaurant in Wichita.

Toyzol drove, and Alice and Lynpeex sat in the back seat. The conversation drifted to all sorts of pleasant, non-controversial, benign topics. "What Dad had cherished most during our life on the farm," Alice said, "was his productive and highly reliable bull, *Fiasco*. To this day, I can't figure out if Dad's sense of irony drove him to give the bull that name, or if the bull's inability to father many males had earned him the name."

She touched Lynpeex knee and added, "When I was little, I'd ask Dad if he'd like to see *Fiasco*'s mate give birth to a baby girl or a baby boy, and Dad would say: *I really don't care, sweetheart.* He'd pause then add: *I really don't care if it's a big boy or a small boy.* Then while laughing at his own remark, he'd reach down with his big farm-gnarled hands, hoist me up, tuck me into his chest and arms, while tickling and kissing me—and rejoicing."

Both men laughed, and Lynpeex said, "How moving is that!"

Alice continued, "Dad, who had a sixth-grade education, was a master at achieving the inadvertent."

"Oh," Lynpeex said, unaware of what she meant; he assumed it was a positive facet in a person's character.

"He'd occasionally come up with a heroic couplet that you'd think was from Chaucer's *Canterbury Tales* or his *Legend of Good Women*—there are some, you know—or even from Pope. As a good Catholic, you're probably wondering: How did the pope get in here, aren't you?"

"As a matter of fact, I am," Lynpeex said, smiling.

"I'm referring to Alexander Pope who in his day unfurled many heroic couplets and whose philosophy is now popular on both coasts: the east coast and the left coast, where secular humanism is rampant. Pope's *Essay on Man* sums up that aspect of our current culture, *not* our net-serve culture, mind you. As I recall, he opens that *Essay* in this heroic couplet:

> *Know then thyself, presume not God to scan;*
> *The proper study of mankind is man.*

Now Dad was no Pope, but one evening at supper while talking about *Fiasco*, he uncorked a heroic couplet that lingered in my mind and would, in time, lead me to give birth to what—many years later—I labeled *Trunk Thoughts*. Here's what Dad said:

> *It's time for our culture to trace in full,*
> *All that it owes to the seed of the bull.*

He wanted people to honor the bull, whether we live in rural or urban America: in Samsville, Kansas or Santa Barbara, California—or in the steel city of Pittsburgh, Pennsylvania."

"Or the Mountain State of West Virginia," Lynpeex added.

Alice continued: "Think, boys, of all the milk that we drink, the meat and cheese that we eat, the leather that we wear and use for furniture, the way of life that is the farm. Many state universities and colleges, as you well know, will fold if kids from the farms didn't attend them."

"We've seen that happen, haven't we, Bob?"

Toyzol added, "So true, Mrs. Goe."

"You boys wouldn't be here if Winterpeace College didn't close," she said. "Many people would be unemployed if they didn't work in meat or cheese or furniture factories or in restaurants that serve elegant meat dishes. Those of us who live on the Great Plains and who claim to be poets and writers must prod and urge our nation's inhabitants to salute the seed of the bull."

"Sounds good to me," Lynpeex said.

"Me too," Toyzol added.

The conversation in the car also touched on the ways of a retired veterinarian in Samsville, on supermarket tabloids, television commercials, Notre Dame football, vanity publishing in the book world, estate auctions in central Kansas, and the portrayal of a militant urologist as sketched in a cartoon that Toyzol had seen in a magazine.

"My cleaning lad," Alice told the men at one instance, "is a witty and imaginative fellow. He recently wrote a short story that explores the dawn of appendix transplants. One afternoon he confided in me (tongue-in-cheek, I presume): *I long for the day when head transplants will become popular, so I don't have to wear my Denial.* That's the name the young chap gave to his Elvis-pompadour hairpiece."

When they arrived at the outskirts of Wichita, Alice directed them to the restaurant. At one point, their car stopped at a red light behind a Ford pickup truck with two white-on-black tailgate stickers in dialogue. Printed in all caps, the sticker on the left asks:

WHAT DID YOUR HONOR

ROLL KID ACCOMPLISH?

And the sticker on the right, an implied response to that question, boasts of the ongoing achievements of the truck-driver's kid:

MY SON—A BULLY—STARTED

THREE HOMESCHOOLS SO FAR

Alice silently read both stickers, then spoke: "Now, Bob, if the guy ahead of you fails to move when the light turns green, please resist all temptations to give him a *courtesy horn*. It'll be misinterpreted out here."

"After reading those stickers," Toyzol said, "I'll do what you say, Mrs. Goe: I'll remain calm and wait for him to move."

"For all I know," Alice said, "that green-and-gold cap he's wearing might have embossed on it the words: PACKING HEAT. I've seen several baseball caps with those colors and words on them in Samsville."

"So, the prudent thing to do," Lynpeex said with his prairie-horn encounter gentle on his mind, "is *not* to use your horn out here."

"Out here and elsewhere," she quickly replied.

— ❧ —

In time, the light turned green and to the relief of all three, the man in the truck ahead moved at once.

"The place we're going to is like *The Four Seasons Restaurant* in New York, where editors and agents have power lunches," Alice said.

The three looked forward to a seven-course dinner.

CHAPTER THIRTY-NINE

WHILE EATING, THEY THANKED HER AGAIN AND again, and they assured her that the money will be used for years and years to come in providing good scholarships for needy students from Appalachia.

"To be honest with you, Mrs. Goe," Lynpeex said, using a phrase that she had told him not to use, "we had absolutely no idea we'd be getting a single red cent from you, not one bronze cent."

"And even after you read that subtly suggestive postscript in *Gladys of the Great Plains*, the story I gave you before you left?" she said. "I thought that'd give it away."

"I tried to read the story on the plane," Toyzol said, "but I was too tired. Exhausted in fact—not in a physical sense but mentally, if you know what I mean. Never made it to the postscript."

"But we can laugh about all that now," Lynpeex said.

The three laughed at her quirky ways and the splendid results from them, and they laughed at their blunders. "As they say," *Hyphen* exclaimed with a smile that flashed his white teeth: "All's well that ends well."

"And it ended well for us," Lynpeex said. "Thank you, Mrs. Goe."

"You don't need to do that," she said.

"Oh yes we do," both spoke at once. Then Lynpeex added, "We most certainly do."

They discussed the success of *Editors and Their Turkeys*, and she told them about her other literary pursuits. That led Lynpeex to ask Alice to consider Royalle College as a repository for all her writings: books, articles, stories, poems, letters, manuscripts, diaries, and so forth. He said, "Our first-rate librarian has a doctorate and she'd catalogue and preserve your work for posterity."

Alice respectfully declined their offer, telling them that she had decided to give all her published and unpublished materials, along with her book and vinyl-record collections, to the Carnegie Library in her town. The library had also asked for the desk from her study, for the typewriters that she had used during her writing career, and for the paintings that she and Frank had brought back from Paris in 1927. Alice agreed to the request. Lynpeex touched her hand and said, "We understand."

She did, however, ask the men for a favor. "When you return to your college," she said, "would you please consider introducing into higher education the country's first *Doc Award*. The award should carry an honorarium of five thousand dollars—an odd number, you see— and it should be given annually, preferably at graduation, to a professor at Royalle College. The professor you honor should be a member of the *male* species: that's important to me. And he should be competent as a teacher to give the award credibility, but lacking charisma and other things in many other ways—much like the award's namesake in the Seven Dwarfs."

The men laughed and laughed, and *Hyphen* said, "Oh we've got our share of charisma-free male profs." Both felt that the Vespa-man would be a good candidate for what she had called "an ambivalently coveted award."

"Believe me, we've got candidates galore," Lynpeex said and touched her hand. "And only you, Mrs. Goe, have the wit and wisdom to come up with such a fun-sounding way to honor them."

The men laughed again as she deadpanned: "Thank you—*Doc*."

— ⁂ —

Also during dinner, the men of Royalle College asked about the themes in her novel, and she noted that she "might try to weave all sorts of themes—I like to call them strands—into the story."

She offered a litany of possible strands that could be woven into the fabric of the novel. She offered them in rapid succession, indicating to the men that she had been thinking hard about the project.

"The literary novel," Alice said, "could explore a radical therapy for loneliness in the life of a widow on the Great Plains and elsewhere.

"It could deal with the life of an elderly and creative widow who feels the thrill of liberation from the vortex of a paranoid man. That part of the novel, like others, would be autobiographical, you see."

"We see," Lynpeex said.

She touched his right hand and continued, "The novel could also serve as an allegory on the writer in society, given that your cash cow, Alice Princeton Goe, is like the overwhelming majority of word-jocks: a struggling writer.

"It could certainly be seen as a critique of the loss of privacy in our modern culture, a concern that was so dear to my departed husband Frank, and now is dear to me, and to both of you, I presume."

"Yes, to us also," *Hyphen* said. "Isn't that right, Tim?"

"Indeed, it is," Lynpeex said.

"The novel could be a commentary on the intersection of business courses and the humanities in our colleges and universities.

"The novel could even examine in a strange way the neglected principles of negotiations. You two were good negotiators, very good negotiators, in case you're wondering.

"It could be a work for the literary boy scouts of academia, the ones that James Joyce loved to keep occupied.

"It could be a novel that illustrates the adage that we had talked about: *Truth is stranger than fiction.*

"It could be an experiment in the novel as a play, the play as a novel. This grows out of my love for dialogue.

"The novel could illustrate how honesty and integrity—in the context of large sums of money—carries its own rewards.

"The novel could unravel and explain the bizarre undertakings that college presidents and their assistants have to endure before acquiring a financial gift for their beloved college."

That last theme caressed the men's faces, and they smiled. Toyzol winked at her and flashed his Lombardiesque hyphen. She winked back as if to say: "I just anointed your man with the nickname *Doc.* Now your job is to run with it."

"I don't know much about novel-writing," Lynpeex said, "but it seems to me *all* these themes could be incorporated into the work."

Both men expressed deep interest in reading the novel after she completes it, and she assured them that she would forward them a copy to read in manuscript form.

She also told them that she would appreciate whatever feedback they would offer her, given that they had played an extraordinary role in developing the novel's storyline.

"It'll be a slice from my life," Alice said. "No, no, check that: it'll be a slice from *our* lives. And if the novel works, then it'll be more than a simple novel to entertain. As the good folks at the Samsville's Café would say: *That if is a big sucker.*"

"They use that same expression in Royallestown," Lynpeex said.

— ☙ —

Toyzol's prostate lit up, so he excused himself and went in search of the restroom. Lynpeex shifted the conversation to the many poor students from Appalachia that the college has been serving for years—and continues to serve.

When Toyzol returned, Lynpeex changed the subject slightly by asking her: "If you're to summarize the content of your projected novel in one brief sentence, what would that sentence be, Mrs. Goe?"

Alice looked up at the ceiling and said: "I'll give you two related summaries. One with *you* as the focus, and the second, *me*. The novel will explore the ways of an octogenarian widow—a writer and a small-town philanthropist—as she tempts two handsome and honorable men with her wealth and traps them in a comic quandary."

"And the second one," Lynpeex said.

"The second one is this," she said. "When one thinks of an elderly woman in a small town in Kansas or Nebraska or Wisconsin or Michigan—you name the state—the image that comes to mind is that of a lonely church-going widow with little education and no cultural pursuits, living in a clapboard house located on or near Main Street. My novel will shatter this stereotype."

"And do you have a title for it?" Toyzol asked.

"I've got a tentative title," she said. "Before I tell you what it is, I must inform you that novels in America, and I suspect even in Europe, tend to be read by many more women than men."

"Is that a fact?" Lynpeex said.

"Yes, it is," she replied. "Editors believe the minute women stop reading fiction, the novel will die. Men enjoy military history, biography, memoir, mostly nonfiction. I want to write seriocomic prose for women. For now, I plan to title the novel *She's a Quirky Millionaire*. Needless to say, it'll be like most first novels—auto-biographical."

"Our families, Mrs. Goe, are most grateful to your quirkiness," Toyzol said, reached out and touched her hand. Lynpeex nodded, smiling.

— ❧ —

While waiting for the desserts to arrive, Alice told the men how delighted she was to be out at dinner with them and how much she was enjoying talking about her writings, the college, nicknames, small towns, and, of course, Virginia Woolf.

Mentioning Virginia Woolf reminded her of another writer she liked to quote. "You know, Tim," she said, "this dinner and the fellowship we're enjoying, as you had mentioned on the phone, is a form of gratitude, a loud and visible form of gratitude, if you know what I mean."

"Well," Lynpeex said as the desserts arrived, "we wanted to show our gratitude. That's the least we could do."

"Deep gratitude," Toyzol added. "Very deep gratitude."

"This fine dinner says it—stentoriously," she stated. And just as the men began to wonder what that word meant, she slapped them with a passage from a modern writer: "Gladys Bronwyn Stern used to say: *Silent gratitude isn't very much use to anyone*, and your gratitude in this fine dinner is anything but silent. I'm most appreciative."

"We are too," both men said at once and continued talking on various topics while Alice ate her cheesecake, and the men their mango ice cream.

"Our Lord put it best when he said: *It's more blessed to give than to receive*. I'm feeling the blessing in the giving, and I know there's also a blessing in receiving, and you're showing that," Alice said while the waiter was refilling their coffee cups.

At one point, Lynpeex said, "You managed to make our first visit to Kansas an unforgettable one."

"That's good to hear," she said.

"I agree," Toyzol added.

"With whom?" she kidded him.

"Both of you," Toyzol said, smiling.

"What one single moment," she said while making eye contact with Toyzol, "do you remember from your visit?"

"Boy that's hard to say—to single out one memorable moment," Toyzol said. "There were so many."

"But there must have been one that *really* stood out," she said, "one that you'd share with a close friend or a spouse."

"If I were to offer one," Toyzol replied, "I'd say when we first met you, and you spoke about your *trunk thoughts,* and you asked me to come up with one on command. My failure wasn't memorable. What was memorable was your move at the time. Do you remember that? When you pretended to be another woman and left us alone for a while. That move, as Tim said then, made us feel as if *we were squirted with verbal mace.*"

Alice remembered that move and laughed. "That verbal mace label was very clever."

"Speaking of clever," Toyzol added, "during one of my prostate fits, I came up with a trunk thought that I wanted to share with you and Tim, but there was too much tension in the air at the time, so I held it in."

"Held what in?" she kidded. "Care to share that now? We're in a tension-free zone, and I'm always up for a good trunk thought."

"Be happy to," Toyzol said. "It's an old chestnut that I once saw written above a urinal in a hotel in Wheeling. It went something like this:

No matter how much you shake and dance,
Those last drops will end up in your pants.

That'll be a good one for the cars of literary urologists and for—"

"The car trunks," Alice interrupted, "of the elderly folks in Florida, where the golden geezers are awash in prostate problems."

"While we're on this subject," Toyzol said, "another thought, really a question, just navigated my mind."

"Love your metaphor," she said. "You're a poetic MBA. Didn't know they make your type."

"In West Virginia, they do," Toyzol winked.

All three laughed. "Seriously," Toyzol said, "poetry has been on my mind lately, and I've got a poetry-related question for you, Mrs. Goe. Some might consider it to be in bad taste. Should I ask it, anyway?"

"It all depends if it's highly offensive or a wee-bit offensive," Lynpeex said. "Consider that before deciding."

"What do you think, Mrs. Goe, should—?"

"Oh, go ahead, Bob," she said. "An off-color word here or there doesn't bother me."

"Okay," Toyzol said. "Here's the question: Is it a paradox when the brewers of beer—a delightful drink—make the kiss of the hops look like and bubble like—urine?"

"In the mind of a skillful and imaginative poet," she said, "a witty and striking paradox could connect these elements."

"How?" Toyzol asked.

She drifted into a pensive mood, hesitated, bit her lower lip, and said: "A poet could delve into the perspectives of a guy with prostatitis. To that guy, urine is not distasteful but delightful. That's just a quick thought, and not a good one, that comes to mind, a thought that might connect beer and urine into a paradox. Frankly, I'm not adept at thinking on my feet and coming up with good insights. I was better at that when I was younger. But you see what I mean by connecting the two elements?"

"Speaking of elements," Toyzol told her, "I've also got a couple clean ones, and I'd love to hear your response to them."

"Ok-ay," she said, injecting a subtle reluctance into her agreement.

Even though he sensed that, Toyzol said: "Heat pops tiny drops of corn into white flakes we call popcorn, and cold pops tiny drops of rain into white flakes we call snow. Now, is there a connection between these facts?"

"I've got to think about all that. For now, let's just put it this way: you've got elements and perspectives here that a good poet could grapple with and weave into a poem." She added slowly: "Is this *okay* with you?"

Toyzol smiled and said, "Some people read between the lines, but I *hear* between the words, and I hear you saying: *Get off my back*! Correct?"

"You got it, son. There's a time for mental hernia—that's our net-serve culture label for heavy thinking—but it's not now." She looked at Lynpeex, smiled, and asked: "What about you, dear Tim. Is there one moment from your visit that lingers in your memory?"

"You and Bob just hinted on what I remember most: the paradox drill beats them all. I just couldn't believe we were out here on the Great Plains of Kansas doing that drill in pursuit of funds for Royalle College."

Alice laughed and said: "If that's the case, let me give you a paradox that deals with your hair."

"Or lack of it," Toyzol interjected. All laughed.

"When the barber cuts Tim's hair," she spoke to Toyzol, "he charges him extra. Do you see a paradox embedded in this comment?"

"Frankly, I don't," Toyzol said.

"Neither do I?" Lynpeex added.

"Oh, my, my, you MBAs," she said. "You miss the point again."

"And the point is?" Lynpeex asked.

Both cocked their ears to listen: "The barber not only cuts Tim's hair," she said, paused, smiled, and added, "but he also hunts for it."

— ✐ —

"What about you, dear Mrs. Goe?" Toyzol kidded. "Is there a moment or two from your first encounter with us that stands out for you?"

"Yes," she said. "When Tim called me *Mrs. G*. Remember that?"

"Oh, yes I do," Lynpeex said. "You lashed out and lectured us, and in so doing, you spoke to my bladder."

"If you spoke to the bladder of—" Toyzol hesitated then added, "our charisma-free *Doc* Lynpeex, then you *activated* mine: I wet myself."

She winked at Toyzol as if to congratulate him on his quickness and wit, and said, "And I'll never forget Tim squirming in anger when that man driving behind us drilled him with that loud and obnoxious horn of disgust—even though Tim felt his driving wasn't *disgust worthy*."

"It wasn't only loud and obnoxious," Lynpeex said, "but it was also a long and sustained horn: anger-laced."

"Also, I enjoyed telling you about the three joys of life, and I recall the perplexing expressions on your faces when I told you that *sneezing* was one of them," she said. "I still think it is—though not in a pizza if you're allergic to flour and want to hold a job in a pizza place."

— ✐ —

When they finished their dessert, Lynpeex paid for the meal and left a generous tip for the server. He told Toyzol, "Please bring the car to the front. We'll meet you there."

Toyzol followed orders. The college president and the small-town philanthropist sat in the back seat. Lynpeex teased the driver by saying, "We'll be going to Main Street in Samsville, sir."

"Will do," Toyzol said and leaned to his right, motioning with his arm and hand as if he were setting a cab's mileage-counter on *Start*.

The drive to Samsville takes a little less than two hours. Alice and Lynpeex talked about all sorts of topics—the weather, sports, music, food, and art on the Great Plains—leaving Toyzol to concentrate on driving.

As they neared the town of Gluesiville, Toyzol spotted the golden arches of a McDonald's restaurant. He took the exit, drove to the restaurant and announced, "Sorry, my dear friends, but the old reliable prostate is at it again. It's like an adding machine: you can always count on it. Need I say more?"

"Please don't, *Hyphen*," Lynpeex said. Alice smiled.

"Whatever you say, *Doc*," Toyzol said, slapping that title with affection on his boss. Toyzol parked in the restaurant's lot, excused himself, and shuffled his way to the bathroom.

"Poor Bob," Lynpeex told Alice, "his prostate acts up all the time at the college. Frequency in urination is the result."

"When that used to happen to my dear Frank," she said, "he'd go to the doctor and get it massaged. It wasn't fun, but it gave him temporary relief. They probably still do that."

"Oh, Bob has had that treatment many times and he really dislikes it because it hurts so much."

When Toyzol returned, he apologized for the unexpected stop and said, "I promise you, my dear friends, this is our last stop until we arrive in Samsville—I hope."

"Out here," she said, "we have a saying that we playfully associate with promises, and it could easily apply to prostate promises."

"What's that?" Toyzol asked.

"Prostate promises are like pie crust: made to be broken."

— ∽ —

They arrived in Samsville at twenty-five minutes past eleven. Alice invited the men "to please come in and chat a little longer. I've got something to give you, and I'm really enjoying your company."

"We are too," both spoke at once as they entered the house. She went to the study and picked up from a round ornate mahogany antique table two hardback copies of *Editors and Their Turkeys*. She exchanged glances with the men, autographed the copies using the nicknames *Hyphen* and *Doc*, smiled, and handed them the books.

"You know, every author wants to write a book that the reader can't put down," she told the men. "Well, that's not me. I wanted to write a book that you *can* put down—but that you *can't resist* coming back to it. And I hope I achieved that in the feathers in your hands."

"If this book isn't in our library," Lynpeex smiled as he spoke, clutching his copy and tapping an index finger on the cover, "I'll make sure three copies are ordered at once: two for general circulation and the other copy for the Royalle College Archives. I'll also ask our small-town librarian to order a copy for their collection."

"You should also order," Toyzol said, "a copy for your nephew."

"The struggling writer?" Lynpeex said.

"Yes," Toyzol said. "What do you think, Mrs. Goe?"

"I'm biased, of course," she said. "But I know struggling writers love to read books on writing. There's a whole industry out there that specializes in such books: how to write, how to publish, how to deal with rejection, how to get a literary agent, and so forth."

"Such books help them overcome their struggles?" Lynpeex asked.

"Maybe slightly," she said. "You can teach writers the basic ways and techniques that might help them improve their craft, but in the end, you can't make them into good writers if they don't have those innate gifts that come from Almighty God."

"Is that so?" Lynpeex said.

"In my opinion, it is," she said. "Let me give you an analogy: you can teach runners how to improve their running skills and techniques, but in the end, you can't teach them *speed*. That's innate."

"Now I see why my nephew continues to struggle," Lynpeex said.

"Writers undergo many struggles," Alice said, "and almost all the books on writing and publishing are written in a serious mode. Not this one, and that's why my publisher loved it. My book assumes that success often breeds boasting and arrogance; frustrations stimulate humor and wit. So, when I wrote my book, I tried to do it in a light touch. Enjoy—and share with others."

Hearing Alice's comments, Lynpeex made a decision: "We will also order copies for all six members of the English department." He paused then added, "Better yet: for the entire college faculty."

Toyzol said, "Great decision, Tim—all fifty-six country squires."

"That's a good take on the life of small-college professors," Alice told Lynpeex.

"In large universities," Lynpeex said, "if you don't publish, you perish. But in small colleges like ours, if you don't publish, you languish."

"Whatever you guys do," Alice addressed them while smiling, "I'll remain most grateful. I know publishers and authors love it when their books are sold in bulk, and you guys are doing that for my turkeys." She paused then asked: "Do you like the dust jacket and its art?" Before they could respond, she continued, "A woman at club dislikes the cover's art because it doesn't look like anything she recognizes. But she likes the way big and small feathers are artfully used as fonts and letters that spell out the book's title."

"It's an eye-catching cover," Lynpeex said. "The art draws you in, and I too like the feather-font design." He turned to the title page and added, "From what I know, the publisher is a distinguished one. Right?"

"A big one," Toyzol interjected, "an influential one. Correct?"

"Yes, to both remarks," she said as the three remained standing. "Do you notice anything peculiar in the publisher's name?"

The men re-focused on *Garvin, Akers & Sheridan.* "It uses the ampersand," Toyzol said, "like Barnes & Noble."

"You're right," she said. "But there is something else in it that came up during your first visit—and you guys found it funny."

They stared at the title page and remained silent. Lynpeex said in a quizzical manner, "You're saying the two of us found it *funny*?"

"Yes, *funny*," she said. "I'm alluding to an inside joke that needs three elements to fly: my hearing, ants, and the publisher's acronym."

The men laughed and Toyzol kidded, "Just for the record, Mrs. Goe," Toyzol said, "I want to inform you that *gas of the ants* wasn't funny during our visit."

"It wasn't?" she said.

"It was *hilarious*," Toyzol said.

Before leaving, each man leaned over and hugged Alice. Lynpeex said: "Thank you very much, Mrs. Goe, for your generosity and care for young people in poverty-stricken Appalachia. Your wit, I might also add, is priceless." When they hugged her, they also kissed her left cheek.

"And now," Alice said sadly, "you'll be on your way home."

"Before we go," Toyzol, who sings tenor in his church's choir, told Alice: "I'd love to sing for you the refrain from Hazel Dickens's song: 'West Virginia, My Home.' In my opinion, she's the Mountain State's best singer. I hope you like this:

West Virginia, oh, my home.

West Virginia's where I belong.

In the dead of the night,

In the still and the quiet,

I slip away like a bird in flight,

Back to those hills,

The place that I call home.

Thank you for everything, Mrs. Goe. We love you—dearly."

— ✂ —

Throughout their time with Alice, Lynpeex had a question that strobed his mind—and kept strobing—but he failed to ask it.

Indeed, he didn't want to ask it. He refused to even mention it to Toyzol, for he didn't want to appear in the least bit ungrateful for the two million dollars.

The question would haunt him for years: "What did our friend, Alice Princeton Goe, the writer and small-town philanthropist, do with the remaining five million dollars?"

The men went back to their motel room and slept comfortably that night. The next morning, they drove to Wichita's Mid-Continent Airport, flew to Pittsburgh, Pennsylvania, picked up their Buick from long-term parking, and drove home to Royallestown, West Virginia.

— ✂ —

In Kansas, Alice started to make serious plans on what to do with the remaining five million.

When Frank was alive, he and Alice had befriended an unmarried middle-aged man in Samsville, an ambitious writer who had struggled in his attempts to get a book manuscript published by a major commercial house in New York.

The writer's wealthy parents had died in an automobile accident. Being their only offspring, he inherited all their money—which they had, like the Goes, kept private. Very private.

In time, the middle-aged man and Alice had agreed to establish in Samsville a unique writer-related institution in American culture. The two met with a lawyer in Wichita and drew up the necessary legal papers that formalized their plans. Alice's five million dollars were to go towards establishing and sustaining the institution—one that they hoped would nurture the town's economy by attracting streams of visitors for years to come to their hometown.

In her diary, she wrote: "What Paul and I had agreed upon will be revealed a month after my death. My role in establishing the institution and my financial contribution to it will remain anonymous."

CHAPTER FORTY

ALICE CONTINUED TO EMPLOY JACK, AND IN TIME the Jaycubsons had their first child, a daughter they named Elise. One Saturday afternoon, while Alice was working on the fourth draft of her first novel, Jack placed his Elise in her stroller, pushed her past the high school's football field, then in front of the tennis court, and meandered towards the Little League baseball field.

Two teams were playing. One had traveled from Gluesiville, and the other was the *Samsville Stallions*. Parents of the players along with their aunts, uncles, and grandparents were there. Many spectators were cheering, clapping, and enjoying the game.

Umpiring at home plate was the son of the only African-American family in Samsville. The umpire's father was a physics teacher at the high school, and his mother, a Registered Nurse in her early forties, worked for Doc Addison, Samsville's only physician.

The umpire grew up in Samsville, played shortstop and pitched for the *Stallions* of his boyhood. He is a second-year student at the Yale Divinity School, now home for the summer.

Jack pushed the stroller to an area behind the fence not far from home plate to observe the game. Between innings, he greeted and chatted with the umpire, a fellow member of the Presbyterian church in town and a long-time friend of Jack's wife, Lisa.

The umpire had started to referee the *Stallions'* home games during his senior year in college when the team broke the gender line and invited two girls to play—even though the team had enough eligible boys. Most umpires are paid for their services, but the divinity student volunteered his time. "You get paid," Jack once teased the umpire, "in other ways."

That day, the umpire was being paid handsomely, Jack thought. While the game was in progress, a tall muscular man—who had a head full of white-and-black hair greased with Vitalis Hair Tonic—yelled and yelled at the umpire, questioning his calls and his eyesight, irritating him to the point where it became unbearable.

So, the umpire called timeout, ripped off his brown padded mask, turned around and stared at the complaining fellow who, Jack would later learn, was a father of a player on the *Gluesiville Elmers*. Clutching the mask in his right hand, the umpire leaned towards the fence and spoke in a loud voice that all the spectators could hear: "Sir, please listen to me. I *am* the umpire. I make the calls. I call them as I see them, and I call them *fair*. Why? Because that makes me feel good. Understand?"

Many spectators applauded. The umpire turned, faced the pitcher, and continued the game. Jack felt the umpire's comment was an original zinger, befitting a volunteer umpire who is also an Ivy League divinity student from the Great Plains.

Jack was standing next to a father who at one point started to clap and shout *a-da-boy* as his son dribbled (thanks to a late swing and to an attention-challenged second baseman) a hit through the infield. The proud father asked Jack, "Did you see him *drill* that solid single into right field?" Jack nodded, smiled, and told himself: "It looks like we've got another parent who thinks he's got a Mickey Mantle in the making."

There is a fellow in Samsville, a member of the United Methodist church that Alice attends, who often reminds his friends that he is a close relative of the famed New York Yankee slugger. "Like me," the fellow would often say, "Mantle was born in Spavinaw, Oklahoma."

When the fellow's Oklahoma relatives would visit him and his family in Samsville, the *News-Free Gazette* would record the Okies' visit and mention their Mantle connections. The paper would also report how many days the visitors had spent in town, the names of the people who had visited the visitors, the dinners or picnics that those visitors had attended (or were planning to attend), and the day the visitors planned to leave.

The Mantle name had earned a special place in the folklore of that little town on the Kansas prairie, and it earned an extra-special place in the mind of a hardcore realist like Jack.

— ❧ —

After watching three innings, Jack tipped the stroller on its back wheels and guided it out of the park. He pushed it on the sidewalk and headed to Blackmore's Baked Goods.

That was the town's only bakery, located next to the stucco building that housed People's Savings and Loan and across the street from the town's only bank: Samsville State Bank. (The town's four-aisle grocery store, Henry's, didn't have a fresh-bakery section.)

At Blackmore's, Jack picked up two loaves of Italian bread, a dozen chocolate-chip cookies, paid for them, and watched the beefy bearded cashier-owner-baker lean over and present little Elise with a free chocolate-chip cookie.

Jack squatted, touched the chin of his two-and-a-half-year-old daughter, and whispered in her right ear, "Sweetheart, what do we say to Mr. Blackmore?"

"Tankoo," she said as she looked up. The two adults smiled and exchanged goodbyes.

Jack pushed the stroller out the door and guided it for fifteen yards or so to the town's only hardware store: *Mildred Anderson's Daughters*, a place whose name was patterned after *Ernst and Sons Hardware* in downtown Lawrence. Alice had asked Jack to "get the very best wheelbarrow at *Anderson's*."

At *Anderson's*, Jack greeted a dark-haired, thirty-year-old, bearded and pudgy clerk, a son-in-law of Mildred and (the late) Herman Anderson. "I'm looking for the Cadillac of wheelbarrows," Jack said. "What do you have in stock? It's not for me, but for Mrs. Goe, and she told me to get the very best in the shop."

The clerk left Jack and went to the back of the store to look. He came back with a red plastic wheelbarrow and said, "This is the only kind we have: one size fits all dirt, you might say."

"Would you please," Jack asked as he glanced at the shiny wooden handles of the wheelbarrow, "charge it to Mrs. Goe's account?"

"Will do," the clerk said. "You want to take it with you?"

"She'd rather you deliver it," Jack said. "She asked me to tell you to tabulate her account, and she'll pay you on delivery."

"Will do," the clerk said, sneezed, and added, "God bless *me*."

Jack felt that remark was strange. He scolded himself for failing to follow up the clerk's sneeze with the *bless you* formality that is often hurled at the sneezing residents of Samsville.

The clerk reminded Jack of his failure in a manner that Jack felt was "very small-townish—at once subtle and blunt, and sort of witty."

Moments after that, the store's radio, set on an AM station that often played popular country music, began to play Glen Campbell's "Wichita Lineman." The clerk told Jack, "My dear cousin, Lilo, is in the Navy, and he's now stationed in Hawaii and loves it there. He tells us the Navy always plays that song over the base's PA system whenever the USS Wichita pulls into Pearl Harbor."

"It's a great song," Jack said.

"Sure is," the clerk agreed. "I love the local flavor it has. It's my favorite song of Glen Campbell."

"I like it too. That song and 'Galveston' are among my very favorite Glen Campbell songs. Both are likely to endure."

"Yes, sir," the clerk said. "I certainly agree."

The clerk snapped his red suspenders, turned around, and plucked, from a small box filled with sand and planted with American flags, a flag the size of a dollar and mounted on a straw. He handed it to little Elise.

She accepted and followed her dad's cue by saying, "Tankoo."

— ❦ —

Jack strolled to the small clapboard house that he and Lisa rented on Melissasal Street. It was two blocks away from his in-laws' handsome red-brick two-story structure where Lisa was born and where she had lived all her life until marriage.

At home that afternoon, Elise took a nap and Jack worked for a while on a four-drawer antique dresser that he and Lisa had bought at an auction held in an Amish town in central Kansas where horses lumber along, pulling buggies that roll and rock and squeak as the horses defecate on the peaceful prairies. The oak dresser had layers of white paint that Jack was removing with turpentine in a slow and methodical manner.

Following that work, Jack spent the early part of the evening preparing supper for his wife who had gone to Wichita with four women from the young-adults Sunday school class at their church. Lisa called their excursion "a field trip to check out a brand-new shopping mall that had five prestigious New York-based stores. My growing reputation for shopping," she told him, "could be compared to a fat man's belly."

"What do you mean by that?" he said. "When I say that my reputation is like a fat man's belly," she said, "I mean that it's always with
me and goes ahead of me. Do you see?"

"I do now."

Other thoughts drifted in and out of his mind while preparing
dinner. He thought of his favorite uncle in Conroe, Texas, the one
who had just retired from the navy at the rank of Rear Admiral.

Jack thought it might be fun to honor and entertain his wise uncle,
a supporter of Jack's football career and a bibliophile, by starting a
literary journal and have all the items in the first issue written by
A. P. Goe but published under different pen names.

This, he felt, would display Alice's talents in a variety of genres:
poetry, short fiction, and essay. He knew she had many unpublished
items in all three genres—items she hoped to publish in due time.
He considered several titles for the journal and decided on one that
might connect with Alice's wit: *Front Admiral Review*.

"I'll propose my idea to Alice and see what she thinks. I hope
she'll see how her love of writing is beginning to rub off on me,"
he told himself as he placed another layer of boiled pasta in the
lasagna dish.

Another thought he had entertained led him to consider working
as a volunteer coach for the junior high school football team in the
fall. All paid positions, full or part-time, were taken.

Lisa felt that Jack, as she once told her mother, "makes a fine—I'd
even say, an extraordinary—homemaker, but, Mom, he's devastated
by being educated and without a full-time job."

On one occasion Jack felt so desperate, he told Lisa, "I wouldn't
even mind one of those full-time jobs where I envision the mantra
to be: *Minimum wage, minimum work*—maximum *anger*."

— ✍ —

Alice had a full-time job: working on her novel, and as usual, she would discuss—at times, obliquely—her work with Jack.

After all, Jack had unwittingly sent her in search of a plot for a novel. In time, Alice would pay Jack handsomely, and she did it in a way that pleased him and Lisa.

CHAPTER FORTY-ONE

ALICE WORKED HARD ON HER FIRST NOVEL IN which she and the men from West Virginia are stars. Her deluxe cleaning lad and her departed husband also play key roles in the novel.

Jack knew that Alice had a tendency to weave into her fiction some of her friends from church and women from her literary club. One day he told Alice at a coffee break, "When I first started working for you and realized that you wrote fiction and poetry and creative nonfiction, I kept reminding myself that I must try to remain as *colorless* around you as I could possibly be."

"Why's that?" she asked.

"Because writers tend to work their friends and acquaintances into their prose or poetry. Isn't that true?"

"It's true."

"And you do?"

"Yes."

"And you'd prefer it if your friends were interesting and colorful. Isn't that the case?"

"Sure is."

"So, you see my logic?" he asked. "By being *colorless*, my chances of not making your writings would be greater than if I were a colorful guy. And it would have worked, too, if not for your fascination with my humble hairpiece." Jack took a sip of coffee and smiled. "I'm just kidding, of course. I'd love to be in your literary undertakings, Mrs. Goe—provided, of course, you do me and my *Denial* in a positive light."

"Well, Jack," she said, reached out, touched his hand, and added, "you succeeded admirably in being colorless, but you're still going to make my first novel."

"Do you have a title for it?"

"I went through many during the writing process. You know, by contract, the publisher has the final say-so in title selection."

— ❧ —

When she finally completed the novel, Alice came up with a long title that she liked: *She Twirled Them Like a Pizza Maker Twirls Dough.* That's the title she settled on when she mailed, in the summer of '84, the manuscript to her publisher in New York.

Her editor liked Alice's poetic title but felt it was way too long. "Long titles," the editor wrote in a letter to Alice, "often come with those doctoral dissertations where the coma begins with the subtitle. We plan to use the spirit of your title.

"We think you're going to like the two-word title we selected: *Twirling Men.* It works on different levels and underscores the men's thoughts, thanks to the dizzyingly strange amusement park-like ride you take them on in the novel. Other levels of meaning are also suggested by the new title, giving the artist who will do the cover a concrete image with which to work."

The publisher went with the two-word title, and Alice was happy with the book's editing, design, cover art, and font selection. She envisioned a handsome hardback book, one that she knew would *not* be sewn in signatures.

Sure enough, when it appeared, *Twirling Men* wasn't sewn in signatures, and it wasn't clothbound. It had a strip of cloth on the spine, but the rest was cardboard. She expected all that. "If a university press had published the book," she wrote in her diary, "I would have had a fine clothbound book with an attractive dust jacket, but I would have paid for all that in sales. Mine is the only book that I had ever seen where the title is written on a twirling pizza. To some that might appear gimmicky: to me, it's clever, very clever indeed."

Thanks to several pre-publication reviews, to good publicity, and to the splendid performance of *Editors and Their Turkeys*, A. P. Goe's *Twirling Men* got off to a tremendous start.

In early October, she forwarded three copies to Royalle College: one for the library and the other two for the Lynpeex and Toyzol families. A brief letter accompanied the books. The letter states:

> Dear Tim and Bob:
>
> Here it is at last. Hope you enjoy it. Thanks for all your help and cooperation. The minute I receive the first royalty check on it, I shall designate it for Royalle College, and I'll sign it and mail it to you guys at once.
>
> You'll note that I carefully incorporated all the changes that you had so kindly asked me to consider making after you had read the manuscript. Remember what I told you on the phone: I made all the changes cheerfully. They improved the book.
>
> All other income—from paperback rights, film rights, translation rights etc.—will also come your way.
>
> Cheers,
>
> Alice

Immediately after receiving the books, Lynpeex and Toyzol called Alice and thanked her. They also sent her two separate thank you cards, and each enclosed pictures of their families with the cards.

Both men began at once to read the entire novel. Lynpeex finished reading it in a day—a long day—but it took his sidekick a week. Both were pleased with her witty and imaginative portrayal of their actions and of life at their college.

When Lynpeex finished reading the novel, he called Toyzol, who was watching the *Tonight Show Starring Johnny Carson*, and told him of his plan to invite Alice to be the college's commencement speaker in late May. "After all," Lynpeex said, "she's an accomplished author who had already visited and liked the campus, and after reading this novel and knowing what we know about her, I'm sure she'll give a great address."

"Go for it, man," Toyzol said. "She'll love the invitation."

The next day, Lynpeex called Alice, and she cheerfully accepted. "But let me tell you, Tim," she said: "I'll give an unconventional speech."

"That'll be fine with us," Lynpeex said. "Can't wait to see you again—and with your permission, we'll alert the media."

"But please," she said, "don't mention the donation I gave the college in introductory remarks or in a news release. My publisher and I would, however, appreciate mention of my books."

"We usually bestow upon our graduation speaker an honorary doctorate," Lynpeex said. "I trust that'll be acceptable to you."

"Absolutely—*not*," she said. "Now, if you're inviting Father Hesburgh of Notre Dame, then an honorary degree would be proper. That fine priest has many honorary degrees, more degrees than a thermometer. But in case you're wondering: I'm no Father Hesburgh, and I would appreciate it if you don't send me on an identity crisis."

Lynpeex laughed and said, "Fine with us, Mrs. Goe. We'll push your books and stay away from the degrees and mention of the donation."

"My publisher would love that, Tim," she said. "If the speech is memorable and if the media is there, it might translate into sales for my books. A writer has got to help push her books, you see."

"You know best," Lynpeex said. "We'll also help."

After they concluded the telephone conversation, Alice spoke to herself: "I want to give a speech that'll get my books in the news, a speech that'll get on the wire services and help sell more books. I want to write a speech that *will be* quoted in its entirety."

That was the challenge she gave herself. She had many months to think about the speech. She remembered the Frenchman Blaise Pascal, who was a philosopher, a mathematician, and a scientist. She remembered that Pascal once wrote a long letter to a friend and attached a postscript to it. In the postscript, he noted: "I'm sorry I wrote such a long letter; I didn't have time to write a shorter one." She had plenty of time to write a short speech.

— ☙ —

Two days before commencement, Lynpeex drove to the Pittsburgh airport to pick up Alice. The minute he saw her, he waved. When she got closer, he hugged and greeted her: "It's *so good* to see you, Mrs. Goe."

"I'm *so glad* that's the case," she said, smiling.

As the two drove to the college campus in West Virginia, he asked her if she would like to stay in the bed-and-breakfast inn where she and Frank had stayed during the Virginia Woolf conference, or if she would like to stay in the guest room in the president's house.

She opted for the bed-and-breakfast place near Mountaineer Hall in the hopes of connecting with fond memories of the literary conference. "Hope you're not offended by my request," she told Lynpeex.

"Not at all," he said. "We simply want you to be *very* happy."

A stage for commencement was set up in the college's football stadium. There, Lynpeex gave a flowery introduction to "our *Spiffy* lover from the Great Plains." Alice got up, walked to the podium, turned and looked at the president, said "Thank you, Dr. Lynpeex," and continued:

> This year as usual, many commencement speakers will credit Winston Churchill with a *stupid* remark.
>
> The speakers will exhort graduates: "Always remember the words of Winston Churchill: *Never give up on your dreams, never, never, never, never give up.*"
>
> That's Churchill out of context! In context, he said: *Never give in. Never give in. Never, never, never, never—in nothing, great or small, large or petty—never give in, except to convictions of honor and good sense.*"
>
> Churchill was smart enough to qualify his remark. He said, "*except* to convictions of honor and good sense."
>
> Many speakers often misquote Churchill's words, and they leave out the "*except*" part.
>
> That's sad. It's like claiming that the Bible says: "There is no God." The Bible *does say that.* But in context, it says: "The *fool* has said in his heart: *There is no God.*"
>
> May divine wisdom inform—your "*excepts.*"

Alice pronounced her last sentence with authority, splicing it with a long pause. She stared at the audience for five seconds, but refused to use what she felt was "the anemic and hollow *thank you* remark that insecure speakers often dribble at the end of rambling and dull orations." Then she headed back to her seat next to the college's president.

A stunned Lynpeex stood and hugged Alice and whispered in

her left ear, "Great speech, Mrs. Goe." He marched to the podium, readjusted the tilt of the microphone, and leaned forward. Then he turned, looked at Alice, and said: "I know your speech is shorter than Lincoln's 'Gettysburg Address'—certainly shorter, much shorter, than my introduction."

— ❦ —

At a private dinner that evening, Alice, Lynpeex, and Gloria, his wife who had prepared a dish of vegetarian lasagna, touched on all sorts of topics.

At one point, Alice told the couple that she had considered writing her adventures not as a novel, but as a work of creative nonfiction. After saying that, she quickly assured Lynpeex: "If I did that, Tim, I would've asked for your permission and approval, of course, given the sensitive nature of the entire matter."

"Had you done that, Mrs. Goe, what title would you have given to the book?" Gloria asked. "I'm curious."

"As a matter of fact, I had a tentative title for it."

"And that was?" Lynpeex asked.

"*Small-Town Philanthropist*, and for a subtitle, I thought: *An Elderly Widow Beats the Wit Out of Two Male Fundraisers*."

"*Hyphen* would've loved that title as much as I do," a smiling Lynpeex said. "But I'm sure happy you decided to go with *Twirling Men*, and I love the fact that it's doing so well."

At another stage in the dinner conversation, Alice, alluding to her commencement address, spoke directly to Gloria: "I hope people don't take the central thrust of my address the wrong way. Maybe I should've developed my main point with illustrations. For example: if a boy dreams of becoming an NFL quarterback, and if he tries and tries but has major difficulties throwing a tight spiral at the high school level, should he keep trying and trying? Or should he *give up* his dream and go in pursuit of something else?"

"I'd say, try something else," Gloria responded.

"Agreed," Lynpeex said.

"Wouldn't pursuing something else," Alice said, "constitute what the great Winston Churchill in his wise *except* refers to as *good sense*?"

"I hear you, Mrs. Goe," Gloria said. "I like your reasoning."

"And this reasoning," Alice added, "applies to many graduates who might wish to be aerospace engineers or neurosurgeons or astronauts or Sumo wrestlers or, heavens forbid, first-novelists with big publishers. Sometimes giving up on these noble pursuits makes *good sense*."

"Sure does," Gloria said, remembering her Hollywood aspirations.

As they continued to eat, Alice asked Lynpeex a question that fascinated Gloria. "If the head of the *Playboy* enterprises, Hugh Hefner, decides to give your school seventy million dollars with no strings attached, would you as president recommend that the board of trustees of Royalle College accept the gift?"

"You say no strings attached?" Lynpeex said. "None whatsoever?"

"Yes, none," Alice said, smiling. "Only old ladies attach strings."

"In other words," Gloria smiled and added while glancing at Alice, "you don't have to build the Hugh Hefner Memorial dorms on campus."

"There's no need to do that," Alice said, smiling. "But here's the catch: the college *must issue* a news release about the gift."

"I tell you what," Lynpeex said. "As a devout Roman Catholic in good standing with our church, I'll gladly go before our board, composed of men and women from various denominations, Catholic and otherwise, and I'll enthusiastically urge them to accept the generous gift by saying: *The money is the Lord's money, and the devil has had it long enough!*"

— ❧ —

In its coverage of Royalle College's commencement, the local paper printed Alice's entire speech and added some biographical elements on the "elderly and accomplished writer from the Sunflower State."

A reporter for one of the wire services picked up and re-worked the story that had appeared in the Royallestown paper. She called Alice, interviewed her, and obtained lots of information about her published books *Editors and Their Turkeys* and *Twirling Men*: information that the reporter assured Alice—"I *will* weave into the story."

At one point during the telephone conversation, the reporter asked: "Is that the shortest speech you had ever given?"

Alice hesitated slightly and said, "Yes."

Numerous newspapers throughout the country ran the wire-service story under various headlines. One read: "Churchill's Forgotten *Except*." Another headline proclaimed: "Shortest Commencement Address Ever?" A third headline printed in a small-town paper in western Nebraska stated: "A Brief Octogenarian's Graduation Speech." A fourth headline from a paper in New Hampshire noted: "The Churchill Few People Know."

In the story, Alice is quoted as saying: "The world would be a better place and many persons' lives would be enriched if we heed the wisdom in Churchill's *except*."

The editor of the *News-Free Gazette* in Samsville called the director of public relations at Royalle College and asked for a printout of the remarks that President Lynpeex had used in introducing Alice.

The director, using the office's newly purchased fax machine, sent a copy of the president's remarks to the editor who counted the words in those remarks and compared the total with the words in the speech. The "introductory remarks were more than twice as long as Alice's 148-word speech." The editor noted this much in his article on the speech.

Newspaper accounts of Alice's speech helped sales of her books. One day in early June, Alice's editor at *Garvin, Akers & Sheridan* called and told her: "We're all very pleased with *Twirling Men's* performance so far. Now that you've earned back your entire forty-five thousand dollar advance, you'll be receiving royalty checks in the months ahead. Congratulations again."

Twirling Men remained in hardcover for its first three years. Then a paperback edition was printed. On the Christmas after the college had received the donation of two million dollars, Lynpeex and Toyzol started a tradition of sending Alice two separate Christmas greetings. Lynpeex would send his first, and a week later, Toyzol's card would follow.

Both gentlemen also noted her birthday. Every year, the two would go to the campus bookstore, purchase a card and a thoughtful memento of Royalle College, and send them to her.

— ☙ —

Alice was aging gracefully, and she had other publishing plans that she frequently shared with women from her writing group.

Jack continued to write poetry, and thanks to Alice's influence, he started to explore his storytelling gifts.

Alice also had to do something with her house.

CHAPTER FORTY-TWO

ONE MORNING IN THE WINTER OF '87—A LITTLE
more than a year following the publication of *Twirling Men*—Alice
sat in the kitchen of her house on Main Street. She sat and looked
at the snow parachuting past a leafless maple tree and settling in
the spacious yard.

She waited for Jack to take a break from his cleaning tasks, and
while waiting she had a daydream of a long, long life. She attrib-
uted that dream to her genes (her parents had reached the age of
ninety) and to her reasonably good health, nurtured by an alcohol-
free vegetarian diet that she had started to keep while in college
and by plenty of light but regular physical exercise.

She exercised by walking everywhere in town: walking to the
bakery almost daily, walking to the bank, pulling a wire cart and
walking to the grocery store, walking to the library. "When your
lovely town is only a two-square mile on flat land," she once told
Lisa, "you should always walk everywhere—summer or fall, winter
or spring. Always."

Alice was born in the closing years of the nineteenth century,
and she felt, if all went well, she could live through the twentieth
century and into the twenty-first. That would make her one of those
rare persons to have lived in three centuries.

"If the time comes when I have to go to the nursing home," she wrote in her diary—after she had distributed the seven million dollars with no fanfare or publicity in order to safeguard her coveted privacy—"then I would do what most of my friends from our women's club had done. I would enter the nursing home and surrender to the place the checks I'm receiving from the Social Security office."

Samsville's sparsely populated home encouraged that arrangement. "From what I understand," Alice added in her diary entry, "the Manor is pleased with all the local people who come to it. After all, we're living in small-town Kansas, and an occupied room with adequate pay is a lot better than an empty room with no pay. Given the economy of our region, this is convincing reasoning, I trust."

In time, Alice had her book collection moved to the Carnegie Library. She also gave the library her desk, her manual and electric typewriters that she had used early in her literary career, and the seventeen paintings—two of which are abstracts—in her house. Four of those paintings were bought in 1927 from artists in the Latin Quarter in Paris.

— ❧ —

On Saturday October 19, 1991, Alice invited Lisa and Jack to her house for morning coffee. That day she asked them if they would be interested in "buying" her house and all the furniture in it. They said they would. Alice insisted on an incredibly low price for the house.

The price was so low that the Jaycubsons felt extremely uncomfortable agreeing to it. While the three talked about it, Lisa said, "Some people bargain and bargain when they buy a house, trying to bring the price down. We're de-bargaining, trying to bring the price up, way up where it should be to appear fair, as it were."

"Some people," Jack added, "want an arm and a leg for a house, but Mrs. Goe doesn't—"

337 S. SAL HANNA

"Even want a pinkie for hers," Alice said. "I want to give it to the two of you. You've been so good to me all these years."

Two months earlier, the house next door to Alice's was sold for ninety-two-thousand dollars. The new neighbor, a retired farmer, widower, and gun enthusiast, moved in and placed on the front lawn his security system's sign—a white board, the size of a briefcase, with red letters on it. The sign, nailed to a long stake, had four words painted in all caps:

BAN IDIOTS
NOT GUNS

Noticing that sign, Lisa said, "If we buy your house—and please don't misunderstand me, Mrs. Goe, because I say this tongue-in-chee—"

"A good place for a human tongue," Alice interrupted.

"Then we too can plant on our lawn a sign that says in bold letters:

TWO IDIOTS
WITH GUNS
LIVE HERE

That'll make for a refreshing," Lisa added, "meet-and-greet gathering."

"Totally," Alice deadpanned. "Witty signs make good neighbors."

"Hey, you two," Jack said, "this sign and the one Lisa imagines in front of two houses could make for a captionless cartoon in a magazine."

"And if one insists on having a caption," Lisa added, "Mrs. Goe's *Witty signs make good neighbors* could be used." The three laughed.

The fair-market value of Alice's house was ninety-six thousand dollars, and the three agreed on a token price of ten thousand. Alice didn't want to see the money, but she insisted that the Jaycubsons commit to give the money to their church in weekly increments of hundred dollar bills.

"For about two years," Alice told them, "you'll have to take with you to church every Sunday one of our Founding Fathers, the beloved deist, Benjamin Franklin. I prefer—no, I insist—you do that rather than write a check. Okay?"

The Jaycubsons laughed and agreed to the deal and the request, in Lisa's words, "with joyful reluctance." They shook hands and hugged.

— ✧ —

Having sold the house, Alice at the age of ninety-three moved to The Manor, the only nursing home in Samsville.

The Manor had many empty rooms. Jack and Lisa would visit her frequently, and they would enjoy caring for her. Lisa would often read to her books written during the first half of the twentieth century, and she would do so for two reasons: one, she loved Alice; two, Lisa had not read many literary books, and she felt it would be an educational experience.

Alice's hearing declined slightly, but her eyesight remained strong enough for her to do some reading (and writing) on her own. She kept her yearly subscriptions to *The New Yorker*, *The Paris Review*, and even the *National Lampoon*.

She also kept her subscription to the *National Review* edited by William F. Buckley Jr., a hero of hers. She watched him regularly on PBS's *Firing Line*. Alice enjoyed Buckley's wit, accent, mannerisms, and ironic style, and unlike her college-educated friends in Samsville, she always read thoughtful conservative *and* liberal thinkers.

She donated the four forums to The Manor's library, making it perhaps the only manor in a small town in Kansas, or on the Great Plains, for that matter, with issues of *The Paris Review*.

In Samsville of the nineteen-eighties and early nineties, a social movement, small but significant, began to take shape—much as it had done in other parts of the country. The movement intrigued

Alice, but it would have disappointed, even infuriated, her late husband, Frank.

Parents throughout the nation began to homeschool their children, keeping them away from public and private schools: Protestant, Catholic, or even non-religious ones. In Samsville, the ABC School (short for the Academy of Baptist Conservatives), which attracted students from nearby towns, saw their enrollment decline, thanks to homeschooling.

"I can understand homeschooling," she told Jack one day, "if one lives in a dangerous drug-infested neighborhood in big cities like Wichita or Chicago or New York or Cleveland or Los Angeles or Detroit, but I wonder how appropriate homeschooling is to small towns like ours. My dear Frank, as you know, was a public school teacher, and this rising homeschool movement would've made him furious. As for me, homeschooling is a choice parents make, and it could be a well-advised choice for some. And I suspect homeschoolers these days do what Frank and I did often in our school days out in western Kansas."

"What's that?"

"Memorize," she said. "It would be unheard of these days to do in *public* schools what we did: memorize long sections from the King James translation of the Bible. We also memorized classic poetry and even some prose. Milton's sonnet on his blindness is one that I can still recite."

Alice recited the entire sonnet for Jack, and she recited Psalm 139, Lincoln's Gettysburg Address, and much to his surprise and delight: the prologue to Tennyson's *In Memoriam*.

"How impressive is that," Jack exclaimed. "Wait till I tell Lisa about all this. She'll be impressed."

CHAPTER FORTY-THREE

LIKE OTHER RESIDENTS IN THE CLEAN AND WELL-kept Manor, Alice had a private phone in her room. She would use it on rare occasions to call her friends in town, or to answer their infrequent calls.

But telemarketers in the nineteen-nineties would always call her number, much as they would call the numbers of many other retired and elderly folks living in Samsville-like manors or in their homes in large and small towns throughout the country.

On a rainy Friday evening in May, Alice felt she'd had enough grief from unsolicited and unwanted calls. She dealt with her discomfort by confronting the telemarketers (usually males) in a unique way.

First, she asked her few friends who would occasionally call her to stop calling for at least one month, and she encouraged them to visit her in person. She informed them: "I plan to ask a young male friend to place on my answering machine a rude message to those annoying telemarketers."

Then she gave Jack a copy of the message and some homework. "I'd like you to consider listening to samples of rap music," she told him, "because if all goes well, the message should sound like a slice from that genre—a slice calculated to end all those calls."

After Jack did his homework, he came to her room to record the message, and Alice exclaimed: "Now let's see if you can imitate a gifted, energetic, loud, lively, and angry rap artist from Detroit. The art here is to stimulate a *playful flicker of fear* in a pesky caller." The message:

> Thanks to you and other
>
> telemarket callers and **asses,**
>
> a judge in **court**
>
> ordered me to **report**
>
> to the mother of all **classes.**
>
> Do you know what that **is?**
>
> a class—worthless as **piss,**
>
> devoid of **bliss,**
>
> a class without **category,**
>
> judge says it's **mandatory.**
>
> They call the **class**
>
> *Anger Management*—
>
> for those who vowed to **kill**
>
> the harassment by unleashing
>
> their will in a lethal **drill.**

Alice believed that in a big-city newspaper when an article is written on a controversial subject, the article gives rise to a buzz. But in small-town America, the reverse happens: a buzz is started about an unusual (or peculiar) action, and that buzz usually leads to an article in the newspaper. This was the case with her message on the answering machine.

The message led the *News-Free Gazette* to do a front page feature story with a picture of Alice and Jack, her freshly anointed rap artist with the Elvis-pompadour hairpiece. Written by *Hot-Type,* the nickname of the newspaper's editor-reporter, the engaging article quotes Alice who claims: "Even telemarketers could use a bit of humor every now and then."

The article reproduces the entire message and places in bold letters those rhyming words that rap artists love to pounce on. The feature also devotes five paragraphs to *Editors and Their Turkeys* and nine paragraphs to her most recent book, *Twirling Men.*

When one of the major wire services picked up the article, Alice told Jack, "I'm so happy to hear that the article is running in numerous papers throughout the country—and mostly in the Sunday editions."

The article gave Alice's two books, which were still in print, new life, much to the delight of the books' publisher in New York.

"Sales of *Editors and Their Turkeys,*" a person at the publishing house wrote and told Alice, "have increased substantially, and sales of *Twirling Men* have hit the ceiling again and are heading through the roof. We plan on printing new editions of both books." That pleased Alice. The letter concludes by noting: "Of course, we attribute all this to you and the unusual way you're able to get publicity for your books. You did that with your graduation address earlier and now this. You can't buy the kind of publicity that feature stories on the wire services can bring to a book. We're all so very happy for you—and us."

After reading the letter, Alice declared to Jack: "Well, well, what do you know! The bizarre in book marketing works again. Funny what an answering machine message can lead to these days, eh?"

— ❧ —

Much to Alice's disappointment, Jack remained unemployed, a smart college-educated philosophy major (now rap artist) living in a small town in Kansas. When word processing came to Samsville,

Jack taught Alice how to use the computer to write her prose and poetry and letters. The promises of the new technology thrilled her.

She would often exclaim to Jack: "How in the world did we ever get along with those manual typewriters or even with electric ones? Word processors to us now are like what yellow pencils, the word processors of yesteryear, were to white paper."

"Interesting comparison," Jack said.

"While we're talking about computers," Alice said, "let me tell you what I told Martha after she had bought for the library three brand-new color computers from the Radio Shack in Wichita."

"Lisa and I thought," Jack said, "that those additions to the library would improve service and get the library moving into the digital age, and we felt Martha ought to be congratulated for going in that direction at her age. In fact, Lisa sent her a thank you note for doing that."

"Oh, Lisa is always so thoughtful, Jack," Alice said. "You're blessed to have her for a spouse."

"Thank you," he said smiling. "And she's blessed indeed to have me—and the *Denial* she made me buy."

"A couple of months ago when the brand-new computers were delivered to the library building," Alice said, "Martha was so scared that someone might break into the library and steal them, that she sat here while visiting with me and we talked about what could be done to secure them. She wanted, as I remember, to find a way to have them chained or bolted to the tables, but I discouraged her from doing that."

"Why?"

"Because out here in our small town that's virtually free of crime, that would look too barbaric, I thought."

"Did Martha agree?"

"She did," Alice said. "In the end, she used a way I suggested—a way that I felt would work just as well as a chain. And I was pleased when she saw wisdom in my suggestion, and even more pleased when my strange way was tested."

"Oh, what did you suggest?"

"I told her to print in large, dark, bold letters a sign and tape it to both sides of each computer," Alice said. "If you want the sign to look professional and authoritative, it should be laminated, and it should state the following:

PLEASE REMEMBER
TO DISCONNECT
THIS COMPUTER'S
THEFT ALARM
BEFORE MOVING IT
FROM THIS ROOM.
THANK YOU

And you know what?" Alice added, "Martha followed my idea, and the sign—a gentle reminder and *not* a nasty threat—worked."

"How do you know that?"

"Four months after they bought the computers," Alice said, "the room in which they are located was scheduled to be painted. And the workers who were there to paint moved all the books and art pieces and tables and chairs and other furniture out of the room, but they went to Martha's office and asked her to come and disconnect the theft alarm. They said they didn't know how to disconnect it, and they didn't want the alarm to go off and disturb the patrons."

"Were there theft alarms on the computers?"

"Of course not," Alice said. "But those workers didn't know that. So, Martha told them: *That's been done already. Please feel free to go ahead and move them.* And they did."

Jack touched Alice's hand and said, "Even from your room in the

Manor, you're helping make life a bit more civilized for the rest of us in Samsville." He smiled as he added, "In a manner of speaking, you *are* Samsville's moral wizard."

— ❧ —

Jack stood up and told Alice, "Maybe I should be on my way home. Lisa wants me to cut the grass today."

"Before you leave," she said, "I'd love it if you read for me Psalm 46 from the King James translation of the Bible." She pointed to the Bible resting under a lampshade on the small nightstand next to her bed. "Frank gave me that Bible on our wedding day. I still cherish it, even though the print in it now appears mighty small."

Jack read the entire psalm, and he read it slowly and in a loud voice. When he finished, she asked: "Did you notice the command in verse ten of that psalm? It tells us: *Be still and know that I am God.* Many people in our culture are always on the go, doing this and that, hurrying from place to place, spinning like dogs trying to catch their tails. In my opinion," she said as she stood up to give him a goodbye hug, "we all need to be still and meditate for at least ten minutes a day—unless we're very busy, of course. And if that's the case, then we need to be still and meditate for a much *longer* period."

"Oh, the wisdom of old age," Jack said, as he hugged Alice.

"Not quite."

"What do you mean?"

"It's age-old wisdom: it's God's eternal wisdom."

"I see."

"There you go again with your *I see,*" she said, and placed her right arm around his waist. "I'd rather hear that than *I disagree.*"

"If I do disagree, Mrs. Goe, I'd certainly tell you. We developed an honest relationship from way back."

"Sure did," she said. "And I'm grateful for that. Here's something I'd like you to remember long after I'm gone. It's a thought based on my personal observation."

"I always like that."

"And it's this," she added. "An adult believer with a sixth-grade education, like my father, can find the Bible to be intellectually and spiritually satisfying, and a highly respected poet, say, T. S. Eliot or an accomplished Yale professor (and for an example, I'll use one whose books I love to read, Jaroslav Pelikan) can also find the Bible to be intellectually and spiritually satisfying. No other book that I know can do that. Not one. But the Bible can—and does."

"I'll have to think about that."

"While you're thinking," she said, "here's another idea for you to ponder. It comes from Dostoyevsky's *Brothers Karamazov* where he says: *Young man, be not forgetful of prayer. Every time you pray, if your prayer is sincere, there will be new feeling and new meaning in it, which will give you fresh courage, and you will understand that prayer is an education.* I often quoted that to my Frank when he was a young man; and here I'm quoting it to you in my old age."

— ☙ —

Almost daily, Jack would visit Alice in the Manor, and they would always have coffee together.

Lisa's teaching duties and her work with the drama group at the high school had consumed most of Lisa's time during the weekdays, but she would usually go with Jack on the weekends.

CHAPTER FORTY-FOUR

ONE SATURDAY MORNING WHEN LISA AND JACK were at the Manor to see Alice, they heard her make a peculiar remark.

Alice—ever the observant and witty woman—said to her beloved friends: "Today, our dear Lisa is dressed in her fashionable jeans that are torn but patched in places that aren't torn."

All three smiled, and Jack excused himself and went to run some errands in town and at Gluesiville, but Lisa stayed with Alice. Lisa sat next to her and listened to her speak about a book that she had seen discussed in a magazine article. The book, *A Father's Story*, is by Lionel Dahmer, the father of the serial killer, Jeffrey Dahmer, the cannibal who had lived in Milwaukee, Wisconsin. "This is a thoughtful article about a sad book dealing with a disgusting, repulsive, and horrible criminal whose ways are beyond our comprehension," Alice said.

"I wonder," Lisa said, "if that revolting Dahmer tragedy, a very disturbing tragedy, was on *Saturday Night Live*."

"Don't know," Alice said. "But I do know that our culture is so warped that it makes fun of tragedy, however devastating it is."

"You're right. Look at what *SNL* is doing now, week after week, with the O. J. Simpson murder. That's a real shame, isn't it?"

"Yes, it is," Alice said, "especially when you know that loved ones had been lost forever."

"Those comic programs on television show absolutely no mercy. They'll make hamburger out of every cow you can imagine. No sacred cows with them, you know. They'll even make fun of the pope."

"And that's always in bad taste," Alice said. "In my opinion, there should be some sacred cows in this world, I think."

"Hear, hear. I certainly agree with that."

"Now, please don't think I hate comedy," Alice said. "I love good comic programming, but I love it more when it's done with taste. Let's get back to that Dahmer tragedy and *Saturday Night Live*."

"Good idea."

"My thinking on that situation is this," Alice said. "If I were a writer for that popular show, I might've done something related *not* to the gruesome Dahmer murders—I have too much respect for the families of the victims. But I would've made fun of Dahmer himself—if that's possible: making fun of him without referring to his victims."

"How would you do that?"

"I'd show Dahmer in his prison cell," Alice said. "And I'd show him reading a famous book by a very famous American expatriate author, a macho American author."

"Who's that?"

"Ernest Hemingway," Alice replied. "And you know what that book would be?"

Lisa thought for a few seconds and then said, "No, I don't."

"C'mon, think," Alice told her. "If Jack were here, he'd come up with the correct title right away."

"Well, he's not here, and I don't know," Lisa said and felt slightly offended by Alice's remark. "I give up. Please tell me."

"Are you ready for this?" Alice asked. She paused, looked at Lisa's feet, and gradually moved her eyes up Lisa's entire body until the two women made eye contact. "I'd have him reading Hemingway's *Farewell to Arms*."

Lisa had a notion of snapping at Alice and saying: "That's sick, Mrs. Goe. That's absolutely sick, disgusting, and stupid." But Lisa held back that thought and refused to laugh. "That title," Lisa thought, "might be funny to Jack, and it might be diplomatic to laugh at Alice's comment, but I don't see it that way—not at all."

— ℰℐ —

Lisa recovered from her anger and offered to read to her elderly friend. Alice requested a selection from her favorite magazine.

"*The New Yorker* came in yesterday," Alice said. "Let's go over the cartoons first, and after laughing at those, you may read what appears to be interesting from the shorter pieces in the magazine. How's that?"

After Lisa flipped through the pages of the magazine and the two laughed at several cartoons, Lisa read from the magazine's early pages. Following that Alice said, "It seems to me the design of those early pages in *The New Yorker* hasn't changed in years."

"You know a lot more about that than I do," Lisa said. "And I believe you. I've always loved *The New Yorker*'s cartoons."

"Speaking of cartoons: if you want to make a little extra cash, you might consider sending the Hemingway-Dahmer-cartoon idea to the folks at *The New Yorker*. They might buy it. Who knows?"

"There's no way I'd do that, Mrs. Goe. That kind of humor doesn't appeal to me one bit—not one bit."

"Well, maybe Jack will do it," Alice said. "He's adventurous."

"And if he goes adventuring in that Hemingway-Dahmer domain,"

Lisa said, "he'll have one-heck-of-an-angry woman to deal with. If he thinks I'm bossy now, imagine how he'll feel if I'm bossy *and* angry."

Lisa didn't want her visit to end on the "angry woman" note, so she read a few psalms from the Bible to Alice, even though Alice's eyes remained good enough that she could still read—and write— on her own. And Alice frequently did both.

The two women enjoyed being together, but on rare occasions, Lisa felt uneasy with Alice's offbeat (almost wicked) humor. That day, Lisa felt that way. But Alice didn't want Lisa to leave angry at her, so she suggested other cartoon ideas to her.

"I've got three cartoon ideas that won't make you angry," Alice said. "Care to hear them before you leave?"

"Sure."

"A good cartoon idea," Alice said, "could be a sketch of a person washing his or her hands in the bathroom of an elegant restaurant in New York or Chicago or Wichita or any other big city. The sign, taped on the wall near the sink or the paper towels or the hot-air blowers, should state: *Employees must wash their hands before returning to work. Customers must wash their hands and faces.*"

Lisa laughed, and Alice said: "Another idea could be a captionless cartoon that shows a person in front of a hockey goal. The person should be a unique goalie—a massive Japanese Sumo wrestler."

"Intriguing," a smiling Lisa said.

"Last evening," Alice continued, "a fellow came to play his guitar and sing at *Friday Festivities*. Many of us went to listen; his performance gave me a cartoon idea."

"The six-foot-plus, middle-aged fellow with a tan Martin guitar and an *Arc de Triomphe* moustache played and played, and on the table in front of him was a large glass jar—a huge jar—with a few dollars in it. And you know what was written in all caps in red, white, and blue and taped to the outside of the jar?"

"What?"

"The word TIPS," Alice said. "Yes, he wanted TIPS."

"That's a common sight with many performers around here and elsewhere. I've seen many artists with similar jars pleading for tips."

"And that's why I think it makes a good topic for a cartoon."

"What's funny in that?" Lisa asked.

"A person leaving the tip."

"Don't see humor in that."

"The humor," Alice said, "will be in having a person dropping in the see through jar *not* another dollar or five or even ten. All that paper money would be redundant, you see." Alice paused, then she added: "The person should be dropping in the jar a unique tip, a classic: one that would be the focus of the cartoon. Are you listening?"

Lisa leaned forward to listen with care, "I'm all ears."

"The cartoon, in my opinion, should show a person playing the guitar and singing, and another person near the tip jar with a deposit in her hand. The deposit should be an index card with one word on it, and that word should be lettered in thick, large, dark caps: IMPROVE."

CHAPTER FORTY-FIVE

In the mid-nineteen-nineties, Jack—Alice's one-time cleaning lad, yard worker, coffee partner, literary critic, and talk-therapist—became a technology trainer.

He introduced Alice to the increasingly popular word-processing technology and to the dawn and promises of the Internet.

One afternoon, after Jack had finished setting up an e-mail account for Alice at the manor, he went home, to her old house on Main Street and sent her a brief e-mail that began: "Hello, Mrs. Goe: Your DCL here."

It was the first e-mail in her Inbox, and for a subject heading he wrote: "Farewell to the Ink Age." When she opened the e-mail and read it, she was puzzled by the words that followed the greeting. She felt the letters DCL referred to some computer jargon, but she wasn't sure. So, she called and asked Jack what they stood for.

"Aha," Jack told Lisa after talking to Alice, "I wonder if Mrs. Goe is at last beginning to lose her sharpness?"

"Why do you say that?" Lisa asked.

"She couldn't figure out what DCL stood for in my e-mail."

"I can't either," Lisa said.

"They're the initials for words she used in referring to me with her friends at club. From what I understand: I was her *Deluxe Cleaning Lad.*"

Lisa laughed and said, "Well, with your education and all—you're a lot more than an ordinary cleaning lad."

"Guess so," a despondent Jack agreed.

Alice's response to that first e-mail led her to feel that the new electronic way of passing information is, as she later told Jack, "likely to make writers, editors, literary agents, and others forget about the phone or the printed letter and embrace the promises of the blinking cursor. It looks like e-mail will become the voice of our fingers."

She replied to Jack's e-mail by sending him four ideas for possible cartoons for *The New Yorker.* (She was always looking for ways to help him make a little extra money.) The first idea states: "Draw a picture of a couple sitting in a booth at a small-town diner and have a person speaking the caption that should say: *This is a good down-scale restaurant.*"

And in the second idea, Alice suggests a captionless cartoon that should have the following: "Draw a sketch of a muscular-looking man, holding a pointed unexploded copper bullet in the two fingers and thumb of his right hand, and draw the man placing the bullet between his teeth and biting it."

For the third idea, Alice wrote: "Sketch two persons standing near a casket at a funeral home. One person should tell the other in the words of the caption: *Old Man Lester: he could sure dim a room with his frown.*"

And the fourth idea has "a couple sitting in their living room reading. One interrupts the other by asking in the words of the caption: *Honey, is there a difference between having an affair and meeting the needs of a person whose spouse had outsourced sex?*"

Alice hoped Jack would seriously consider submitting these

ideas for consideration by *The New Yorker*, and if they reject them ("an act they're good at," she'd often tell herself,) then he should consider other magazines, newspapers, or even literary journals that publish cartoons.

Before long, Jack found himself introducing Alice to the ways of the dawning Internet: to the presence of websites, to the notions of surfing the Net, to enlarging the print on the screen, and to the availability of numerous resources for all age groups.

Alice—who continued to have a sharp and witty mind well into her nineties—found the Internet to be full of promises for writers, but to people like her late Frank, she saw the Internet as a threatening place. "To paranoid people like my beloved Frank," Alice told Jack, "the Internet is equivalent to hospice care."

— ℰℐ —

Someday, Lisa or Jack might write about Alice's years in the nursing home. "For even there," Lisa says, "Alice remained witty and creative, thoughtful and kind, wise, winsome, and imaginative."

One Sunday afternoon during a visit to the Manor, Lisa told Alice about the sad situations with her two brothers. "Bill is having marital and financial problems. His wife left him and their ten-year-old son; she went to Topeka to live, in Bill's words, *with an old high school flame, a dude who reconnected with her thanks to our newest curse: the Internet.*"

Dan, her other brother who never married, has problems with bill collectors. He works full-time as an orderly in the Gluesiville hospital, living paycheck to paycheck.

Aware of Dan's situation, one fellow from Wichita approached Dan and told him: "I've got this great plan that'll get those annoying bill collectors off your back, and all you have to do is pay me. I'll take care of all your debts." The man explained the plan in detail to Dan, who shared it with his sister.

Lisa, who respected Alice's wisdom, fleshed out the fellow's plan to Alice and asked her: "Should Dan take this unsolicited offer?"

Alice asked a few questions, assessed the responses, and told Lisa, "If I were Dan, I'd refuse the offer. It's full of hidden traps." Alice paused then added, "I know the times are tough, but at least Dan is gainfully employed, and at this stage in his life, it's better—much better—for him to swat a lot of little flies than fight a big elephant."

"Got you," Lisa said. "Thanks for your advice. I'll pass it on."

— ❧ —

One sunny morning, Jack was doing part-time yard work for the Samsville Manor. He was asked by his boss to use a new gas engine leaf blower that the Manor had purchased. Jack followed orders.

He strapped on his back the small yellow engine, and he turned it on full blast. It was a noisy engine, and the fumes from it blew and swirled behind and in front of his head. In his right hand, Jack held a wide firm plastic hose that was about a yard long. The hose would blow the leaves into a neat pile. Then Jack would point the hose at the newly formed pile, and he'd blow the pile away to another area. Moments later, he'd point the hose again, and he'd launch the pile to yet another area.

Alice sat on a rocking chair at the Manor's porch and watched Jack, who had strapped the bright-yellow machine on his back as if he were still a college student carrying a book-bag. That machine, Alice thought, will now add more noise and fume pollution to our peaceful little town on the Great Plains.

Later she told Jack, "We'll be losing something special if we abandon the bamboo rake or the metal rake for the leaf-blowing machine. This machine may be compared to the modern-day *e-scroll*. But the hardback book, like the rake or the spoon, is a perfected technology. The book, you see, is the enduring and noble legacy of the ink age."

CHAPTER FORTY-SIX

WHEN ALICE REACHED THE AGE OF ONE HUNDRED and three, the staff at the Manor, working closely with the staff at the Samsville library, held a modest birthday party in her honor.

Her friend Martha Stuneburn, who was then in her early eighties, helped organize the party. Martha had retired from her work at the library but remained active in her church and community.

The birthday party was held in the Reference Room of the library, the room with the stained-glass windows and the blond-oak tables, the same room where special meetings of the Women's Literary Association—such as guest speakers, film viewing, high teas—would be held.

At the party, Alice slouched in a Victorian armchair and offered a few remarks in which she said: "Thanks to the good Lord, my days have been long in the land of the living, starting at the close of the nineteenth century, spanning the twentieth, and now into the twenty-first. I have lived in three centuries. All those days—except for the times when my dearly departed Frank and I would travel—were spent in our beloved Kansas."

Three weeks after that party, on a hot day in late July, shortly after a dust storm had swirled outside the Manor, the end came.

Years earlier, Alice had entered into her word processor a will. She printed two copies, signed them, and placed them in two envelopes. She sealed the envelopes, signed over the sealed part, and wrote in red ink: "To be opened the day I die. Alice Princeton Goe." She gave an envelope to Jack and Lisa and kept the other on her bookshelf.

"The day I die," she told Jack, "please take the sealed copy of the will and open the envelope in the presence of our Methodist pastor."

Jack followed Alice's request, and the pastor agreed to carry out all her wishes. The will states:

Having a sound mind, I write this document: my *Will*. When I die, I would like to see the following take place under the direction of Lisa and Jack Jaycubson, two of my long-time friends. They have in their possession a sealed and signed envelope containing this document.

First: I refuse to prove my death by having my body presented as evidence for public viewing at a funeral home. I request the workers at the Niselly-Donne Funeral Home to prepare my body for immediate burial.

Second: please place in the newspaper an obituary that lists my date of birth and death. The obituary should simply state the following: "Alice Princeton Goe authored three books published by the New York-based house: *Garvin, Akers & Sheridan*. The titles of her books are these: *Editors and Their Turkeys* (creative nonfiction), *Twirling Men* (a seriocomic novel), and *Waiting for the Mail* (poetry). Her book output is so meager, she often joked, it should guarantee her inclusion in the hardback edition of *Who's Who in Merited Oblivion*. She also published short stories, poems, and essays in literary journals here and abroad. The Carnegie Library in town had requested and received all of A. P. Goe's unpublished work. Throughout her stay on earth, Alice loved the Bread of Life—and always prayed for peace."

Third: the money in my only bank account at the Samsville State Bank should be divided in the following way. All the funeral expenses should be paid. What remains should be divided this way: thirty percent goes to Samsville's Methodist Church; thirty percent to the Carnegie Library in town; and thirty percent to our town's Manor, where I lived my last years. The remaining ten percent should go to the Jaycubsons. The living tithe to the Lord, the dead to friends.

Fourth: I request that my funeral service be simple. In the church service, I would like Jack Jaycubson to read whatever Holy Scripture pastor would assign to him. I want absolutely no eulogies. None. That's God's job. He'll say, "Well done, good and faithful servant"—if the good Lord feels I deserve that.

Fifth: I would love it if people attending the service in Samsville will get to hear two songs from the poignant albums of Kate Wolf, who I feel is the best poet-singer of the twentieth century. She died at forty-four but left us a rich legacy. The songs I hope Pastor will consider playing are in the album *Close to You*, released in 1981. The songs' titles: "Love Still Remains" and "Eyes of a Painter," a song Frank would have loved.

— ☙ —

At the service, the pastor stated: "Many will say—and some have already said this—*Alice's soul is now in a better place*. That's partly correct. I say partly because her soul is *not* only in a better place. Her soul, my sisters and brothers in Christ, is in the *best* place."

The pastor had copied both Kate Wolf songs onto a tape and placed the cassette player on the podium. He pushed the play button and she began singing, "Love Still Remains."

After that, the pastor told the hushed crowd in the packed church, "Alice also requested that I play for you another song by this great singer: 'Eyes of a Painter,' a song, she felt, her late Frank would have loved."

When the song ended, the pastor took a deep breath and exclaimed, "I don't know about you, but I love these words:

His school was the prairie, the sage, the wild berry

The quail, the wide-open sky

Now, my friends, thanks to Alice, I'm hooked. I plan to sit in my study and enjoy all of Kate Wolf's albums. She's an extraordinary talent."

Then he switched to literature. "As some of you know, Alice loved the work of T. S. Eliot. In his famous poem titled *The Waste Land*, Eliot writes of a corpse being planted. He doesn't use the word buried. In that context, permit me please to say: our beloved Alice will now be *planted* next to her beloved husband Frank in Samsville's Peaceful Acres."

Years before her death, Alice had implored Jack "to pick and design—with wicked creativity—my tombstone." In time, he did, and the result is a white marble slab, the shape of a yield sign but larger, set on a five-foot stone post. Her name is carved on the left slant of the triangle, her dates are on the right slant, and across the top, these words appear:

Staircase on the Prairie

— ❧ —

Alice was in her early nineties when she informed Jack of the six words ("A Naked Staircase on the Prairie") that she wished to have on her stone. "I know," she told him, "this *Dada*-like epitaph will stir up all sorts of controversy in our little town."

"Especially, the first two words," he said. He persuaded her to drop the first two, but she insisted on staying with the last four. "There will still be some controversy with the four words," Jack said, "but with that word *naked* out of there, the controversy won't be so bad."

"As a dead person, I'll be okay with controversy, I think," she said. "If—or when—the folks start to gossip, you, Lisa, and Martha will deal with that, and I'm certain you'll do it with a creative flair."

Sure enough, the minute the stone went up on a Tuesday in early August, the town's gossip switch was flicked on, and the mill ran nonstop. The epitaph's hidden meanings were pursued by citizens in the café, the bank, the bakery, the high school, the grocery store, the street corners, the tennis court, the ice cream stand, the kitchen tables, and the drugstore.

Lisa, sensible Lisa, urged Jack to consult Alice's pastor and ask him if he would allow Jack to speak for ten minutes during the Sunday morning service on the epitaph that lit up the gossip mill in town. "It'll be nice," Lisa told Jack, "if people stop looking for hidden meanings and allow the poor woman to rest in peace—in Peaceful Acres. You know, honey, we need to do something about that."

One Saturday afternoon, Lisa and Jack visited the Methodist pastor in his church office. The pastor liked the idea. "*Hot-Type* will probably be in church," the pastor said, "and he'll probably work some of your remarks into an article for the *News-Free Gazette*. You two might end the gossip."

In his remarks in church, Jack said: "With my deep and abiding respect to Mrs. Goe's gifted friends in the Women's Literary Association and to every citizen in town, allow me to say that as one who had cared for her house and yard for years, I came to know Alice very well. The four words that form the metaphor on her stone are calculated to create an eternal flame—not a flame of gas that results in an ongoing and costly gas bill , but a flame of air."

Jack paused, a long pause. He looked at the people in the pews, turned and glanced at the pastor sitting to his far right, and then added while speaking in a loud and distinct voice: "Half the words on the stone have the word *air* in them. If you look carefully, you'll note that the dots on the letter 'i' are not carved in the conventional-circle pattern, but they are carved in the shape of a flame. This means that our beloved Alice, a bestselling author, will live on as an eternal flame of air—a fresh and constant breeze on the prairie. We must *yield* to that thought, my friends—hence the shape of the sign."

Jack knew that Alice's immersion in modernity had given rise to her perplexing epitaph. Explaining all that—and the two words that were omitted—would have been difficult, and it would have given rise to more unfortunate speculation. So, he tapped his knowledge of Alice and came up with the flame explanation. It was Jack who had asked the carver of the stone to dot the "i" with a large and distinct flame-shaped design instead of a circle.

Jack's explanation would have pleased Alice in two ways. One, he refused to fabricate a story and, in effect, lie. Two, he defused the gossip by his cogent and creative take on the metaphor.

— ❧ —

As the pastor had predicted, *Hot-Type* wrote a front-page story in the newspaper. He quoted extensively from Jack's remarks, and he went out and took colored pictures of the gravestone (with tight shots of the flame) and printed several with the story on the front page. Lisa, Jack, the pastor, and others found *Hot-Type*'s work commendable.

Martha Stuneburn, the town's librarian emeritus, was overjoyed with Jack's presentation and *Hot-Type*'s article. She wrote a long letter to the editor in which she noted: "The epitaph that our Alice

Princeton Goe had written for herself (and that has been stimulating all the recent talk in town) is vintage Alice. Like some of her literary pursuits, the epitaph is on the enigmatic side . . ."

Martha added, "These days, our intellectuals speak and write about secular humanism and our post-modern culture, but our beloved Alice was lodged in modernity. And she loved being there . . . As a retired librarian and a long-time friend of Alice, I wish to affirm that she was—and through her writings will remain—our town's perpetual breeze on the Kansas prairie."

Perhaps the most surprising letter to the editor printed in the paper came from an assistant football coach at the high school. He wrote: "Many Samsville residents know that Alice's husband, Frank, played football in high school and college. Alice and Frank loved to watch some college football—and a great deal of professional football—on television. For years, I lived next door to them. We would often watch NFL games together and reminisce, while wood surrendered to flames in the fireplace, on the days of quarterback Johnny Unitas of the Baltimore Colts or Bart Starr of the Green Bay Packers or Bill Wade of the Chicago Bears or the ever so portly Lou Groza of the Cleveland Browns. Groza's work as a lineman and as a pouch-carrying placekicker had fascinated the Goes . . ."

The coach concluded his long letter by noting: "Alice also took interest in the Pittsburgh Steelers of the nineteen-seventies. She loved their handsome coach, Chuck Noll, and she liked their colorful logo. It's an abstract logo, placed on one side of the helmet (the only NFL team to do that), injecting the Steelers, in Alice's mind, with a touch of modernity."

— ❧ —

The most consequential letter sent to the newspaper was typed on a yellow unlined sheet. The writer's name and address were omitted.

Hot-Type and his part-time assistant speculated on who might have written the letter, but they failed to come up with a specific name.

At one point, *Hot-Type* told his assistant: "To me, the correct use of hyphens is the smoking gun that leads me to believe that the letter is written by one of Alice's college-educated colleagues in their literary club, but I don't have a specific name." The entire letter states:

Dear Editor:

All this talk about A. P. Goe's tombstone—its shape and the words on it—is small-town stupid.

Alice left us a beautiful legacy in all her writings. Now we honor her memory with an enduring and artfully designed stone.

Instead of seeing wisdom in her four-word poem: *Staircase on the Prairie*, many in town are offended by a tombstone that looks like a _ _ _ _ing yield sign.

Disgustingly yours,

A Long-Time Resident

P.S. It is beneath my dignity to use the f-word, but I dare you, Mr. *Hot-Type*, to exercise your freedom of the press and do two things: one, print this letter using the censored word; two, print the letter WITHOUT this postscript.

"I've been at this paper for forty-seven years," *Hot-Type* told Tommy, his part-time assistant who also worked part-time at Henry's, the grocery store, "and in all those years, we never printed—and, believe me, we were never *even tempted* to print—an unsigned letter."

"Oh," his assistant said.

"But we will indeed print this one."

"With the f-word?"

"Yes, sir," *Hot-Type* said and watched his surprised assistant drop his jaw, open his eyes wide while raising his eyebrows and wrinkling his forehead. "We'll assert our freedom, and I'll call it a career—and retire."

"*What!*" snapped a startled Tommy Wyse. He took a deep breath and in disbelief asked: "Did you just say—*retire*?"

"Yes," *Hot-Type* replied, "and the job will be yours. Printing this unsigned letter will lead many in town to call for my firing or resignation. I own the paper, so I can't be fired, but I can—and will—retire, and when you take over, you'll have the freedom to set the paper on whatever course you feel is appropriate for the twenty-first century."

"Thank you, *Hot-Type*!" Tommy exclaimed. "Goodbye, grocery store! Hello, newspaper!" Referring to his wife, he added, " My dear Amanda won't believe it. At last, a full-time job in the writing and editing field."

"Don't thank me," *Hot-Type* spoke softly as Tommy extended his tattooed arms and hugged his boss. "Thank the author who from her grave is stirring up all this. Our dear A. P. Goe just got you a job."

Tommy smiled and said, "When she was alive, she employed my good friend Jack, and now that she's dead, she gets me a job. Wow."

"If she had witnessed this entire spectacle happen to someone else, she would've found a way to work it all into her prose," *Hot-Type* asserted. "Alice was a remarkably creative woman who wasn't afraid of words."

"If you write your memoirs in the years ahead," the editor-elect told the retiring editor, "this whole situation is likely to appear in it."

"Righto. It'll make an intriguing chapter."

That evening at supper, a calm and happy Tommy told Amanda—a full-time bank clerk and a Samsville native—about the anonymous letter and *Hot-Type*'s response to it.

"That letter generated a major piece of good news for us," he said. "You always claimed: *One good word, strategically placed, can get you a job in a small town.* Now I see what you mean. In my case, the magic word that, in effect, led to my full-time job is—"

"*Retire*," she interrupted.

CHAPTER FORTY-SEVEN

In Samsville, Kansas, the Carnegie Library has a spacious room that displays the Goes' art collection under carefully configured track lighting. A large painting of a wheat field, done by an artist in Paris's Latin Quarter and bought by the Goes in 1927, is at the center of the display.

The room also has all the published literary pieces of A. P. Goe. Her unpublished writings (with a few exceptions) remain in boxes, and the librarian is working, however slowly, on reviewing and placing them in appropriate files.

Hardback books from Alice's personal library—many being first editions with clean dust jackets and in mint condition—are in the room, which also houses her collection of "Little" and literary magazines.

Alice's oak desk and the typewriters that she had used are in the room. Anchored above the door is an unpainted slab of wood with the following words carved in it:

ALICE PRINCETON GOE MEMORIAL ABODE

The word *Abode* stirred a dispute between the librarian and the members of the town's library board whose task is to oversee the work of the library. The board is composed of three retired farmers, a banker, a barber, and a high school English teacher, the board's only female. The barber pushed hard for *Abode* because he felt "the 'A' in *Abode* goes nicely with the 'A' in *Alice*." He felt Alice would like to use that word.

But the librarian disliked the sound of the word *Abode*, and she felt Alice would also. She lobbied for *Room* or *Collection* but failed to get support for either, so she suggested *Archives*, and she graciously told the barber: "The 'A' in *Archives* goes nicely with the 'A' in *Alice*." The barber resisted the librarian's logic and taste. He made a motion to use *Abode*. The motion passed five to one.

— ☙ —

The librarian, who had succeeded Martha Stuneburn, felt that the board had used the dispute to settle an old score. Months earlier, the librarian—a Samsville native and a Phi Beta Kappa graduate from a small college in Iowa—had acquired for the library's spacious Reading Room an abstract cherry-wood sculpture that cost slightly more than two thousand dollars.

The attention-riveting wooden sculpture is titled *Our Conscience*, and it is the work of Joan Freyoni, a close friend of the librarian. Both had attended the same grade school, high school, and church in Samsville, and they were roommates in college for four years. As kids, the two joined the 4-H Club and Girls Scouts; they grew up as if they were sisters, and they remained so after college.

While writing the check, the librarian winked at Joan and said: "I know I'm going to hear about this, but I'll handle the situation using the wisdom that I once heard in the Samsville Café." She stopped writing for a moment, looked up at her friend, and added: "When I was a little girl, I sat with my parents in a booth at the café. Next to us, sitting at a round table, were farmers, dressed in overalls and hats and boots, smoking pipes or cigars, and talking about all sorts of topics. I sat in our booth and eavesdropped on their conversation. At one point, one farmer told the rest: *There are times when you'll get far more done if you decide to ask for forgiveness and not permission.* It's in that spirit that I'm now purchasing *Our Conscience* for the Carnegie Library collection."

Alice would have loved that spirit. The sculpture would have reminded her of the four-color abstract art piece used on the cover of *Editors and Their Turkeys*. To the board members, that spirit was a threat. They expected the librarian to seek their approval to purchase an item that costs more than a thousand dollars. But the librarian knew the board would veto a request to buy an abstract sculpture that didn't look like something they recognized. Still, she went ahead and bought it, and later she defended her decision.

Speaking to the entire board one Tuesday evening in early April, the librarian stated in her impromptu remarks:

> As you all know, the cherry-wood sculpture is by our own accomplished artist, Joan Freyoni, who has been awarded many honors for her work.
>
> I'll admit: it's an abstract, and that's not typical of the art you see around here. Consider this, my friends: it's easy to draw or paint or make a sculpture of a boot. You bring a boot, set it in front of you, look at it, and make a copy of it.
>
> Likewise, if you want to draw or paint or make a sculpture of a truck, a table, or a vase, that too is easy to do. You draw or paint the concrete item that you see.
>
> And, if you want to draw or paint or make a sculpture of a navel—or parts above or below the navel—that too is easy to do. And as we all know, that's done—all too often, perhaps—by all sorts of artists.

But if you want to draw or paint or do a sculpture of a *conscience*, what do you do then?

A boot, a truck, or a vase are concrete items. But *conscience* is an abstraction. How do you draw or sculpt it?

You guessed it: an abstraction merits an abstract, and what our own Joan Freyoni had done—and brilliantly, I might add—is an abstract titled *Our Conscience.*

A heated discussion ensued between the board members and the wise, shrewd, soft-spoken, and self-assured librarian. When forgiveness soothed the anger of the men, the discussion shifted to where the sculpture should be placed in the library. The librarian—feeling triumphant and happy—argued for "the library's showcase: the impressive Reading Room with its solid oak tables and stained-glass windows."

At one point, the barber said, "How about placing the thing in the room we're refurbishing for Alice Goe's stuff?"

"I'll respectfully say no to that," the librarian said in a calm voice. "Besides, it's not a *thing*: it's a noble and remarkable work of art, and Alice's writings are not *stuff*, but the fruits of a gifted writer."

"Forgive me for calling it stuff," the barber said. "The sculpture belongs with her writings, which after all, put our little town on the map."

"I agree with the map part," the librarian said.

"I do too," a retired farmer said. He paused, scratched his beard, snapped his blue suspenders, and added, "Putting us on the map is what Mrs. Goe has in common with the *Misplaced Mansion*."

That comparison led the librarian, teacher, and banker to smile. The barber and farmers laughed. The *Misplaced Mansion* is a three-story Victorian edifice on the edge of town. Retired farmers who gather daily at the town's only café for fellowship and Folgers coffee feel the ash-colored brick mansion belongs in a big city and not on the Kansas prairie, hence the place's nickname. For years, an elderly retired banker from Wichita had lived in the house, but he died, and the place was for sale.

"My dear friends," the librarian said, "Alice Princeton Goe is no longer with us, but she lives in the characters she created and the works she wrote. We connect with her voice and personality whenever we read her work in print. There is a living person there, you see."

"There sure is," the teacher said. "Sure is."

"Thank you for saying that," the librarian said. "Future generations of Samsville residents will also enjoy her work in the years ahead."

"You're right," the teacher said. "But not only is Alice alive and well in the work she had written, but many of the people that she had written *about*—whether they like it or not—are also alive and well, thanks to her prose and verse." She paused, made eye contact with the barber and the banker, and said: "Some artists create on canvas and wood; our Alice created persons and places with words."

With that remark, the meeting came to an end, and the principle of asking for forgiveness instead of permission had worked again.

— ℘ —

After the meeting, the men left the library. But the English teacher stayed to visit with her friend, the librarian.

The two sat in the librarian's office and talked about the earnest and aging barber and his well-intentioned but ill-advised ideas. They also brought up Harold "Curley" Hayward, one of the farmers on the board whose wit always delighted the entire committee. At one point, the librarian said, "Did you like the way Curley scolded the board for being so darn tight? When he did that, I thought he's going to vote with us."

"I did too," the teacher said.

"And I loved it," the librarian added, "when he lectured the board by saying: *If we don't watch out, the staff at the library will begin to claim that our board is so tight, it can squeeze shit out of a buffalo nickel.*"

"And he's right, isn't he?"

"Sure is," the librarian said and offered another example from Curley's wit. "During one board meeting months ago when you were on vacation, Alice's name came up and Curley spoke about her writings as having *a humor sensor*. The barber corrected him and said: *You mean to say, 'a sense of humor'?* Curley snapped at the barber and said: *Oh Stan, you, more than any other person in this town, should know that all sorts of people these days claim to have 'a sense of humor.' I'm sure many come to your shop. But the Alice I knew had 'a humor sensor' like no other.*"

The two walked towards the library's main door. "I loved the way you framed Alice's writings by saying she created persons and places with words," said the librarian.

"Thanks," the teacher said. "I enjoyed *Editors and Their Turkeys*, and I still feel sorry—and happy—for those two learned hillbillies from West Virginia that Alice tormented and delighted in *Twirling Men*. That gifted and creative woman had a wickedly engaging sense of irony."

"I'll say," the librarian agreed and turned the key that locked the library's door. "She's as original a thinker as you'll find out here. I've been looking at some of her unpublished writings and—"

"You mean all those boxes downstairs?" the teacher asked.

"Yes," the librarian said. "We've got many boxes of unpublished material, and as time becomes available, I've been trying to organize and catalogue her writings; I'd love to have a professionally trained librarian assist me, but given the dismal state of the farm economy out here and our buffalo-nickel board, there's no way they'll approve such a hire."

"You're right about that," the teacher said. "No way."

"I'm doing my best on the cataloguing and filing."

"Do you enjoy working on her material?" the teacher asked and answered her own question. "I bet you do."

"Yes, I do," the librarian said. "To be more specific, let me mention the book-length manuscript that I started to read the other day; it deals with what Alice calls the *net-serve culture* of the Great Plains. The four hundred-plus page manuscript has this title: *Board Games Are the Blues Poor White Folks Sing on the Prairie*. I'm not one for long titles, but I absolutely love this one."

"I do, too," the teacher said. "Love the poetry in it."

"I'm confident," the librarian continued, "Alice's work is original and significant, just the kind of work that'll provide a Ph.D. student in literature or social and intellectual history with a dissertation topic. A. P. Goe could be seen as a regional writer from the Great Plains, though I believe her writings transcend our region."

— ∽ —

Both women stood on the entrance's top sandstone stair. A boy, wearing a Little League *Samsville Stallions* t-shirt, rode a red bike on the sidewalk below; the bike had a black banana seat and balloon tires.

The freckled-faced boy was holding the bike's handle with his left hand, and with his right he was holding and licking an ice cream cone that he had bought at the town's summer hangout *Ye Olde Sweet Tooth*, a seasonal business owned by Samsville's only dentist.

The boy looked up at the women and greeted them using their last names prefaced with a Miss for the librarian and a Mrs. for the teacher. Both women, members of the same United Methodist church that the boy and his parents attend, returned the boy's greetings.

"Now isn't that sweet?" the teacher said referring to the polite boy. "That reflects manners and maturity beyond his years."

"It's sweet, cute, and poignant, I'd say," the librarian responded. "You see reflections of the manners taught at home."

"And at scouting," the teacher said. The teacher returned the conversation to the board meeting and said, "You kept your cool this evening."

"Thanks," the librarian said. "It wasn't easy."

"How did you like Curley's jovial comparison of Alice to the *Misplaced Mansion*?" the teacher asked. "Wasn't that hilarious?"

"Love that guy," the librarian said. "I've heard Alice compared to other writers, but never to a building. If nothing else, that underscores her uniqueness." She paused then added, "Alice Goe is a misplaced writer. She might've thrived in a vastly different manner had she been born and raised in a highly cultured urban or university setting."

"Curley made his remark with a smile," the teacher said.

"And it helped defuse the tension of that moment."

"He probably believes his claim. Don't you think?"

"I'm sure he does," the librarian said. "And if I know Alice, she would've enjoyed the comparison that was offered by a humorous farmer. She loved and respected the farmers of the Great Plains."

"And I believe she would've been proud of you," the teacher said. "That's the feeling I get from reading her work."

"If our Alice had attended this meeting," the librarian said, "she would've stayed in the background and reflected on *Our Conscience* and the discussion it had generated. She'd write an account of our discussion, a creative-nonfiction piece that fleshed out the facts and then transcended them by capturing the *reality* of the situation."

"I suspect," the teacher said, "it'd be a comic account."

"You're right," the librarian said. "Alice loved offbeat humor, and, to quote Curley, her sensor would lead her to see humor in places most people would miss."

"And she did all that," the teacher added, "by way of making serious points."

"That she did," the librarian said. "While going through her diary the other day, I came across a a philosophic idea in which she claims that life orchestrates four seasons: *wisdom, pain, love, and humor.*"

"Interesting."

"And in a long diary entry that's really an essay, she explores the rhythm and harmony in the four seasons. The entry has a clever aphoristic title: 'Wisdom and Pain Love Humor.' "

"Did she ever publish it in a literary forum?"

"That I don't know," the librarian said as the two began to walk down the stairs. "If Alice were to write a piece that captures the spirit of tonight's meeting, she'd turn to her beloved T. S. Eliot and title her piece: 'The Love Song of a Feisty Abstract.' "

CHAPTER FORTY-EIGHT

Before exploring the institution that Alice had helped establish, a quick look at what became of others is in order.

Joan Freyoni still has her sculpture in the library's Reading Room, and she is now a James Joyce devotee.

Jack wrote a first novel that he refuses to print privately or to post electronically. He is searching for a literary agent. "So far," he says, "the agents I contacted are either overworked or don't like my work."

Lisa continues to be the main provider for the family by teaching math and directing drama at Samsville High. Their daughter Elise is a sophomore in a small liberal arts college in Quincy, Massachusetts.

Editors and Their Turkeys is still in print and is selling well year after year. *Twirling Men* is in its seventeenth printing, and royalties from it continue to go to Royalle College. The two men who had played crucial roles in the novel retired after twenty-seven years of service. Throughout those years and even in retirement in Florida, they remained in touch with Alice.

In the Sunshine State, one had his prostate removed; the other had a colon resection. Both would have liked to go to Alice's funeral, but their health issues kept them away. Their new office is the doctor's office, and their motto is "Geezers Rejoice."

Rita Todd, Alice's editor at *Garvin, Akers & Sheridan*, claims, "Alice's prose books are very active items on our backlist; they work while we sleep. But *Waiting for the Mail*, her poetry book, is in a coma."

Though the film rights to *Twirling Men* had been optioned, no movie has yet been produced. In time, this may change. In the film, Lisa and Jack, Tim, Bob, and Frank will be major characters. There will be all sorts of minor characters. The stars will be Alice and her beloved Kansas.

— ❧ —

Royalle College had received a two million dollar grant from Alice, and the college continues to get all the royalties from her books.

The remaining five million stayed in Samsville. It went towards a cultural institution that Alice and a wealthy friend had agreed to establish. When Alice was in her early eighties, she and Paul Paxolord drove to an attorney in Wichita, an out-of-town attorney, to safeguard their privacy, and the two formally drew up plans to give birth to—and for Paxolord to nurture and sustain—a literary institution in American culture.

Thanks to Alice's five million dollars and to four million from Paxolord, the two established an institution that was to open after her death. The charter listed Alice Princeton Goe and Paul Paxolord as founders, and Paxolord as its first curator.

Other than having her name listed in what she considered to be the "private legal charter," Alice requested to be *completely anonymous* in all matters released to the public about this brand-new institution.

She didn't want the people of Samsville to know that the Goes were millionaires. "I'll be overjoyed," she told Paxolord after they left their Wichita attorney's office and were driving back to Samsville, "if the good people in town continue to assume that I'm your typical small-town thousandaire, or better yet—paycheck-to-paycheck hundredaire."

Paul smiled, reached over and touched her hand.

Alice added: "Please, please, Paul, I don't want my name or my late husband's name to be associated in any way with the place even though I fully support its mission; have complete trust in your vision for it; and, most importantly, have confidence in your leadership skills."

— ∾ —

Located in the *Misplaced Mansion* of Samsville, Kansas, the institution has become a cultural oasis on the Great Plains—a hall of fame for unknown writers. Paxolord had commissioned Joan Freyoni to design and paint the sign near the Hall's entrance.

The large sign shows a thick hardback book with a blue dust jacket. The book's spine notes in italics: *Est. in 2003*. The title, lettered in white paint and all caps, states UNKNOWN WRITERS HALL OF FAME. The lower part of the jacket omits an author's name and lists in italics what Alice had selected for the Hall's motto: *We're in Kansas forevermore.*

A larger version of this sign appears on a billboard located at the edge of a wheat field near Exit 8, the highway exit that leads to Samsville.

Twelve years after the Hall was established and visited by many people, a book came out about it titled *A Hall of Fame for Unknown Writers*. Published by a university press in Texas, the seriocomic book has a handsome cover that features green and gold wheat fields, scattered clouds, and a blue Kansas sky—all serving as the backdrop to the book's title carved on four strips of wood, glued to a post, planted on the periphery of a field.

The book explores the origin and contents of a unique Hall, one that inducts not people but pieces, unpublished items by unknown writers. The back cover sketches the book's content:

> After thirty-six years as book editor in New York, Robin retires and moves back to her girlhood home in Oberlin, Ohio. She takes with her copies of items she had kept in a special file.
>
> The items had come not from literary agents but directly from writers, reflecting their quirky, original, creative, passionate, ironic, even bizarre voices. All the items enlighten and entertain.
>
> *A Hall of Fame for Unknown Writers* is Robin's story as she reproduces the comic items and nominates them for induction into America's first (and only) hall of fame for unknown writers, where the motto reads: "We're in Kansas forevermore."

The back cover also has an excerpt from the book that offers readers a feel for the book's content by recording some of Robin's thoughts and actions during her first visit to the Hall in April of 2006:

> To me, an elderly non-Kansan, the motto implies that the writers whose pieces are ensconced in that Victorian mansion are unhappy campers. I hear them saying, "Like it or not, we're stuck in Kansas."
>
> Before leaving the Hall, I signed the guestbook. Others had also. Some wrote comments. I copied several into the palm-size notebook that I carry in my purse: "Fine job," "Charming," "Design a Hall flag and fly it," "The Rejection Room rocks."
>
> "Mom took me on many field trips," a homeschooler wrote, "but this is Weirdoville." A sketch of a smiling face trailed this comment.

Another comment winked at ambiguity by proclaiming the Hall to be "Done with taste." An illegible signature, the kind that announces a writer's convoluted identity, followed this comment.

One visitor wrote: "A splendid tribute to writers from the ink age." Another used a calligraphy pen and wrote a phrase in Latin: "*In risu veritas*" (In laughter, truth).

The book is prominently displayed in the Hall's souvenir shop on the first floor. Visitors often pick up the book, admire its cover, read passages from it while smiling or laughing. Many take the book to the cash register and pay for a copy.

The attendant at the souvenir shop once told Paxolord: "From what I've noticed, the people who end up buying the book almost always head to the Hall's guestbook and write benign observations, or suggestions, or thoughtful comments—or even wisecracks."

In the Hall's basement, there is a small used bookstore. The store carries select literary hardback books authored by reasonably unknown writers. There is also a coffee shop in the basement where people have been seen drinking cappuccinos or caffé lattes or espressos while reading their copies of *A Hall of Fame for Unknown Writers*.

Paul Paxolord had cooperated fully, and happily, with the author, so when he received his inscribed and signed copy of the 299-page book, he read it in one day. He read it again a week later.

On a balmy day in June, he relaxed in an oak rocking chair set on the Hall's wrap-around porch, smoking a hand-crafted meer-schaum pipe, reflecting on his life, and wistfully glancing at the restful prairie. Alice's aphorism—*Regrets are the rummage sales of life*—cruised his thoughts.

"Would Alice," he asked himself, "be impressed by the book's cover, design, content, wit, and presentation? Or, would she dismiss my cooperation with the author as a rummage sale?" He paused, then added, "She'd probably smile and say, *Upscale rummage sale.*"

— ❧ —

In his first floor office in the Hall, Paxolord has all of Alice's writings that had been published in books, magazines, and literary journals. He would occasionally connect with her by reading her work.

One morning, he sat in his office, reached up and pulled from an antique bookcase a copy of a literary quarterly that had published an extensive essay by Alice dealing with her visit in 1927 to Sylvia Beach's bookstore in Paris: Shakespeare and Company. With a mug full of coffee in his hand, Paxolord began reading Alice's reflections.

To his delight, he found himself interacting with Alice, joining her as she unfurled and explored her love for those European and American expatriate writers and editors who had lived in the cultural ghettos of Paris in the first half of the twentieth century.

"In this period," Alice writes, "literature flowered in the lava of two world wars."

ABOUT THE AUTHOR

S. Sal Hanna often jokes that his name has a "flagship version in S S Hanna." Under this version, he published two books with university presses.

The University Press of Colorado published BEYOND WINNING, a sports memoir. And Iowa State University Press published THE GYPSY SCHOLAR, a book that was reviewed in PUBLISHERS WEEKLY with these words: "*Well written, fast paced, funny and enjoyable, it deserves a sizable audience.*"

A third university press published a book written by Hanna. He uses a pen name for this book and weaves its title, content, and publisher into A HAIRPIECE NAMED DENIAL.

Besides writing, Hanna dabbles in art. He created large abstract sculptures of metal, stone, or wood and placed them in his house's spacious backyard.

"One day," Hanna recalls, "my dog was out exploring an area near a metal sculpture, sniffing for a spot on which to contort his body into the question-mark posture. Noticing that, I asked myself: 'What's my best friend thinking? Could he be asking me: *Are you a better artist with words?*' "

www.ingramcontent.com/pod-product-compliance
Lightning Source LLC
Chambersburg PA
CBHW030629020726
47493CB00006B/1631